Revenge at the Rodeo

REVENGE AT THE RODEO

GILBERT MORRIS

Fleming H. Revell
A Division of Baker Book House
Grand Rapids, Michigan 49516

Copyright © 1993 by Gilbert Morris

Published by Fleming H. Revell
a division of Baker Book House Company
P.O. Box 6287, Grand Rapids, Michigan 49516-6287

Second printing, May 1993

Printed in the United States of America

Library of Congress Cataloging-in-Publication Data

Morris, Gilbert.
    Revenge at the rodeo / Gilbert Morris.
        p.   cm.
    ISBN 0-8007-5457-3
    I. Title.
    PS3563.08742R47 1993
    813′. 54—dc20   92-591

Scripture quotations in this volume are from the King James Version of the Bible.

To
Lucille Montgomery
and
Jann Smith
There's nothing like
high tea
with two fine ladies of quality!

Contents

1   A Case of Nerves   9

2   A Call from Dallas   27

3   "You're No Good to Anybody!"   46

4   Under Cover   63

5   The Corral Club   76

6   Second Warning   92

7   "Too Good to Be True!"   110

8   Sixkiller's Roommate   124

9   A Visit to Church   142

10   Dani Gets a Call   155

11   The Drop   171

12   Good-bye to a Friend   186

13   Feeding the Ducks   197

14   Waiting for Megan   210

15   Captain Little Gets Some Volunteers   225

16   A Woman in Black   240

Contents

17   Late Movie   253

18   Sixkiller's Hour   265

19   Deep River   273

20   "What Could Be in His Heart?"   288

21   Greet the Brethren   304

1
A Case of Nerves

*S*tocking *masks distorted their faces, pressing their noses flat and rounding all the sharp planes—making them appear like half-formed creatures. More terrifying than the grotesque smoothness of their features was the absence of any expression. The eyes were dulled behind the sheer material, and all mobility of feature that marks humankind was blunted, metamorphosing them into nightmarish monsters.*

Dani could not seem to move as they emerged from the darkness of the doorway. Helplessly she watched, a thin soundless scream rising in her throat as they separated, almost like a single entity becoming two separate forms. Each carried a gleaming automatic weapon that reflected the overhead lights of the gymnasium. One moved slightly ahead and to the left and began to lift the muzzle of the gun upward as he crossed the gleaming oak floor.

He wore new blue jeans, a black knit T-shirt, and a black stocking cap pulled almost to his eyebrows. He moved mechanically, his steps precise as if he were doing a drill of some sort. With the same sort of robotlike movement, he swung the rifle up to bear on the group that stood watching him.

In a second Dani clearly noted the delicate hands, long, tapering fingers like those one might see on a concert violinist or a brain surgeon.

As she realized that Ben would never be able to get to his gun in time to save them, Dani felt herself reaching for her .38. Her mind was screaming, but her nerves seemed frozen, and it was like trying to move underwater. One hand touched the rough, knurled butt of the weapon. Her fingers closed about it, and as she pulled it free from the holster she found herself looking into the muzzle of the gunman's weapon. It was like looking down a tunnel, and as she brought the .38 into firing position, grasping it with both hands and laying the bead on the chest of the man facing her, she suddenly found that she could not pull the trigger.

Time froze, and even as she tried to pull the trigger, her mind screamed, I can't do it! I can't kill a man!

But then she saw the thin finger of the assailant whiten as he began to squeeze his trigger, and the faces of the children behind her flashed through her mind.

With a spasmodic reaction, she squeezed the trigger, and the roar of the exploding powder filled her ears. She could smell the cordite and feel the kick of the .38 as it flew upward.

Then she saw the bullet strike the chest of the dark-clad figure. It drove him backward, as though he had been struck by a huge, invisible fist. As he threw his hands up in a wild gesture, the weapon arced into a parabola, swiftly reflecting gleams of light as it spun end-over-end through the air.

He sprawled flat on his back, one hand thrown over his head, and in a flash Dani could see the scarlet blood begin to pump, sending a jet of crimson that soaked the black knit shirt he wore. Like a miniature fountain it gushed, staining the heaving chest the brightest red she had ever seen. . . .

Danielle Ross came out of the dream suddenly—as she always did—with a wrenching motion that brought her up, clawing at the air frantically. Her eyes snapped open, revealing the dim, familiar outlines of her bedroom, and she fought to choke back the scream that gathered in her throat.

The dream was always the same. Even as she flung herself out of bed and stood trembling, with her eyes shut, breathing in a short, gasping manner, the vision of the still body of the gunman with his chest incarnadined would not leave. With desperate urgency, she flung herself into the bathroom. The harsh, brilliant lights of the fluorescent fixtures over the large mirror drove the image away, but she pulled off her nightgown and stepped into the shower. The blast of cold water took her breath, and she stood under it until her body cooled and the water lost its shock.

Finally, she turned the water off, stepped outside, and dried herself slowly with a thick, yellow towel. She moved carefully, keeping her mind off the details of the dream, as one walks warily around broken glass with bare feet. *It's coming more often*, she thought, dusting herself with scented powder. *Three nights in a row.* Driving that thought from her mind, she focused her attention on getting dressed. It was still dark outside, but the glowing face of the clock beside her bed told her it was six minutes after five. Too late to go back to bed—even if she had dared to do so.

Prolonging the rituals of putting on makeup and fixing her hair, she methodically followed the familiar routine while listening to the new Praise album. As always, it had a soothing effect on her spirit, and by the time she was ready to get dressed, the shock of the terrible dream no longer seemed so unbearable. It was not gone, she knew as she stood before the closet, trying to decide what to wear to work. No, it lurked somewhere in the dim corridors of her memory, waiting until she was relaxed before it would come back to torment her.

As she stood there, the phrase, *You have killed a man*, swept through her mind as it had a thousand times since she pulled the trigger and watched a man's life flicker out. She had learned to quickly occupy her mind with something—anything—when it came, and now she suddenly pulled a dress from the closet rod and whirled away, saying aloud, "Well, I was a fool to pay so much for this thing—but I'll wear it to work all the same!"

She admired it as she had when she had first seen it at the exclusive shop, and quickly she slipped it on. Going back to the closet, she stepped into a pair of purple pumps with three-inch heels. She walked to her dresser, fished out a heavy gold chain, slipped it over her head, then put on a pair of heavy gold hoop earrings. Picking up a purse to match the shoes, she turned to look at herself in the mirror. The dress was a saronglike affair, made of sheer cream-colored polyester and cotton voile. It was much more feminine than other dresses Dani usually wore to the office. Now as she stood there admiring it, she suddenly looked at herself as well as the dress.

A tall, shapely young woman of twenty-six, with a pair of gray-green eyes, deep-set in a squarish face, stared back at her. *The nose*, she thought as always, *is too short and the mouth too large.* But the coloring and fine texture of the skin offset that, and the deep tones of the auburn hair cut just over her collar were the envy of most women.

Abruptly she turned and walked to the dressing table again. Picking up a bottle of Oscar de la Renta perfume, she applied it liberally, taking a perverse pleasure in the gesture. "You could smell good a lot cheaper than this, Ross," she murmured. Then after one more look, she turned and left the apartment.

Dawn was breaking as she pulled into the Camellia Grill on St. Charles Avenue. The air was thick and hotly oppressive, a foretaste of the humid heat that would blanket New Orleans by ten o'clock. The Camellia, a small, white building with pillars in front, was crowded, but she found a place at the counter, and Leroy Plotts came to stand before her, a broad smile crossing his black face.

"What'll you have, Miss Ross? A waffle?"

"That'll be fine, Leroy. And coffee."

She need not have told Leroy that, for he knew her habits well. Soon she was eating the golden-brown waffle, and when she was finished, had another cup of coffee. Leaving a tip for Leroy, she left the Camellia, got into her red Cougar, made an illegal U-turn on St. Charles, and drove rapidly to her office.

Ross Investigations was located on Bourbon Street. Once the locale had seemed rather romantic to Dani, but over the past months it had become just another street. Parking was terrible, and the tourists flocked like lemmings to the area, hoping to see and possibly get involved in sin. Dani was not tempted by the canned sex and tawdry commercialized evil that had soaked into the street over the years, but the parking had driven her up the wall. That had been solved when she had lent a helping hand to an elderly woman, Mrs. Clara DeBreaux. Mrs. DeBreaux had been terrified of a suitor who had resented it when she had refused to marry him. She had called Dani, who had at once sent her best investigator, Ben Savage, to have a talk with the man. Dani never found out what Ben had said, but Mrs. DeBreaux had never heard from the man again. Her gratitude was overwhelming, and in addition to the fee, she insisted that Dani park her car at her home, an off-the-street Bourbon Street residence surrounded by a high brick wall, only a block from Ross Investigations.

Dani parked the Cougar, noting that Mrs. DeBreaux was not up, then moved to the street and walked quickly to the office. As Dani climbed the steps, she thought again how it might have been better to locate the office in a more reputable section of New Orleans. Being on Bourbon Street, she thought wryly as she unlocked the door, was like trying to carry on a business in the middle of a Ringling Brothers' three-ring circus.

Flipping on the light, she paused at her secretary's desk to grab the mail, then moved through the door into her office. Light streamed through the tall windows that lined the street side of the office, and the pale sun brought out the rich glow of the antique walnut desk and the shelves along the wall. She threw back the curtains, glanced out at the ironwork that framed her small balcony, then sat down at her desk.

For ten minutes she sorted through the mail, separating the junk from the legitimate items. The junk she tossed into a wastebasket, the legitimate she sorted out according to priority. It was the act of a woman who liked order, who wanted things to be classified logically.

This part of her character had made her a competent CPA and a good private detective. The other side of her nature lay carefully hidden from public view, controlled by an iron will. Beneath the facade of smooth control lay a volatile set of emotions that could explode like Mount Vesuvius. She had learned long ago that when she gave way to this side of her nature, she exhibited a wildness that could injure those who got in her way—as well as herself.

Ben Savage had long ago penetrated this level of Dani's makeup. "You're like a bottle of nitroglycerin wrapped in pretty satin paper with a lacy bow on top, Boss," he had said, studying her carefully. "You look as sweet and cute as Shirley

Temple—but if you get nudged, you explode like a land mine!"

She thought of that as she sat in the leather chair, and a frown creased her brow. She looked up suddenly at the picture of her great-great-grandfather, Colonel Daniel Monroe Ross, which dominated the wall to her left. He was a fierce-eyed man dressed in Confederate gray with a red sash around his waist and a mouth like a steel trap. Dani stared at the picture, thinking of how her father had often told her, "You get your stubborn streak from that old confederate rebel, Dani!"

Dani sat quietly, thinking of her ancestor and of the blood and carnage he had endured through the agonizing Civil War. He had written a straightforward account of that desperate charge he had made with General Pickett, the futile and courageous attempt of the Confederates to take Little Round Top. Her grandfather had allowed the rigid curtain of iron courtesy and control to drop when he penned the last sentence: "It was a bold maneuver, doomed to failure—and my heart weeps over the friends I left on that dreadful hill!"

Dani looked up at the stern eyes, then murmured softly, "I don't guess you'd be proud of me, Colonel, making such a big thing of shooting one man." As she spoke she heard the outer door of the office open and then close. Getting to her feet, she walked quickly out of the room to find her secretary, Angie Park, settling down at her desk.

"Oh, hello, Miss Ross." Angie greeted her with a slightly startled look. "I didn't know you were in your office." Angie was an attractive woman of twenty-eight, with genuine blond hair and soft blue eyes. "Anything you need right now?"

"Get Al in here as quick as you can, Angie."

"He'll be in at nine—or so he said last night."

Dani gave Angie a quick look. "You were out with him?"

Angie shrugged with a weary gesture. "He's better than sitting at home watching a crummy TV show." Then she shook her head. "Not really. Every time he asks me out, I say, 'No more!' But then the walls start to close in, and I find myself fighting him off again."

Dani opened her mouth to give some advice, then closed it abruptly. Al Overmile was one of her investigators, an ex-cop who was handsome in a crude way. He was a weight lifter going fat; he drank like a fish; and he was a womanizer. Al had put all the moves on Dani early in their relationship and would try it again. Only two of his qualities kept her from firing him: He worked cheap, and he knew a lot of people from his days on the police force.

"Send Ben in as soon as he gets here," Dani requested abruptly, then left the room, closing the door behind her. Angie looked after her, shook her head, and started working. She only looked up at nine, as Al Overmile came through the door.

"Hi, lover," he said loudly and came around the desk, lowering his heavy head in an attempt to kiss her.

"Never mind that," Angie responded crisply. "Dani wants to see you. And you'd better not try to kiss *her!*"

Overmile shrugged, then asked, "She still in a rotten mood?"

"Just don't come on strong, Al," Angie advised. She pushed the switch on the intercom, announcing, "Al is here, Miss Ross."

"Send him in."

Overmile winked at Angie and suggested, "Maybe we better go out again tonight, take up where we left off." When Angie ignored him, he blushed and walked into Dani's office, shutting the door with extra force.

Angie didn't have to use the intercom to hear some of what went on, for almost at once Dani's voice rose to an angry pitch. It was impossible to make out any details, but when Al came sailing out the door, ten minutes later, his face was red and his lips were set in a grim line. He didn't slam the door, but shut it carefully.

"Nice interview, Al?" Angie queried innocently.

"Peachy! Gimme all the reports on the Williams case." He took the thick file that Angie fished out of a drawer, then without a word walked over to the other desk. He took off his coat and lit a cigarette, then began turning the pages slowly. "She said to send Ben in as soon as he gets here," he muttered angrily.

The interview with Overmile had pulled Dani out of the calm mood she had achieved. He was an irritating man, and only by keeping rigid control over herself did she ever manage to retain a civil manner toward him. When he had come sailing through the door with that smile that she'd seen so often on his face, it had pushed her over the edge. She'd intended to ask him to go over the facts of a case he'd worked on, but he'd made the mistake of putting his hand on her shoulder in what was supposed to be a friendly gesture but was actually a caress. Dani quickly blasted him verbally and sent him out of the office. She had wished for one instant that she were a man like Ben Savage, so she could have *thrown* him out bodily.

When she grew angry, it was imperative for her to find something to *do,* some activity to help her regain her calm. Going to a drawing board by the window, she sat down on a high stool and soon was engrossed in making a scale drawing of the home of Mr. Adkins Cole. He had hired her to create a security system for his art collection, and for several days she had taken pleasure in laying in the fine lines that made

17

the drawing. She had a knack for such work, and as she studied the print was soon lost in the job. Ben would have to design the circuits and switches that would circumvent a would-be burglar, but she enjoyed laying out the drawing of the house.

Time passed, but in the silence of the room, Dani was unaware of it. From time to time faint voices or the sound of a car wafted up from the street, but Dani was lost in the intricacies of the drawing. She worked steadily, carefully, and stopped only when she discovered that the pen she used was out of ink. Irritated at having to stop, she moved to the cabinet that held her supplies and picked up a small bottle of black ink. It was a new bottle, and as she walked back to the drawing board, she found herself struggling with the stubborn cap. She had strong hands, but the cap resisted her. Finally, she took a deep breath, grasped the bottle firmly, then applied all her strength.

The cap came off suddenly, and its release caused Dani to give the bottle an involuntary jerk—which sent the entire contents of the bottle right across the bodice of her new dress. Unbelieving, she stood there staring down at the hideous black blot that was spreading over the sheer cream-colored material. Superimposed over that she saw again the form of the gunman with the scarlet blot spreading on his chest as he lay dying.

Dani began to shake, and she turned with a muted cry and ran to the small bathroom. She stripped off the dress, then seeing that the slip was stained as well, took it off. She leaned against the wall, her eyes tightly shut, and tried to think of something else. The image of the dying gunman was gone, but she was terrified that it might come back. She began to pray, asking for help, and finally the tremors lessened. Straightening up, Dani tried to think what to do. She had no other clothing at the office, none at all. She resolved to keep an outfit in her office in the future, but that didn't help her now.

Finally she reached down and picked up the slip. It was not stained as badly as the dress, and she washed it under the cold water, using the hand soap. Though the stain remained ugly, she ended by putting on the slip, then turned to the dress. It was terrible! The porous material had drunk the ink, it seemed, so that a huge blot at least eight inches wide covered the bodice. She began washing the dress, but it was hopeless. The water just spread the stain over a wider area.

For a long moment she stared at the ruined garment, then drew her shoulders back. She walked over to the window and spread the soaking dress over a chair so that the sunlight would dry it out.

As she turned around, the door opened and Ben Savage walked in.

He took two steps into the room, then stopped dead still. His eyes, usually hooded and sleepy, flew open at the sight of Dani in her slip, staring at him with an expression he'd never seen before.

Dani stood there, paralyzed by the sight of him. For one brief moment, there was total silence. Ben had just started to turn and leave the room, when her voice caught him. It was a voice he'd never heard from her, filled with white-hot anger. "Just come barging right on it, Savage!" she exclaimed, her eyes flashing. When he didn't answer, she added, "Just a regular old voyeur, are you? Get your jollies by spying on women in their underwear?"

"That's it," he said evenly. "Thought you knew I was that sort of chap."

"Get—get out of here!" Dani ordered between clenched teeth. "And you can just keep on walking as far as I'm concerned."

"Easy to do."

Dani stood there as he turned and walked out of the room, and as soon as the door closed, she began to cry. She slumped into her chair, buried her face on her arms, and her shoulders heaved. Finally the spasm passed, and she lifted her head. Tears had blurred her makeup, and her hands were trembling. Finally, she flipped the switch on the intercom. "Angie?"

"Yes?"

"Send Ben and Al away. Lock the outer door, then come in here."

"Yes, Miss Ross."

Dani could not seem to get up. She sat there stiffly until Angie came in. "Oh, Dani! What in the world . . . ?"

"I—spilled some ink all over my dress, Angie. You'll have to go to a shop and get me something to wear." Angie's presence seemed to stiffen her, for she got to her feet and picked up the stained dress. "Just get a lightweight jacket—you know my size."

"I won't be long."

Dani stopped her as she reached the door. "Did Ben—say anything when he left?"

Angie shook her head. "Not a word."

Dani bit her lower lip, admitting, "I was too hard on him. He caught me off guard." She attempted to smile. "I guess he looked pretty mad, didn't he, Angie?"

Angie shook her head, "You know Ben. Nobody can tell what he's thinking." She hesitated, then asked, "You want me to try to find him?"

"No, you get the coat. I'll find him myself."

Luke Sixkiller found Dani sitting at her desk, staring up at the portrait of a soldier in a Confederate uniform. He followed her gaze, then asked, "Relative of yours?"

"My great-great-grandfather."

The Indian glanced at the stern face looking down on the room, and grinned. "He probably took a shot at *my* great-great-grandfather."

"Wrong army, Luke." Dani smiled. She studied the man, who took a seat across from her, and added, "He was in the Confederate Army. I guess your great-great-grandfather had his troubles with the Union generals."

"Way the story comes down," Luke mused, "it was the generals who had trouble with *him*. He never did surrender. Just sort of petered out."

Dani smiled at Sixkiller. He was a powerful man of thirty-five, with the blackest hair possible and high cheek bones proclaiming his Sioux blood. He was one of the most *physical* men she'd ever known. For one thing, he carried 190 pounds on a frame only five feet ten inches tall, and none of it was fat. He had a solid, thick chest, and a neck that any wrestler would have been proud of. But for all his strength, he was quick as a cat, and if half the stories Dani had heard about him were true, he was a dangerous man to cross. The criminal world, she had been told, had a saying: "Don't try to buy Sixkiller."

He lay back in his chair, his dark eyes half-closed, but she knew that meant nothing. He never seemed to pay attention, yet he was aware of everything that happened. "What you need the fuzz for, Dani?" he asked lazily. Sixkiller was chief of detectives for the New Orleans Police Department, and the two of them had worked together from time to time.

Dani was a little embarrassed, a fact that drew Sixkiller's quick attention. She was, he knew, a woman of tremendous self-possession, not easy to shake up, but she was obviously troubled now.

"Well, Luke, to tell the truth, I'd like a favor," she admitted. Her cheeks were a little red, and she ran her hand through her hair nervously. "I don't know how to say this—but I can't find Ben."

Sixkiller's dark eyes glowed with interest. "Where'd you lose him?"

"Well—to tell the truth, we had a little argument."

"You always have arguments with Ben. This must have been a doozie!"

"Not really. Oh, Luke, it's ridiculous! I can't even talk about it without feeling like a fool!"

"Lay it on me."

Dani told the story, feeling more self-conscious than she could ever remember. She ended with, "And that's all there was to it. I yelled at him, but I've done that before. It's been three days now."

Sixkiller suggested innocently, "Maybe we'd better re-enact the crime. You just shuck out of those duds, and I'll come in—"

"Oh, Luke, don't *you* start on me!" Dani shook her head. "I think something may have happened to him. He doesn't answer his phone, so he's not at his apartment."

"May just not want to answer the phone. I *never* want to answer a phone. He's probably at his place with a bottle and some young chick consoling him."

"No, he's not."

"How do you know?"

"Because I *went* there!"

"He probably saw you coming and wouldn't come to the door."

"I went inside. He's not there, Luke."

His heavy black eyebrows lifted. "You have a key to Ben's apartment?"

"No!" Dani snapped. "I jimmied the lock."

Sixkiller found that delightful, but kept his face stern. "Breaking and entering. Could get you five years at St. Gabriel's. Are you confessing?"

Dani usually liked his teasing, but now she was upset. "Luke, he's been involved with some rough characters. One of them may have decided to pay him off."

Sixkiller nodded, seeing how serious she was. "I'll see about it." He got to his feet, then gave her a sardonic look. "But you may have to get another cop."

She stared at him without understanding. "Why?"

"You don't know?" He laughed softly. "Read today's paper. And watch the six o'clock news. I'm in the news, kid."

"What is it, Luke?"

"Police brutality," Sixkiller explained. "Story is I beat a suspect with a baseball bat."

"Luke!"

"Yeah, you'd suspect a nice guy like me of a thing like that?"

"But—they must have some sort of grounds," Dani objected. "Who were you supposed to have beaten up?"

"Sweet Willie Wine." He grinned as Dani's mouth drew tight with shock. "Gets you, doesn't it? Here Sweet Willie had done in at least three people that I *know* about, and one of them a woman. But now he's just a poor misunderstood boy who needs acceptance."

Dani shook her head. "What happened?"

"He tried to resist arrest. I caught him breaking a guy's knees with a bat. I took it away from him, and he resisted. The guy he was working over was sort of a friend of mine. Just a plain guy who got behind on his payments to a big-time gambler."

"What's going to happen?"

"I'll probably get fired." Sixkiller shrugged. "If Willie were just your average white Anglo-Saxon Protestant, nobody

23

would ever hear of it. But the militants need something to scream about, and the American Civil Liberties bunch hasn't got a good *cause*, so they'll probably jump in for some of the headlines."

"Can I help?"

"Sure. Have dinner with me tonight. We can go parking, and you can soothe my ragged nerves."

"You never had a nerve in your life!" Dani scoffed. "But we can go out tonight."

"Parking?"

"No, you idiot!" She laughed. "We'll plan how to find Ben and how to keep you from getting fired. Pick me up at seven."

Dani enjoyed the date with Sixkiller, but he refused to talk about either his own problems or Ben Savage. He kept her amused, but when he took her to her door, he said, "Well, you can ask me in, but I'll refuse. I know how girls like you are!" When she smiled, he sobered. "Ben's in town."

"He is? But where is he?"

"Right now I don't know, but he's been seen two or three times with a woman. Good-looking dame with black hair. Guy who told me about it said he'd never seen her before."

Dani stood there uncertainly. "I need to see him, Luke."

"Yeah. Well, I should have something for you tomorrow. I'll look into it myself."

She smiled wanly. "Thank you, Luke. I'm a lot of trouble, aren't I?"

"Tons," he agreed. "I'll call you tomorrow."

She leaned forward and kissed his cheek, "You're a sweetheart, Luke Sixkiller."

He stared at her. "Wow! I haven't had a kiss like that since my Aunt Ethel was at my fifth birthday party." Then he left, moving competently down the hall and disappearing down the stairs.

But Dani didn't need his call, for the next day at ten o'clock Angie's voice came over the intercom, "Ben's here."

"Send him in!" Dani ordered quickly. She got up from her chair and waited as he entered. "Ben, I'm sorry for the way I yelled at you the other day," she confessed at once.

Savage came to stand in front of her desk. He nodded briefly. "It's okay. No scars or anything."

She saw that he was not himself. His hazel eyes were usually bright, but now they were not. "Is something wrong, Ben?" Dani asked.

He was not a large man, no taller than Sixkiller, but with none of the policeman's bulk. He weighed 175 pounds, and his years as an aerialist, with the circus, had given him a trim form. He had a squarish face with deep-set eyes protected by a heavy shelf of bone, in the manner of some of the Slavic race. A scar ran across his brow, disappearing into his left eyebrow, and his short nose had been broken.

"I've got to leave town for a while," he announced.

Dani stared at him. "Ben, I said I was sorry."

"Got nothing to do with you," he told her evenly.

Dani twisted the ring on her finger. "How long do you think you'll be gone?"

"Can't say. Better hire another guy."

His brevity was not unusual, for he was not a talker. She asked, "Where will you be going, Ben?"

He shook his head. "I'll be moving around a lot. Be hard to say."

Suddenly Dani grew angry. "You don't have to do it this way, Ben! If you want out, just say so."

"All right," he responded evenly, his eyes watching her. "I want out."

Dani felt shocked by the words and suddenly realized how

25

much she counted on his being around, but she kept her face still. "Fine with me. I'll have Angie make out your check."

He nodded, and when she spoke the words to Angie, he offered quietly, "I'll try to keep in touch." He hesitated, then added, "I know you're having a hard time over shooting that guy. Hate to leave you with it."

Dani felt a wave of self-pity rise, and to cover it she said, "Never mind all that, Ben. I know you've got a new playmate. So why don't you just get out of here and take off with her to the beach or somewhere?"

Savage stared at her, and for a moment, she thought he was going to change his mind. But instead he turned and walked out the door without another word.

Dani sat down abruptly, her legs suddenly very weak. She had a tremendous urge to lower her head on her arms and cry, but she kept her jaw locked. Finally she called out, "Good-bye, Ben Savage—and good riddance!"

2

A Call from Dallas

I don't like the way Dani looks."

Daniel Ross and his wife had walked from their house down to the pasture to call Dani to breakfast. She had arrived the evening before, stayed the night, and had risen at dawn to ride her horse. They stood there, watching, as she drove her horse, Biscuit, in the pattern around three orange barrels.

As always Daniel admired the way the rider and the animal became one in the intricate maneuver, and he waited until Dani pulled the rust-colored quarter horse to a stop before turning to look at his wife. "I don't either," he agreed quietly. "She's healthy enough, though."

A single line traced across Ellen's brow. "Oh, physically she's all right. But her nerves are bad, Dan." Ellen Ross, a tall, ash-blond woman of forty-four, pushed a wisp of hair away from her brow. "She's not sleeping very much, and she's hard to get along with. That's not like her."

"No, it's not." Daniel pulled himself up from the fence post he'd been leaning against; he was a tall man with beautiful white hair and thin, patrician features. "It's that shooting. She can't shake off killing that man. I don't know if she ever will."

Dani was walking Biscuit toward them, and Ellen spoke quickly, "She needs help, Dan. Have you talked to her?"

"Tried to. But she's got it all locked up." He added hurriedly, "Don't say anything to her right now, though." He lifted his voice, demanding grumpily, "What kind of riding is that? I could do better myself!"

Dani pulled Biscuit to a halt and slipped to the ground, her thin white T-shirt soaked with sweat. Taking a handkerchief out of the pocket of the worn Wrangler jeans, she mopped her face. She put the square of cloth back, slapped the horse on the neck, then smiled briefly. "Biscuit thinks so, too, Dad. He gets downright disgusted with me when I don't come up to his standards."

The two began to talk about the fine points of barrel racing, and Ellen stood there watching them. *She's closer to Dan than she is to me,* Dani's mother thought, but without jealousy. *They're so much alike. She's always gone to him with her problems, just as Allison comes to me.*

"I'll go get breakfast," she announced. "And you wash that horse off your hands before you come to the table, Dani!" She walked back through the dew-covered grass, toward the two-story plantation house, entered the kitchen, and found her fifteen-year-old daughter sitting at the table, reading a book. "You do the toast, Allison," she commanded, pulling a large, cast-iron skillet from a shelf.

"I thought we were having pancakes," the girl objected. Putting the book down, she took the wheat bread from a box and began mortaring it generously with yellow butter.

"There's no time for that this morning," Ellen said. Taking a large bowl of eggs from the refrigerator, she glanced over at the girl. "Don't put so much butter on that bread. I'm trying to lose weight."

"Well, I'm trying to *gain*, Mother," Allison snapped. "I can't go around looking like a skeleton!"

Ellen suppressed a smile, for she knew Allison was sensitive about her figure. Actually she was like a young filly, leggy and a little awkward, but already her figure was beginning to form, and soon she would be a beautiful woman. "You can stuff yourself with milk shakes, but the rest of us are fighting the battle of the bulge."

Allison sniffed, but she had a naturally sunny disposition, so passed on to another subject. "Is Dani going to stay for the weekend? I hope so! She can help me with that dumb old geometry! What good is that old stuff, anyway?" She slapped a slice of buttered bread into the Munsey toaster with great force. "I think it's all part of a communist plot!"

"You can't read novels and do gymnastics all the time," Ellen pointed out. "There are other things, and math is one of them. It'll be good for you," she added, vigorously stirring the eggs she had broken into a large green bowl.

"Did *you* like it, when you were in school?"

Ellen thought of the straight D's she had made in geometry and chose to ignore the question. "Don't you bother Dani too much, Allison."

Allison looked up quickly, her large blue eyes wide. "Why not? She's not still in a slump because she shot that man, is she?" When her mother hesitated, she continued defiantly, "Why, she *had* to do it! I'd have done the same thing myself—and I wouldn't have worried about it for one second!"

Allison was bragging, Ellen knew, for the girl could not bear to hurt anything. There was no way to explain to the youngest of her children what a terrible burden killing the man had been for Dani.

29

"Don't say anything to her, Allison," she repeated firmly. "Your sister is having a very hard time. Just be sweet and show her lots of love." Glancing out the window, she observed, "Here they come. Set the table—and don't mention the shooting."

Dani came in, smiling at something her father had said, and by the time she had washed, the food was ready. She came back and sat down across from her mother. As soon as the blessing was said, Allison wanted to know, "Dani, will you help me with my dumb old geometry tonight?"

"Allison, you let Dani eat her breakfast," Ellen warned, giving her younger daughter a stern look. Then she asked, "You'll be staying all weekend, Dani? We haven't seen much of you lately."

Dani shook her head. "Afraid not. Too much work piled up at the office." Then she smiled. "But I'll be here again tonight, Allison. We can whip the geometry out after supper."

"Well—I've got an announcement to make." Dan was shoveling the scrambled eggs into his mouth, but swallowed to speak more clearly. He grinned at Dani. "I had a talk with Doctor Pascoe today. He says I'm as good as new and that I can go back to work." Washing down the eggs with a stiff jolt of black coffee, he added, "Now you can let the old man handle the hard stuff."

Dani was nibbling at a piece of toast. Ellen noticed that she had hardly touched her eggs, just shoved them around with her fork. Now she gave her father a straight glance. "Is that so, Dad?"

"Well—yes," Dan said with just a slight hesitation. Then he nodded emphatically. "Oh, he's cautious, but he gave me a go-ahead."

"You didn't tell me that, Dan," Ellen countered.

"Guess I forgot. But I'm all right, he said."

Dani pointed the toast at him as if it were a loaded gun. "Dad, I think your heart attack had a bad effect on your morals."

"What does *that* mean?" her father demanded.

"It means you've taken up lying." Dani took a bite of the toast but kept her eyes on his face. "I had a little talk with Doctor Pascoe myself, just yesterday."

Daniel Ross looked, Ellen thought, like a little boy with his hand caught in the cookie jar. She knew him well enough to realize that he was guilty and asked, "What did the doctor really say, Dani?"

"He said that Dad was much improved and that he could come to the office for a few hours a day, as long as he did no strenuous work."

"Well, that's what I said!" her father protested quickly, his face slightly flushed.

"No, you didn't say that." Dani took a sip of her coffee, studying him clinically. "Your exact words were 'Doctor Pascoe said I'm as good as new.'"

"Oh, for heaven's sake, Dani!" her father protested. "That's what he *meant!*"

"No, it's not. And you're not going to come to the office and work yourself into another heart attack."

The two of them were staring at each other over the table, and Ellen thought suddenly how much they looked alike. They were both very stubborn people. She intervened at once, "I talked to Doctor Pascoe, too, Dan. And he told me the same thing he told Dani. So you can stay at the office a few hours, a couple days of the week."

"Good grief!" Daniel Ross's face was scored with chagrin, and he added irritatedly, "Man can't call his soul his own, what with these fuddy-duddy doctors and whining women!" Then he shook his head, coming up with a weak smile. "I should have known better than to try to fool a trained investigator. Well, will it be all right with everyone if I go in for a few measly hours today?"

Dani nodded. "Yes. You can sit at your desk and study the case files." She got up and went around to run her fingers through his hair. A smile came to her lips, but she promised sternly, "I'll send him home at noon, Mother."

"Sherlock Holmes never had to put up with this!" he growled.

"Holmes was a bachelor, dear," Ellen remarked, then smiling sweetly, added, "'He that hath wife and children hath given hostages to fortune.' Don't eat the rest of those eggs. You can almost see the cholesterol on them!"

After Dani left to change for work and Allison scrambled to the highway to catch her school bus, Ellen followed Dan into their bedroom. As he changed, she said, "Thought you'd put one over, didn't you?" She came to stand beside him as he knotted his tie in front of the mirror. Putting her arms around him, she gave him a hard squeeze. "I knew you'd try something like that."

He tightened the blue and maroon tie, then gave her a kiss. "I'm about to go nuts, Ellen." He nodded. "I mean it; I've thought lately I'd rather be dead than crazy."

"I know," she whispered. "But be careful! I know how you are when you get on a case. But you've got to stay around a long time. Rob and Allison need you. Dani needs you." She looked up at him and whispered, "And I need you most of all, Dan!"

He held her quietly, then stepped back. "God's going to take care of me, Ellen. He didn't get me through all this to let me die. I'll take it easy, but Dani needs help. Ben's been gone for two weeks now—and Dani's taken up all the slack."

"Has she heard from him at all?"

"Not a word." Dan slipped into a light tan coat, kissed her, then promised, "I'll be back about noon."

He found Dani waiting in the foyer. The two of them drove to town in separate cars. Angie looked up as they entered the office, a smile touching her lips. "Well, now we can get some work done around this place!"

"Hi, Angie." Ross smiled. "You're looking great."

"See to it that he goes home at noon, Angie," Dani commanded sternly. "Run him out with a stick if you have to. Come on in the office, Dad."

"Let Angie fill me in on the broad picture," he suggested, and he turned toward the door. "Hello, Luke," he said as Sixkiller came in.

"Back at work?" Sixkiller asked, shaking hands. "Good to see you, Dan."

"Just a part-time errand boy." Daniel shrugged.

"Better than me."

Dani gave Sixkiller a sharp look. "What does that mean?"

"Means, I'm unemployed."

"No! They didn't fire you over that Stevens charge!" Dani replied sharply. "Nobody believes you used excessive force on Sweet Willie."

Sixkiller shrugged, his dark face impassive. "The police commissioner does. Suspended me for three months."

"I'll give the commissioner a call," Dan Ross offered, frowning. "He ought to know better than that!"

"He's paying back a favor to someone," Sixkiller explained. "Got his tail in a crack, and I'm the fall guy." Some of the fatalism that made up the man suddenly came through as he admitted, "Could have been worse, Dan. The do-gooders tried to get him to fire me. He refused to do that. 'A little vacation, Luke,' is the way he put it when he gave me the news."

"What'll you do until then?" Dani asked.

"Drink whiskey and chase women." Sixkiller's dark eyes gleamed, and he let his left lid droop in a slight wink that only Dani's father saw. "What about it, Babe? If I get me a bike, you wanna get a black leather jacket and split? Shake off the shackles of middle-class morality?"

"You'll have to get my father's permission," Dani replied.

"Okay by me." Dan Ross nodded. "You need to broaden your outlook, Dani."

"Well, thanks a lot!" Dani objected indignantly. "Father of the year, that's what you are, Daniel Ross! Just for that, I *will* go out with this hooligan!"

Sixkiller grinned. "I thought we'd have a bite at McDonald's, then catch Championship Wrestling at the Arena. Tonight it's Chainsaw Bart against the Hungarian Beast, Texas style. Ought to be a fine contest. Pick you up at seven."

Dani laughed, but to her chagrin, he *did* take her to the wrestling match! First he took her to Tavern on the Park, an 1860 landmark with a spectacular view. They began their meal with shrimp remoulade, crabmeat St. Jacques, and fried alligator, and finished with desserts of homemade bread pudding and chocolate mousse.

"You're unemployed," Dani pointed out when the check came. "Let me take care of it."

"Nope, I cashed in my old-age pension," Luke said. Then he looked at the tab and his eyebrows went up. "It'll just about cover this little snack."

They left the restaurant, and when they were in the car, Dani asked, "Where to now?"

"I told you today," he reminded her as he started the engine. "The wrestling matches."

"Oh, Luke—!"

"You ever been?"

"Well, no. . . ."

"It'll broaden your cultural base."

Dani stared at him, then laughed. "All right. Let's go."

He took her to the arena, and for the next hour she sat there, stunned. The wrestlers were huge, some of them fat, some sleek and padded with muscle. They posed and screamed with rage, pounding each other into the mat with awesome power. But the audience attracted Dani's attention, and she spent more time watching purple-haired old ladies screeching like banshees and cursing like sailors than she did watching the wrestlers.

After an hour, when the tag-team match was over—a contest between two huge bearded men who lacked front teeth, wore overalls, and called themselves the Hillbilly Horrors and two sleek men who were billed as Captain Democracy and the Freedom Kid—Sixkiller sighed. "Well, it goes downhill from here on."

On the way to the Ross home, Dani questioned, "Luke, it's beyond me. Why do people watch such stuff?"

"You didn't like it?"

"It's so—*phony!*" Dani slumped down in the seat and thought about it. "You know when one wrestler gets the other by the wrist, then puts his foot on his jaw—and *kicks* him in the face?"

"What about it?"

"Why, just *one* kick would half kill a man! But they kicked and kicked, and nobody even got hurt, not really. I mean, they pound on each other and throw each other around, but you can see it's all practiced. Why would anyone watch a sport like that?"

"It's not a sport," Sixkiller shrugged. "It's a drama. Used to be a sport. Back in 1936 George Hackenschmidt and Ed Lewis wrestled for the world's heavyweight wrestling championship on the level." He took the Porsche between two semis in a careless fashion, then continued, "Lewis got a head-lock on Hackenschmidt, and the two stayed locked on the canvas for nearly an hour. Can you picture the audience tonight watching *that*?"

"No!"

"Right! So when the wrestlers found out that the crowd wanted action and crazy stunts, they gave it to them. But what it really is, Dani, is some kind of morality play. It's always good against evil."

Dani thought about it, then nodded. "That's right. One of the wrestlers was always a good guy and the other one a rotten villain."

"Now you got it! So the fans go to scream for the good guy and to spit on the bad guy. That's what it's all about."

"But can't they *see* it's not real?"

"Naw. It's as real as the soaps, wouldn't you say? Those guys appear to get hurt and shed blood once in a while, so the real fan will say, 'How about all that blood, hey? What about that?' And the wrestlers sometimes put capsules in their mouths, to spit out what looks like blood. Some of them will nick themselves with a little blade. A teaspoonful of blood looks bad when it's on a man's eyes."

"It's all just a show," Dani concluded. "It's not real."

Sixkiller said nothing until they pulled up in front of her parents' home. When they got to the door, he maintained, "Nothing much is real in this world, Dani. Most of the stuff I see is just as phony as professional wrestling."

Dani turned to face him. "But not all of it, Luke."

He hesitated, then nodded. "Right. There are some splashes of light in the dark."

"Why, that's beautiful!" Dani said, looking at him in surprise. "Is it poetry?"

"Never read the stuff," he denied quickly and then would have kissed her, but the door opened. He turned. "Hey, Dan, you really are old school, aren't you? Waiting for the boyfriend to bring little Dani home from the high-school dance."

Dan Ross didn't smile. "Come on in, both of you."

"What is it, Dad?"

"It's Ben," he reported. He bit his lip and handed her a slip of paper. "This is the number for Baptist Hospital in Dallas. He's there."

"What's wrong with him?"

"I don't know. They wouldn't tell me much. The only identification he had was your card, as his employer. They want you to call right away. Ask for Doctor Rogers."

At once Dani moved to the phone and dialed the number. "I'm Danielle Ross. Let me speak to Doctor Rogers, please." She waited, tapping her foot anxiously. After what seemed a long time, she spoke into the mouthpiece, "Yes, Doctor Rogers, this is Danielle Ross. Yes, he works for me. What's wrong?" She listened without comment, and both men saw that her face turned pale, and her fingers were white, so tightly did she grip the phone. Finally she said, "Yes, I'll be in as soon as I can get there, Doctor. Be sure he gets the best you have."

"What is it?" her father asked as soon as she replaced the receiver in its cradle.

"He's in a coma." Dani's voice was steady, but she put her hands behind her to conceal the trembling—something both men noticed. "He's been badly beaten and hasn't regained consciousness since he was brought in." She suddenly straightened up, announcing, "I'm going to Dallas."

"You don't need to drive, Dani," her father suggested.

"I'm all right!"

Sixkiller put in, "I'm unemployed, remember? We'd better take your car, though."

Dani nodded. "Thanks, Luke. I'll get an overnight case."

When she left, Dan confided, "I'm glad you're going." He hesitated, not knowing how much Sixkiller knew, then added, "She's been having a problem anyway, and this won't help."

"She shook up over killing that guy?" Sixkiller nodded in answer to his own question. "Yeah, I've seen it eat on her. Look, Dan, I'll stay with her, drive her back and all. Try not to worry, you and Ellen."

Dan took a deep breath, then found a piece of a smile. "You're a good guy, Luke. We'll feel a lot better if you are with her. And if she wants to stay, that's okay. I can handle things in the office. Get a little help, if we need it."

"Won't help her if you kill yourself working, Dan."

"No. I'll watch it."

They talked quietly until Dani came down. Ellen was with her, and they said their good-byes quickly. "Call when you get any word, Dani," Ellen called out as they got into the car.

"I will. Go to bed and don't worry."

As the car pulled out of the driveway and headed for the interstate, Ellen whispered as an echo to Dani's parting word: "Don't worry." She turned and leaned against Dan's chest. "Has any parent ever figured out how to do that?"

He held her tightly, peering at the red gleam of the taillights as they faded, and shook his head. "No—and no parent will. Come on inside and we'll say a prayer for her. And for Ben, too."

Sixkiller took Interstate 10 through Baton Rouge, then at Lafayette took 49 North. Except for a detour at Alexandria, where the cloverleaf was being completed, he sent the Cougar flashing down the highway at speeds up to ninety. Once, just past Shreveport, he was stopped by a state trooper, but he showed his badge, told a lie about his mission, and was waved on. Interstate 20 out of Shreveport ran straight into Dallas. Although it was a little over 500 miles from New Orleans to Dallas, it was only 8:15 A.M. when they pulled up in front of Baptist Hospital.

Dani got out of the car, her legs so stiff from the long hours of sitting that Luke had to catch her as she staggered. She said with a grimace, "Quick trip, Luke."

"Yeah, Can you make it now?"

"Sure."

They entered by the front door, and the gray-haired lady at the information desk told them, "Ben Savage—yes, he's in intensive care. That's on the third floor."

They took the elevator to the intensive care waiting room. Two men and one woman—all looking worn and haggard— sat in the uncomfortable-looking chairs covered with green vinyl. All three looked up as Sixkiller and Dani entered, then dropped their eyes.

"We'd like to see Ben Savage," Dani explained to the nurse who sat behind the desk.

She looked at them, then ran her pink fingernail down a paper, stopping at a name. "He's Doctor Rogers' patient. Have you talked to the doctor?"

"No. Is he in the hospital?"

"I don't think so. You'll need to speak with him. But Mr. Savage can only have one visitor, and only for ten minutes every four hours."

Dani shook her head and was about to argue, but the waiting woman, who sat beside the door, got up and stepped closer. "Are you Miss Ross?"

"Yes." Dani looked at the woman, who appeared to be in her middle twenties. She was dark, with very black hair cut short, brown eyes, and a squarish face. "This is Lieutenant Sixkiller."

"I'm Ruth Cantrell." She hesitated, then glanced down at the two men. "Could we have a cup of coffee? There's a cafeteria on the first floor."

Automatically Dani responded, "Yes, of course." She and Sixkiller left the waiting room with the woman, who said nothing until they reached the cafeteria. "You drove all night, I expect. The food is good here."

Dani saw that Ruth Cantrell was having difficulty of some sort. The ceremony of eating together would probably loosen her up, Dani decided. "Sounds good. You hungry, Luke?"

"Sure."

The three of them got trays and soon were settled at a table in a corner of the room. The cafeteria was only half full, and they had some privacy. Dani at once bowed her head and said a silent thanksgiving. When she looked up, she saw the other woman staring at her.

"I—I guess you'd better know about me," Ruth began, then seemed to grow hesitant.

"You're the girl Ben was with in New Orleans, aren't you?" Dani guessed. Sixkiller nodded imperceptibly, for she fit the description he had gotten from one of his men, who'd seen the pair several times.

"That's right," Ruth said. Then she lifted her head and looked directly into Dani's eyes. "My maiden name was *Savage*."

Dani blinked with surprise, then nodded slowly. "You're Ben's sister, then?"

"Yes."

"You look like him." Dani took a sip of coffee and studied the woman. The resemblance to Ben was clear, now that she knew the relationship. Ruth had the same wide cheekbones, short nose, and crisp black hair. Like Ben, she had a slightly European cast to her features, and there was some of his caution in her eyes. Dani suddenly remembered how she had practically run Ben out of the agency over this woman—and realized with sharp discomfort that she had been almost jealous over his interest in her.

"Ben's in terrible shape," Ruth said, biting her lower lip. "I—I guess you'd better know the whole story?"

She broke off suddenly and stared at Sixkiller with obvious doubt.

"It's all right," Dani quickly assured her. "Luke's a good friend of Ben's. You can talk in front of him."

"Well—all right." Ruth looked down at her hands, then up again with a show of determination. "It's all my fault that he's hurt."

"Better start at the beginning, Ruth," Dani advised. "Why did you come to New Orleans?"

"I came to get Ben to help me. But I wish I hadn't!" She shook her head, and misery filled her dark brown eyes. "I didn't know who else to go to for help."

"What kind of help?" Sixkiller asked, almost idly. He made a tough shape as he lounged in his chair, but something in his face seemed to give the woman confidence.

"Ben and I haven't been real close since we grew up," she began slowly. "But we always stuck together when we were kids. It was a rough time for us—I guess Ben's told you some of it?"

"You tell us again, Ruth," Dani nodded. "We need to know everything."

"All right. I was married to a man named Larry Cantrell. He was no good. Beat me up and ran around with every woman he could find. He was a crook. Got killed in some sort of drug thing. The police say he probably tried to hold out on some hard guys, and they killed him. All I got from him was bruises and a hatred for men." She sipped her coffee, bitterness in her eyes, but then she shrugged and went on.

"I stayed away from people for about a year after Larry was shot. I'll never know why, but he took out an insurance policy and made me the beneficiary. I got $20,000 in a lump sum. Lived on it for a few months, then I went to stay with a friend who owns a ranch in New Mexico. It was great there," she remembered wistfully. "Nobody trying to hustle me. And what got me were the horses."

"What kind of horses?" Dani inquired suddenly.

"Some quarter horses, some thoroughbreds." Ruth smiled. "And some mixed breeds. My friend, Rhonda, she was a barrel racer." She smiled and nodded at Dani. "Ben told me you have a horse, that you used to race yourself."

"That's right."

"Well, maybe you can understand," Ruth said, her eyes expressive. "Rhonda taught me how to ride, and I was good! Had a natural gift. Guess it runs in the family, Ben being an aerialist and all. He told me it probably took the same kind of timing to race a horse as it took to work the trapeze. Anyway, I went with Rhonda to some rodeos and found out I was good enough to win—some of the time. So finally I took some of the money and bought a horse and started rodeoing."

"How'd you make out?" Sixkiller asked.

"Not bad. I made over three thousand dollars the first four months. So I got the bug. Bought a trailer and a truck and went on the circuit. It was good for me," Ruth stated quietly. "I got rid of most of the hatred I had for men."

"And you found one you didn't hate at all?" Dani suggested.

Ruth stared at her, then smiled. "Ben said you were a smart one, Dani. Yes, I did. Clint Thomas."

"Hey, he's been the All-Around Champion Cowboy for a couple of years!" Sixkiller exclaimed in surprise.

"Three years," Ruth corrected him. "We started dating six months ago."

"Anything serious?" Dani asked.

"It is with me," Ruth confided. "We've talked a little about marriage. We're not engaged, but we will be."

Dani studied the woman carefully. "What trouble sent you to Ben?"

Ruth gave Sixkiller a straight stare. "It's something that's going on in the rodeo. I'd heard of something like it in Chicago and Detroit, but it's new with us." She frowned, then quavered, "Someone is threatening the performers, mostly the big-time stars."

"What kind of threats?" Dani demanded.

"It's always a phone call. Clint's gotten two of them. A man says, 'You pay me a thousand dollars, or your horse will wind up with a broken leg.'"

Sixkiller nodded. "Just the old protection racket in a new form. Lots of it in the big cities. A storekeeper gets a word that if he doesn't cough up protection money, his store will get bombed. Mafia stuff, some of it."

"Has anyone tried to stand up to the threats?" Dani asked.

"Tilman Yates did. He was in second place national for bull-dogging. When he got the threat, he just laughed. But the next week his horse had his leg broken. Had to be destroyed."

"What'd Yates do?" Luke wanted to know.

"Went to the cops, but they couldn't find anything. Then a week later, Tilman told us he'd gotten another threat. He was mad over the horse and said he'd sleep next to his new horse with a loaded forty-five. But it didn't do him any good."

"What happened, Ruth?" Dani asked.

"He was beaten up." Ruth bit her lip and shook her head. "He was in the hospital for two months."

"Who did it?" Sixkiller demanded.

"Nobody knows. Somebody caught him coming out of a tavern in El Paso. He was pretty drunk, the witnesses say. The attacker took him to an alley and smashed his knees. He'll never ride again."

"So now everyone pays up?" Dani guessed.

Ruth stared at her. "Not Clint. He swears he'll never pay a cent."

Dani sighed and then nodded. "So you went to get Ben to find the one behind this racket."

Ruth looked miserable. "Yes, I did. But it didn't work."

"What happened to Ben?" Dani leaned forward on her elbows. "I guess he plunged right in?"

"Yes. Everyone knew he was out to find the crook. But he didn't have a chance."

"How'd they get him, Ruth?" Sixkiller demanded. "Ben's a pretty tough guy. Smart, too."

"Nobody really knows." Tears rose to Ruth's eyes, and she pulled a handkerchief from her purse. "He told me day before yesterday he thought he had some kind of lead; then he disappeared. Nobody saw him until a couple of kids found him in an alley on the south side of town, unconscious."

"What does the doctor say, Ruth?" Dani inquired.

"Oh, he's like all doctors, I guess—afraid to say much of anything. But Ben's better now than he was yesterday. I can see that. Got a broken collarbone and some internal injuries. But it's the head injury that's the worst. Doctor Rogers says he can't be sure how bad it is." She began to weep helplessly, and the people at other tables began to cast covert glances toward their table.

"I'll talk to the doctor," Dani offered." We'll pray that he'll be all right."

Ruth got control of herself and gave Dani a wan look. "Ben said you were real religious," she told her. "I'm not, but I wish

I were. Do you think if I promise to go to church God will help Ben get well?"

Dani felt her gaze and the weight of Sixkiller's attention. Suddenly she was weary of having her faith put on trial. She wanted to shout, *Why don't you stop trying to buy God? Do you think he's some sort of huckster, trying to bargain for your grubby little soul?*

But she kept her face still, saying only, "God wants to help us all, Ruth. Let's go back to the waiting room."

As they left the cafeteria, Sixkiller remarked quietly, "You missed a good chance for a sermon there." Then he took her arm and gave it a comforting squeeze. "But I think Ruth and I got the message!"

3

"You're No Good to Anybody!"

Funny how we count time," Sixkiller remarked as he stared up at the ceiling tiles of the waiting room. "Sometimes we count it by seconds, like when we're in a dentist's chair and he's boring into a molar. Every second's a month." His neck began to ache, and he pulled himself up stiffly from where he'd been sprawled, trying to rest his head on the back of one of the hard chairs. Rubbing the nape of his neck, he flexed his heavy shoulders. "But sometimes it drags on like a slow-motion movie. Like now. All we count now is a ten-minute visit every four hours."

Dani lifted her gaze, startled by the sound of his voice. They had been alone in the waiting room for nearly four hours, and the silence had sunk into her. She arched her back, nodded, then said, "That's Einstein's theory of relativity, Luke."

Sixkiller grinned, his teeth very white against his bronze skin. "It is? Well, if it's that simple, I could have saved him a lot of trouble." He looked at his watch, then informed her, "Half-hour before midnight. You want some coffee?"

"I guess not."

"Well, I do." He came to his feet, commanding as he left the room, "Hold the fort."

Dani nodded, thinking how bad it would have been if Luke hadn't been with her. Dr. Rogers had come by for a quick visit but could offer no promises. "He could wake up at any time," he stated, but had not said what they all were thinking—that Ben might *never* wake up. Ruth had gone home at noon, asleep on her feet, and the two of them had sat in the waiting room hour after hour. Dani had gone in to see Ben at noon, but the sight had shocked her. He had been very pale, and the glowing faces of the dials, the tubes that ran into his body, and the machine noises frightened her. She had stood by his bed, reaching down once to let her hand rest on his forehead, but he seemed drained of life, and she left the room quickly at the nurse's word.

Sixkiller had picked up on her mood but had not rushed to comfort her with platitudes. When she had told him how Ben looked, he'd stood there, his big hands at his sides and a brooding look in his ebony eyes. All he said was, "Ben's a tough one. He'll make it."

But ignoring her protests, he had made her leave the waiting room. "Nothing to do here until four o'clock," he had announced firmly. "Let's take a walk." Luke had practically dragged her outside and walked her hard, stopping once in a while to look at some ducks in a small lake. "Mallards." He nodded. "Like to have one of them all roasted with some wild rice." They were tamed by their stay and came out of the water, waddling up and quacking for handouts. One of them was not a mallard, and Dani asked with interest, "What in the world is *that* duck? Or *is* it a duck?"

"Sure it's a duck—a Muscovy duck."

Dani stared at it. "That's the ugliest duck I've ever seen in my life!"

"To you, maybe." Sixkiller shrugged. "But to a female Muscovy duck this one may be the Robert Redford of the duck world."

Dani smiled and watched the bird, which was very large and black, with short legs. But he had a tremendous red wattle right in front of his eyes and what looked like red warts scattered around it.

Sixkiller informed her, "They're good laying ducks. People raise them for the eggs."

"How do you know so much about ducks?" Dani asked.

Sixkiller gave her a sly look. "I'm an Indian. Us noble savages know lots of stuff you palefaces don't," he teased.

He had taken her back to the hospital a few minutes before four o'clock. When Dani came out of Ben's room with the report that he looked no better, Luke had suggested, "Let's feed Handsome some bread; then we'll go get some Tex-Mex food." He had driven her to a small convenience store, bought five loaves of bread, and they had gone back to the pond and fed the ducks. Handsome, as they called the Muscovy, was a bully, keeping the mallards from the food by headlong rushing and horrible hissings.

"Reminds me of some of my relatives," Sixkiller had remarked, and Dani had laughed.

Afterward he had taken her to El Patio and practically forced her to eat a good meal. Then he had driven to a motel a few blocks from the hospital and gotten two rooms. When she had protested, he had simply pushed her into the room with the words, "Lie down. If you can't sleep, at least you can rest."

She had taken a shower and lain down. To her surprise, she had dropped off to sleep. Two hours later his knock had awakened her, and she had felt refreshed as they went back to the waiting room.

Ben seemed the same, and Sixkiller said when she came out and gave her report, "Let's take a drive." Then he had driven her around the city, commenting, "God made the country, man made the town. Us Sioux had a good thing going until you white guys came along and screwed it up."

They got back to the hospital at a quarter to eight. There was still no change. Dani stood beside Ben's still figure, prayed, and felt frightened. He had not moved once during any of the visits. When she went out, she worried, "Luke, he's bad. I wish the doctor would come."

She had refused to leave the waiting room, for the nurse had mentioned that Dr. Rogers usually made his rounds at midnight. Now, sitting alone, she realized how skillfully Luke had maneuvered her, for her nerves would have been frayed if she had remained in the waiting room all day. He was one of the hardest men she had ever known, but she knew now that beneath that hard muscle and tough manner lay a sensitive spirit.

Suddenly Dr. Rogers came through the door, calling, "Miss Ross?" Dani sprang to her feet eagerly. "Come along," he directed. "We'll see how he's doing."

She followed him down the hall, walking rapidly to keep up with him. He was in his sixties, a tall man with long legs, a thatch of white hair, and a set of steady gray eyes. He said nothing at all, and she stood back as he read the charts without comment, then moved next to the bed and looked down at Ben. Dani moved opposite him as he reached out and lifted an eyelid and peered into Ben's eye with a lighted instrument.

49

When he straightened up and glanced at her, she could read nothing in his expression.

He had a very thick southern accent—a South Carolina one, she discovered later. "Ah can't tell you anything new, Miss Ross. Like Ah said before, this kind of injury—well, theah's no way to make a prognosis." He frowned and shook his head, looking down at Ben, lost in thought. He appeared very tired, and his lips were pulled together in a tight seam.

"Can't you tell me *anything*, Dr. Rogers?"

He brought his gray eyes back to study her. "You his lady friend?"

Dani flushed, then explained quickly, "I'm his employer."

Dr. Rogers looked at her as if she were a specimen under a microscope. A hint of humor touched his eyes, though he didn't smile. "Must be a pretty good workuh for you to come all the way heah to sit with him."

"We're—good friends, Doctor," Dani said quietly.

He nodded. "Ah see that. Well, the good news, Miss Ross, is that theah's nothing bad wrong with him—that we can *find*. He's got a very bad concussion, but I've seen worse cases snap out of a coma like this and never have a minute's problem. The *bad* news is that theah may be somethin' we can't find. That brain heah—" he put his hand on Ben's forehead and frowned, "—well, it's the most complicated object on God's earth! Just one little wire out of place—and the whole machine shuts down."

"You think he might die?" Dani asked, keeping her voice steady.

"I don't think so, but he might. And he might live and nevah think a logical thought again."

Dani kept her gaze locked into his, and stated evenly, "I'm going to believe he's going to be completely well."

Dr. Rogers nodded briefly. "Bettuh to think that, Miss Ross. But it's out of my hands. Not much we doctuhs can do with something like this."

She knew he was telling her to be prepared for death, but she declared, "I'm a Christian, Dr. Rogers. Ben may be beyond your help, but he's not beyond God's help."

He had heard it before, she could tell, and had no doubt seen men and women who had been prayed for die. But he merely nodded and offered, "I'll let you know if theah's any change, Miss Ross."

He left abruptly. Dani put her hand on Ben's forehead and prayed quietly. When the nurse came in, she left the room and found Sixkiller waiting. "What's the doc say?" he asked.

"He says that he can't do anything. Ben might wake up all right at any time—but he might not make it." Then she squared her shoulders and pronounced firmly, "But I'm trusting God to bring him out of it!"

Sixkiller felt sudden admiration for Dani, for though he was not a Christian, he had made some close observations of the young woman before him. He saw that despite the fatigue and pressure that marked her face and made her strong shoulders droop, she was not giving up. He encouraged her, "Ben's lucky to have you in his corner." Then he called, "Come on."

"Where to?"

"I'm going to put you to bed." Sixkiller took her arm and led her out of the waiting room as if she were a recalcitrant child. He spoke of other things as he drove her to the motel. When they got to her door, he ordered, "You sleep eight hours. I'll see Ben at four o'clock. Then you can see him at eight." He hesitated, then warned, "This may be a long-time thing, Dani. You've got to take care of yourself."

Dani looked at him and smiled. "I don't think so, Luke," she disagreed, leaning forward and kissing him on the cheek.

"It looks as if I've got you to take care of me." She turned and stepped inside the room, leaving him to stare at the door for a full minute. Then he turned and walked to his own room, his face thoughtful as he touched the spot on his cheek that bore a trace of her lipstick.

Dani opened the door the next morning at seven to find Sixkiller waiting. "Let's go eat," he suggested. On their way to the hospital he told her about his visit at four o'clock. "Gave me kind of a shake, you know?" he admitted, keeping his eyes on the traffic. "I mean, Ben's always been so active—and when I saw him all pale and still, well, I didn't much like it. Never was much good around sick people."

They found Ruth at the hospital and with her was Clint Thomas. She introduced him to the pair, and Dani felt the power of his hands in the brief handshake. "Glad to know you, Miss Ross," he greeted her in a soft baritone. "But too bad it's got to be under such tough circumstances." He was not a large man, which surprised Dani for some reason. Wiry and strong, he was no more than medium height, with stiff black hair and deep-set black eyes. He had a cleft in his chin and was not handsome, but Dani knew he would draw the attention of women. He was, Ruth had told her, thirty-eight years old and divorced.

"Glad to meet you, Clint," Sixkiller exclaimed, then added, "I was there the night you rode Tombstone."

Thomas gave the muscular Sixkiller a keen look and smiled ruefully, "Well, I'm glad you were there that night, 'cause nobody's rode him *since* then!" He looked suddenly at Dani. "Are you two—ah—going together?"

"I'm—ah—trying my best to talk her into it, Clint," Sixkiller retorted. "Not much luck so far. May be she won't have an Indian on the place."

"Oh, hush, Luke!" Dani sputtered, then turned to Ruth. "You go in this time. Luke and I will be here all day."

Ruth nodded and left, and the three of them sat down to wait. Sixkiller asked Clint how he had done lately, and Thomas spoke easily. "Got kind of a hold on number one—but that ol' Bake could take that away anytime, Luke." He spoke openly of the money he'd made thus far, and Dani sat there listening, trying to read the man. She'd only known Ruth a few hours, but she was Ben's sister and was in love with Clint Thomas. This man was no grocery clerk; in his own small world, he was king. That did things to people, Dani realized. It made despots out of some, brought out benevolence in others. She had kept up with the world of rodeo years ago, in high school, and was aware that the stars in that world drew groupies. There would be plenty of women for Clint Thomas—easy women, who would ask nothing more than his notice, at any price. Some men could handle that, and some women, too—but many became users, tiring quickly of what came so easily and always looking for a new thrill.

Ruth came back after the brief visit, announcing, "He's just the same." Dani persuaded her that there was no need for staying and suggested, "You can come back and see him at four o'clock. Luke and I will be here."

Ruth said, "All right, Dani, if you think so."

Clint offered, "Hey, if there's anything I can do—maybe help with the expenses, anything?"

But Dani recommended, "Just take care of Ruth." She stood there, watching the pair leave, and at once asked, "What did you think of him?"

"Clint Thomas? I guess he's okay." Sixkiller's brow wrinkled, and he added, "He's got a rep as a woman chaser—but any guy in his shoes would have women after him."

53

"I hope he's all right. Ruth doesn't need another bump right now."

"Well, let's go feed Handsome," Sixkiller proposed. They got the bread and sat down under a small oak beside the pond. The sun was hot as it rose, but the sound of the waves lapping the shore and the reflection of the small tree quivering in the water brought a peace to the place. Dani threw bread to the ducks, watched them gobble it down, and laughed as Handsome carried on his eternal war to hog all the food.

She went in to see Ben at noon. Ruth came at four—this time alone—and then Dani went in at eight. She went out for a sandwich and for another walk, then called her parents, giving them her brief and unsatisfying report on Ben's condition. "I'd better come home tonight, Dad," she suggested.

"Don't worry about the office," he insisted. "I talked to Mel this morning, and he can help fill in until you can get free." Mel Hartz was an ex-investigator who had once worked for Daniel and if he was on the job, there was no problem with her father.

The hours moved slowly. During the midnight visit Dani was startled. She had gone into Ben's room, and in the solitude was praying audibly and fervently for him. Her prayer was for God's will to be done, but she cried, "O God, I don't *know* your will for Ben! And until I do know it, I'm going to pray for you to bring health to his body. He's in your hands, not the hands of the doctors—!"

At a faint noise she broke off and looked up to see with some degree of shock that Dr. Rogers had entered the room and was standing right across from her, considering her with a level gaze. "Oh—Dr. Rogers! I didn't hear you come in!" she told him apologetically.

He smiled, the first smile she'd seen on his lips, and granted, "Well, I gathered you weren't talkin' to me, Miss Ross. And I nevuh want to interrupt when someone's talkin' to God."

Dani asked quietly, "Do you believe in God, Doctor?"

"Yes, Ah guess Ah do." Dr. Rogers shrugged. "But Ah'm not on as good terms with him as you are." Then he broke off and looked down at Ben, putting his fingers on the strong throat. "He's no bettuh, Miss Ross. In fact, he's worse. The longer he stays in this coma, the worse it is. Could go into a bad condition."

Dani bowed her head, then raised it suddenly. Her eyes were gray-green, the strangest color Rogers had ever seen, and her lips were tight with determination. "Doctor Rogers, let me stay with him," she requested. "I won't do a thing. All I want to do is stand beside him."

The doctor knew the answer he should give to that request, but for some reason that puzzled him, he refused to give it. Intensive care, he well knew, was to keep people *out*. But after the silence in the room had run on for a few seconds, he nodded. "Don't see any harm in it," he admitted. He considered Dani, then cryptically added as he turned to leave, "May even do some good."

Dr. Rogers poked his head in the waiting room, explaining, "Youh young woman, she's goin' to stay with Mistuh Savage." Then he cocked his head, an admiring look in his eyes. He smiled. "She's a *pistol*, ain't she now?"

Dani stood beside Ben for nearly four hours, moving almost not at all. Occasionally nurses would come and read the gauges, make notations, then leave, but they didn't speak to her.

The time meant nothing to Dani. It might have been minutes or seconds for all that she knew. She had prayed for long periods before—but this was different. She lost, for perhaps the first time in her life, *self-consciousness*. Like most other people, Dani was always conscious of herself, even when praying. But as she prayed for Ben, at some point, she—Dani Ross—was no longer a factor in her spirit or her thoughts. She was engaged in a holy argument with God, and the only thing in the universe was God and the need—Ben's healing.

Finally, she moved into a state of consciousness of her surroundings, and it was like coming from one world to another.

She saw that Ben's eyes were open!

"Thank you, Jesus!" she whispered and leaned over. "Ben, can you hear me?"

Savage's eyes regarded her, but he didn't speak. Once she thought his lips moved, and she was *certain* that there was recognition of her in his eyes, but soon he closed his eyes again.

Dani straightened up. "I'm going to believe you, God, all the way to the cemetery! He looked at me—and he *knew* me!"

She left the room, and Sixkiller, taking one look at the stars in her eyes, came to his feet, his face alive. "He's better!"

Dani nodded, unable to speak for a moment and he took her in his arms. She wanted to weep, but struggled against it. "He opened his eyes, Luke—and he *knew* me!"

She never told anybody about that time of prayer, but when the doctor came in at four, she met him and told him what had happened. He looked at her carefully, then shrugged. "Both of you can come in."

He led Dani and Sixkiller to Ben's bed, and as soon as he touched the forehead, Savage's eyes opened. "Well, now, this is *bettuh!*" Dr. Rogers exclaimed. "Don't try to talk, young man. Just let me take a look." He stared into Savage's eyes, then straightened up. "Are you awake?" he asked.

Ben looked at him steadily, then nodded slightly. "Fine! Fine!" the doctor commented. He moved to the charts, ran his eyes over them, then came back to stand beside Savage, looking down on him. "You've had us worried. Do you know this young lady?"

Ben's head turned slightly, and his eyes fell on Dani. His lips moved, and then he moistened them. "Hello, Boss," he whispered huskily.

"Ben!" Dani's eyes filled with tears, and she had to grope for a handkerchief. Sixkiller handed her his and she dabbed at the tears that ran down her cheeks. "Ben—" she quavered, her voice rough, "You're all right."

Dr. Rogers observed Savage's response as Dani spoke to him, then ordered, "Well, now, what this young fellow needs is some rest. But I wouldn't be surprised if he wasn't out of this place and in a private room befoah long!"

He led Dani and Sixkiller out of the room and turned at once to announce, "He's going to be all right, Miss Ross. His eyes are fine—absolutely clear." Then he hesitated before saying carefully, "I told you this might happen. And the charts say that he started gettin' bettuh while you were sittin' with him. Now, I suppose you're going to say it was God's doing?"

"Yes, I am, Doctor!" Dani declared firmly. Then she gave him a militant look and asked sternly, "Whose doing do *you* think it was that brought him back?"

Dr. Rogers shook his head soberly. "Well, not *mine*, Miss Ross." Then he smiled, adding, "As a physician I have no answer, but as a seeking man, I'll have to say that I think it actually *was* God who did the work."

He left on that, and as he had said, Ben was moved to a private room. Delighted, Ruth fell into Dani's arms, tears streaming down her face. They all went out and ate at a fast-food place, but at noon the next day they all filed into Ben's room.

He was sitting up, looking alert, despite the greenish bruises on his face. Though Ben winced when he moved, his eyes were bright and aware. He watched them come in, then greeted Sixkiller with, "Not enough criminals in New Orleans to keep you busy?"

"None of my business how many crooks there are in New Orleans. I've been suspended. Police brutality."

Ben wanted to hear about it, so Sixkiller gave him a quick rundown. Then Savage greeted Dani, "Hello, Boss. Who's minding the store?"

"Dad's working some, and Mel is filling in." She wanted to touch him, but instead tried to act tough. "I knew as soon as you got out of my sight this would happen."

Savage's lips curled upward at the corners, and he nodded. "Well, Sherlock got tossed off a cliff by Professor Moriarty."

Ruth came to her brother and bent down to kiss him. "Ben, I've felt so *awful!* It was all my fault."

"How was it your fault that I was stupid?" he asked. Disgust swept his features as he added, "I might as well have worn a sign: STUPID DETECTIVE HERE—COME AND BEAT HIM UP."

"How'd they get you?" Sixkiller asked.

"Why, a guy called me up and said he had a lead on who was making the phone calls. And I just went there and let him hit me over the head."

"Did you see who it was?" Ruth inquired.

Disgust larded Savage's voice as he answered, "No. He told me to meet him out on the edge of town. Said he'd be in an eighty-nine Camaro. Well, the Camaro was there, and like a sucker I walked over to it. There was a guy in it. I bent down to speak to him, and he knocked my brains out. I guess he must have taken a few licks after I was out, too."

"You'll be out of commission for a while, Ben," Dani pointed out. "You've got a broken collarbone and some nasty bruises. As soon as Dr. Rogers says it's all right, we'll take you back home."

Savage stared at her stubbornly. "And just let Ruth go down the drain?"

Ruth interjected, "Oh, Ben, don't be muleheaded! You're in no shape to follow me around from one rodeo to the next! And now that everyone knows you're a detective, you'll never be able to find out anything."

"I can handle it."

Dani grew suddenly angry. "Ben Savage, if you think I've got nothing to do but drop everything and come running every time you get in a jam, you've got another think coming. Now, you're going back to New Orleans, and that's all there is to it!"

"Am not!" he snapped.

For the next ten minutes the three of them tried to talk Ben into going home. Finally Savage declared, "You're always trying to run a man's life, but you're not going to run mine."

Sixkiller broke in, "Hey, let's give the patient a little rest, okay?"

Dani saw that Ben's face was pale, and she bit her lip in chagrin. "I'm sorry, Ben," she apologized.

"It's okay."

The room was quiet, until Sixkiller commented, "I thought you were a smart gal, Dani. I'm just a dumb flatfoot, but I know what to do."

All three looked at Sixkiller, and he grinned suddenly. "You've got a horse and trailer, Dani. You know how to ride a barrel race. Do I have to spell it out for you?"

Dani stared at him, her eyes blank with shock. Finally she gasped, "Do you mean I should go undercover and find whoever's making those calls?"

Ruth exclaimed, "That's a wonderful idea! And you'd get paid, Dani!"

Dani stared at her. "Paid by whom?"

"By me," Ruth announced promptly. "And by the rest of us. I'll be paying for the rest of my career, if this thing goes on. Maybe I can get the others to go in, and we'll hire you to work for us."

"Sure, and you might pick up a few bucks in the barrel races," Sixkiller urged.

Dani stood there, unable to speak. Finally she snapped, "I won't do it!"

The silence ran on, and then Savage requested, "Luke, will you and Ruth step outside for a minute?" He waited until the two left, then said, "I hear you prayed me back to life."

Dani, expecting something else, flushed. "God healed you."

"Dr. Rogers said it was you." Savage looked at her strangely. "I don't think he's given to rash statements. Thanks."

Dani reddened, then took the hand he put out. "Oh, Ben, I was so scared!"

He held her hand, instead of releasing it, and she didn't know what was in his mind. His eyes were fixed on her, and finally he insisted, "Boss, you've got to do it."

Dani stiffened and tried to pull her hand away, but he held it fast. "Ben, that's a crazy idea, and you know it!"

"No, it's not crazy," he murmured. He was looking at her hand, and then he put his other one over hers and looked up into her face.

"I can't leave the agency. Dad would work himself to death."

"No, he wouldn't. You find this guy and put him down. I'll take care of the agency."

His answer took the wind out of her sails. She stood there, her hand held in both of his, and tried to think, but her mind was blank.

"Boss," Ben gently pointed out, "You're no good to anybody the way you are!" She tried to jerk her hand away, but he held it. "You killed a man, Dani. No getting away from that. He's dead, and all your tears won't bring him back."

"And will it bring him back—if I do this job for Ruth?"

Savage shook his head, and his voice was even as he replied, "No, that won't bring him back—but somehow you've got to accept the fact that you killed him. A change of scene might help. Maybe give you time to think it through—or pray it through."

He fell silent and released her hand. She stood there, her mind racing, but nothing came. Then she took a deep breath, her breast stirring as she acknowledged, "Ben, I don't think I'll ever get over it. But I'll do it. For Ruth's sake, if for no other reason."

He smiled at her, and the smile made him look much younger. "I'll owe you one for this, Boss," he said. "Tell Ruth, will you?"

Dani went to the door and opened it. When the two others came in, she announced, "I'll give it a try, Ruth. Probably won't do a bit of good, and you won't owe me if I don't come up with the crook."

Ruth was delighted, but Ben quickly demanded, "Ruth, have you told anyone about Dani, that she's a private investigator?"

"Not a soul! Not even Clint!"

"Good, keep it like that. Once Dani's found the killer, the others can kick in their share of the fee. Then Savage shook his head. "It's a risky business, Boss. I wish you had somebody to watch your back."

Sixkiller spoke up, "Oh, well, Ben, I've been watching her for a long time. I may as well watch her back for a change of pace."

"Never mind watching my back or anything else!" Dani snapped.

"I mean it," Sixkiller insisted, then gave her an odd look. "Hey, I'm an Indian, and I was raised on a horse ranch in Oklahoma. Give you one guess what I grew up hoping to be?"

Savage's eyes gleamed, and he said, "I'd guess a rodeo star."

"Give the man a cigar." Sixkiller grinned. "And I was pretty good, too. If I'd stayed with it, I might be giving Clint Thomas a run for his money. But I became a cop instead. Only now I'm an ex-cop—at least for three months." A hint of laughter gleamed in his eyes, and he quipped, "Well, now I get to play cowboy for three months—and watch the elegant Miss Danielle Ross!"

Dani stared at him. "You mean—compete in the rodeo?"

"Sure. I might even win the All-Around!" Sixkiller drawled.

Savage warned, "Watch your step, Luke—and Dani's, too. This bird hasn't killed anybody yet, but I think he might be the type. So you two watch yourselves."

Dani regarded him carefully, then said, "Ben Savage, you planned all this. I have a feeling that you did. Is that right?"

Ben looked at her with an innocent gaze, then said blandly, "Well, Boss, if you say you've got such a feeling, I guess you do." Then he smiled and said, "I'll mind the store while you catch the crook."

4

Under Cover

Ben improved dramatically, so much so that two days after he had regained consciousness, Dr. Rogers said, "No sense keeping you heah. You can go home anytime."

Luke had driven the Cougar back to New Orleans, so Dani rented an LTD from an agency, to make Ben more comfortable on the long trip. While the nurses were getting Ben ready to check out, Dr. Rogers had a word with her. "He's doin' fine, but keep him still foah at least a week." He regarded her, his shock of white hair and youthful gray eyes making a striking contrast. "Maybe I'll call you when I get anothah patient who needs moah help than I can offah."

Dani took his hand and smiled at him, suggesting, "It would be much better if you'd get yourself on praying ground, Dr. Rogers. And I think you're headed that way." She had spoken with him several times and knew that God was working in him. But one thing she had learned about sharing her faith, and that was to give God time to work. A seed needed time for growth. So she merely invited, "Call me sometime, Doctor Rogers. I promise not to preach at you too much."

"I don't reckon that would hurt me too bad," he commented slowly. Then the nurse wheeled Ben into the hall where they stood, and he ordered sternly, "Now you stay put, boy! You heah me? Just let the womenfolk pamper you for a while."

Savage put his hand out, smiling. "Yeah, I'll do that, Doc, and thanks."

"Bettuh thank the good Lord."

"Sure." Ben watched the doctor disappear at his usual rapid pace, then looked up at Dani. "I don't guess you'd consider letting me walk to the car?"

"I would not!" Dani moved beside the wheelchair as the nurse stepped into the hall and began to push it. "I'll get the car," Dani told them and headed at once for the huge parking lot. Pulling up under the canopy marked DISCHARGED PATIENTS, she waited until Ben got inside. He moved slowly.

"Hurts pretty bad?" she empathized.

He settled himself carefully on the passenger's side and took a deep breath. "I feel as if a herd of elephants walked all over me." Then he shrugged and came up with a grin. "Stripes are for the back of fools, the Book says."

She pulled away from the hospital, then concentrated on getting out of Dallas. An hour later they were coasting down Interstate 20. Neither of them said much, and it was not until they passed Shreveport that Ben admitted, "I'm glad to be out of that place. Always hated hospitals." He looked out at the countryside flying by. "That apartment of mine's not much, but it's better than the best hospital room in the world."

Dani didn't take her eyes off the road as she commanded, "You're not going to your apartment. You're going to stay with my parents for at least a week, maybe longer. And I don't want any argument."

Savage turned slightly to look at her, the movement sending pain through his chest. She was wearing a pair of khaki shorts and a pale blue shirt with a small grinning bear over the left breast, and the morning sun touched her auburn hair with glints of gold. He thought, not for the first time, *She'll never be a beauty contest winner,* and was glad of it. Those who did win such things seemed to him like large Barbie dolls, every one like every other one, turned out and processed by the dozens.

He admired the strength of the jaw, the firm pressure of the wide mouth, and the air of competence in the gray-green eyes. *Just a little bit more, and she'd be mannish,* he thought, continuing his examination. But there was no danger of that. There was nothing at all masculine in the full sweep of her breast or in the fine bones and delicate fingers that rested lightly on the wheel. Even the directness of her manner was not the driving hardness that one sees in aggressive males, but a firmness not unmixed with gentleness.

"Go on," she ordered suddenly, turning her gaze on him, her lips turned up slightly in a smile. "I know you're going to argue."

Savage *had* intended to protest, but seeing that she expected that, he settled down in the seat more comfortably, saying lazily, "Me? Why should I argue about that? I think it'll be great! Your mother's the greatest cook in the Western world." He was aware that she was staring at him, and went on, "The problem with you, Boss, is that you just don't understand men. We *love* to be babied and cuddled. You ought to read some of these new books on how to keep your man. I'll pick one up for you at the supermarket next time I'm there. It'll do wonders for your personality."

Dani was speechless but knew that he was teasing her. He took a perverse delight in doing so. Therefore, she replied coolly, "Fine. I'm glad you're showing some sense for once."

They pulled into the front drive just as the shadows were beginning to grow long. The entire family, including Rob, who was in his freshman year at Tulane, came out to greet them. They all swarmed over Ben, especially Allison, who had an awesome crush on him, until Ellen sharply directed, "Well, don't crowd the poor man, or he'll be back in the hospital!" Shooing them away like chickens, she went to Ben with a smile. "Come along. I'm going to feed you and put you to bed."

Savage looked embarrassed—a phenomenon that Dani had never seen and that amused her. He glanced at Ellen and confided, "I see where your daughter gets her bossy ways." But he did look haggard, and Ellen hustled around during the meal, hovering over him, then leading him firmly to the spare bedroom.

"He looks as if he got run over by a semi, Dani," Rob observed. He was a tall, gangly young man and could never seem to get enough to eat. "Must have been a pretty tough cookie to take Ben down. How'd it happen?"

Dani told them the bare facts of the case, then glanced at her father. "Did you tell them?"

"Just your mother," he replied. Then he leaned back and listened while Dani filled Rob and Allison in on the plan.

"I may not be gone too long," she ended, shaking her head. "It's a long shot, and if the crook is smart, he can cover his tracks."

"Gosh!" Allison exclaimed woefully. "You have *all* the fun, Dani!"

Dani stared at Allison, then shook her head. "It won't be a vacation. I had a friend who rode the barrels professionally, and I saw enough to find out it's *work!*"

"And dangerous, too," her father remarked later, after the meal. He and Dani were washing the dishes. "From what you've told me, this fellow can play rough. A horse maimed and two men badly beaten—both of them pretty tough fellows, too." He put the dishcloth on the rack, then turned and suddenly put his arm around her, looking down at her. "I can't spare you, Dani."

She leaned against his chest, holding him tightly. She had been through a terrible time when he'd had his heart attack. Just the thought of losing him made her panic, for they were very close. Now she murmured, with her faced pressed against his chest, "That goes for me, too. You be careful. Let the work pile up until Ben gets back to the office." She held on to him for a moment, then pulled back and kissed him. "You have a time with me, don't you, Dad?"

"Terrible!" he agreed with a smile. "Takes up all my prayer time, just keeping you in order." Then he stepped back, got a cup of coffee from the pot, and wanted to know, "What's next?"

"Get ready for the Astrodome," she said. "Luke and I will start there. Everyone will be there—including the Creep, as Clint Thomas has decided to call him. I've got to get set up—trailer, truck, and so on."

"Use my Silverado," he offered. "That's the biggest expense. It'll do the job, and I won't be using it."

"That *would* be a help, Dad. Thanks a lot. Think I can pick up a good used trailer, and then Luke and I are on our way."

"Glad he's going with you." Daniel nodded. "He's a tough one. You know, I think the Lord may have gotten him suspended just so he could go along and protect you."

Dani laughed and gave him a quick hug. "You're an incorrigible hyper-Calvinist!" she exclaimed as she left the room.

"Why, no," he called after her. "I just think what is to be will be—even if it never happens!"

Sixkiller had followed Dani from New Orleans in Ben's battered '83 Ford. The policeman had not thought it would be a good idea to drive the gleaming new Porsche, so he had swapped with Savage. The upholstery had a broken spring on the driver's side, which punctured him constantly. Just outside the Houston city limits he passed Dani, waving her into a Dairy Queen.

"Looks like Ben could get a decent car!" he complained, snapping hungrily at a greasy cheeseburger.

When he finished eating, he pulled a stick of gum out of his pocket, peeled it, then stopped to stare at it. "Guess I better start using Skoal."

"Don't you dare!" Dani sputtered. "That snuff dipping is the nastiest habit in the world."

"Better get used to it, sweetheart." Sixkiller grinned. "Most of the riders are tobacco worms. You'll just have to snuggle up to them, snuff or no snuff."

Dani sniffed, saying tartly, "I have no plans for *snuggling* up to anyone!"

"No?" Sixkiller asked, arching his heavy eyebrows. "That kind of throws a monkey wrench into my plans. But I better warn you, morals aren't all that high on the rodeo circuit." He put the gum in his mouth, chewed it slowly, then added philosophically, "No, most of them have the morals of minks—so keep your guard up. You go on in. Wouldn't be too smart for us to get there at the same time."

Dani agreed and got into the Silverado. Moving into the traffic stream, she thought of the job ahead of her. Having Luke around might make the job safer—but she had no illusions about her chances of success. She had regretted taking the job, knowing that if the Creep (she and Sixkiller had both picked up on Clint's name for the criminal) had any sense at all, it would be like trying to find one particular fish in the Mississippi River!

An hour later she pulled into the Astrodome parking lot, finding the section that was filled with the contestants' vehicles. Horse trailers of all makes and conditions, from battered one-horse trailers with peeling paint to elaborate four-horse rigs, gleaming and ornate, were packed closely together. She found a place for her rig, parked it expertly, then got out and backed Biscuit out. "Here we are, Biscuit," she murmured as he stamped the ground, glad to be free from his confines. "And I never felt so out of place in my life!"

She looked around for the corral where the horses were kept, but paused in confusion. A tall, well-built cowboy turned suddenly out from a line of trailers, leading a beautiful bay horse. "Looking for the corral?" he asked.

"Yes."

"I'm headed that way," he said with a smile. "Come along." As she fell into step with him, he wanted to know, "First time in the Dome?"

Dani answered at once, having already planned her background story. "First time *anywhere*." She laughed at the surprise that flickered across his face. "I mean, it's my first time at a professional rodeo. I'm green as grass."

"That right?" he drawled. "I'm Bake Dempsey. Welcome aboard. Maybe I can give you a hand."

Dani looked at him quickly, for she recognized the name. Ruth had said that was Clint's closest rival. He was a handsome fellow with curly red hair and dark blue eyes. "I'm Dani Ross," she introduced herself, then added quickly, "Well, I may be green, but I'm pretty good at getting in with the top riders. You're having a good year, aren't you? Going to beat Clint Thomas out for All-Around this year?"

He shot a sudden glance at her, and she saw that she had touched a nerve. He shook his head and mourned, "Clint's a hard man to beat." Then he changed the subject. "You ride the barrels?"

"Just an amateur." She nodded. "I competed in high school and then in college. Now that I'm getting to be an old woman, I wanted to find out what the big-time was like. Silly, isn't it?"

Bake Dempsey gave her a frank look, taking in the clear eyes, the fine complexion, and the smooth lines of her figure. "Well, now, Grandma." He grinned. "Better do it before that ol' wheelchair gets you! I can see you're ready for the nursing home." His eyes were bold, filled with frank admiration, but he shook his head and answered her question, "No, Dani, it's not silly." He thought about it for a moment, then admitted, "Most of us are here for the same reason, I guess. We like horses, sure, but few of us would risk our necks and travel like crazy if the arenas were empty."

He led her out of the lot, and as they moved toward what seemed to be a small corral, he added, "Show biz, that's what it is. We'd all break our necks just to hear that crowd holler."

"Well, I'm not likely to hear much of that," Dani remarked. "But I knew I'd never be satisfied until I tried it."

"Sure." Dempsey nodded. "Looks like you got a good horse for it. That's half the battle won. Come on, we can leave our mounts here while we go pay our entry fees."

Leaving their horses in the small corral provided for the horses of contestants, they passed through the Dome, a gigantic stadium seating over 60,000 people. It had five chute gates at each end. At each line of chutes a tall tower rose, which accommodated the timing judges, the rodeo announcer, and other officials. The arena itself had been plowed and replowed until the dirt had turned to powder; if this were not done in an indoor arena, the sod would become packed, hard as concrete. The chutes were newly painted white, so that the big red numbers on each stood out clearly.

Bake Dempsey led her past the open area behind the chutes, where the pens for the cattle and horses were, then into a large room where several officials were taking entry fees from a line of contestants.

"Looks like everybody had the same idea," Bake declared as they took their place in line. "Wait until the last minute to sign up." It was a busy place, and everyone knew Dempsey, it seemed. Nearly every cowboy who passed after getting his fee paid spoke to him, and those who came in made it a point to speak to him. Most of them gave Dani a careful study, and more than one grinned and made a remark about her to Dempsey.

"Hey, Bake," a small wiry cowboy, an older man with a wrinkled brown face and faded blue eyes greeted him. "This pretty little filly your main squeeze now?"

Dani's face reddened, but Dempsey was amused. "Well, not yet, Tom, but give me a little time. Want you to meet Tom Leathers, Dani. This is Dani Ross, Tom." He gave the older man a friendly slap on the back, adding, "Tom was All-Around a few years back. You want to know anything about horses, you go to him, Dani."

"Well, I can tell you one thing," Leathers said, taking off his hat, "and it ain't about hosses. You watch yourself with this here cowboy, Dani. He thinks he's the big bad wolf, and pretty little girls is all Red Riding Hood!"

"Aw, come on, Tom!" Dempsey protested. "I'm just a little ol' lamb!"

Leathers shook his head and grinned, then moved out of the room. "Great guy," Bake commented. "Been around forever."

"Does he still compete?" Dani asked.

"Not so much. Does pickup work mostly. Guess he's like I'll be when I get too old to ride. Like an old fire horse who hears the bell. But I'll have my brains scrambled before then. Tom was so good he never got hurt bad. He was—"

"Bake, where've you been?" A shapely blond woman in her mid-twenties appeared and possessively took the cowboy by the arm. "We held the party for you last night."

"Got held up in Oklahoma City. Burned out a wheel bearing." Bake nodded at Dani. "Hey, this is Dani Ross, Ruby. Going to give you some competition. Ruby Costner, Dani."

Dani felt the pressure of the girl's light blue eyes and knew that she was being stripped, analyzed, weighed, and computed. But Dani smiled and put out her hand. "Worry about somebody else, Ruby. I'm a rank amateur. This is my first professional shot. I'll probably fall off my horse."

"I doubt it," Ruby said but she relaxed slightly. "Glad to see you." She hesitated, then asked, "You two known each other long?"

"Almost fifteen minutes." Bake grinned. "We just met in the lot."

"I won't give you any unasked-for advice about barrel racing or horses, Dani," Ruby confided in a friendly manner. "But don't let yourself get caught in the chute with this cowboy."

Dempsey gave Dani a worried glance. "Hey, that's two bad marks I got in two tries. Don't listen to 'em, Dani."

Ruby laughed and patted his arm. "She won't find you in church, Bake, but he's really fairly respectable—among this bunch, I mean." She was a forthright girl, and Dani suspected that she was not overly respectable herself. There was too much makeup on her face, too much aggression in the way she put her hand on Dempsey, and something too sensuous in her full-figured body. "Clint talked the management into giving all the contestants a big bash at the Corral club tonight.

You be there, Bake, and you come, too, Dani." She gave a slight smile, which made her lips voluptuous, then added, "You may change your mind about going into this business, after one of Clint's parties!"

"Sounds like a real orgy instead of a party," Dani observed. She watched Ruby leave, noting that almost every man watched her pass. Then she asked innocently, "Are you going?"

Bake Dempsey hesitated slightly before nodding. "I guess so." Then he perked up and offered, "If you'll go with me, I could introduce you to everyone."

Dani grabbed at the chance to enter his world. "I'd like to go, Bake."

"Great! It'll probably start about seven or eight. You got a place to stay?"

"Not yet. Just pulled into town."

"Well, you can get a room where I'm staying, maybe. But it's pretty full in all the hotels. You'd better call now, to be sure. Not pushing, you understand, but the town fills up during rodeo."

"I'll call as soon as we pay our fees."

She spent the rest of the afternoon getting settled, and as Bake had said, getting a room was difficult. She got one only after Bake got on the phone and sweet-talked the girl at the desk, promising her a couple of tickets to the rodeo. Dani settled Biscuit, then went to her room, rested, and took a quick nap. When she awoke, it was still early. She showered, washed her hair, and worked on her nails as she listened to a teaching tape by a British Bible teacher. Finally she slipped into her new clothes, fancy-dress Western wear. She had gone to a store in New Orleans that specialized in that sort of clothing and bought two outfits.

Dani chose a pair of tight, hip-hugging, straight-leg pants and a frilly shirt. When she had protested to the clerk that it was too immodest, the young woman had grinned. "You want modesty, go to a bingo game, Honey. This one *is* modest, compared to most. You look great in it. Some of the girls who've peaked look awful in a thing like this. I can't afford to tell them they look like overstuffed sausages, but they do. Still, this is what's being worn in fancy western dress."

Dani had not liked the outfit, but her experience told her that she needed to look the part she was playing, so now she stood staring into the mirror with distaste. "Looks painted on!" she objected in disgust, but there was no help for it. The pants were silver lamé, and she picked up the baby-blue western hat with rodeo-cowboy crush and tried it on. It made her face look square, but it was what was worn, the girl had said, so she sighed and gave up.

At seven Bake came by with two other cowboys and knocked loudly on her door. She was soon to learn that cowboys knew no other way to knock on doors. "Honey, this is Wash Foster and Fighting Bill Baker. This is Dani Ross, you birds, and don't handle the merchandise," Bake warned.

Baker was short, very muscular, and had a good-natured face that was considerably battered. He had a bullfrog voice and a pair of calico eyes. "Hi, Dani. Good to meet you."

"Hello, Bill." Dani smiled. His hand was hard as oak and calloused, but he didn't try to hold hands with her the way some men did.

"How are you, Wash?" she asked.

"Mighty fine, fine as silk!" Wash Foster was about thirty, with a set of muddy brown eyes and a thatch of blondish hair. He was no more than medium height, and when he moved, Dani saw at once that he had a stiff right arm. She saw also that he was very perceptive, for though her eyes had rested on the bad arm for no more than a split second he caught the look. He said nothing more, but Dani realized that he was sensitive about the handicap.

"Well, guess we got to go." Bake shrugged. "But if we had any sense we'd go to the library and read a book." His dark blue eyes gleamed suddenly, and he laughed. "You don't know where I'm from, do you, Dani?"

"No, Bake."

"Bucksnort, Tennessee. Now go on and laugh! It's an awful name, but nobody ever forgets it. Anyway, we had a guy who was the town drunk. Name was Tom Fender. Stayed drunk as much as he could, which was just about all the time. Well, one Saturday afternoon, when I was just a kid, I met him downtown. 'Where you going, Tom?' I asked him." Bake shook his head slowly. "That was years ago, but I never forgot what Tom said. He gave me one of the saddest looks I ever saw on a man's face, and he said, 'I'm going to get drunk, Dempsey—and do I dread it!'"

Fighting Bill Baker laughed loudly. "Hey, I know what that's like, I been there myself. But it ain't rained wisdom in these parts for quite a spell, so let's go get drunk. I shore hope I don't have to whip J. D. Pillow! Hey, Bake, do you think I can whip him, or what d' you think?"

They all wandered out to Baker's car, a late-model red Cadillac, and as he drove recklessly to the Dome, he and Wash Foster carried on a long, involved argument about a horse named Frying Pan that had been dead for years. Dani sat with Bake in the backseat. Once he told her, "Ruby called me the Big Bad Wolf. I'm not—but there are plenty of that breed around."

"You offering to be my big brother and keep them fought off, Bake?" she asked.

He gave her a swift grin, "Well, I ain't *that* honorable yet!"

5

The Corral Club

The Corral Club was a private club on one level of the Astrodome, used by sponsors, their guests, and other dignitaries of the city and the rodeo. When Dani entered the main lounge, which was furnished in a Western decor complete with the huge heads of mounted longhorns on the wall, she saw that the party was already in full swing. Some of the women were young and pretty, others were not, but all of them wore Western wear. And the clerk who had sold her the two outfits had been right; all the women's clothing was skintight, and most women wore either gold or silver lamé pants.

Scattered around the room were a number of contestants, easy to identify by their Wranglers and their youth and health. The others were better dressed, mostly overweight, and were somehow less *used* than the men who actually rode the bulls and the horses. Four bartenders were busy behind the long bar, and several pretty girls dressed in very short skirts and

Western shirts moved around the crowd. Everyone seemed to talk loudly, perhaps to override the stereo, which played country-Western music.

Dani saw Ruth with Clint in the center of an admiring group of fans but made no attempt to go to her. Bake took her arm and guided her into the room, threading the way toward an open space along one wall. A man and two women had watched them approach, and Dempsey greeted them loudly, "Hi, Clyde. Hey, Fran, you're looking good!" He hauled Dani around by the arm to face them. "This is Dani Ross. Dani, this is Clyde Lockyear. He's the stock contractor who furnishes the sorry animals us poor cowboys have to ride. And this is his wife, Fran."

Fran Lockyear was an attractive woman of about twenty-eight. She had a Southern look somehow, with red hair and greenish eyes. Although she was beginning to lose the fresh glow of youth, Dani knew she must have been stunning at eighteen—the tall, shapely type that became Miss Mississippi or Miss Alabama. She was wearing a pair of light green pants and an emerald shirt decorated with silver thread. Despite the fact that she was not as slim and firm as some of the other women, her lush figure would catch the eyes of most men.

"Hello, Dani." Fran had a husky voice, and her smile seemed genuine. "Are you from Houston?"

"No, from New Orleans."

"She's starting a new career, Fran," Bake volunteered. "This is her professional debut—riding the barrels."

"Is that right?" Clyde Lockyear's blue eyes showed immediate interest. "You'd better get with Fran here. She was one of the best, when she was competing." He was a small man, no taller than his wife's five foot eight. His round face, coupled with a pug nose and a small mouth, gave him a boyish look. He was overweight, but all the excess flesh was in his potbelly, as symmetrical as a cannonball. Dani noticed that he didn't try to hide it, but let it hang over his belt, and from time to time he ran his hand over it with a caress, as if it were a valued old friend. As he thrust his hand through his thinning blondish hair, Clyde remarked, "Glad to have you in the arena."

"Thank you, Mr. Lockyear."

"Oh, just Clyde," he said with a friendly smile. "Guess there aren't any *Misters* in rodeo."

Fran gave him an odd look, before performing an introduction, "Like you to meet Megan Carr, Dani. Better be nice to her, or she'll ruin your good name."

Dani gave the woman standing beside Fran a startled look, wondering what Fran could mean. Dani nodded. "Well, I'm glad to know you, Megan—I *think* . . . ?"

Megan Carr was a small woman in her late twenties. She had a pair of very direct dark blue eyes and a shock of black hair, cut very short in a boyish style. "Don't pay any attention to Fran, Dani," Megan advised, putting out her hand in a masculine gesture.

"She's a journalist." Clyde Lockyear eyed Megan with respect. "Writing a book all about the rodeo and the riders. Better watch out for her, Dani. She carries a tape recorder and a blasted video camera everywhere she goes. She'll have you taped before you know it." His small mouth pursed into a grin. "She's found plenty of color, I guess. More stuff going on among rodeo folks than on a soap opera. Glad I don't have any skeletons in my closet for you to dig out, Megan."

"Oh, I expect there are a few dingy sheets you wouldn't want hung out in public, Sweetheart!" Fran smiled, but Dani thought her tone held a barbed threat. Then Fran laughed and squeezed Clyde's arm. "Don't worry, it's just the stars Megan wants to get the dope on. Isn't that right?"

"Not really, Fran." Megan Carr shook her head. "What I'm after is the *essence* of the thing. Sure, the most colorful people are the performers, like Bake here, but there are others, you know."

"Like me!" Clyde grinned. "Like to see what would happen if I didn't bring the bulls and the bucking horses along. That's right, ain't it, Bake? You boys can't ride bicycles, can you?"

Bake scowled at him. "I been on some bicycles that got more buck in them than some of them scrubs you been giving me, Clyde," he complained. Then he said thoughtfully, "You know, you got a point there, Megan. Most important man in the show, you know who he is?"

"Who's that, Bake?" Megan asked instantly, her dark eyes alert.

"Why, Hank Lowe!" Bake nodded emphatically. "He's the bullfighter, or the clown," he explained. "And you wouldn't have no bull ridin' if Hank—or somebody like him—wasn't there."

"Oh, come on, Bake!" Clyde protested.

"Fact. You can get a rider off a bucking horse with pickup men, but them bulls ain't afraid of no horse. They go for one just as quick as they'll go for a man. And when a man gets on a bull, two things are sure." He counted them off on his fingers, his face very serious. "One, he's gonna get bucked off or jump off. That ain't no *maybe,* honey; that's a hard fact of life! And number two, when he does hit the dirt, that bull's gonna try to stomp him into jelly, and *that's* likewise a fact, as you well know, Clyde! So I'm servin' notice right now that I'm not climbing on no bull, no way—except ol' Hank is standin' right there to get that critter off me!"

Clyde flushed slightly, and he shook his head. "Well, I guess old Hank does earn his keep. . . ."

Megan nodded, her eyes glowing with interest. "Exactly what I need! One of the unsung heroes, the little people who keep the wheels turning. I did my last book on auto racing, and it's the same. Mario Andretti or Al Unser may get the glory, but if some little guy doesn't come out and change his tires, the hero's just another guy."

Clyde regarded her with sharp attention. "Well, maybe you'll put me in your book." He looked down at his ostrich boots thoughtfully, and when he lifted his head there was a wistful look in his light blue eyes. "When I was a kid, there was only one thing I wanted to do," he shared quietly. "The other guys switched around, changing their dreams every time a new thing hit TV. One week they were gonna be private eyes, the next week it was fast-gun test pilots or pop singers. But not me! From the time I could walk, I just knew there was one thing to be—a bronc rider!"

"I never knew that, Clyde," Bake marveled.

Clyde shrugged and came up with a sour grin. "No reason you should, Bake. I guess every kid gets hooked on something. Other guys knew the batting averages of baseball players or who was gonna win the Heisman Trophy. I was a walking encyclopedia on rodeo. Still am." He nodded. "I can reel off just about any info about riders."

Wash had said nothing during the conversation, but now demanded, "Name a cowboy who won the bareback championship and the saddle bronc title the same year."

"Casey Tibbs, 1951," Clyde shot back promptly.

"You and I had better get together, Clyde," Megan suggested, patting his arm with a warm smile. "I've been spending *hours* poring over all the books on rodeo I can find, and here I've got a walking history book right under my nose!"

"He's that all right!" Fran said with a frown. "Can't carry on a normal conversation without dragging a bull or a horse into it!"

"Well, it put those diamonds on your hand," Clyde contended, with a sharp light in his eyes. His mouth drew down in a pout. "And Megan's got the right idea about her book. Most of the stars aren't much when they're off a horse."

"What about Clint Thomas?" Dani asked, glancing over toward where the cowboy was holding court with an admiring group of fans. "Didn't I read an article that said he had a pretty high IQ?"

An awkward silence fell, so heavy that Dani felt that she had committed some sort of terrible social blunder. Clyde Lockyear's face reddened, and his wife's lips drew into a hard line. Dani felt Bake shuffling his feet, and glancing at him, saw that he was staring down at the floor. He looked up and interjected, "Hey, let me get you a drink, Dani. What'll it be?"

He was trying to break the rigidity of the moment, Dani saw, and decided, *Got to keep my mouth shut until I find out what's going on!* But she said, "Just a Coke for me, please."

Bake stared at her in surprise, and Wash snorted, "Well, now, you ain't no Sunday-school teacher in disguise or a temperance woman, are you, Dani?"

From the first, Dani had known that this moment—or one like it—would come. It always did. Most people drank, and the rodeo crowd, she knew, was a hard-drinking crowd. Her father had put his finger on the problem as they had discussed the undercover assignment. "You're going to stand out like a sore thumb, if you don't drink, Dani," he had opined. "Matter of fact, you'll probably have every sort of fleshly delight pushed at you. What will you do about that?

"I knew a fine Christian policeman. Name was Charley Sutter. He went into undercover, working with the vice squad.

Well, he was in a tight spot. If he got caught, it was his life. He had to fit in, so he did what the rest of them did—all of it, including drinking and sex."

"What happened to him, Dad?" Dani had asked.

"He went wrong. I tried to tell him it wouldn't work, but he insisted it was part of the job. He got on dope, and it was downhill." Daniel had had a look of sadness in his fine eyes as he concluded, "You can't fool with sin, can you? No matter how noble your motives, there's always a harvest."

Fleetingly Dani thought of that conversation as the others regarded her. But she had already made her decision. "Guess I'm just an old fuddy-duddy, Wash." She smiled. "Maybe I saw too many old Shirley Temple movies, but somewhere along the line I decided it wasn't worth it. I won't give any lecture or anything like that," she added quickly. "But I've seen too much grief come from it."

They were all staring at her strangely, and Fran asked suddenly with a hard edge in her tone, "I wonder, if you don't drink or smoke, what *do* you do?"

Dani gave her a level look responding easily, "Not *that* either, Fran."

Lockyear got a kick out of that. He giggled wildly, then gasped, "Well, you're going to be a mighty small minority around this bunch!"

Megan told her, "Maybe I better put *you* in the book, Dani—a natural curiosity." But her tone was kind, and she suddenly remarked, "There's a couple of chairs at a table. Get the Coke, Bake. We'll be over there."

Dani was relieved as Megan pulled at her, and she parted from the others with the words, "Glad to have met you, Fran—and you, too, Clyde."

"Sure, Dani," Fran said, "I'll be interested to see how your experiment works."

"Experiment?"

"Trying to keep pure and rodeo at the same time. Don't think it's ever been done."

Clyde gave Megan a sharp look but had a smile for Dani. "Stick to your guns, kid!"

When the two women were seated, Dani asked at once, "What did I say wrong, Megan?"

"You mentioned Clint Thomas's name, honey." Megan smiled. "Might as well put a torch in a powder keg. But I guess you didn't know."

"Know what?"

"Why, Fran was married to Clint." She laughed, a tinkling sound in the loud room, and put her hand on Dani's arm. "Don't worry about it, Dani. It's just that you've got to get your players straight. Like in a ball game," she explained thoughtfully. "When you first go, the players are all alike to you. But you get a scorecard and learn their numbers, and you listen to what the guy in the next seat says about number 17. Only this is a little bit more touchy than a ball game."

Dani sat back and watched Clyde and Fran as they moved around the room, then let her eyes go back to Clint Thomas. "Maybe you could give me a few hints, Megan," she suggested. "I don't want to put my foot in another bear trap."

"That could happen." Megan shrugged. She sipped the martini she held and thought about it. It was, Dani understood, a habit with her—thinking and analyzing things. *She's probably a good writer,* Dani thought as she waited for Megan to speak.

"I don't have any rodeo background," Megan explained, "so I had to pick up on what was going on from other people. Fortunately, rodeo people like to talk—especially about each other! First, get this straight, Dani. Rodeoing isn't a sport, it's a business. And that means money is at the center of it. Well, there's ego, too," she said. "Everybody wants to be number one, the star. But it's jungle, red in tooth and claw."

"They all seem pretty friendly to me," Dani objected, drawing her out.

"Oh, sure, but it's a small world, very small, and there are feuds that go back for years. Like the one between the Lockyears and Clint. The best I can make of it, Clint dumped Fran, which means she hates his guts. She'd have to, wouldn't she? Then there's Clyde. He got Fran on the rebound, but he thinks—along with everyone else—it was his money Fran took him for. So he watches her like a hawk when Clint is around, and I guess he's sore at Fran because she's still got a yen for Clint, and he can't forget that Clint was number one in Fran's life."

"And Clyde's resentful, I think, of the riders," Dani noted slowly. "They're what he's always longed to be."

"Hey, I'm supposed to be the writer around here, with all the insight," Megan spoke in mock anger. She lit a cigarette, let the smoke curl around her face, then nodded. "I never knew that about Clyde, but a thing like that happens often. That's why you see a forty-year-old man at a high-school football game, wearing his old jacket."

"And why you see a thirty-year-old woman wearing clothes that only look good on a twenty-year-old." Dani suggested.

"Watch it, now! You might be stepping on *my* toes!"

They sat there, talking lightly, and Dani found that she liked Megan very much. As she spotted Bake coming across the room, dodging the heavy traffic, she asked, "Anything more you can tell me, Megan? I mean stuff I shouldn't say out loud?"

"Lots! For one thing, you see that girl over there? Her name's Ruby Costner. When Clint left Fran, he took up with her. They had a real hot thing going, and everybody expected them to get married. Trouble was, she was Clay Dixon's girl, and Clay's been running around looking for someone to bite ever since it happened. He's a mean one, too. That's him—over there talking to the young fellow with the black hair."

"And now Clint's got another girl? The one standing with him?"

"That he has. Her name's Ruth Cantrell. So you have Ruby hating Clint for taking up with Ruth, and Clay sore at him for taking his girl away—not to mention the Lockyears wanting to eat his liver."

"Sounds like a real bad soap opera." Dani smiled, then reached up to take the Coke from Bake. "Thanks, Bake."

The room seemed to swell with noise as more and more people filtered in. Dani met so many people she gave up trying to match names with faces. She spent considerable energy refusing drinks and more refusing invitations to leave the party and find a quiet spot. The smoke was thick enough to walk on after the first hour and a half, and most of the people were half-drunk. She was about to excuse herself when she saw Sixkiller walk into the room. He saw her at once, but did not allow a flicker of recognition.

Bake was hauled away by a pretty young woman with a shrill voice and an octopuslike grasp to where a few couples were dancing at one end of the room. Megan left the table, moving along the edges of the crowd, and Dani could almost see the notes going into her head as she observed the crowd.

Dani finally got up when she heard a loud yell and the crash of furniture breaking. At the far end of the room, near the dancers, she caught a glimpse of a man sailing backwards, propelled as if he were shot out of a cannon.

"Come on, Bill!" she heard Bake shout. "You can whip 'im!"

When she moved in closer, she saw Fighting Bill Baker pick himself up and spit on his hands. Lowering his head, he charged a tall, wiry cowboy who met him with a flurry of blows. The crowd was yelling, and as the two men flailed away at each other, Dani saw that there were two reactions to the fight. The rodeo crowd loved it, but expressions of nervous apprehension covered the other guests' faces. A balding man standing beside her cried, "I'm getting out of here!" and scurried out of the room.

The fight moved from one point to another as the battlers drove each other with wild punches, and finally the tall man went down, his frame collapsing in sections.

"You whupped him, Bill!" somebody shouted, and Baker lifted his hands in a gesture of triumph. "Anybody else want to fight?" he shouted in his bullfrog voice. But there were no takers, and there was a stampede back to the bar.

Dani moved toward the door, but her arm was caught by a strong hand. "Hey, we ain't met, little lady." A huge man, at least six feet four, with tremendous shoulders, pulled her toward him. Immediately she identified him as a real cowboy by his huge hands, scarred and calloused, and his face, which had taken punishment. He had a pair of pale blue eyes and a shock of yellow hair that had been roughly cut.

"I been watching you." He grinned, and she smelled the potent whiskey on his breath. "I'm Clay Dixon. Guess you must be the new barrel racer Wash was tellin' me about."

"Yes. I'm Dani Ross." His grip cut into her arm with unnecessary force, and she struggled to pull away. "I'm not going to run away," she said with a smile.

"Shore not!" Dixon nodded. "Hey, you don't have a drink. Let's go to the bar and get you fixed up."

"Thanks, I'm not having any."

The answer made him halt, and his pale eyes studied her. "Why, you can't spoil a good party like this by not drinking!" He ignored her protest and, keeping his grip on her arm, hauled her across the room. Dani caught Megan Carr's glance and saw her give a helpless shrug of her shoulders, as if to say, *You may as well go with him.*

Dani surrendered, going to the bar with him. There were no stools, and Dixon simply shoved two men aside as if they were furniture, not even aware of their hard looks. "Hey, Barkeep, let's have a couple of drinks!"

Dixon ordered two Bloody Marys, and when the bartender set them down, shoved one toward Dani, commanding, "Drink up, Dani. You're way behind."

Dani watched him drain the glass. When he looked at her, she confronted him, "I know it's a shock to you, Clay, but I don't drink. The way it works is like this—I don't try to stop you from drinking, and you don't try to make me drink. That way we're both happy."

Her simple logic seemed to stun the big man. He blinked his eyes, then shook his head in bewilderment. "Don't make no sense," he muttered. "What the use of a party, when you don't drink?"

"We can talk," Dani offered. "Let's go sit down, and you can tell me about the kind of year you've been having." She moved away from the bar, and after a moment's hesitation, he followed her. They found a table at the far end of the room from the dancers, and when they sat down, she said, "Now, tell me about how you're doing this year. Are you a saddle-bronc rider, or is it bulls?"

Dixon leaned back in his chair, studying Dani, his large frame relaxed. "Why, I ride them all, honey!" he told her. "Ain't nothing with hair that I can't ride—bulls, bareback, or saddle bronc."

"Have you been riding long?" Dani managed to get Dixon talking. It was not difficult, for he was a man who liked to talk about himself. He rambled on for a long time about his career, rather often whistling for a waitress to bring him another drink. Dani listened, sorting out much of what he said, but as he poured drink after drink down his throat, she began to lead his loose talk into another channel. "It seems a shame that a fine rider like you can't win the big money, Clay," she commented innocently. "But I guess Clint Thomas has that all sewed up?"

A look of pure rage flamed in Dixon's eyes. He shot a glance across the room to where Thomas was dancing with Ruth, and Dani saw his huge fist close around his glass, turning white with the pressure. Obviously the big cowboy would rather it had been Clint Thomas's neck. He answered in a thin voice, "He's had all the luck! They give him all the good mounts! But he won't last forever! I'll see him—"

He broke off suddenly, shook his head, and then got to his feet. "I don't wanna talk about that imitation cowboy," he announced. "Let's go dance."

"I'm not much of a dancer, Clay."

"You're good enough. Come on."

He pulled her along, and Dani dangled at the end of his arm, having to scramble to keep from falling. His grip hurt her, and a small cry of pain escaped her lips.

"Dixon, you're hurting that lady." Tom Leathers had come out of the crowd, and the sound of his voice created a small pocket of silence that spread outward.

Trouble has a smell to it, Dani thought suddenly. *And the men who ride bulls weighing almost a ton move in violence the way a fish moves through water.* Now the crowd that had watched Fighting Bill Baker and J. D. Pillow pound each other were drawn almost magnetically toward Leathers and Dixon with Dani locked in Dixon's grasp.

Dixon peered down at the smaller man, an ugly light in his eyes. "Tom, if you don't git outta my way, you'll get hurt."

Leathers looked small and fragile as he stood looking up at Dixon's massive hulk. He was no more than forty-five, but a life of getting pounded by bucking horses and bulls had marked him. He shook his head slightly. "Sure, Clay. You turn the girl loose, and I'll be glad to move."

Dixon cast a quick look around at the crowd, and his lips turned upward in a smile. He had to have fights just as he had to have liquor. But he knew that he could not crush the older man. Leathers was a popular cowboy, having the respect of everyone. So Dixon didn't hit Leathers; he simply stepped forward and brushed him aside with his massive left arm.

Leathers was driven to one side, falling hard on the tile floor. At once a young cowboy with black hair stepped up, needling him, "You're tough on old men, aren't you, Dixon?" Then without hesitation he sent a tremendous blow right into Dixon's face.

Dixon was driven back a single step. He released Dani's wrist and raised that hand to touch his mouth. He looked at the blood on his palm, then with a cry of rage, plunged at the smaller man, his huge fists striking like pistons. The two blows simply destroyed the boy—and he seemed no more than that to Dani—who collapsed with blood streaming down his face from a cut over his eyebrow, laid open to the bone.

Dixon looked at the boy, who didn't move, saying, "Punk kid!"

A flash of motion caught Dani's eye. She only had just enough time to turn her head and see Clint Thomas pick up a wooden chair. Lifting it high, he brought it down with all his might on Dixon's unprotected head. The chair struck with a dull clunking sound, then broke into pieces. Dixon collapsed in a heap, his head split in a gash that ran from front to back, exposing the white gristle of his scalp.

Thomas tossed the wreckage of the chair on the floor, then stood looking down at Dixon's still form. "Well, I didn't make it."

Wash Foster stared at him. "Didn't make what, Clint?"

A smile appeared like a white slash across Thomas's wedge-shaped face. "Why, I thought I could drive him through the floor up to his knees," he drawled, his eyes bright with what seemed to be enjoyment. "Maybe next time I'll use a bigger chair." He turned and walked away, not even breathing hard. He spoke lightly to Ruth, who came to hold his arm, her face pale and her hands trembling.

Dani moved to kneel beside the boy whom Dixon had struck. Pulling her handkerchief out of her jeans, she tried to staunch the blood that welled up from the cut. His eyes opened, and she saw the blankness in them fade as consciousness returned. "You're going to have to have that cut stitched," she said.

He stirred, shook his head, then sat up. His eyes focused on Dixon, where he lay with his bloody scalp exposed. "What happened to him?" the cowboy asked.

"Clint Thomas hit him with a chair after you went down."

A strange light flickered in the boy's dark eyes. Instant outrage filled his voice, "I don't need his help!" He struggled to his feet, and Wash Foster came over. "Boone, you got to get that cut taken care of. Come on."

He led the young man out of the room, and Dani asked Bake, who had come to stand beside her, "Who is he, Bake?"

"Name's Boone Hardin," Bake replied. A puzzled look filled his eyes, and he shook his head. "Seemed to make him mad that Clint took Dixon out. You'd think he'd be grateful, now wouldn't you? He's a funny one, anyway. Don't mix with folks much."

"I want to go, Bake."

"Sure, I guess the fun's about over." They picked up Wash Foster and left the Corral Club. When Bake stopped at the door of Dani's room, he took off his hat and asked, "Well, how do you like the social life on the rodeo circuit?"

"Too rich for my blood, Bake." Dani smiled but a troubled look remained in her eyes. "Won't Clay try to get even with Clint for what happened?"

Bake thought for a moment, then shook his head. "Nope. He'd have to get in line to even the score with Clint. The fellow on top, he's the target."

"Good night, Bake, See you in the morning."

"Yeah, sure."

Dani showered and went to bed, shocked at how the violence at the party had shaken her. She lay there for a long time, reading her Bible, but her mind dwelled on the people she had met.

Somewhere among them, she felt sure, was the man she was looking for. But how to find him? Finally she turned out the light and closed her eyes. For one moment apprehension that the dream of the shooting might return filled her—until she realized it had not come since she had thrown herself into the job. She smiled, saying, "Thank you, Lord—" and fearlessly plunged into the warm darkness.

6
Second Warning

Dani got up before dawn, dressed, and left the motel. She drove around aimlessly, then went into Denny's and ordered a big breakfast. But she felt too nervous to eat more than a few bites, so after drinking three cups of coffee, she left and went to the Astrodome.

Biscuit whickered when Dani came to the holding corral, and she rubbed his velvet nose, feeding him some of the sugar cubes she kept in her pocket. "You're not nervous, are you?" she muttered. "Good thing *one* of us has some confidence."

Turning from the horse, she wandered through the large doors in the rear of the Dome, walking around aimlessly. Even empty and slightly ghostly as it was, there was something deadly that one didn't find in other large arenas. It was, she decided, the fact that other large arenas were for games—but a rodeo was not a game. This was more like the ancient gladiator spectacles in the coliseum, in Rome, where men met not to settle which one could run the fastest or throw a javelin the farthest, but to settle which one would live and which one would die.

A tractor was chugging along under the dim lights, pulverizing the earth into powder, and she paused to watch the geometrical patterns it created in the dirt. The driver was an older man with a shock of white hair and a drooping mustache, and as he spotted her watching him, he lifted one hand in a languid gesture of friendship. She waved back, and thought, *He's not worried. Nobody could get hurt doing groundwork like that. But if he were going to get on top of a fighting Brahma bull in a little while, he'd be worried that he might get his lungs punctured with a horn or his head smashed by a hoof.*

The danger woven into rodeo inhabited the place, specterlike and ominous, Dani decided. Slowly she continued her walk, wondering, as most people do, why men would risk everything for such a cause.

As she saddled Biscuit, she wondered if the cowboys did it just to tackle something bigger than themselves. In life challenges are often vague and unexciting, such as getting up and going to work day after day. But in a rodeo arena it's compacted and concentrated, and she concluded that to escape boredom, men sought out the danger that comes rising up from that powdered dirt, the cattle pens, and the chutes and their gates.

"You have to pick everything to pieces!" she admonished herself and forced her mind away from speculation. After riding Biscuit slowly around the stadium, she dismounted and walked him behind the chutes, which would be filled in a few hours with cowboys waiting to make their rides. At the side of the chutes were pens for cattle and horses: calves for roping in one pen, the dogging steers in another, then closer in, the three groups of animals used for the bucking events—the bareback horses, the horses used in the saddle-bronc event, and the bulls. Some of them were already in place, eating slowly and contentedly. A huge Brahma lifted his head and studied her, not looking very dangerous, all slack-mouthed and benign.

"Don't look too mean, does he now?"

Dani turned quickly to find a man of about forty watching her. He was of average height, very wiry, and dressed in worn jeans and a checkered shirt that had lost all color. Two children stood beside him, a girl of about ten, with auburn hair, and a boy no more than six, with a thatch of tow-colored hair and countless freckles. Both children studied her watchfully.

"Well, no, he doesn't." Dani smiled at the children and introduced herself, "I'm Dani Ross."

"Hey, the cat got your tongue?" the man questioned sharply, when neither child spoke up. He hitched his pants up and came forward to offer one calloused hand. "I'm Hank Lowe," he said easily. "This here is my kids, Cindy and Maury." He nodded as he added, "Guess you're gettin' a little nervous about your ride this afternoon."

"How'd you know that?" Dani wanted to know. "I must look scared to death—which I just about am."

Lowe smiled again. "Nope, you look cool as a cucumber. But Ruth told me about you. Said you'd just decided to rodeo, and today was your maiden voyage."

"Oh, you know Ruth?" Dani saw Lowe's face change slightly at the question and wondered what it meant. "Well, that's right. But right now I'd like to run back home and forget the whole thing!"

"My daddy's the most important man in the whole rodeo!" Maury stared at her with defiance, his brown eyes serious.

Dani replied, "You know, Bake Dempsey says the same thing, Maury. He told me he wouldn't even *think* about getting on a bull if Hank Lowe wasn't there to keep him from getting hurt." The answer pleased the boy, she saw, and she looked with admiration at Lowe. "I don't see how you do it night after night, Hank."

Lowe's weather-beaten face flushed slightly, and he pulled off his hat, slapping it against his thigh to cover his embarrassment at the compliment. "Aw, well, it's a living." He shrugged, then gave her a keen look, a thought coming to him. "Don't guess you're good at arithmetic, are you?"

"Why—as a matter of fact, it was my best subject in school."

"Was it now?" Lowe's homely face lit up, and he started to speak, then bit his lip. "Well, now, I don't want to pressure you, Dani, but I'm trying to get Cindy and Maury through without having to put them in a school while I'm on the road. I've got most of the subjects they need settled. Had to rope and tie just about everybody I know who's seen the inside of a high school, but seems like arithmetic and rodeoing don't hitch."

He paused, looking at her with restraint, until Dani volunteered, "Why, I'll be glad to do what I can, Hank. I'm no teacher, but we can try it, can't we?"

"All right." Cindy shrugged. "I'm no good at it though. I'd rather ride a horse. Ruth was showing me how to ride the barrels—but she don't do that no more." She looked at her father as if he were somehow to blame. "I don't know why."

Seeing the look of embarrassment she had noticed before when she'd mentioned Ruth, Dani took a quick guess at what had happened, but said only, "Well, you can ride Biscuit, if your father says it's all right. I'm not as good as Ruth, but I've got a pretty good horse."

"Sure!" Hank chimed in quickly, his eyes warm with gratitude. "You just say when, Dani, and I'll have the kids ready for their lessons. And you let them ride Biscuit anytime. Cindy's pretty good—and so is this wrangler!" he dropped his hand to rub Maury's mop of hair, then looked at the bull who was eyeing them. "This is Popcorn," he mentioned, changing the subject. "He looks peaceable enough, but he's a cowboy stomper for sure. Always hate to see a young buck on top of him, but Bake's riding him tonight, so it's all right."

The arena was beginning to come alive, now, with animals being moved into the pens. Hank excused himself, "Got to run, Dani. Thanks for offering to help with these two."

Dani smiled as they left, then moved out of the arena. Her ride wasn't scheduled until the afternoon, and she wanted to find Luke. But she didn't see him all morning long and didn't know which motel he was in. At noon, she joined the crowd at the snack bar; as she left with a hamburger and Coke, Megan Carr waved at her from one of the small tables. "Sit down," Megan invited. She was eating a supersized hot dog, piled high with chili and baptized with mustard. "You racing today?" she asked, licking mustard from her upper lip.

"This afternoon," Dani informed her. She picked up the rounded part of the bun, peered inside, then admitted, "I don't know why I got this. I can't eat a thing."

Megan chewed the hot dog and swallowed, studying Dani. "Got some butterflies, huh?"

"Millions!" Dani sipped nervously at the Coke, then shook her head. "I must be crazy, Megan. I used to ride the barrels in high-school rodeos, but the girls here have been doing nothing else all their lives. I'll probably fall off my horse!"

Megan noted the nervous mannerisms of the woman in front of her, and asked calmly, "Tell me about riding the barrels, Dani. I've been talking to bull riders and saddle-bronc riders so much, I haven't had time to get any background on barrel racing. I don't even know the rules or how it got started. Fill me in, will you?"

Dani began to talk, unaware that Megan Carr was not telling the truth, that she just wanted to calm Dani's nerves.

"Well, women didn't play much of a role in rodeo for a long time, Megan. After World War I some girls did trick riding, and a few even rode saddle broncs. A woman named Fox Hastings even entered the bull-dogging, right here in Houston, in 1924, but that was just a freak. There was something called a Sponsor Girl Contest a little later. Girls sponsored by a firm or a ranch were judged on horsemanship and dress, but there was no standardization, and it wasn't much."

Dani picked up her hamburger and took a small bite, thinking about her subject. "In 1945 two women decided to have a real competition—a race that was a figure-eight turn, around barrels or poles, which would show how well their horses were trained. It caught on, and that's how barrel racing got started."

Megan had been eating steadily and paused only to ask, "What exactly are the rules? How far apart are the barrels?"

"No certain distance, Megan. It depends on the arena. There are always three barrels set in a cloverleaf pattern. If arena sizes and shapes allow, the pattern is shaped like a triangle, with the base nearest the start, the base barrels thirty yards apart, and the run to the single barrel at the point of the triangle thirty-five yards from the base barrels."

"How do you win?"

"Why, it's strictly a timed event." Dani nodded. "The barrel racer has a running start. When she enters the arena, she usually takes the barrel to her right first and circles this barrel clockwise. The next two she'll probably circle counterclockwise. The rules say that she has to turn both ways during the three-turn run. The start is twenty yards from the line on which the base barrels sit, and the minimum run at the starting line has to be fifteen yards."

Megan finished her hot dog, and Dani—soothed by the laid-back attitude of the other woman—finished her hamburger. Dani continued to talk, then abruptly cut herself short. "Say, you're a pretty good therapist, Megan!" She smiled. "Got rid of my shakes with your bedside manner, didn't you?"

Megan gave her a steady look. "What's with you, Dani? You're no country girl with stars in your eyes like most of the girls who do this sort of thing. And you're not *country-Western*, either—which *all* of them are." She leaned forward, resting her chin on her hand, studying Dani carefully with a clinical eye. "Why are you here?"

"Why—I guess just to see if I can do it," Dani excused herself lamely. Megan's close inspection alarmed her, and she tried to shore up her credibility. "I've always missed the rodeo atmosphere. And the old eight-to-five job gets pretty boring."

"What *was* your eight-to-five job?" Megan demanded swiftly. "You're college stuff and sharp as a tack. Most riders, men and women, don't want to know anything but horses and bulls. They get all their fun at parties like the one at the Corral last night. And you looked as out of place there as a minister at a racetrack!" She cocked her head, adding, "I've a pretty good feel for people, Dani. Done a lot of prying around. And you just don't fit the pattern."

Dani shrugged but knew there was no way to fool this woman. "Well, I'm running away, if you have to know, Megan. Got into a situation I couldn't handle—so I walked away and left it. Got a little money, so it doesn't matter too much if I win anything racing." She forced a smile, thinking suddenly of her dream. Quietly, she admitted, "Guess I'm nothing but a wimp. Never had any respect for people who ran away from problems—now here I am, leading the parade!"

Megan glanced down at the table, and when she looked up again, her voice was low. "Remember what the old baseball player Satchel Paige said? 'If you hear footprints, don't look back, 'cause something might be gaining on you.'" There was a sad cast on her heart-shaped face, but as if aware that she had let her guard down, she laughed and chattered, "Must be about time for the balloon to go up. What time do you ride?"

"Jay Dember said to be ready at three."

"Plenty of time. Let's go watch the show."

"All right." As they walked toward the chute area, Dani sought more information: "I told Hank Lowe I'd help his kids with math. But I didn't think to ask about a wife."

"Doesn't have one, not now. His first wife ran off with an aluminum-siding salesman," Megan informed her. "Hank carried a real torch for her, or so Ruby tells me. She said the only woman he ever showed any interest in since number one is that barrel rider—Ruth Cantrell."

"I thought she was Clint Thomas's girl," Dani commented cautiously.

"She is, but the way Fran tells it, Hank and Ruth were on the way to a ring. Then Clint waved his long eyelashes at her, and that took care of that." As they came to stand beside one of the chutes where a black horse was kicking a staccato tattoo against the sides of the chute, Megan concluded, "Hank, he's a fine guy, but there's one cowboy I think he'd let a bull stomp without lifting a hand."

Dani gave her a startled look. "Clint Thomas?"

"Got it the first time, Dani. Look, there he is now. He is a hunk, isn't he?"

Dani glanced over to see Clint laughing with two cowboys. She glanced at the black horse, who reached up with his hammerhead to gnash at one of the handlers, and wondered how anyone could be so cool. They were not, she soon discovered. The entire area in back of the chutes was in motion. Stock was being moved up. Clyde Lockyear, wearing high-heeled boots and a white sombrero with a peaked crown, was a blur of motion. He walked continuously down the line of chutes, prodding animals, asking cowboys if they were ready, signaling arena hands to bring up more flank girths, more halters, more snagging hooks.

But the cowboys were just as active, Dani saw. They were constantly milling around the chutes in a tireless, nervous manner. Some chewed gum, not slowly and methodically, but quickly, in nervous spasms. They worked and reworked their already perfect equipment, taking off their hats and looking at the sweatbands. They squatted, they stood, they got up and walked around—then did it again.

Finally the voice of the announcer boomed over the speaker system, welcoming the audience to the rodeo. When that was over, he said: "And now, ladies and gentlemen, the first event on tonight's program is cowboy bareback bronc riding. You'll notice these horses don't wear saddles. The cowboy has to hang on to a standard leather handhold. He is required to have his spurs in the horse's shoulder as he passes the judges and then he is required to spur the horse throughout the eight seconds of the ride. Each cowboy is judged on how well he rides, how well he spurs, and how well the horse bucks. Now it looks like we're ready, so we go to chute number five and a young cowboy from Tulsa, Oklahoma, named Charlie Devoe. He'll be riding Midnight, a real bucking horse!"

A short, heavyset young cowboy settled onto the back of the black horse, looking very nervous, Dani thought. He pulled his hat down, his face tight and pale, then nodded. The gate swung open, and the horse exploded. He hit the dirt kicking, and the rider's head was whipped backward by the charging jolt. He stuck on, but Megan judged, "He was off-balance coming out of the chute. He won't score high."

The ride ended, and the pickup men moved in to take the cowboy off the horse. "A fifty-three for this cowboy."

It was a very poor score. Dani knew. To win or even place in the money required a score in the high 60s. The judges rated each horse on a scale from 65 to 85, depending on how hard he bucked. They scored the rider from 1 to 20, depending on how well he stayed in control of the ride. A good score, such as 88, represented the total of the scores recorded by the two judges.

Bake Dempsey wandered over to where Dani and Megan stood. "Come to see me take first money?" He grinned. He seemed loose, and there was no fear in his face. He nodded over to where Clint Thomas perched on the top rail and eased himself down onto the back of a roan. "Ol' Clint's just a hair ahead of me right now, but he'll be number two pretty soon."

The announcer was saying, ". . . Nineteen ninety-one All-Around Champion. Hails from Baton Rouge, Louisiana. Watch him go!"

They watched the ride, and Bake predicted, "Old Clint got a lemon. That horse ain't worth shucks."

Dani was watching the horse, who was making vaulting, kicking leaps. The crowd yelled but Bake shook his head. "That ain't a dirty horse. He's easy to ride. Don't never give a cowboy any surprises, and once you get the motion it's like sitting in an armchair." The ride ended, and Bake predicted, "Sixty-six." He grinned when the announcer droned out, "And it's a sixty-eight for Clint Thomas."

Thomas walked through the gates, saw them standing there, and came over. He cursed harshly, his face screwed up with anger. "I'm goin' to shoot Clyde if he don't come up with better horses."

Bake laughed, saying, "Well, I appreciate your help, Clint. All us poor mortals just can't grieve much over it when you big stars don't do too well."

He turned and walked to the chutes, not aware of the murderous anger on Clint Thomas's face. Thomas stared at Bake Dempsey with rage in his eyes, but then he suddenly wheeled and caught Dani staring at him. At once he shook his head and forced a rueful laugh. "Can't stand to lose, Dani. Never could."

He stood between Megan and Dani, watching Bake ride a tall, rawboned horse getting a score of 81. When Bake came back, Clint grinned and commented ungraciously, "That was a good ride, Bake." Then he turned and walked away.

Bake complained, "He's like a sore-tailed bear when he loses, ain't he? But then, who ain't?" Watching one of the chutes, he remarked, "Don't know that cowboy."

Dani and Megan turned to see a broad-shouldered man easing down onto the back of a nervous paint. "He looks strong enough that the horse ought to be riding *him*," Dempsey quipped. "But there ain't no man stronger than a twelve-hundred-pound hoss."

The announcer cried out, "And now in chute number 1 we have Luke Sixkiller riding Agony. . . ."

"Sixkiller?" Bake mused as they waited for the horse gate to swing open. "Thought I knew every rider in the country." He watched the ride, which was a good one, and when the score of 76 was announced, Bake murmured, "Not bad." Sixkiller came in and saw them standing there, but did not speak until Dempsey hailed him.

"Hey, Sixkiller, that was a good ride. I'm Bake Dempsey. This is Megan Carr and Dani Ross, case you ain't met them."

Sixkiller nodded, his chest not even lifting from the effort of riding the horse. "Glad to know you, Dempsey. Seen you ride lots of times."

"Well, I never saw you, Luke," Bake commented.

"Getting a late start," Sixkiller curtly explained. He didn't look at Dani especially, but included them all in his invitation, "How about something to drink?"

Megan said quickly, "That'd be nice. You've got time, haven't you, Dani?" She was very efficient, Dani saw, in maneuvering people. They were soon drinking Cokes at the snack bar, sitting at the same table Megan and Dani had occupied a little earlier.

Sixkiller sat back in his chair, physically imposing as always. The smooth muscles of his shoulders and chest arched, clearly outlined beneath the thin cotton shirt, and he exuded a sense of latent power. He was, Dani thought suddenly, like Caesar, the huge Bengal tiger in the zoo at New Orleans. She loved to watch the magnificent animal when he was in repose, looking harmless and sleepy-eyed in the sun. But then he would suddenly rise and stretch; the immensely powerful muscles would spring into relief and the claws extend like sabers. She never looked at Caesar without thinking of William Blake's poem "Tyger, Tyger," particularly the line that called the animal a piece of "fearful symmetry." She had seen enough of Sixkiller in action to know that he had that same quality.

Megan kept probing at Sixkiller, skillfully and never obviously, but her expertise as a reporter failed her, for she was up against an expert in the matter. Luke had spent too many hours grilling suspects to give anything away himself, and it amused Dani the way he easily avoided Megan's carefully laid traps. He gave himself out to be just a "late bloomer," a fellow who'd tried rodeoing a little, but only as a hobby. When Megan pressed him about what sort of work he did, Luke answered, "Demolition work. But the job played out."

Dani gave him an innocent look and asked, "Are you married, Luke?"

"Nope. I'm available, just a lonely old bachelor," he volunteered with a gleam of humor in his dark eyes. "How about you?"

"Just a lonely old maid."

"Sounds like a match made in heaven." Bake grinned. Then he looked up, and his eyes drew down into a squint. "What's eatin' Clint? He looks mad enough to bite somebody." He lifted his voice, calling out, "Hey, Clint, what's going on?"

Thomas stopped abruptly, then seeing Dempsey, came over. "Got another phone call from the Creep," he announced in a voice brittle with anger. His mouth was drawn tight, and he shook his head stiffly. "Wish he'd show his face—I'd like to split his wishbone!"

"Same guy?" Bake asked.

"Sounded the same. Voice was kind of muffled, but it was the same old song."

"Who's the Creep?" Dani asked. It was the first time the calls had been mentioned, and she wanted to know all she could. But Clint stared at Luke, not willing to talk in front of strangers. "Oh, this is Luke Sixkiller, Clint," she quickly introduced them.

"New competition, Clint." Bake nodded, then answered Dani's question, "Some guy is putting the arm on some of us. Threatening to bust up our horses if we don't fork over a wad of cash."

"You going to the police, Clint?" Megan asked.

"No, I'm going to oil my forty-five," Clint threatened grimly. "If that sucker gets near my horse, I'll blow his head off!"

"Can't watch him all the time." Bake shook his head.

"Pay the Creep if you want, Bake," Thomas snorted. "But I can tell you what'll happen. His price will go up. His kind never gets enough! But not me. He can't do anything in the daytime, and I'm going to be around Tarzan for a few nights. Hope he *does* show up. I'll stop his clock!"

"Tarzan's a valuable horse," Bake said slowly, as Clint stomped away. "So is my dogging horse. But I can't spend a lifetime sleeping next to a horse—and neither can Clint. Better just to pay up."

"How many people are paying protection, Bake?" Dani asked.

Dempsey shrugged his shoulders. "I know three or four—but there's more than that. Some people are keeping quiet about paying off."

Clyde Lockyear came hustling by, stopping long enough to exclaim, "Hey, Dani, you better get ready. Barrel riding's the next event!"

Dani got up, the earlier nervousness coming back. "See you later," she threw over her shoulder. As she left Dani noticed that Megan managed to attach herself to Luke as the two men rose. "Good luck, Dani," Bake called out.

She hurried to get Biscuit, then went at once to where Ruth and two other women were already in place. "Thought you might have chickened out," Ruth teased with a smile.

"Nothing I'd like better!"

"You'll do fine," Ruth encouraged her. "You're third, aren't you? I'm before you, but I'll hang around. We can go celebrate your victory later."

Dani was too tense even to smile, and as the first rider got in place, then shot out into the arena, the anxiety got worse. The time of the first contestant was announced, and then somehow Ruth was finished, and Clyde was saying, "Nothing to it, Dani."

She looked down to see his round face peering up at her and nodded. "You'll do fine." He comforted Dani with a smile, and then she heard her name. Holding the reins in her left hand, she spoke to Biscuit and was suddenly propelled into the arena. Though she tried not to think of the thousands of eyes fixed on her, she could not help it. She was out of sync with Biscuit's gait and overran the first barrel badly; then she tried to cut back too sharply, so that Biscuit almost went down. But her spunky horse had amazing balance and scrambled to an upright position. Dani felt so confused and rattled she could not even see the next barrel—but the rust-colored horse could. That was what made a good barrel horse.

Horses used in the other events have moving objects to follow, which capture their attention. But the barrel-racing horse has to boom into the arena, find the first barrel (often under poor light), then spot the others.

Dani barely saw the second barrel before Biscuit was leaning into his turn, and all she could do was hang on instead of leaning into the turn to help the horse. Her poor riding made her a dead weight. Once she caught sight of the third barrel, Dani misjudged it badly and sent Biscuit too close. His shoulders struck the barrel, and even as her horse completed the turn and headed back to the gate, she saw the barrel teeter— then go down, rolling in the dust.

"Oh, too bad for Dani Ross!" the announcer cried. "Let's have a hand for a good try, folks!"

Dani found herself almost weeping with shame as she slid off Biscuit's back. She leaned against his neck, hot tears gathering in her eyes as he tried to nip her gently. She had lost before, but not in front of thousands of people.

"It's no fun losing, is it?" Looking up quickly, she saw the young cowboy who had been knocked out by Clay Dixon, standing close. He was wearing a black outfit and looked very young. As she dashed the salt tears from her eyes, he looked at her with a bitter smile. "At least you're a woman and can cry when things get bad. A guy can't even do that!"

Then he turned and left as Ruth approached, concern on her face. "Oh, Dani, don't mind it. We all knock a barrel down from time to time."

"Silly, isn't it, Ruth?" Dani managed to smile a little. "Here I am just riding barrel to cover up my identity, then squalling like a spanked puppy when I lose!" Taking a deep breath, she went on, "I don't like Clint's idea." When she saw confusion in Ruth's eyes, she asked, "Didn't you know? He got another call for money. Says he's going to sleep beside the horse—with a loaded gun."

Ruth paled, then shook her head. "He's so stubborn! I'm going to try to talk him out of it!"

But she could not, which came as no surprise to anyone. Dani kept close to her, and that night after the rodeo found herself at a smoky bar with the couple—and with Luke Sixkiller. He had whispered, "We gotta work up a hot romance, Dani. Just to make it look good, you know?"

As they danced she finally complained, "You don't have to make it look *this* good, Luke! You're holding me too tight!"

"Oh, sorry, Dani. Just a result of my careful police training."

Clint drank heavily, and when the four of them left for the motel, he said, "Not me. I'm going to bed down with old Tarzan tonight." He gave Ruth a kiss and left despite her pleas.

"I'd sure have to love a horse to sleep in the barn with him," Luke observed when the three of them were ready to go to their rooms.

"He does love Tarzan," Ruth explained in a dispirited tone. "He's had him a long time. Good night, Dani. Good night, Luke."

"She's got it bad," Luke watched her go. "Too bad."

Dani glanced at him. "What does that mean?"

"Why, nothing, I guess, except that Clint Thomas just isn't a marrying man. Just likes women—and they like him."

"Ruth's not like those women, the groupies!"

"No, she's not. Which probably will make it worse when he drops her."

Dani stared at him. She felt tired and disgusted with her ride—and was still not convinced that the undercover thing would work. "You made a good ride, Luke. Did you see my little fiasco?"

"Bad break. You keep watching me, and you'll see some hammerheaded horse kick my rear," he added. "You want to cry on my manly bosom?"

She stared at him, until she realized this was his way of trying to help. "If I don't do better tomorrow, save a place for me—assuming I can get Megan to move over. She was like a leech on you when I left, wasn't she?"

"All over me." Sixkiller nodded. "I had to give the poor kid a break. We've got a date tomorrow night. Better take the old bosom now. May not be available tomorrow," he warned her hopefully.

"Good night, Luke." Dani smiled, then added, "I'm glad you found a room here, not halfway across Houston."

"Yeah, lucky break—a sudden cancellation." Luke grinned at her.

Dani slept poorly that night, finally dropping off to sleep about two or three. Too early, a loud knock on the door brought her up in a fright.

"Who is it?" she called out, struggling into her robe.

"Sixkiller. Open up!"

She pulled the robe together and opened the door. The policeman brushed by her, and she saw that his face was tight, but his eyes were gleaming. "Somebody ruined Thomas's horse," he announced.

"Luke, no!"

"Took Clint out with a club or something, then broke both the animal's front legs."

"How's Clint? Is he badly hurt?"

"He's okay, but I never saw a guy hurt so much over a horse." Sixkiller shook his head, compassion in his eyes. "Cried like a baby—and didn't care who saw it!" Then he snapped, "Get dressed. We're going down there."

He left, and Dani threw on her clothes, telling herself, *It could have been worse. They could have broken Clint's legs.* The image of Biscuit with his legs broken flashed before her. She shuddered at the thought, then left the room quickly.

7

"Too Good to Be True!"

Lieutenant James Stark looked more like an unsuccessful insurance salesman than a member of the Houston Police Department, Dani thought. He was of average height, overweight, and had a pair of weak blue eyes behind rimless glasses. As he looked over the crowd that had gathered around the dead horse, he barked, "Get back there! There's nothing to see!" and gave an irritated wave of his hand.

Stark turned back to face Clint Thomas, who was standing with his head down. "Now, Mr. Thomas," he demanded in a petulant tone, "let me hear this one more time. First of all, you say you were hit on the head and knocked unconscious. What time was that?"

Thomas took his gaze off the ground and stared at the policeman. He was wearing the same blue shirt and Wranglers he'd worn the last time Dani had seen him, but they were rumpled. His hair, usually neatly combed, was mussed up, and he had a heavy growth of beard. "I don't know," he said angrily. "I don't have a watch."

Lieutenant Stark gave him a tired glance and was about to argue, but Clyde Lockyear stepped forward, intervening, "It was four fifteen when I found him, Lieutenant." Clyde was neatly dressed and obviously felt important as he went on, "I'd come down early to check on a sick animal, and I heard the shot. Came running in to find Clint and the horse."

"All right, we'll need a statement from you on that. Now, why did you shoot the horse, Mr. Thomas?"

Clint stared at him blankly, then explained impatiently, "His front legs had been broken. He was hurting."

"And is this your gun?" Stark said, holding up a Colt .45 automatic.

"Yes."

"Do you have a permit for it?"

"No, I don't."

Lieutenant Stark shook his head and lectured Thomas as if he were a naughty schoolboy. "That's against the law, you know. I'm afraid you'll have to do some explaining about this weapon downtown." Then he put the gun in a brown leather case, turned back to Thomas, and asked blandly, "Do you ordinarily sleep next to your horse and a loaded forty-five, Mr. Thomas?"

Clint glared at him. "No. I usually sleep in bed—and it's none of your business who I'm with."

"It's my business to find out if a crime has been committed."

"My horse has been killed." Clint spoke between clenched teeth. "He's a valuable animal, and that's a crime even in Houston, isn't it?"

"Not necessarily," Stark pointed out. "He was your horse, and there's no law that I know of against a man's killing his own horse. Lots of people kill their pets."

Thomas was in bad shape, Dani saw. He had turned pale, and his hands were not steady. "I didn't break his legs," he spat out, attempting to get control of himself. "Look, I've just been hit on the head with a blackjack, my horse is dead. Why don't you start looking for the guy who sapped me?"

Ruth came forward and put her arm around Clint. She had been crying, and she pleaded, "Lieutenant, you'd better know that there had been threatening calls about Tarzan."

"Who are you? And what do you mean threatening calls?"

"My name is Ruth Cantrell. Clint has had more than one call from a man who said he'd maim his horse if Clint didn't pay him money."

"Is that right, Mr. Thomas?" Stark demanded. When Clint nodded, the policeman fussed, "Well, why didn't you tell me? We've wasted a lot of time here. Tell me about the calls."

He listened as Thomas told him, and in the middle of the conversation Stark ordered the uniformed officer, "Monroe, get this area roped off and call the lab." He turned back to Thomas. "Now, let's go where we can talk without all this disturbance."

"Lieutenant . . . ," Lockyear interjected, "I think you might like to know that several of us have received calls from this man."

Stark's gaze went to him, then swept the circle. "Anybody else who's gotten one of these calls come with me." He moved away, followed only by Clint, Ruth, and Lockyear.

"Wonder how many won't own up to getting a call?" Luke murmured. He and Dani stood there looking at the horse. *How would I feel if it had been Biscuit?* Dani wondered and her chest felt a wrenching sensation.

The officer Stark had spoken to was looking around help-lessly. Spotting Dani and Luke, he came up, brow furrowed, and inquired, "Hey, know where I can get a rope to cordon this area off?"

Tom Leathers, standing in the crowd, offered, "You can use mine. It's right over across from the chutes."

The officer gave Sixkiller a quick look and seemed to like what he saw. "Hey, buddy, keep these people back while I get that rope and call the lab, will ya?"

"Yeah, I'll take care of it."

As soon as the policeman followed Leathers out of the area, the crowd broke up. Sixkiller began walking around, his dark eyes searching the ground. He said nothing, but as he com-pleted a large circuit, he stepped closer to the place where the horse lay. Suddenly he took out a handkerchief, bent down, and picked something up.

"What is it, Luke?" Dani asked.

"A clue," he murmured, holding out the handkerchief.

Leaning closer Dani saw a brown leather object.

"It's a sap—a blackjack." Luke nodded. Wrapping it care-fully, he put it in his pocket, then grinned at her. "Nothing is ever this easy. It's too good to be true."

"You don't think it was used to knock Clint out?"

"Probably was, but finding out who it belongs to won't be easy."

"Not if there are fingerprints on it?"

Luke shook his head doubtfully. "There won't be any on the handle. It's braided. You could only find a latent print on the end, the thick part that holds the metal. And leather doesn't take a good print. Anyway, when's the last time you ever heard of a crime being solved through prints?"

Dani stared at him, then looked around to see the police-man coming back. "Are you going to give it to him?"

"No." Luke stared at her, saying no more. When the officer approached with a rope in his hand, he cheerfully called out, "Give you a hand with that, buddy?"

"No, I can handle it. Thanks for watching things."

As Sixkiller and Dani moved away, he outlined his plan, "I'll get this off in Express Mail to our lab in New Orleans. Should know by tomorrow if we've got something."

The news of Tarzan's death swept over the rodeo, not only among the performers and hands, but to the world outside. When Clint's name was called out by the announcer in the calf-roping contest, he added, "And you ought to know, folks, Clint's not riding his own great horse, Tarzan, this time." His voice grew lugubrious as he explained, "Clint lost old Tarzan last night—and that's a big loss for any man!"

Ruth, standing beside Dani muttered, "Why don't they just shut up about it?" Her face was tense. "It's cut Clint all to pieces, Dani. He doesn't have any business riding today— but he won't listen to me." They watched as Clint came out, made a good catch, and threw the calf. The time was good, but Clint didn't smile, and he walked off, disappearing without a word.

Ruth herself was off, for her time was 18 seconds. She came back, not even pausing to speak to Dani. Timing was relative in barrel racing, the championship being decided by the total amount of prize money won over the season.

Ruby moved her horse closer to Dani and leaned down to say, "She's got to go give him a shoulder to cry on—but it won't do any good." Dani saw a cold look in her eyes, and Ruby added, "Clint won't let anybody help him. I ought to know." Her horse skittered, and she pulled him down with a firm hand. "It takes a dumb horse to make him cry! He won't cry over a woman, I can tell you that!"

She was, Dani saw, not sorry over the tragedy, and her ride was very good—16 seconds. Dani mounted Biscuit and watched as a black-haired girl named Tammy Bryan made her ride, but she knocked over two barrels. Coming back, the girl said in disgust, "Well, you can't do worse than second if you don't knock a barrel down, Dani!"

Her name boomed over the speakers, and Dani moved Biscuit into position. She blocked her mind from everything except the ride, the world closing to a narrow opening, and commanded, "Go, Biscuit!" The horse's muscles bunched under her, and he fired out into the arena, turning toward the barrel to the left with only a touch of her hand on the rein. Perhaps it was good that the first ride had been so bad, for this time she had no thought of the spectators. It was as though she were alone in her practice field, just she and the driving horse beneath her.

Suddenly the joy of riding swept over her, and as Biscuit rounded the first barrel, coming so close that her right boot touched it lightly, she cried out, "Go!" and the horse responded with a blinding burst of speed. They took the next two barrels smoothly, and the crowd cried its approval as they drove back toward the entrance.

"And it's 15.5 seconds for Dani Ross!" the announcer boomed. "A fine ride for the little lady!"

Dani pulled Biscuit to a halt, slipped out of the saddle, and was patting his shoulder when Hank Lowe came up to say, "Hey, now, that was one good ride, Dani!" He was wearing his clown costume, for the bull riding was the next event. He had on a huge putty nose and wore red pants held up by green suspenders. A battered round bowler perched over his eyes, and Dani noticed that he was wearing shoes with baseball spikes—for speed and sureness, she understood.

"Thanks, Hank. Now you be careful out there today."

Her concern surprised him, and he grinned. "Sure, Dani." Then he asked, "Think you might come over to the trailer and do a little math this afternoon?"

"How about two o'clock?"

"Just right!" He nodded, a grateful look in his warm, brown eyes. He moved away as the announcer began talking about the bull-riding events.

When Dani went to the space reserved for trailers, she found Hank's easily, as a donkey poked its head around a corner. Behind the animal, Hank was pulling at the halter around its neck. He suddenly looked up to see her. "Here's your teacher, kids," he yelled, and at once Cindy and Maury came piling out the door of the trailer.

"What are you doing with that donkey?" Dani asked curiously.

"Trying to train him," Hank answered, wiping the sweat from his brow. "But, he's too smart for me. To be a donkey trainer, you gotta be just a little bit smarter than the donkey!"

"Aw, Daddy, you're smarter'n that ol' donkey!" Maury objected.

"Maybe so, but I ain't as stubborn." Hank grinned. "Air conditioning's on inside, Dani. Go on in. If they give you any trouble, let me know. They're about as stubborn as Ulysses here is!" he warned her as she went inside with the children.

The interior of the trailer, to Dani's surprise, was neat as a pin. It was not large, but it sparkled, and she said, "You are better housekeepers than I am." She saw a desk that had been placed along one wall, and asked, "Is that our school?"

"If we hurry," Maury piped up, "we can finish in time to see 'Batman.'"

But Dani had come prepared. She had visited a Christian bookstore earlier and made some purchases. She opened the sack and laid out several magazines, which Maury pounced on. "Hey, are these puzzles?" he yelled. Thumbing through them, he boasted, "I'm *good* at puzzles!"

Dani suggested, "Let's see how good you are. You work this one, while I see how good your sister is at algebra."

She found at once that both of the children were very bright. Maury buried himself in the puzzle books, yelping whenever he completed one, and demanding a gold star, which Dani affixed to each completed exercise.

Cindy was cautious at first, but Dani drew her out, and soon she and Dani were laughing together over the silly problems in the math book that Hank had bought. Dani stopped them after a time, bringing out the cookies she had brought, and they washed them down with soft drinks from the refrigerator. Maury went back to his puzzles voluntarily, and Dani led Cindy through some of the mysteries of algebra.

When Dani saw that the girl was getting bored, she exclaimed, "You have such pretty hair, Cindy! But you know what? I think it would be prettier if you fixed it differently. Let's try it."

When Hank came in an hour later, he found the three of them giggling and playing Monopoly. "Hey, you three are supposed to be studying!" he sternly took them to task.

"We *are* studying, Daddy!" Cindy nodded. "Dani's teaching us about mortgages and stuff with Monopoly."

Hank stared at his daughter. "What'd you do to your hair?"

"Dani fixed it," Cindy's eyes sparkled. "Isn't it nice? And she says she's going to take me to a store and buy me a new dress."

"You have to go with us, Hank." Dani nodded. "I know how badly men hate to shop with women, but Cindy and I need your money."

Then Maury piped up, "Dani's even better than Ruth in this ol' stuff."

Dani shot a look at Hank, noting that his face had sobered. "Well, wait until next time, Maury," she warned. "I used up all my good tricks on this first one. Now, let's go spend your money, Hank!"

Lowe took them to a department store, but later when he walked Dani back to her truck, he said, "Don't know how you did it, Dani. I can't get them to crack a book. Sure do appreciate it."

Dani stopped beside her truck. "Oh, I'm new to them. They'll holler loud enough next time. Now that I've won their confidence, I can afford to really pour on the work." She laughed suddenly. "Now you know what a conniving female I am, Hank!"

He looked at her, slim and beautiful in the sunlight, and teased, "Sure, I can see you're a hard number."

She hesitated before mourning, "Terrible about Tarzan, wasn't it?"

He nodded. "I'd like to get the guy who did it. Break *his* legs!"

"Clint's all broken up about it."

"Sure. Even a hairpin like Thomas grieves over losing a horse." Dani did not miss the barbed reference concerning Clint, but said nothing. "Tarzan was past his prime, of course. It was his last year."

"I didn't know that."

"Oh, sure. Clint almost didn't use him this year. Got a new horse last year. Not as good as Tarzan was in his prime, but he will be."

"Hank, are you making a payoff to this man?" Dani questioned.

Lowe looked startled, then slowly he nodded. "A small one. Most people don't know it, but a trained donkey is an expensive animal. After Tilman Yates's horse got ruined, I caved in." His eyes narrowed, and he explained, "It's only a few bucks. Like paying insurance."

"How many more do you think might be paying off?"

"Don't know. This guy is pretty choosey, Dani. I make pretty good, and he don't fool with little people. Guess you think I'm wrong, paying off?" he worried.

Dani shook her head. "I hate the idea, Hank, but I'm not in your shoes, so I don't have any right to judge."

"It's not Ulysses I'm worried about so much," Lowe admitted, biting his lip nervously. He hesitated, then plunged ahead. "Yates got busted up, and now Clint's been knocked in the head. When he called, the guy said if I didn't care about protection for the mule, I ought to think about my kids. He said, 'What would happen to them if *you* got your legs busted and couldn't do your job?'"

"He knows how to work people." Dani nodded. Then she asked cautiously, "Hank, who is it? I mean, is it some Mafia hood who's moving in on all of you?"

"No! It's not a big enough operation for that bunch," Lowe said, shaking his head. "And I don't think it's an outsider, either."

"Why not?"

"Because he knows too much about us. Knew my kid's names. Knew the times I worked." He gave her a strange look, then lowered his voice, "Dani, he's been inside my trailer."

"What? How do you know, Hank?"

"Well, I can't prove it, but when he called, he told me, 'You can keep a picture of Lorrie over the couch, but a picture can't watch your kids.'" He looked directly at Dani. "Lorrie was my wife. She walked out on me."

Dani consoled him, "I'm sorry, Hank. But I admire you for the job you're doing with Cindy and Maury."

"Do my best—but anyway, the guy knew about the picture. He's either been in my trailer or he's talking to someone who has been."

Dani pondered this. "That narrows it down, Hank."

"Not so much as you think. He may be connected with the rodeo, but this trailer's been pretty popular. People drop by all the time, helping with the kids or just visiting. Could be any one of a hundred, Dani. It could be one of the losers."

"Losers?"

"Sure. Lots of guys rodeo and never make any money. There ain't no guarantees, Dani. There's about two thousand members of the RCA—the Rodeo Cowboy's Association. There's about seven hundred of them here right now in Houston, with about five hundred in the bucking events alone. But there's only a few like Clint Thomas making a hundred thousand a year. Behind him are a handful earning maybe fifty thousand and after that about fifty men making thirty thousand a year."

"That's a pretty small crowd, Hank." Dani had not known those figures. "What about the others?"

"All strung out, winning a few thousand a year, struggling to stay on the circuit. Mostly living on canned goods out of grocery stores, traveling five and six to a car to cut expenses, staying in the cheapest motels, borrowing all the time just to pay their entry fees for that next show up the line. Some go on for years like that. Some have families and take temporary jobs during the off season, just livin' for the next year."

"And you think the Creep might be one of these?"

"Could be."

Dani saw that Lowe was getting nervous, so she suggested, "I'll pop in tomorrow for lesson number two, Hank."

"Thanks, Dani," Lowe said, closing the door for her. "Maybe we can go out and eat someplace. The laborer is worthy of his hire."

Dani stared at him. "You know the Bible, Hank?"

He shook his head. "Know it a little—but don't do it." He stood there, watched her drive her truck out of the lot, then turned and walked slowly back to the trailer. On the way, Ulysses reached out and bit him on the arm. Yanking the hurt member back, he cursed the animal. He drew back his arm to strike the donkey, but then suddenly dropped it. "Why not you?" he muttered. "Everybody else does!"

Dani went to Ruth's motel room at once, saying as soon as she was admitted, "Tell me about it, everything."

Ruth stared at her, then sat down on the bed. "Clint didn't get even a glimpse of whoever hit him. He was drinking and sort of dozed off. But he came out of it when he thought he heard somebody coming up from behind Tarzan's stall. He got cracked on the head, and when he woke up, it was over. He couldn't stand to see Tarzan in agony, so he shot him."

At Dani's insistence Ruth repeated what she could remember of the interview with Lieutenant Stark. "He kept asking questions like who could get in, stuff like that. Of course, just about *anybody* could—that's what Clyde told him. There's not much security—just one guy who makes the rounds every couple of hours."

Dani pried at the girl until she got most of the information about the interview, then asked, "What did Lieutenant Stark say he was going to do?"

Ruth looked angry. "He kept asking Clint questions, and I could see he was suspicious. He asked if the horse was insured—stuff like that. He just about came out and said that he thought Clint shot Tarzan himself for the insurance money!"

"Was Tarzan insured?"

"Yes, we all insure our horses, but Clint loved that horse!"

Dani left that alone, knowing that any information she got out of Ruth would be colored by her feelings for Clint. Finally she queried, "Ruth, how much have you paid, and how did you deliver the money?"

"Only two hundred dollars," Ruth replied. "It was just one time, two weeks ago. He called and said to leave the money in a purse on a park bench. He said there were two of them, that one of them would watch after I left. That was in El Paso. I did what they said. Took an old purse, put the money in it, and left it."

Dani questioned her for a long time, then got up, observing, "I don't think the police will do much. But what will Clint do now?"

"He'll kill whoever put Tarzan down!"

Dani gave her a careful look. "That won't be easy, Ruth. He can't carry a gun, and this man is smart. The Creep won't give anyone a chance to corner him."

As she turned to go, a thought came to her. She said in an offhanded manner, "I spent some time with Cindy and Maury today. They're nice kids, aren't they?"

Ruth's cheeks flushed and she admitted, "I—I miss them a lot, Dani. But after I started going with Clint, I just couldn't—"

She couldn't finish, and Dani explored tentatively, "Ruth, you and I haven't known each other long, but—"

"I know!" Ruth snapped. Her lips drew together in a tight line, and she shook her head. "Ben tried to talk to me about Clint. How he's always been a woman chaser. But he's different now, Dani. I know he is!"

How many other women have said that? Dani wondered, but knew that it was useless to talk of it. "I'll see you later, Ruth," she finally broke off. "You haven't told anyone about Luke and me have you?"

"Oh, no!"

"It might get us killed," Dani warned. "Anyone who'd break a horse's legs is hard enough for anything. Be careful."

Ruth sat on her bed, watching the door close, then fell face down on the bed and wept. On the small bedside table the picture of Clint showed the rider in a serious mood, his eyes dark and brooding; they seemed to rest on the shaking body of the girl as she lay there, weeping.

8

Sixkiller's Roommate

The dream came again, not as before, in a series of events—but fragmented. At first only a vague sense of fear, such as one gets when the doctor says soberly, *We have a little problem here,* touched her. Then a sharp picture followed of the faces of people, all filled with fear.

Dani saw Ben springing up and down on the trampoline, his body arching in a series of turns. Then she saw herself standing by a swamp, holding a gun, and she heard the thunderous roar of the weapon and saw the fragments of a cypress tree as the slugs tore into it. In the silence that followed Ben warned, *"Shooting at a tree's not like shooting at a man, Dani. Nobody knows what he'll do when he's got to shoot someone."*

Then she saw the face of the man she killed—not grotesque, as it had been when she first saw him, wearing the stocking mask, but as she had seen it later, when the police had pulled off the stocking and she had stood looking down at him. The blood soaked the black T-shirt, but none touched his face. In her dream she again saw the face of a man who lay in a grave because of the bullet she had put in his chest.

His eyes were open, just as when she had last seen him, but then they had been blank, without expression. In her dream the eyes were alive and staring at her with a terrible intensity. All the other features were dead, but the eyes glared at her and seemed to grow larger—much larger than any eyes she'd ever seen. They swelled up like dark balloons, carrying some sort of terrible indictment.

Dani tried to run, but was frozen, and the eyes grew into flat and ugly oceans. Then a maelstrom, a whirlpool with smooth, black lustrous sides, formed. And she found herself drifting on the flat surface, struggling to keep away from the deadly center. The sides grew steeper, and she began to weep and cry as she slid toward the pit. A dead silence was broken by a thin cry; as she was sucked by the oily, black waters, which had become almost perpendicular, she could see what lay at the bottom of the vortex.

It was the face of the man she had killed, the eyes now glowing with an inhuman light. As she began to scream, he lifted a thin hand, with fine fingers like those of a concert violinist, motioning her toward the cerulean depths—

Dani woke up with a violent start, her entire body jerking, and her outflung arm knocked the lamp from the table beside the bed. As it crashed to the floor, she cried out loudly and sat bolt upright in the darkness. She was weeping, and her breath came in short, painful gasps, as if she had been in a terrible accident.

Just as consciousness came, driving the scenes from her mind, the phone rang.

The suddenness of the loud sound so nearby caused her to give an involuntary jerk and one short, sharp cry. As the phone kept up an incessant ringing, she put her hands to her face, holding them there tightly until the trembling that racked her body abated.

Lowering her hands, she took a deep breath, then picked up the phone. "H-hello?"

"Dani? Is that you?"

"Ben!" she gasped. The sound of Savage's cheerful voice brought a sudden flood of relief. To cover her weakness, she barked, "Why are you calling at this time of the night?"

He didn't answer at once, and when he did, there was concern in his voice. "What's the matter?"

"Matter? You call me in the middle of the night, then want to know what's the matter with *me!*"

"You weren't asleep," he observed flatly. "When people try to talk over the phone after waking up suddenly, they're all fuzzy and confused. What's wrong? You having trouble sleeping?"

Dani gripped the phone tightly. "Stop playing detective, Savage. I'm fine."

"I hate it when people say that," Savage enlightened her. "You ask how they are, and even if their lives are falling to pieces, they say, *Oh, I'm fine! Just fine!* Look, you can tell me. This is Savage's Psychological Service. Hours twelve to twelve, we never close." Then his jocular tone grew gentle, and he asked, "You still having a bad time?"

"Yes," Dani whispered, and the tears came to her eyes. She dashed them away and forced herself to say resolutely, "But it's all right, Ben. I'll get over it. Thanks for—for caring."

"No extra charge." He paused. "I just wanted to tell you not to worry about the office. Your dad's doing fine, looking great. Angie fusses over him like a mother hen with one chick. Sends him home at noon, happy as a clam."

"What about you, Ben?"

"Aw, I'm too dumb to hurt, Boss," he quipped lightly. "Guess I fell on my head too many times when I was in the circus. Doctor says I'm okay. Just a little stiff, is all. Now, what's with Ruth?"

"Ben, whoever is doing this thing injured Clint's horse last night." She quickly gave him all the facts, then ended, "I think he's pretty rough, the Creep, as Clint calls him."

"You're right there. What have you two come up with? Any goodies?"

"Not much. Luke found the sap that took Clint out. He's sending it to New Orleans to check for prints. Says it probably won't help." They talked a little more, then Dani cautiously admitted, "Ben, I'm not too happy about Ruth and Clint."

He responded at once, "He's got a bad record with women. I tried to warn Ruth, but a woman in love doesn't want to hear things like that. She'll change him, she says."

"I know. But maybe's she's right. I hope so, Ben. She's a fine woman, and she deserves a good man." When he didn't answer, she asked tentatively, "Was she serious about Hank Lowe?"

"Yeah—and I wish she'd stayed serious. He's a good guy."

The conversation bogged down, and Dani ended, "Thanks for calling. Do it again, will you? And I'll be calling to let you know how things are going."

"Sure—but one thing, Boss—"

"Yes?"

"I've been meaning to tell you—about that Sixkiller hanging around with you—he's a slick operator with women. Keep your powder dry."

Dani laughed. "It's funny, Savage, but he said exactly the same thing about *you!*" She hung up the phone and got out of bed. As she peeled off her gown and put her shower cap on, she was thinking, *Savage's Psychological Service—not bad for a beat-up acrobat!* As the warm water ran down her body, it seemed to sluice away not only the sweat but the tension that the nightmare had brought. But a nagging thought surfaced as she dried with the skimpy motel towel, *How do I get rid of this thing for keeps? Will I have to live with it—like someone who loses an arm and is never complete?* But there was no answer, and as she dressed she forced the memory of the dream into a small closet in her mind, slammed the door, then locked it firmly.

When the voice woke him, Boone Hardin sat bolt upright and stared wildly around. His back was stiff from slumping down in the uncomfortable chair, and it took him a few seconds to recognize the room clerk standing in front of him.

"What—what's that?" he mumbled, getting to his feet.

The middle-aged man with thick glasses and thinning blond hair smiled apologetically. "Didn't mean to scare you, Son," he said quietly. "But you can't sleep here anymore."

Hardin's back stiffened, and he objected angrily, "It's a lobby, ain't it?"

The clerk shook his head. "Just for paying guests, Son. And you're not registered."

"Don't call me Son!" Hardin snapped. "And I don't need your crummy old lobby, anyways!"

As he turned to leave he bumped into a large man standing beside the chair. "Watch where you're goin'!" the boy sputtered with a truculent air. He would have passed but the man put a big hand on his arm and pulled him to a stop.

"Your name's Hardin," he said. "I saw you put up a pretty good ride on Firecracker two nights ago."

Hardin had not looked at the big man but now he did. "Oh, yeah—" he nodded, then identified the other, "You're Sixkiller, right?"

"Yeah." Luke saw the clerk waiting. "I'll take care of it. No more problem."

"Well, it's not my say, boys." The clerk shrugged. "The manager—he told me no more guys sleeping in the lounge."

Hardin mumbled, "Who needs this old lounge!"

Sixkiller studied the boy, noting the circles under the dark eyes and the unwashed black hair falling across the forehead. "Where's your gear, Boone?"

"Oh, out behind the bushes."

"Go get it." Sixkiller nodded. "Got two beds in my room. No sense one of them going to waste." He saw refusal forming in the boy's proud eyes, then laughed and slapped him on the shoulder. "I've camped out in a few lobbies myself, Boone. Besides, if you keep on riding as good as I saw you the other night—and if I keep on getting tossed off on my head, like tonight—you'll probably be offering me a bed in *your* room!"

The ease of the big man and the grin on the wide lips made it all right. "I'll be right back."

When Boone dashed out the front door, Sixkiller wandered over to the desk. "Put down two in my room, buddy," he ordered. "Don't tell the kid."

"Sure! Hate to see young guys having it so rough." He nodded approval at Sixkiller, adding, "No charge. Good to see you guys hang together."

When Hardin came back carrying a battered green suitcase, Sixkiller led him to the room. "Take that bed, Boone." Then he directed, "You take a quick shower. I've gotta have something to eat." Then he forestalled the boy's refusal, saying casually, "Never could stand to eat alone. Get moving, cowboy, I'm starved."

As a matter of fact, Sixkiller had eaten after the last show, but he saw the signs of hunger on the boy's pale face. He picked up a book and read while the boy showered and dressed, then the two of them left the motel. "There's a pretty good little place I found over close to the arena," Sixkiller commented as they got into the car. "Not fancy, but good chow. Cheap, too."

Half an hour later the two were seated at a table at Andy's Steakhouse. "Name of the place is a little deceptive, Boone," Sixkiller told him as the waitress came over. Then he gave the order without asking Hardin. "Bring us two chicken-fried steaks, two baked potatoes, and some vegetables to go with it, Beautiful." He grinned.

"Anything else?" the tall waitress returned his grin with a provocative gleam in her blue eyes.

"I can think of a couple of things, Honey, but a gal like you has probably got a tough boyfriend. I can't afford to get beat up, so just bring us two slabs of that good apple pie with ice cream on top."

She giggled, gave the order back, ending with "apple pie a la mode with ice cream on top. Right at you!"

At first the boy tried to conceal his ravenous hunger, but soon he gave up and attacked the steak in a feeding frenzy. Sixkiller toyed with his, cutting it into two sections and finally admitting, "I'm not as hungry as I thought, Boone. My daddy taught me wasting food was the unforgivable sin. Wish you'd help me out with this."

After the pie, the two men sat there drinking coffee, and Sixkiller saw that the food had practically drugged the young cowboy—that and lack of sleep. Luke yawned hugely and drawled, "Like to stay up and jaw with you, Boone, but I can't keep my eyes open. Let's go get some sleep."

"All right." Boone almost dozed off in the car, but when they got to the room and were getting ready for bed, he opened up a little. In answer to Luke's seemingly careless questions, he told a little about himself. He spoke of his mother freely—except when he mentioned the hard life she had led. Then his voice grew unsteady, and he quickly changed the subject. He'd been raised, he said, in a small town just outside St. Louis. When he didn't mention a father, Sixkiller asked "What about your dad? What's he do?"

Sixkiller didn't miss the anger that pulled the muscles of Boone's face taut, and the boy's voice was spare and tinged with concealed anger as he bit out, "Never knew him."

At once Sixkiller changed the subject, talking about horses, and found that the boy had one blazing ambition, and that was to be All-Around Cowboy. He had undressed and slept in a pair of faded shorts. The youngster was well-built, but his wiry frame did not have the muscle that would be there in a few years. Lying there with his eyes closed, Boone's voice grew more slurred, and finally he dropped off in the middle of a sentence.

Sixkiller got up and took the billfold from the boy's faded Wranglers. There were two single dollar bills, which brought a frown to Sixkiller's face. He found four pawn-ticket stubs in one pocket, a snapshot of a bay horse with Boone mounted and smiling, and a Missouri driver's license. In the "secret" fold that all cheap billfolds have, he found the most interesting item—a picture of Clint Thomas, the All-Around Cowboy for the past three years and a newspaper clipping in which he was quoted as saying in response to a reporter: "No, I'm never going to get married again. Women and kids slow a fellow down!"

Sixkiller stared at the clipping and the picture and put his dark eyes on the sleeping boy. *Guess every young cowboy's got to have somebody to look up to,* he thought, slipping the wallet back in the jeans. But as he lay in the darkness, the corollary to his thought came: *But I wish Boone had picked one with a little more character.* Then he murmured softly as sleep overtook him, "I guess character doesn't make a guy sit on a thousand-pound horse any better!"

The next day Boone stuck to him like a burr. Sixkiller paid for breakfast, and that afternoon the boy made a good ride. Seeing how nervous Boone was, Sixkiller stayed close to him as the saddle-bronc contest drew near. "I don't know anything about this horse, Luke," the younger man worried. "Don't have no idea what to take on him."

"Why don't you ask somebody?"

"Why, I don't want to do that!"

"You're a fool if you don't," Luke commented and, seeing Fighting Bill Baker standing close, called out, "Hey, Bill, you ever ride this hoss?"

Bill came at once, nodding. "Shore have. Take about a thumb and a fist." He gave Boone a nod, adding, "You can fit a ride on this one, kid, but rake him as soon as he hits the gate. He'll soldier on you, if you don't!"

"About a thumb and a fist?" Boone asked, holding up a clenched fist with the thumb extended.

"Maybe a little more. He nearly fetched me once."

Knowing exactly where to hold the rein on a saddle bronc was important. If a cowboy held the rein too high, he had no control, and the horse could put his head down between his feet and pitch. But if the rein was held too far toward the neck, the horse could jerk the contestant right over his head.

"You got to share what you know with the other guys, Boone," Sixkiller advised. "It's a pretty select club, and you

132

may get in a brawl with another cowboy, but here at the chutes, you forget all that."

It was, he saw, a new concept to Hardin, and the young man sat digesting it as the announcer continued, "And your next event, ladies and gentlemen, will be cowboy saddle-bronc riding. In this event the cowboy must have his spurs in the horse's shoulder as he passes the judges; he must spur throughout the duration of the ride; and he must not touch the horse or himself with his free hand. Neither may he lose a stirrup. Now coming out of chute number two on a mighty tough horse, King Tut, a young cowboy from Santa Fe, New Mexico, Stan Ketchell!"

"Get on your horse, Hardin," Clyde Lockyear called out, and Boone took a deep breath.

Bill Baker and Luke both positioned themselves, Bill saying, "Easy, now, hoss . . . !" The animal flinched and trembled as Boone let his weight down, and Luke shook him by the mane to distract him from what Hardin was doing. Leaning first to the right and then to the left, Boone guided his boot tips into the small stirrups. Finally he settled his full weight on the horse's back. At once the horse started and jumped, trying to rear, but Luke held him with a firm grip on the halter.

It was the worst moment of the whole affair, for if a rider got thrown in the chute, it was bad news. But the horse settled down, shuffling nervously. The announcer called out, "And now Boone Hardin, a young cowboy from St. Louis—coming out of chute number one on Breakneck!"

The gate loader waited for his signal. Boone nodded, ordering, "Let me have him," and the gate swung open. Breakneck hit the open space, and Boone spurred him in the shoulders, right out of the chute. When the horse hit the ground on the second jump, Boone hit the shoulders again, but not too high. He went to the cinch and camped for one jump as the blood pounded between his ears, all that pounding that a man had to take when he got on a bucking horse. He went to the shoulders again and from there on out spurred about eight inches in front and the same distance behind. It seemed like a half hour before he heard the gun, kicked both stirrups away, and ignoring the pickup men, vaulted off Breakneck, feeling hot and clean and happy.

As he walked back, Boone kept his head down, until the announcer spoke excitedly. "That was as good a ride as we've seen from a young man in many a year, folks. Remember that name—Boone Hardin!"

Luke was waiting for him and hit the shoulders of the young cowboy, grinning. "You son of a gun! Just for taking first money, *you* can buy the steaks tonight!"

"Don't know if it'll be first," Boone protested.

"If you don't get at least an eighty, we'll shoot the judges!"

Then the announcement came, "And that ride was worth eighty-seven points, ladies and gentlemen. . . ."

Tom Leathers and Fighting Bill Baker gave the boy a slap on the shoulder, and so did several others. Then suddenly Clint Thomas came up, saying, "That was a good ride, Hardin."

Boone nodded shortly. Sixkiller saw the strange expression of shock and something else that washed across Boone's face as Clint appeared. When Hardin spoke, it was a mere grunt, "Thanks," with little life and nothing in his face.

Thomas stared at him, surprised, then walked away toward his chute.

Later, when Boone was standing beside the bull he was going to ride, Sixkiller carelessly noted, "You didn't have much to say to Clint, Boone. You jealous of him?" Suddenly aware that his question had brought the young cowboy's guard up, Luke added, "I guess all of us maybe would like to take his spot."

He said no more but studied the bull until Hank Lowe came to stand beside him. "Hank, what the blazes do I do with this bull?" Luke asked.

Hank grinned broadly, "I guess it don't matter so much what you do with him as what he does with you, Luke." Then he stared at the banana-horned bull with a big splotch on his hip. "He's a good one, Luke. He'll buck straight away, but he'll really show out for you."

"Must be eight feet tall." Luke shook his head. "Don't know if my legs will reach his belly."

He climbed aboard the bull and got his grip on the rope, which was looped like a noose around the animal's middle. It was braided flat and had a handhold like the flat handle of a duffel bag. He put his gloved hand in this loop, knuckled down, and Hank, standing on the chute, pulled all the slack out of the rope. When it felt right, Luke took the free end of the rope, laid it across his palm, then wrapped it behind his hand. His glove had been resined, as had the bull rope, and with his free hand he pounded his riding hand shut.

"How's that feel?" Hank asked.

"Okay."

Then Hank was gone with his helper, Rocky James, to get into position. When the bull shot out, they worked in tandem, racing along on each side of the bull, about four feet away from the animal, staying back far enough so as not to interfere with the ride, but close enough so that they could get there quickly when the rider finished.

He was a good bull, bucking wild and strong, but Luke had no trouble. He stayed on until the timing horn made a loud "Uggaah!" and the ride was over.

Somehow Luke flipped over the bull's shoulders, doing an almost complete somersault in the air and landing close to the bull's shoulder. But the bull rope had gotten twisted, and he was tied to the bull.

The crowd screamed, and Luke scrambled to his feet. But the bull was so tall that he was jerked off his feet at every jump. It was a terrible strain on his arm, and he thought of one man who'd had his back broken in just such a way.

Suddenly Hank Lowe appeared. While Rocky James kept the bull distracted, Hank twisted at the rope, and Luke fell free. The bull went bucking on down the arena, and Hank helped Luke to his feet.

The crowd gave them a great hand, and Luke said with a straight look, "Appreciate it, Hank."

"Sure."

Despite the accident, Luke got a good score for his ride. Seeing that Boone was talking excitedly to Bake Dempsey, he decided to find Dani. He discovered that she was not scheduled to race that afternoon, and when he failed to find her at the arena, he called her room. When she answered, he suggested, "Let's get together for some detective talk. How about the pool? Nobody would ever notice us there."

"I didn't bring my suit."

"Neither did I, but I'll pick up something at a store."

"You think I'd let you buy me a swimsuit?"

"Hey, I read *Cosmopolitan* all the time," he assured her. "Be cool." He stopped off at the store, came out of the swimwear department in ten minutes, and was knocking at Dani's door fifteen minutes later.

"Slip into this little number," he said.

She opened the sack and pulled out what seemed to be a fat piece of black string. Her eyes widened, and she threw the suit back at him. "You idiot!"

"You don't like it?" he lamented, shaking his head in amazement. "The girl I bought it from said it was the latest thing."

Dani moved to shut the door, but he stuck his foot in it. "Here, I got this one, in case you were too prudish for the real thing." He watched as she took out the plain, one-piece black suit.

"Probably won't fit," she muttered and turned to go inside.

"Oh, it'll fit, all right," he called out as the door shut. "I've been doing research."

Dani slipped into the suit, threw a bath towel over her shoulder, and made her way to the pool. Two small girls were playing in the shallow end, watched by their mother, and two women were sunning themselves on a pair of plastic benches. Luke came sauntering down the walk. He was wearing a black suit with a silver fish on it. As he walked by, both the women followed him with their eyes. Dani didn't blame them, for he was impressive, a flat stomach ridged with muscles, an arching chest, and not a spare ounce on him.

"Suit's okay," he observed, giving her a look and throwing down his towel. "I found one that fit your personality better—but it had a flaw on the knee."

"Race you for supper," Dani said, ignoring his jibe. "Six laps."

They lined up and plunged in, but it was no contest. Dani left him behind on the first lap, and though he churned the water into froth, she ended two laps ahead of him. He pulled himself out of the water with a smooth motion, explaining sourly, "I've been sick."

Dani laughed, and the two of them lay down on towels. "Wish I were an Indian," Dani said with an envious look at his smooth, copper skin. "I never had a good tan."

"We'll have a ceremony." He was lying flat on his back, his eyes closed. "I'll make you a blood brother. Doesn't hurt much. Then you'll be a squaw."

They lay in the sun, the heat baking them, and once he got up to go get some ice water. When he came back, she told him that Ben had called. "Says we better be careful."

"Yeah, he'd lose his job if anything happened to you." Sixkiller rolled over and propped his head on his elbow. He reached out and ran his fingers down her cheek. "Know what? I got a new roommate."

"I'm afraid to ask!"

"It's that kid, Boone Hardin." He told her how he'd taken the boy in, then how he'd gone through his identification.

"You did that when he was asleep?" she demanded. "You have no morals!"

"Sure I do." He nodded. "I just don't use them much in my line of work. But it's a good thing I don't. Found out something about the kid. He carries a picture of Clint Thomas hidden in his billfold."

Dani thought about it, then shrugged. "I guess lots of young cowboys look up to Clint. He's the champion."

"Sure, but later, when Thomas came over to speak to him, the kid froze up. Hardly spoke to Clint. I didn't dream it, either. We all noticed it."

Dani turned over and let the sun soak into her back. "Well, Officer, what conclusion have you drawn from all that?"

Sixkiller shook his head, saying, "Nothing." A shadow fell across his face, and he shaded his eyes. "Hey, Megan," he called out. He sat up, adding, "Go get suited out. I'll race you in the pool. Already beat everybody else."

Megan shook her head, "Don't have a suit."

Dani sat up and spoke with a straight face, "Why, you could let her have the one you bought, couldn't you, Luke?"

For once the muscular Sixkiller was caught without a word. "Aw, that was a joke, Dani."

"Make him give you the key, Megan," Dani insisted. "But if you wear that suit, better hire a bodyguard. It's pretty daring."

"Give me the key, Sweetie," Megan grinned. "I feel like doing something daring." She took the key Sixkiller fished out of his small pocket, then left.

While she was changing, Dani told Luke, "Ben was right about you. He said you were the skirt chaser, not him."

Sixkiller grunted, and when Megan came down the walk in the skimpy suit, Dani teased, "There's a scientific name for bulging eyeballs, Luke. Wish I knew it, 'cause you have a bad case of it."

Sixkiller gave her a scowl, then nodded at Megan. "It looks great, Megan. This puritan here said it was too immoral for her."

Megan laughed and seemed to appreciate his admiring look. She had a good figure. Shaking her hair with one hand, she challenged him, "Let's race."

Sixkiller got up, then asked, "Are you a good swimmer?"

"Intercollegiate freestyle champion." She nodded. "Let's go."

She beat Sixkiller even more decisively than Dani had, and when they got back to the towel, Dani explained, "He's been sick."

Sixkiller grumped, "Back in the good old days, women had enough sense to let men beat them. Now you've given me an inferiority complex."

"You don't have a complex, Luke." Dani winked at Megan. "You're really inferior!"

They lay in the sun, joking and swimming from time to time. It was pleasant and the tension eased away from all three of them. Finally Megan began talking about her book, but she said almost at once, "This thing about Thomas's horse—I don't know how to think about it. The rodeo is violent, but it's a—" she tried to find a word, then finally shrugged her shoulders. "I guess I'd call it a *clean* violence. Breaking the legs of a horse gives me goose bumps."

"The Creep is getting everybody to understand he's serious," Luke nodded. "I'd guess he'll start putting the screws on tighter."

"Got any ideas, Megan?" Dani asked.

"I'm no detective. But Clay Dixon would be a natural. He hates Clint, and he's mean enough to do just about anything."

"But not too bright," Luke objected quickly. "It takes a pretty shrewd operator to put all this thing together. How does he actually get the money? In the mail? That'd be easy for someone to trace."

Dani told him how Ruth delivered her payment, then Megan chimed in, "It's always a drop—or so I gather. Ruby paid off, and it was just about like what Ruth did. Same thing with Bake Dempsey. He's been hit pretty hard."

"How'd you find out about Bake?" Dani inquired.

"Oh, we've gone out a few times. Not too difficult to get a guy to talking."

"I've got lots to tell," Luke noted. "But my lips are sealed." He gave Megan a careful look. "Now if you'd like to try to worm *my* secret out of me . . . ?"

The two women laughed, and Dani stood up. "I'm going to wash my hair."

"You riding tomorrow?" Megan asked.

"No. Not until Monday."

"What will you do all day tomorrow? It's Sunday."

"What I always do. Go to church."

Megan gave her a straight glance, then asked, "Mind if I go with you?"

"Sure. We'll have breakfast, then go."

As Dani walked away, Sixkiller remarked, "Better not wear that suit to church. I don't think these Texas Baptists are liberated enough for that."

"Why don't you come along?" Megan demanded. "You need it."

Sixkiller grinned at her, then sobered. "All right, Megan."

Megan looked toward where Dani was vanishing between two buildings. "Know what, Luke? I'm not much for church."

"Didn't think so."

"No, but I've got to find out if Dani Ross is real." She turned her eyes on him, saying slowly, "I've known lots of women, Luke—but I need to find one who's real! I can't figure out if she's really as good as she seems or if it's all a big act."

9

A Visit to Church

I'm not sure I can go through with this."

Megan Carr halted suddenly, staring at the small white church set back off the road under a cluster of small oak trees. "You two go on."

"Nothing doing," Luke Sixkiller insisted, taking her arm firmly. "This was your idea."

"You can't drag her into the church, Luke," Dani pointed out.

"Sure I can!"

Megan glared at the burly Sixkiller, but the humor of the thing got the best of her, and she allowed a smile to touch her lips. "Oh, all right! You can let go of me, Luke. I won't run away."

Dani glanced at her two companions, noting that Luke seemed almost as ill at ease as Megan. She had been surprised when the two of them showed up at breakfast, but now she smiled, teasing, "It's no worse than a root canal. Come on."

Leading them up to the small white building, she stepped inside the foyer, and the three of them were met by a tanned, silver-haired man who smiled and greeted them, "Good to see you. I've got three fine seats close to the front."

He led them into the auditorium, which was almost filled, and as they took their seats, Megan muttered under her breath, "I'd just as soon be in the bleachers." Settling down between Dani and Luke, she looked around cautiously, taking in the simplicity of the church, which was as plain as a Shaker meeting hall. The walls were bare, broken by tall, opaque windows, and the pews were of oak, worn smooth by much use. A platform spanned the entire width of the building, occupied by musical instruments, including piano, keyboard, drums, and several guitars.

"I don't remember any drums in the church my grandmother took me to," Luke noted, with an interested look at the stage. "Looks about like a rock stage." Then he peered carefully at the musicians and shook his head. "But those aren't rockers. Not enough hair, and they have clear eyes."

The worship service began without any announcement. A dozen or so young people came to stand behind microphones, and a red-haired young man playing the keyboard hit a note, then sang in a clear tenor voice:

> Bless the name of Jesus,
> Praise the name of Jesus,
> Sing unto the king of Israel.
> Bless the name of Jesus,
> Praise the name of Jesus,
> Sing unto the king of Israel.

Then the chorus swelled into a grand anthem, filling the room as they sang:

Glory, glory, glory to his name forever!
Glory, glory, glory to his name!

Megan felt awkward and out of place but was taking in the spontaneous quality of the worshipers. Her experience at church had been limited to formalistic and highly structured worship, and the obvious joy of the congregation caught her off guard. Not only the vigorous singing but the actions of the worshipers caught her attention. Many lifted their hands in an expression of thanksgiving; others clapped in time to the music, and the movement seemed to bring to the chorus an ineffable sense of joy and excitement.

The singing continued for at least thirty minutes, with no direction or interruption, and both Megan and Luke lost their sense of awkwardness. From time to time, Megan stole a glance at Dani, noting the air of ease as Dani closed her eyes, lifted her hands, and sang in a strong contralto voice. Megan glanced at Sixkiller, the two of them isolated in the midst of the joyful singing, and he lifted one of his heavy black eyebrows as if to ask, *Well, is this real or not?*

Megan had come partly out of curiosity and was accustomed to bringing her talents as an investigative reporter to bear on any situation. She was trained to stand outside of things, to weigh them objectively and without any emotional involvement. But as the singing went on, for some reason, she found herself unable to keep her distance from what was going on. Her firmest concept of religion was that it was a stern duty, an exercise that people went through, a rather unpleasant matter that had to be done, much like a trip to the dentist.

But the faces and the singing and the obvious pleasure of the people in this service shook that long-standing belief to the foundation. Time and again her eyes would go to the singers, especially to the most unusual one. A young woman, no more than twenty, was singing with great joy. She would lift her hands, and with tears running down her cheeks could still smile with obvious joy. She had lustrous brown hair and a beautiful complexion—and she was blind.

Megan, like many other people, had been plagued since childhood by a fear of blindness. There was no physiological basis for this fear, since she had perfect vision and had never experienced eye problems of any sort. Nevertheless, many bad dreams had plagued her, even past adolescence, and a shiver went over her at the sight of the young woman. During one of her worst bouts with the phobia she had vowed, *I won't live without sight! I'll kill myself first!*

But there was such joy in the face of the young woman, that it was obvious that she had found something that made her handicap bearable—and even more than that, for when she sang a solo in a pure, clear voice, there was no doubt about the joy and happiness that were hers.

Megan sat down when the worship service was concluded, disturbed as she seldom was. Her hands trembled, and she clasped them together tightly so that Dani could not see them. A tall man in his early thirties stepped to the platform, then turned to face the congregation. He had a pair of crackling blue eyes set in a craggy, bronzed face, and his hands were so large the Bible he held looked very small.

Megan expected some sort of introduction, perhaps a joke to loosen the crowd up, but he ignored all that.

"We have celebrated the Lord in praise and worship," he told them with a smile. "Now we will go to his Word to find out *why* we worship and praise him. And this morning we will find such a cause in John's Gospel, chapter four, verses five through nine." Dani opened her Bible and laid it halfway over Megan's lap so that they could both follow as the minister read:

Then cometh he to a city of Samaria, which is called Sychar, near to the parcel of ground that Jacob gave to his son Joseph. Now Jacob's well was there. Jesus therefore, being wearied with his journey, sat thus on the well: and it was about the sixth hour. There cometh a woman of Samaria to draw water: Jesus saith unto her, Give me to drink. (For his disciples were gone away unto the city to buy meat.) Then saith the woman of Samaria unto him, How is it that thou, being a Jew, askest drink of me, which am a woman of Samaria? for the Jews have no dealings with the Samaritans.

The minister paused, looked out over the congregation, then bluntly stated, "Jesus made two bad mistakes—or so many of his contemporaries would have said. First, he spoke to a national enemy. The Jews hated Samaritans with a passion, so much that they would go miles out of their way to avoid passing through their country. Then he spoke to a woman—which no orthodox Jew would do. Women were, at that time, chattel to be used." Looking over the congregation, he added, "We hear a lot about the feminist movement today, but to find out the truth about how women are treated, look at those parts of the world where the gospel of Jesus Christ is preached, and you will find that women are protected and cared for as precious and worthy of all respect. Then you go to the lands where Islam is strong, or Buddhism, or any other form of religion. What will you find? Women bought and sold, treated worse than animals, in many cases! But Jesus Christ honored women as no other leader before or since!"

Megan straightened her back, and Dani stole a glimpse at her face, finding shock written on her features. Megan listened hard as the minister traced the Scriptures, giving instance after instance from both the Old Testament and the New of how women have always been specially favored by the God of the Bible. It was another blow at one of Megan's theories, for she had swallowed the party line of the militant feminist leaders that Christianity and the Bible were the enemies of "true womanhood."

She leaned forward, her eyes fixed on the preacher, who was reading the story from his Bible in a more excited tone, his eyes flashing.

> Jesus answered and said unto her, If thou knewest the gift of God, and who it is that saith to thee, Give me to drink; thou wouldest have asked of him, and he would have given thee living water. The woman saith unto him, Sir, thou hast nothing to draw with, and the well is deep: from whence then hast thou that living water? (John 4:10–11)

"This woman was hungry for God, I think," the minister stated. "But she took one look at Jesus and doubted that he could do anything for her. 'The well is deep,' she said, and I think she was talking about more than the well they stood beside. She was speaking, I believe, of the difficulties men and women have in getting to God. Then she said with doubt in her voice, 'Thou hast nothing to draw with.' In other words, this woman was saying something like, 'There are thousands of priests. There's a temple and many places of worship. None of these have ever helped me, and how can *you*, a poor man with no sign of any authority, do what they haven't been able to do?'"

The congregation sat listening intently, Megan noted, while not missing a word. Then the preacher looked out, and his eyes caught Megan's, holding her gaze. "You may have asked the same question in a different form. The woman of Samaria asked, 'How can you help me? I don't see anything in you to make me trust!' And you may have said, 'Well, Christianity doesn't work. My problems are so terrible that there's noth-

ing in religion for me!' But in verses thirteen through fifteen we see that Jesus *did* have something to draw with:

> Jesus answered and said unto her, Whosoever drinketh of this water shall thirst again: but whosoever drinketh of the water that I shall give him shall never thirst; but the water that I shall give him shall be in him a well of water springing up into everlasting life. The woman saith unto him, Sir, give me this water, that I thirst not, neither come hither to draw.

"Do you see what has happened?" the minister demanded. "This woman suddenly realizes that her whole life has been dry and barren! No matter how many pleasures she indulged herself in, they never lasted! Pleasures never do. The next day she had to go back for more, and then more, and there was never anything that satisfied. So when she said, 'Give me this water,' she was saying, 'I want something that will satisfy this thirsting in my soul! Something that I won't lose but that will always be there!'"

Then he spoke slowly, and it seemed to Megan that he was looking only at her, speaking only to her: "I think there are some in this house this morning who are feeling what the Samaritan woman felt so many centuries ago. Some who are tired of the shallow answers of the modern world, with its empty promises of fulfillment that never come to pass. And that's who the gospel is for—those who long for peace of heart and peace of mind. But even though you long for this, you may do what this woman did. For with all her longings for peace and despite her hatred of the empty life that she led, she began to argue with Jesus! When Jesus said, 'Go, call thy husband, and come hither,' she said, 'I have no husband.'"

Again the room was quiet, and the pastor said, "She was lying, trying to cover up what she was. Ashamed to admit that she'd led a terrible life. Aren't we all like this? For Jesus said, 'Thou hast well said, I have no husband: For thou hast had five husbands; and he whom thou now hast is not thy husband.'

"Do you see what Jesus was doing? He was bringing this woman to the point where she could see herself as a failure. For God can do little with us as long as we think we are able to handle our own lives. Almost every great man and woman of record in the Scripture had to be broken before God could begin his great work. And we are no different, for the gospel is based on grace and free will. God will change you and give you this water of life—but he can only do it for those who will *permit* him to work in their lives. That's the one thing God will *not* do for you—he will not override your will!

"What was this woman lying about? The failures in her life—in this case a life spent in immoral conduct, a series of adulterous affairs. It's easy to point a judgmental finger at her, for that sort of sin is easy to identify. But the Book of James says, 'Whosoever shall keep the whole law, yet offend in one point, he is guilty of all.' God doesn't have a list of 'little sins' as opposed to 'big sins'—for when we break *any* of God's laws, we've offended him, the Holy One of Israel."

For some time the sermon continued, and Dani was intensely aware of the effect it was having on Megan. She prayed quietly for her and for Luke Sixkiller as well. Luke was listening intently, but his immobile face gave no sign of the sort of impact the sermon was having. But Dani had learned long ago not to be disappointed in the response of people to the gospel. She knew the message of God was like a seed—it took time to lie fallow before the fruit was seen.

Finally, the minister said, "So this woman came to Jacob's well on a very common, ordinary errand. But she encountered Jesus Christ—and when she gave herself to him, nothing could ever be quite so ordinary and common again." He spoke

149

of how she ran back to tell the people of her village about the man she had met at the well. "She said, 'Come, see a man, which told me all things that ever I did: is not this the Christ?'"

He closed his Bible and stood there, a tall shape in the sunbeams that fell from the lofty windows. Finally he commented, "He told her all she did. Which means he accepted her, and we must believe from what the Scripture tells us, that she from that day drank of the water of life. That she found the peace and joy that we in this room sang of earlier."

He paused, then asserted, "Life is made up of two things—a crisis and a decision. Some of you are at the time of crisis. You've tried the world, and it hasn't satisfied. You have looked at religion and said, 'You have nothing to draw with—nothing that will give me peace of heart.' But there is One who can do that, who loves you so much that he gave his life to bring this peace to you. That's what the cross is about. Not a gold ornament you may wear around your neck—but an ugly instrument of death where Jesus bled his life away. As he gave his life, he cried out, 'It is finished!' *What* was finished? Humanity's hopelessness was finished, for the death and resurrection of Jesus did the one thing for us that we could never achieve by our own efforts. The gospel of Jesus is that we can now believe on that One who died, and by that death we can find God. That is the decision you must now make. Will you all stand?"

Megan's legs trembled, and unconsciously she leaned against Dani, who put her arm around her. The minister explained, "This is that part of our service when we pray for those who are in need. Some of you may need physical healing; some of you may need to find peace through the gospel of Jesus Christ. Will you come as we begin to pray?"

Dani felt the tremor run through Megan's body, and Dani hesitated. It was always a hard decision for her—to choose just how direct her actions should be at such times—but she whispered quietly, "Would you like me to pray for you, Megan?"

Megan's eyes suddenly filled with tears, and she was swept with an anguish of spirit such as she had never known. For years she had closed up her emotions in a tight little box, nailing the lid down securely. But now they were rising powerfully, so strongly that she could only stand clutching the pew in front of her with all her strength. She hated displays of emotion and struggled in vain to staunch the tears that rose to her eyes, blinding her; she tried to keep the sobs that rose in her breast from issuing forth.

Then Dani spoke again, "Megan, I think it's your time to let Jesus Christ take over. He loves you so much! Won't you just let him have your life and do with it whatever it takes to give you peace in your heart?"

A war raged inside Megan. Terrible memories of her childhood came, memories of abuse that she had buried deeply, so that they only came in dreadful nightmares. Voices, or thoughts like voices, seemed to whisper to her: *Don't do it! Don't let anyone control your life! You'll have to give up so much!*

Megan seemed caught in a fierce storm, with violent winds pulling and shoving her. She could only stand there, trying to hang on to something. The sound of people praying reached her ears, but she could not make out the words. Yet she sensed that there were others going through the same torment of doubt that was sweeping over her. She heard someone singing about Jesus—and every time the name *Jesus* came to her ears, it felt like a knife slicing into her heart.

The agony did not lessen, and suddenly she could not stand. Dropping to her knees, she laid her forehead on the hard edge of the pew, smelling the furniture polish and the fragrance of old wood. She pressed harder, needing the physical pain to draw her thoughts away from what was happening inside—but the emotional chaos swirled still, and finally she began to weep freely, as she had not done since she was a girl.

As she wept, she was conscious of Dani's arms around her, of her voice as she prayed fervently. How long this went on Megan never knew, but there came a time when she cried out in desperation, "O God! O God! Help me!"

Dani's voice came strong and quiet and joyful, "Just tell God you're tired of your life, Megan, and ask him to make you a new woman. Ask in the name of Jesus!"

Megan at once gave up on herself. She saw the long empty years that lay behind—and, knowing that the same lay ahead, began to call on God. Almost at once, as she breathed the name of Jesus, the storm within her spirit began to abate. A sense of utter trust and dependency came to her, like nothing she had ever known. With great, shuddering sobs she relaxed and would have fallen to the floor, if Dani had not held her.

For a long time the two women knelt there, both weeping. Luke Sixkiller stood, not knowing which way to look. The service had impacted him, but he could see that Megan was going through something foreign to him. The pastor had been walking around, stopping to whisper a word to one here and there, and he glanced down at the two women, then gave Sixkiller a keen look. Luke braced himself, expecting a sermon. The pastor said nothing, only fixing his blue eyes on those of the other man. The policeman who had intimidated killers and rapists with a look from his own black eyes, could not hold the minister's steady gaze. He dropped his eyes, then turned and walked quickly out of the church.

Outside, he was amazed so see a slight trembling in his hands. He stared at them, murmuring in shock, "I didn't think anything could make me do that!" He walked around nervously, while the two women tarried. Finally they emerged, and Sixkiller looked closely at Megan's face. It was swollen with weeping, and tears had made a trail through her makeup, but there was something different. He had admired her greatly, for he had seen a toughness in her that he himself possessed. But now that had somehow been transformed. A new aura of vulnerability wreathed Megan's face, and there was a softness on her lips that had been missing.

"Ready to go?" he asked awkwardly, trying to appear nonchalant.

"All ready, Luke." Dani smiled.

The three of them got in the car, Sixkiller in the back, watching the two women carefully. Dani spoke easily about the service: "He's a fine preacher, isn't he?"

Megan nodded, sitting there possessing a thoughtful silence. But Sixkiller answered slowly, "He's got a pair of eyes on him. Reminds me of an old boss of mine. Only different." He didn't speak about his own reaction to the scene, but when they got out at the motel he went away at once, anxious to get out of the presence of the two women.

"I think Luke's in shock." Megan smiled, watching him leave hurriedly. Then she took a deep breath and shook her head. "I know I am."

Dani gave her a sudden hug, exclaiming, "I'm so happy for you, Megan! You're going to be a great Christian!"

Megan looked at Dani with an odd expression. "Is that all there is to it, Dani?"

"All there is to being a Christian?" Dani echoed and shook her head so violently her auburn hair swirled in the sun, sending off golden glints. "Of course not! It's the *beginning*, Megan! You're a baby, that's all. Now you'll begin to learn how good it is to have a friend. Not only *the* Friend, but other friends. Like me."

Megan said slowly, "I feel so peaceful, Dani. But will it last? What will happen when trouble comes?"

"Jesus will be right there, Megan!" Dani encouraged her, with a glad light in her glowing eyes. "He'll never leave you nor forsake you." She laughed, adding, "Come on, let's get something to eat. Then we can talk about it!"

The two women disappeared into the motel, and the sun threw its rays down on the trees and on the large calico cat that dozed in the shade of the roof.

10

Dani Gets a Call

Dani awoke early Monday morning feeling some degree of agitation. Several times she had seen people make professions of faith that did not seem to last. Would Megan turn out to be one of these? She lay in bed, stewing over the thought that the pressures she knew would come to bear on Megan might be too great. For a while she prayed earnestly; then finding herself wide awake, Dani got up and dressed, putting on faded jeans and a denim shirt with large buttons. Quickly she went to the restaurant.

The waitress had just brought her a short stack with bacon when Ruth walked in. Dani waved at her, motioning her to the table. As soon as the other woman sat down, Dani asked, "How's everything going?"

Ruth's short black hair was not brushed as neatly as usual, and a worried expression drew a pair of vertical lines between her eyes. Shaking her head in an abrupt gesture, she answered, "All right, I guess, Dani. I didn't sleep much." A short, heavyset waitress with a mop of blond hair came up for her order—toast, juice, and coffee—and when the girl was gone, Ruth said briefly, "Well, to tell the truth, I'm worried about Clint."

"He still grieving over his horse?"

"Sure, but it's more than that. He's not riding well, for one thing." She leaned her head down, taking her chin in one hand; a dark brooding appeared in her eyes as she added sourly, "Well, neither am I, for that matter. My concentration is off, and you know what that means."

The waitress returned with juice and coffee, and Ruth drank the juice at once, making a face. "They must trample the oranges with their feet!" she complained. Then, taking a sip of scalding black coffee, she stared across the room. "Clint's the same way. Maybe all of us are alike in this crazy business. We don't get paid unless we win, and when we don't win, the bills start climbing. And that makes us more tense—which means we get a little more uptight."

"But Clint's made a hundred thousand dollars this year," Dani exclaimed. She took a morsel of pancake, put it in her mouth, and chewed it slowly. It was not as good as her mother's, but not bad for restaurant fare. "And he's still number one in the rankings."

"It sounds good." Ruth nodded. "But you don't know how fast he can go through money. He's fighting the IRS, and nobody wins much off those people!" She took another swallow of coffee. "He gambles, too, and even though he won't say, I think he's lost quite a bit."

"He's still number one, Ruth."

"He's thirty-eight years old, Dani. That's an old man in this business. You ever look at the faces of the guys who ride the rough stock? Most of them in their early twenties—some of them even younger! A man can only take so much of getting snapped like a whip on the back of a bronc. Even if he doesn't get a serious injury, that daily pounding will get to him."

"I've seen that." Dani shook her head. "When I asked Tom Leathers if he'd ever been badly hurt, he told me, 'Why, no, not serious. I had my head tromped on. Had my nose broke, and my legs been cracked a couple of times. All my vertebrae except two have been knocked out of place. Had a couple of teeth knocked out. One time a horse stepped on my mouth, cracking all my back teeth, and I had to have ten fillings. Nothing really serious though. If I ever get hurt real bad I might quit.'"

"Sure, that's the way they all are," Ruth commented. "And when a man's thirty-eight he can't shake it off like he did when he was eighteen." The waitress brought her toast, and she sat there, nibbling at it, talking mostly about Clint. Finally she said, "He's worried about the future, Dani, for the first time in his life. He sees Bake edging closer to the number-one slot, and he knows he can't do anything else. He's got no money saved, so it makes him edgy. Losing Tarzan was hard, and he swears he'll kill the man who did it."

Dani looked up, and seeing Megan enter, motioned her to come over, comforting Ruth, "He won't do that, I guess. Whoever it is, he's going to be hard to catch up with."

Dani smiled at Megan. "You look chipper this morning."

Megan returned her smile. "I slept like a baby all night. Haven't done that in a long time. I guess there's something to this business of being a Christian." She caught the surprised look that swept Ruth's face and laughed. "That's right, I've hit the glory trail, Ruth. Next thing you know, I'll be toting a Bible around and getting rid of my makeup."

The waitress returned, and Megan ordered eggs and bacon, then sat back in her chair, looking refreshed and content. Ruth examined her carefully, before admitting, "I didn't know about that, Megan."

"All Dani's fault." Megan grinned. "She hauled Luke Sixkiller and me off to church yesterday, and I got converted. Better watch out for this girl, Ruth; she's not a Bible thumper, but she's got her wiles."

"Oh, Megan . . . !" Dani protested, but Megan laughed at her, excused herself, then said, "Don't mind anything I say, Dani. I'm just so—so peaceful!" There was, both women saw, a new quality in Megan. She had been outgoing enough, but there had always been a wall between herself and others. Now it was gone. While the journalist sat there smiling and talking rapidly as she ate her breakfast, Dani saw that Ruth was shocked by the change in Megan. Dani herself felt relieved; obviously Megan was overflowing with a new assurance.

They ate breakfast, Megan telling the story of her conversion with no trace of reticence. When Ruth asked her tentatively if she thought it would last, Megan replied, "It's lasted all day and all night, Ruth. I guess I'll have a few down times— but no matter what comes from now on, something happened to me in that church. It was always hard for me to ask anyone for something. Too much pride, I guess. But when I cried out and asked God to help me—why, he *did!*" A look of wonder crossed her heart-shaped face, touching her blue eyes, and she quietly continued, "Nothing's the same this morning. Lots of old problems, sure—but something inside me now that makes them all look small."

"That's the peace of God." Dani smiled. "The presence of Jesus Christ inside."

Ruth sat there silently as the other two women spoke, and when they got up to leave, she was so subdued that Dani noted it. "I know you're worried, Ruth," Dani acknowledged. "But God cares for you. Don't forget that."

"It just looks so—so hopeless!" Ruth cried out.

Megan gave Dani a quick look, then put her arm around Ruth. "Don't give in. I've got an idea that this thing won't last too much longer."

Dani shot a glance at her, demanding, "Have you got something, Megan?"

Megan only shook her head. "Nothing I can talk about. Not yet. But I've got my tape recorder running and the old video, so watch out!" Then she smiled cheerfully. "Just give me a little time, girls!"

She refused to say more, and as she left the restaurant, Ruth observed, "She's so different, Dani! She's always had a lot of confidence, but she's sort of bubbling over now. Is that the way getting converted makes you?"

"Sometimes it does." Dani nodded, but her thoughts were on other things. "It bothers me, Ruth—what Megan just said. If she's got something, I'd like to know it."

"Maybe you ought to tell her the truth."

They were walking to the parking lot, and Dani waited until they were in the car and on the way to the Dome before she admitted, "I can't decide. Maybe I will tell her. She's a sharp lady, Ruth. And we could work together on this thing."

She spent two hours with Biscuit, practicing her runs, then grooming him carefully. As she brushed his tail, she thought suddenly of how her life had been linked with the rust-colored horse. She had always loved the sturdy quarter horse, but her duties had prevented her from spending much time with him. Now every day she was with him for long periods, and she slapped him fondly on the neck, dodging as he nipped at her, playfully. "You ornery critter!" She smiled and gave him three cubes of sugar. His velvet-soft lips tickled the palm of her hand, and he nudged her side, begging for more. She gave him all the cubes she had, then said brusquely, "Now, that's all there is, you panhandler. And if you knock a barrel down this afternoon, I'll sell you to the soap factory!"

As usual, the barrel-racing event came late in the program, so Dani went behind the chutes to watch the other events. In the saddle-bronc competition, Bake won first place, with a score of 78, on a hammerheaded bay; Clint came in a hair behind him, with a 77. Dani noticed that when Bake jibed, "Hey, old man, you've got to do better than that if you want to hang on to that All-Around Championship this year!" Thomas gave him a glowering scowl and walked away without an answer.

"You shouldn't rub it in when you win, Bake," Dani warned.

Bake gave her a look of surprise. "Why, we all ride each other, Dani," he said at once. Then he frowned. "I reckon Clint thinks he's beyond a little kidding. But his head won't be so swelled when I take the number-one spot this year."

Dani suddenly realized that Bake, for all his amiable ways was a predator. He stared after Thomas with a hard look in his dark blue eyes, and his wide mouth was drawn into a mere slit, all humor gone. Dani thought, *Bake's nice enough—but the rodeo is his life. And the only way to make it in this world is to win. That means putting your body and your life on the line day after day—and it means that all the other contestants are in some ways the enemy.* Bake could have enough desire to do anything he had to for the championship, she decided. *He could even have been the one who knocked Clint out and broke Tarzan's legs.*

But the hard, angry look in Bake's eyes was gone, and she put the idea out of her mind. She watched the team roping event, admiring the skill of the horses as much as that of the riders. The bull riding was next, and as she moved across the packed earth, she found Sixkiller and Wash Foster helping a young cowboy named Pete Dubois settle down on a gray bull.

Dubois was a tall fellow with a shock of yellow hair and a pair of light blue eyes. He was pounding his rosin-soaked glove into place around the handhold, his face serious.

"Fit a ride on him, Pete," Foster said. Dubois nodded, and the gate swung open. The bull came out bucking in a stiff-legged, jolting way that snapped the rider's body like a piece of rope. They were going down the fence line right in front of the first row of the grandstand, when suddenly the bull kinked his back, sending Dubois off between him and the fence. The cowboy was up at once, but the big bull swung his huge horns in a scything motion right and left. Clearly Dani heard a whump! whump! sound that made her stomach grip tightly.

Hank Lowe and Rocky James were there instantly, waving their hands in the bull's face, but as they lured the huge animal away, Dubois staggered backward, then fell in a deathly limp way.

"Get him!" Clyde Lockyear was the first man there. He took one look at the boy, then shouted, "You guys—let's get him out of here!" He directed four cowboys to pick up the limp form, and even as they carried Dubois out of the arena, the announcer cried, "We need the ambulance in the arena. Hurry, please. Clear those gates! We have a man hurt!"

Dani could not move, and when the four men, led by Lockyear, came right by where she was standing, one glance showed her that Dubois was writhing, with blood flowing from his nose and his mouth. He clutched his chest, and Bake muttered, "He caught a good one, I think."

The rodeo went on, the announcer droning out the names of the contestants as the chute gates flew open and the bulls came charging into the arena. Dani saw Sixkiller moving toward one and despite herself she caught his arm, saying, "Luke! Don't do it!"

He paused and looked down at her. She saw that his mouth was in a hard straight line. But he only said, "I'll see you after the ride."

Tom Leathers and Fighting Bill Baker were waiting to help him get aboard, so Bake stood beside Dani. He had heard her plea and finally asked, "Why'd you do that? Beg Luke not to get on that bull? You two got something going?"

Dani blinked her eyes in surprise, but answered quickly, "Seeing that boy hurt made me sick, Bake. I—I don't want to see Luke get injured. Or you either."

"No way to keep from getting hurt. Goes with the territory." Then he nodded at Sixkiller, who was asking for the gate. "But that bull's not going to hurt anybody much. He's about as reliable as one of those critters ever get."

The gate swung open, and Sixkiller stuck on the animal's back like a burr. The buzzer sounded, and just at that moment, Luke, preparing to leave the plunging animal, was caught off guard. The bull gave an unexpected lurch of his hindquarters, which threw Luke forward, then tossed his head high. Luke caught the full force of the bull's uplifted head right in the face, and as he left the animal, he staggered blindly.

Dani cried out, but Bake announced, "He's okay! Didn't catch the horn!"

So it appeared, for as Lowe and James drew the bull away, Sixkiller seemed to recover. He threw his head back, then stood with his back straight as the announcer called out, "He's all right, folks! A fine ride by Luke Sixkiller!"

Dani watched as he came through the gate, met by Ruby Costner and Boone Hardin. They positioned themselves on each side of the burly rider, leading him away. He tried to protest, but Ruby said firmly, "You come along with me, Luke. I've had lots of experience with banged-up bull riders!"

"Wants to play nurse, I'd guess," Dani muttered.

As the three disappeared, Bake said, "He's in good hands now. Ruby's pretty good at taking care of a man."

Dani frowned, but Ruth Cantrell had entered the arena, leading her horse. "Almost time for the barrel race," she said. Dani left to get Biscuit. By the time she got back, two of the girls had already made their race. She moved into position, thinking of the sound of the horns striking against the chest of Dubois and then of Luke's head being driven backward by the force of the bull's devastating blow. It threw her timing off and her ride was bad.

She rubbed down Biscuit, fed him, then waited for the rodeo to end. Afterward Dani went to Hank's trailer and spent nearly two hours with the children. They were bright young-sters, and after they had satisfied her with their work, Cindy begged to ride Biscuit; of course Maury demanded equal rights. Dani took them to the corral and saddled Biscuit, and they spent an hour there. As Cindy was riding, with Maury behind her, Hank and his assistant joined Dani by the corral. Both men were tired and dirty, but Hank seemed glad to see her. "Kids do all right with their arithmetic, Dani?"

"Sure did." She hesitated, then asked, "Did you hear any-thing about the cowboy who got hurt?"

The two men exchanged glances, and Hank told her soberly, "It's not good. He got some internal injuries. Could be real bad."

Rocky James, a thickset man of thirty, had bulging shoul-ders and moved rather painfully when he was out of the arena. He usually had little to say, but now he suddenly threw down his hat, his face angry. "We're all crazy!" he cried bitterly. He began to curse, but Hank stopped that at once.

"Shut up, Rocky! Watch your mouth!"

James glared at him, then picked up his hat and walked off without a word. "You have to excuse Rocky, Dani," Hank explained quickly. "He was on top of the game once, but got hurt. Matter of fact," he added with a shrug, "he stays hurt."

"I don't see how either of you survive," Dani admitted.

"Well, I don't either. I've been at it for a long time, and I've had my share of wrecks. But Rocky's had every bone in his body broken, including his back. He knows a lot about bulls, but he's lost a step. The bones don't heal as fast now, and the falls hurt worse."

"For you, too, Hank." Dani nodded. Then she asked, "Why don't you get out of it?"

He gave her a swift look, then glanced down at his feet. "Meant to last year. I've got a horse ranch in Colorado. Nice little place. But it gets lonesome, you know?" Pain came to his eyes, and he faltered.

Dani understood his problem at once. "You were planning to marry Ruth and make a home there?"

"Yeah, that was it."

"I'm sorry, Hank."

He shook his head, then tried to smile. "One thing about being in the rodeo business, Dani. You learn how to lose. I've been throwed by many a horse, so losing Ruth was just another spill."

"No, it's not like that, is it, Hank?" Dani pointed out gently. She put her hand on his arm, looked at him carefully, then said, "You're doing a fine job with your children. I'm sorry it didn't work out with Ruth, but there'll be another woman for you."

Lowe gave her a startled glance, then found a shy smile. "Well, I've always been kind of a one-woman man, Dani. But thanks for your interest." He gave a look toward where Rocky James was stalking into the gates of the Dome, and said thoughtfully, "I'm worried about Rocky. He's been taking butazolidin."

"What's that, Hank?"

"What vets give to horses with swollen joints."

Dani stared at Hank. "He's taking horse medicine?"

"That and maybe other stuff. He's strong, Rocky is, but in the morning he can hardly get going, he's so beat up." He shook his head, adding, "He can't do his job. Going to have to get a new guy after this season."

"What will he do?"

Lowe's cheerful face grew sober, and he shrugged saying glumly, "Don't know, Dani."

Dani left, feeling depressed. As she got to her car, she found Boone Hardin leaning against Luke's car. He glanced up when she appeared, and Dani asked, "How's Luke, Boone?"

"How should I know?" An acerbic note flavored the young cowboy's short answer, but he shrugged his shoulders. "Ruby took him to that fancy motor home of hers. I went inside, but she got Luke down on a bed and we put some cold cloths on his head. Then she ushered me out."

"It looked like a pretty serious blow, Boone."

"Aw, not all that bad," he answered. "Got a knot on his head is all."

"He needs to see a doctor."

Boone shrugged again, trying to look the part of the old, experienced rodeo hand. "If we went to the doctor every time we got a lick, they'd have to close the rodeo down." He heaved himself up, wondering, "You going to that party Clyde and his wife are throwing tonight?"

"Oh, I guess not, Boone."

"I am. And if I get a chance I'm going to knock Clay Dixon on his rear."

"That didn't work too well the last time," Dani warned him.

Boone blushed suddenly, but stubbornly insisted, "He got in a lucky punch. And this time I won't need Clint Thomas to break a chair over his head."

Dani studied Boone carefully, but made her voice casual. "You don't like Clint, do you?"

At once the young cowboy set his lips and shook his head. "He's a good rider." It was no answer, but something in young Hardin's face made Dani realize that he would say no more.

"See you later, Boone," she said, then got into her truck and left the parking lot. The air was still hot, but she left the windows down, letting the breeze wash over her face. As she threaded her way through the afternoon traffic, she tried to shake off the depression that had fallen on her.

It troubled her that she seemed to be getting no place with the investigation. She tried to tell herself that it was going to take a break of some sort, a handle she could use to wedge the case open. So far, there was almost nothing to investigate. The one thing she had decided was that whoever was behind the thing was no outsider. Being careful not to give herself away, she had talked more than once to several of those who were paying off the Creep. Almost all of them had given her something that made her conclude that it was an inside job. Ruth had agreed, "It's always the same one who calls—at least from what I can pick up from the others. But the calls can come anyplace. I got one in Oklahoma City and one in Lake Charles. Ruby said he called her when we were in Fort Smith, Arkansas, and two nights later Bake got one in Nashville. It's somebody who's always around, and mostly it's a pretty small world."

But that meant almost nothing, Dani thought. It could be one of the stock handlers or a pickup man—even one of the judges. By the time she got to the motel, she wanted only to forget it, so she stripped off her sweaty clothes and lay down on the bed for an hour, sleeping soundly. She woke up with a start, then stayed in the shower for twenty minutes, letting the cool water sluice away the pressures. The phone rang, and she ignored it, but when it continued insistently, she stepped out of the shower and, grabbing a towel, made a wet track to the small table beside the bed.

"Hello?"

There was a brief silence, then a voice said, "Well, now, Miss Ross, you're a hard young lady to catch."

Instantly an alarm went off in Dani's head, and she thought, *It's the Creep!* But she kept her voice steady as she demanded, "Who is this?"

"Why, I understand you call me the Creep, Miss Ross. But I never let a little thing like name-calling disturb me."

Dani had never heard the voice before, she was sure of that. She had a good ear for voices and could recognize instantly any that she knew, but this one was not one of those. It was a man—she was certain of that. Not that it was deep; it was a tenor voice, higher than that of many women. But there was, she decided, something masculine in it.

"I suppose you know why I'm calling?" Mockery laced the voice, and he made it sound as though it were simply a matter of minor business of some sort.

Dani warned, "You're wasting your time. I don't have any money."

"Oh, now, let's not begin on a bad note, Miss Ross. Or may I call you Dani?"

"I don't want you to call me anything," Dani rapped out, making a quick decision. "If I hear from you again, I'll call the police." Then she slammed the phone down. The water was dripping from her body, puddling the floor, but she ignored it. She stood there staring at the phone, and as she had expected it rang again at once.

"Hello?"

"Now, this isn't smart, you know?" The voice hardened, and he went on, "Look, I know you're not making a lot of money. And I'm not going to ask for a lot. That wouldn't be smart, and I'm smart, Dani—very smart! And I think you're smart, too. It's like insurance. You pay a premium, then you're covered."

Dani didn't want to cave in too quickly, so for several minutes, she argued with the caller. Finally she repeated, "I can't pay much."

"Only a hundred dollars, Dani. You won that much yesterday. And you're going to win a lot more; I can see that. You've got what it takes. Why, I've seen every great barrel racer in the business, and you're as good as any of them."

"Never mind the snake oil!" Dani told him. "I'll pay your 'premium' this time, but you leave me alone after this."

"Well, I can see you're upset, so we'll just get down to business. There's a party tonight, thrown by Clyde Lockyear and his lovely wife Frances. You be at that party—with the money in your purse."

"What do I do with it?"

"Just have it, Dani. You'll be told what to do sometime during the party."

"All right."

"Fine! Fine! We're going to get along, I can see that!" The voice changed slightly, and Dani could sense a dangerous quality in the speaker as he added, "But one word of warning—nothing personal, I promise you—just don't try to get smart. Like if you told the police, you'd be very sorry." He paused, then sneered, "Remember Tarzan? You wouldn't like for Biscuit to wind up with his legs broken, screaming in pain, would you? It's not a nice sound, even when it's someone else's horse. But when you love an animal like you love Biscuit—well, it's almost unbearable."

"I—I won't call the police."

"Now, that's fine! I knew you were a smart girl!"

The phone went dead, and Dani stood there, staring at it. The threat to Biscuit had caused a raw shock to run along her nerves, and her hand was so unsteady that she missed the cradle on her first attempt to put the phone down.

Mechanically she dried off, then brushed her hair. When she had gone over her hair with a curling iron, she glanced at the clock. It was nearly seven, and the party would start at eight. Her first thought was to find Luke, but he didn't answer his phone, and she remembered that he was with Ruby. Next she thought of calling Ben, but she shook it off. He could do nothing.

For a long time she sat down in a chair, thinking hard, and finally she made a decision. She got up and dressed, wearing one of the two fancy outfits she'd bought in New Orleans—silver pants and an orchid shirt, both fitting like gloves. She fixed her hair carefully, pulling it back and adding a silver bow to hold it in place. She put on silver hoop earrings and sprayed cologne on her neck and wrists.

Finally Dani walked over to her suitcase, which lay in the bottom of the small closet. Bringing it to the bed, she opened it, then reached into the zippered section on one end. It contained only one object, and she removed it slowly, then stood staring down at it as it rested in her hand.

A lady-detective model, she seemed to hear Ben's voice, and the moment he'd given it to her flashed before her eyes. *Holds five slugs instead of six, which makes it lighter. A shorter barrel and a smaller grip. Just right for a woman to slip into her handbag,* he'd said.

There was a lethal beauty in the gun, and Dani felt admiration for the smooth symmetry but revulsion at the knowledge of the deadly power that lurked in the weapon.

Her hand trembled, and she swayed slightly, fighting off the memories that began to swarm in her mind's eye, but finally she set her jaw and put five loads in the empty chambers. Snapping the cylinder shut, she moved to the dressing table, picked up the small silver clutch bag, dropped the .38 inside, then turned and left the room.

11
The Drop

Luke came awake slowly, his head throbbing as if a pile driver were attacking his brain. He went through one of those wild and frightening moments of complete disorientation, fear sweeping over him as he tried to figure out where he was. He was lying down, and there was a damp cloth over his face. Only when he reached up and yanked it away did a sense of presence come ebbing back.

He was lying on a pale blue couch in Ruby Costner's motor home, and as he sat up slowly, trying to keep his head as still as possible, he thought of the hairy head of the bull ramming him. The thought coupled with the act of sitting up brought a grunt and at once he was aware of a movement to his left. Ruby came into his line of vision, knelt down to his level, and said, "Honey, are you feeling better?"

"Better than what?" he demanded, his voice thick and slurred. He blinked and tried to get up, but she pushed his shoulders down. "What time is it?" he asked.

"Oh, it's about six," Ruby told him. "You've only been asleep a couple of hours."

Luke tried twisting his head slowly. When his head didn't fall off, he questioned, "What was that pill you gave me, Ruby?"

"Just some kind of pain pill I got a year ago. It sure works good, doesn't it?"

"Dandy." Luke focused his eyes on her. She was wearing some sort of sheer, peach-colored robe that shimmered under the overhead light. He had never seen her in anything but the standard dress for rodeo girls—worn Wranglers, western shirt, and a big hat. Now as she leaned over him, he caught the scent of soap and perfume and girl. "I need a drink of water," he whispered. "My tongue feels like it's growing mushrooms."

"I'll get it," Ruby offered quickly. She rose and went to the small refrigerator and as she removed the ice said, "You really took a hard lick. I was afraid you were hurt bad, Luke." She brought over the tall glass of ice water, and as he drank it thirstily, suggested, "This is better than going to that old room of yours, isn't it?"

Luke vaguely remembered arguing with her that he was able to go to his room, but she insisted on bringing him to her place. "Yeah, it sure is." He looked around slowly, taking in the compact kitchen, which included a dishwasher, noting the fine stereo with twin Bose speakers, and the compact but comfortable arrangements of the lounging furniture. The key color was pale blue, but the curtains were coordinated, as was everything else. "This is all right, Ruby." He nodded. "Must have cost a bundle."

"About two thousand dollars a foot," she told him. She sat down beside him on the couch, her leg pressing against his.

"I got tired of motel rooms, and you can't take a three-bedroom house with you on the road."

"Had it long? It looks pretty new."

"I got it two years ago." She hesitated, then seemed to decide something. "It was a present from Clint."

Sixkiller studied her, thought of what she had said, but only commented, "It's plush."

"Does that shock you?" Ruby asked. "You've been around a little. You're probably thinking, *He didn't give it to her for nothing*. Aren't you?"

"Not thinking much of anything, Ruby," Luke responded evenly. "Guess that bull butted out what few brains I had. But I made me a rule a long time ago. I let people do what they want."

"Pretty good rule," Ruby agreed. Suddenly she leaned against him, her body pressing against his arm. It was an open invitation, and she sat there, watching him carefully. "What do you want to do right now, Luke?"

Sixkiller was tempted. She was a beautiful woman, and his experience told him that she was his for the taking. Somehow he felt a sudden tiny warning that he had experienced a few times. More than once in his duties as a policeman he had heard it—or felt it—and he had some scars to prove that to ignore whatever it was could be dangerous.

He closed his eyes, muttering, "I've got to get up. Head's still swimming." Using his injury as an excuse, he figured, would prevent Ruby from getting angry. He slowly came to his feet and discovered that he didn't really need an excuse. The room seemed to tilt as he stood up, and he reached out to gain his balance. "Whole world is out of joint," he muttered.

Ruby stood up and put out a hand to steady him. "Maybe you better go to bed. You're pretty shaky."

"No, I'd rather stay up."

Ruby bit her lip, considered him, then confessed, "Well, I was going to the party Clyde and Fran are throwing. I don't guess you feel up to that."

"Better than going to bed," he told her. "If I pass out, just ignore me."

"I've got to dress. Maybe you should eat something. Help yourself to what's in the kitchen."

As she moved to the rear of the motor home, to change, Luke waited only until the bedroom door clicked shut, then at once began searching the place. His head ached, but he lost the dizziness and moved only slightly less quickly than usual. There was little to be gleaned from the kitchen, but across from the couch was a compact desk, and with one ear cocked toward the bedroom, he went through the contents.

If Sixkiller had been asked, "Why are you shaking down Ruby's place?" he would have answered, "Because it's there." He was by nature a curious man, and his years on the police force had nurtured that tendency. But even more than that, he was interested in the relationship between Ruby and Clint. He had already heard of it, so her "confession" that they had lived together came as no shock. If she had not told him about the arrangement, he would have found evidence of it in the desk—a bill of sale from Clint Thomas to Ruby Costner for the motor home, with a price of one dollar. *This rig must have cost thirty big ones,* Luke thought. *Clint's fun comes pretty high.*

He went through the drawers quietly and efficiently, finding several letters from Clint—and one from Clay Dixon. He scanned through Thomas's letters, finding the last one interesting. It was brief and contained a final release: *I've told you, Ruby, it's all over. Now let's act right about this thing. We've had fun, but these things all come to an end. We can still be friends, but that's all.*

Sixkiller looked at the letter from Dixon—more a note than a letter actually. Luke studied it carefully, one page, printed in large block letters, much like a child's crude effort: IF YOU DON'T DUMP CLINT, I'LL KILL YOU FIRST AND THEN HIM!!!

It was signed *Clay Dixon* in cursive. Luke replaced it carefully, thinking of the hulking Dixon, trying to picture him as the man who was bleeding the performers. Finally he shook his head, muttering, "He's not bright enough."

He looked quickly through the remaining drawers and almost missed the most interesting thing of all. In the back of the bottom drawer was a brown-leather blackjack with a plaited handle—exactly like the one he'd found close to where Clint had been lying with his head busted. Taking out a handkerchief, he wrapped it up and slipped it into his pocket. *Not what you'd expect to find in a lady's desk. Can't see Ruby breaking that horse's legs—but she's mad enough at Clint to have let him have a sock in the head.*

He was sitting on the couch when Ruby came in. Getting to his feet, he said, "Good thing you're driving. I'm seeing double."

Ruby grinned at him. "If this party is like all the rest, you'll be right in style. Everyone gets pie-eyed drunk anyway. Come on."

The Watering Hole was as seedy as most dives in the area, Dani decided as she drove into the concrete lot—a lot of blue neon and windows all painted over. Inside she discovered the usual long bar, propped up by what seemed to be a gathering of zombies. People floated around like fish in an aquarium, darting here and there to shout intimacies over the din of about a hundred others determined to shout their own. Above this a six-piece country-Western band with a short, chubby blond belted out a plaintive song.

As she entered Dani was met by Clyde Lockyear. He grinned at her, a roly-poly figure with the face of cherub. "We got a place in the back, Dani. C'mon with me," he invited.

As he took her arm and steered her through the noisy room, Dani thought that few places were sadder than the insides of the million and one joints that line the outer limits of America's cities. Misplaced persons of emotional culture. Bunnies ravenous for romance, yet settling for what they call "making out." She took in some of the futile, acne-pitted young men, right out of high school, thrown into a world surfeited with unskilled labor, forced to take jobs sacking groceries at food marts. Most of them, she noted, were moving around the dance floor with some semblance of excitement, but beneath it all there lay a desperation—as if they had to keep moving to avoid considering the emptiness of their lives.

Somewhere, Dani thought soberly, *They must have had at least a hope that if you are sunny, cheery, sincere, group adjusting, and popular the world is yours. The world of barbecue pits, diaper service, percale sheets, and friends for dinner.* The entire room seemed the antithesis of that—some sort of murky cavern, hidden away from all that was light and good and wholesome.

"Right in here," Clyde said, opening a door and stepping back. "Got a pretty good crowd here. Glad you could come."

Dani stepped into a long, narrow room with tables set up along the walls, where two Mexican bartenders were busy mixing drinks. Six or seven round tables covered with red-and-white checkered tablecloths were scattered around the room, and a stereo belted out a song by George Stuart.

"Hey, come sit with us, Dani!" Fighting Bill Baker yelled from a table where he sat with Hank Lowe and Boone Hardin.

But Clyde took a firm grip on her arm. "Nothing doing, Bill," he called back, his high tenor voice rising above the music. "Go get your own girl!" He steered Dani to a table near the back of the room, where Fran was sitting with Bake Dempsey and Megan Carr. "Look who I found," he announced. "Sit down, Dani. We got lots to eat and all you want to drink."

Dani sat down, and Bake rose, offering, "We got all kinds of Tex-Mex stuff, Dani. Let me get you a plate." He moved across the room to a long table loaded with Mexican food. Soon he slapped a huge platter before her, loaded with enchiladas, tamales, refried beans, and tacos, and a huge glass of some red liquid. "Eat all that, and you'll be fat and pretty, like me." He grinned.

Dani tasted the enchilada, then made a face. "I see you found the hot sauce," she quipped.

"No such thing as Mexican food that's too hot," Bake contended. He began eating, saying between huge mouthfuls of the spicy food, "You better enjoy that punch, though. It's the last chance you'll have at one of Clyde's parties to drink anything that ain't alcoholic."

"That was a good ride you made yesterday," Fran praised Dani. "If you got a faster horse, you'd be in the big money soon." Every other woman in the place had come in Western dress, but Fran Lockyear wore a strapless lace-over-satin dress with a double-tiered V front, cut very low. It was a delicate shade of aqua, which picked up the glints in her greenish eyes. A small fuchsia flower and a pair of classic sling-back pumps of the same shade completed her outfit. Two enormous diamond earrings flashed as she turned her head, and the diamond on her left hand would have supported and fed an African village for ten years.

"Thank you, Fran." Dani nodded. "Guess I'll just stick with Biscuit."

"He's a pet, I suppose?" Fran frowned and shook her head, sending gleams and yellow flashes from her earrings. "Not a good idea, Dani. If you get too fond of an animal, you'll let up on him. That's rule number one—use up your animal, if you have to." She glanced at Dani, then ordered abruptly, "Come on, Bake, dance with me."

Clyde watched them leave, then took a swallow of amber liquid from his glass. "That's her way with people, too, not just horses. Use them up, then throw them away."

Dani suddenly became aware that Lockyear was drinking steadily. He didn't yet slur his words, but pronounced them very carefully to cover up. She tried to change the subject by saying, "I've heard that Fran was a fine barrel racer, when she was competing."

"Sure. She's fine at everything she does." Clyde took another swallow, then stared down into the empty glass. The music throbbed heavily, but he seemed oblivious to his surroundings. Finally he lifted his eyes to meet Dani's and commented, "She'll use me up one day, just like her horses."

Dani felt awkward, as she always did when someone revealed a tragic flaw. She had heard Clyde say that all he ever wanted was to be a bronc rider in the rodeo, and now she understood that all his money and success were hollow victories. *He'd give it all away just to be a rodeo performer—even one as low on the scale as Wash Foster!* A wave of pity for the little man with the paunch and the weak eyes overcame her. "You make it all work, Clyde. If it weren't for your stock, there wouldn't even *be* a rodeo," she encouraged him.

He gave her a startled glance and a slight smile touched his lips. He pulled himself up, studied her, then spoke approvingly, "I heard you were religious, Dani. But you're more than that." He reached out and put his pudgy hand on hers, and a warmth filled his eyes. "You're kind. I don't see a lot of that in my world."

"Hey, are you two holding hands?" Both looked up to see Megan returning to the table with a plate of food. She was smiling at them as she sat down and added cheerfully, "Watch out for this one, Dani. He's a real charmer."

Her words pleased Clyde Lockyear, and for a time the three of them sat there, talking. When Bake brought Fran back, the cowboy promptly claimed Dani, and soon the two of them were dancing in the large room. The music was loud, the room was dark and crowded, and Bake was squeezing her tightly. Dani laughed and pulled back, objecting, "You're hanging on to me as if I were one of those steers you bulldog, Bake!"

"Aw, Dani." He grinned. "You're *lots* better looking than any steer I ever dogged!" Then he asked, "You cheer Clyde up some?"

"He's not a happy man, Bake."

"Well, *I* would be, if I had his cash!"

"No, you wouldn't."

Her abrupt statement made him miss a step, and he paused to look at her carefully. With a rueful laugh he admitted, "You're right. I guess Clyde would give every penny he has, if he could rodeo." Then he made a face. "And when he married Fran, he just made it worse. She throws it up to him all the time."

"Throws what up?"

"That Clyde's not the man Clint Thomas is."

Dani stared at him. "That's pretty rough, Bake."

"You've seen her, Dani. I guess you're smart enough to see what she is. A man-eater. Why, she's been after me for a long time, but I got better sense than to fool with a married woman."

"Afraid Clyde would shoot you?"

"No! Not ol' Clyde—but I know *Fran* would, if I gave her cause!"

After the dance, they returned to the smaller room, and for the next hour Dani watched people drink and busily fended off those who tried to get her to join in. But all the while she remained alert, wondering how the instructions for handing the money over would come. A black telephone sat precariously on one of the food tables, wedged in between cheese dip and lunch meats, and it rang several times. Each time she stiffened, expecting that it would be for her.

At one point, Sixkiller drifted by. She got up at his offer to dance, and when they were moving around the smoky dance floor, she demanded tartly, "Well, did Clara Barton get you patched up?"

He gave her a lazy look, saying innocently, "You mean Ruby? She's got a tender heart, Dani. Can't stand to see any of us poor cowboys suffer!"

"I notice she was sticking to you like a Band-Aid!"

He grinned broadly. "She's a suspect. I'm keeping a close watch on her." When Dani scoffed at that, he nodded. "Sure. I found a clue in her motor home."

Dani listened as he told of finding a blackjack exactly like the one he'd sent to New Orleans for lab work.

"What does *that* mean?" Dani asked. "Did you hear from New Orleans about the other one?"

"Yep. No prints but a few flakes of dead skin caught in the webbing. All we have to do now is test everybody who could have dropped it, and we'll maybe have something. Shouldn't take long—only about a thousand people could have dropped it." Then he frowned, adding, "But this second one, I can't figure it. Maybe they come with Crackerjacks or something."

Dani broke in abruptly, "I got a call tonight. . . ."

Sixkiller listened, his face taut with interest. When she had finished, he insisted, "If you go to make a drop, I go as a tail."

"He'll be looking for that, Luke."

"I can be invisible."

Dani argued with him, and they finally went back into the party room without settling it. Dani said only, "One thing, if I get a call, look around the room."

"Ah-ha!" Luke tapped his temple with a forefinger. "If he's in the room, he can't be calling you, right? So we eliminate anyone who's in the room from being the Creep."

"My, you got it the first time!"

"I didn't finish the third grade for nothing, Baby!"

When they walked into the party room, Clyde Lockyear was calling for quiet, having to shout, "Hey! Shut that music down, will ya?" Someone cut Willie Nelson off right in the middle of an off-key note, and Clyde nodded. "Now, before you all get too drunk, we're gonna have a talent show." He waved his hand at the groan that went up, insisting, "We got some folks here who can sit on a bucking horse, but there's more to life than that."

Wash Foster yelled out, "Hey, Clyde, if you want this bunch to perform, you better let us all get *more* drunk, not less!"

Dani had gone back to sit with Bake and Fran, and as Clyde went on, Fran shook her head. "We go through this at least once a year—usually when Clyde has had too much to drink."

Megan looked at her. "What kind of 'talent' is he looking for?"

"He's not looking for much from anyone else," Fran informed her wearily. "It's just a chance for him to show off."

"What does he do?" Dani inquired.

"Oh, he's a pretty good singer." Fran shrugged. "Sooner or later you'll find out he could have had a great singing career."

As Clyde persuaded one of the couples to dance, Dani looked at Sixkiller. He caught her gaze, but not a sign crossed his smooth face. Under Clyde's insistence, some of the crowd began to enter into the spirit of the thing. But by the time two or three of them had "performed," there was little skill called for. Several of the cowboys' "talent" was telling stories, most of them pretty raw. Several couples danced to the stereo, none of them showing half the skill that the cowboys showed on riding stock.

"Reminds me of show-and-tell, back in the second grade," Fran complained. She got up to leave the room, warning, "Clyde's going to be next. I've learned how to judge these things."

She had not been gone over three minutes when people began calling out, "Come on, Clyde! Let's hear a little singing!"

Clyde held up his hand in protest, objecting, "Aw, you've all heard too much of me!" But he allowed himself to be persuaded and went over to a small spinet piano. Sitting down, he ran his hands over the keyboard expertly and moved right into a smooth version of "Ain't Misbehavin'."

Dani listened, then said to Megan, "He's good, isn't he?"

Megan nodded. "Yes. He might have had a shot at a singing career—at least he might have made it back in the old days, when people sang on key and the words made sense. He's like Perry Como, all smooth and easy."

"Too bad all the song lyrics say today is 'Mama, mama, yeah—I love you bay-bee!'" Dani agreed. She applauded when he finished and liked the next song, which was also a golden oldie— "Moon River."

For twenty minutes Lockyear sang, but not all the nostalgic songs. Someone called out, "Let's hear 'Shake, Rattle, and Roll,' Clyde!" and he kicked his seat back, stood up, and did an imitation of Jerry Lee Lewis.

Megan laughed as he finished. "Well, he doesn't look like the killer, but he sure sounds like him!"

Lockyear, Dani discovered, had the gift of mimicking people. It was not new to the crowd, for someone called out "A little Ray Charles, Clyde!" and he sat on the stool, swaying and singing "Georgia on My Mind." He did a credible Elvis, a fair Hank Williams, Jr., and an incredibly accurate Conway Twitty.

The crowd ate it up, and Clyde was in his element. He went from one song to another, sometimes in his own smooth tenor, but often using his ability to imitate other singers.

He was doing "Smoke Gets in Your Eyes" in a Tony Bennett manner, when Tom Leathers suddenly appeared beside Dani. Leaning down, he whispered, "Telephone, Dani."

Dani almost jumped as he spoke, but managed to smile. "Thanks, Tom."

She made her way to the phone, and just as she picked up the receiver, Clyde moved into a piano-pounding rendition of an old Chubby Checker number. Dani closed one ear with her left hand, and pressing the receiver tightly against the other, said, "Yes?"

"Ah, Dani, glad I caught you." It was the same voice. Dani asked, "What is it?"

"Why—it's premium time, of course!" There was a touch of surprise in the voice, but instantly he recovered. "Now, listen carefully. Leave the party and go into the parking lot. There's a 1990 Ford Ranger pickup sitting by itself in the northeast corner of the lot. The license number is LEM-4431. The door is unlocked. Put the cash on the floor under the driver's seat. Go back to the party. You got that?"

"Yes."

"Dani, don't be clever. Remember Biscuit. He'd scream if I broke his legs."

He hung up, and Dani turned to see Sixkiller watching her carefully. But she shook her head, saying no with her lips. He shrugged, and when she nodded at the crowd, he began going over it carefully.

Dani moved to the door and left the room, noting that Megan seemed to be aware of her leaving, but others were jumping up and down to Clyde's playing. The crowd had not thinned out, and one tall man tried to stop her, saying, "Hey, Doll, let's you and me have a drink!" But she eluded him and stepped out into the darkness.

The parking lot had no lights at all. Only a faint blue glow from the neon sign affixed to the front of the building illuminated the area. It was a starless night, and as she walked across the lot, with her heels clicking on the concrete, a shiver ran up Dani's back, and her nerves began to tingle. The sound of the raucous music floated on the still night air, the thumping of the bass hitting like a muted hammer.

The Ranger sat isolated from all the other cars, and as she reached the door, she gave a look over her shoulder, as a sudden noise jarred against her nerves. But it was only a car door slamming on the other side of the lot. It was invisible in the darkness.

Opening her purse, she took out the envelope with the money, opened the door of the pickup, then placed it under the seat. She slammed the door firmly, then marched quickly back to the Watering Hole. But instead of going through the main room, she turned left, down a narrow hall that she had spotted coming in. Two rest rooms and a door marked MAN-AGER faced each other, and at the end of the short hall stood a door marked EXIT.

Slipping the night lock, she opened the door quietly, stepped outside, then closed it. It made almost no sound. She bent and removed her boots. When she had straightened up, she reached into her purse and pulled the .38 free. It was cold to her touch, and the very act of holding the knurled stock in her hand brought a wave of revulsion into her throat.

But Dani took a deep breath and moved across the lot, the concrete hard under her feet and the .38 grasped in her hand. Somewhere far off in the distance, a train whistle moaned, and as its echoes faded, she silently melted into the darkness.

12
Good-bye
to a Friend

As Dani approached the pickup, the .38 in her right hand seemed to grow heavier. It was the first time since she had shot the gunman at Dom Lanza's that she had been in a situation that demanded that she use it. Now, as the bass guitar throbbed strongly, it almost seemed to become a second heartbeat for her—heavy and ominous, like a distant drum foretelling danger.

She stepped into a pothole in the cement, jarring her teeth and missing her stride. Her grasp on the Special tightened out of reflex, and for one terrible moment she thought the gun would fire. But she only stood there in the hot, silent darkness, breathing in short, shallow gasps. Her hands became so sweaty that she wiped her left on her shirt, then transferred the gun and wiped the other. The spicy food she had eaten rose in her throat.

The train whistle moaned again, far off but no less mournful for that, and she made herself move forward. Her knees were shaky, but she forced herself to ignore the weakness that threatened to overcome her and crept closer to the pickup.

Finally the outlines of the Ford were clear, and she stopped dead still. There was no sign of motion, but she knew that picking up the money would not be long delayed. Her instinct told her that the Creep worked on a tight schedule, and at any moment someone might arrive at the Watering Hole and park beside the Ranger.

Then a sound touched her—approaching the truck from the far side—and it was like a live wire hitting against her nerves. *Wearing boots,* she thought, moving closer and straining her eyes in the darkness. The footsteps grew louder, then stopped as if the person were listening. Dani stood stock still. Apparently satisfied, the walker moved again, and Dani saw a form appear. A man came closer, moving to stand beside the pickup. The sound of the door opening reached Dani.

One moment's pause, then the door closed, and at that moment Dani ordered sharply, "Hold it right there!"

A sudden grunt of surprise sounded, and as she took a step forward, she saw that he was turning to run. She drew the hammer back on the .38, and the sharp, clear, clicking sound must have shaken his nerves for the man cried out quickly, "No! I ain't moving—don't shoot!"

Holding the Special in both hands now, Dani barked, "Both hands on the cab—*quick!*"

The man instantly turned, and the slap of his palms on the top of the cab assured Dani. She moved forward with more assurance than she felt, but let no hesitation appear in her voice. "Spread those legs! If you move, you've had it!"

She held the gun in her right hand and frisked him with her left, standing far back, the way Savage had taught her. The man was not armed. Dani stepped back, then directed, "Lock your hands behind your neck, then turn around."

He obeyed, and she pulled the penlight from her shirt pocket. Turning it on, she threw the slender pencil like beam of light into his face—then cried out in surprise, "Tom Leathers!"

Leathers flinched both from the light that blinded him and from the sound of her voice. She kept the light in his eyes, and he stood with his hands locked behind his neck, his eyes tight shut, and his mouth pulled into a grim line.

"That's you, ain't it, Dani?"

"Yes, it's me."

She said no more, for the identity of the man had caught her off guard. At one time or another both she and Luke had gone over a list of possible suspects. As she stood there, holding the gun on the cowboy, she remembered clearly that both of them had eliminated Tom for all practical purposes. Dani recalled that she herself had said finally, *He's just a broken-down old cowboy, Luke. I gave up trying to see guilt or innocence in faces some time back—but Tom Leathers has the most honest face I ever saw.*

Now Leathers stood there, batting his eyes against the thin beam of light, and his face was haggard. He was a pretty tough fellow, Dani knew, and had led a hard life, but she could see that his lips were contorted in an effort to keep them from trembling.

"I never thought you'd be the man doing all this, Tom," Dani told him, disappointment in her voice. "But I've got to turn you in."

"Dani—" Leathers spoke in a cracked voice, not at all like his usual easy manner. "I know what this looks like—"

"It's not a matter of 'looks,' Tom," Dani broke in. "You're the only one who could get the money. Nobody else knows about it but you and me."

"Dani, it ain't me!"

She heard the urgency in his voice, but shook her head. "Tom, you've *got* to be the one."

Leathers requested, "Dani, can you lower that light a little? I ain't goin' anywhere."

She shifted the light downward, warning, "I'll shoot if you make a wrong move, Tom." Yet she was aware that this was boast. Her hand jerked spasmodically, and she removed her finger from the trigger, letting it rest on the outside of the guard. *I couldn't shoot him!* she realized suddenly, but he couldn't be allowed to find that out. "Just keep your hands where they are."

"Sure, Dani," Leathers said. He took a deep breath. "You've heard this guy on the phone, Dani. You know he don't sound nothing like me."

"You disguise your voice."

"I ain't no actor!" he pointed out wearily. "I can't talk no other way than how I do."

"You're the one who came for the money, Tom."

"Sure—and it ain't the first time." He leaned back against the truck, his seamed face looking old and tired. "Go on, call the cops," he suggested. "It don't matter much no more."

Dani stood there, irresolute in the darkness. She studied his face, then replied, "I'd like to hear your story, Tom."

He looked at her, his faded eyes a record of broken hopes and empty dreams. Finally he shrugged. "About a month ago I got a call from this guy—the one Clint calls the Creep. 'Course I'd heard what was goin' on—we all had. How he was making some of the fellows pay up or get their horses ruined." He paused, thinking how to put it. "I laughed at him, Dani. 'I ain't got a dime, and I ain't got a horse. What can you do to me?' That's what I told him. And it was the truth."

"What did he say?" Dani prompted as he seemed to be finished.

"He said, 'You've got a pair of legs. What would you do if both of them got broken? You'd be away from rodeo for a long time. Who'd pay your hospital bills? When you did heal up, in six months, who'd give you any kind of job?'" Leathers uttered a short, humorless laugh, then said, "He knew me pretty well, Dani."

"How's that?"

"Why, he knew that the one thing that matters in my life is to be where the rodeo is. It's all I've ever had. I ain't got much now, but if I had to be out of rodeo, I'd blow my brains out."

Suddenly Dani felt that he was telling the exact truth. "Let me guess the rest. He told you that you wouldn't have to pay him any money, but you'd have to pick up money from all the others."

Leathers stared at her. "You're a quick one, Dani! That's what he said." He dropped his head suddenly, a forlorn, lost figure.

Dani thought of A. E. Housman's poem, "To an Athlete Dying Young." It spoke of a fine young athlete who died before he had time to grow old and lose out to other men. And she understood clearly for the first time, the poignancy in the lines:

> Eyes the shady night has shut
> Cannot see the record cut. . . .
> Now you will not swell the rout
> Of lads that wore their honors out.

Tom Leathers, she decided, *had* lost out, chasing fame and money, only to discover at the last that these things were phantoms.

"All right, Tom," she spoke quietly and lowered her flashlight. "I believe you. But I want to hear all about it."

He stared at her and slowly unclasped his fingers. "I ain't proud of myself, Dani," he admitted in a thin voice. "But one thing—he offered me money, but I never took it!"

"Sure, Tom." Dani let the hammer down on the .38 and put it back in her purse. "I want to get back to the party. I'll get away as soon as I can, but I'll be at the little diner down from the Dome—the Blue Goose. I'll meet you there."

He only nodded, and Dani turned and walked back across the pavement to the Watering Hole. She found her boots, thankful that nobody had stumbled across them, and put them on. The exit door was locked, so she entered through the front door and made her way back to the party. The so-called talent show was over, and she saw Sixkiller watching her. She nodded slightly at him, then went back to her seat.

"What was that all about?" Megan asked curiously. "I saw you leave." When Dani hesitated, she backtracked quickly, "Never mind, Dani. My reporter's nosy ways get the best of me."

Dani was glad Megan didn't press it, and she made herself wait thirty minutes, time enough for the party to go into another phase—extreme drunkenness, more or less. Clyde stared at her owlishly, saying, "Better have a drink, Dani."

"No, I'm tired, Clyde." She smiled and complimented him, "You're a fine musician. I'll look forward to more of your songs."

He flushed with pleasure, his round face beaming. "Oh, it's not like riding a bull, Dani."

"Don't put yourself down, Clyde," Dani suggested. Getting to her feet, she added, "God gave us all something. You've got so much; don't grieve over what you don't have."

He stared at her, soberness washing over his face. "Good advice, Dani. I wish I could take it."

She said, "Good night, Clyde. Tell Fran I had a good time. See you tomorrow, Megan."

As she had guessed, Sixkiller made his way out of the room, seemingly by accident. "Told Ruby I had to get some air," he explained when they stepped outside. "What's up?"

Dani briefly sketched her encounter with Leathers. "I think Tom's a victim, but maybe I'd better talk to him alone. We don't want to be seen together too much."

"All right, but watch yourself." He suddenly reached out and ran his hand down her cheek. "I'm getting used to having you around."

She stood there, the feel of his hand solid on her cheek, then nodded. "I'll be careful. You just watch yourself with Ruby."

She found Leathers at the Blue Goose. It was an out-of-the-way place where they weren't likely to be seen. As soon as they got coffee, Dani demanded, "Let me have all of it, Tom."

As he drank coffee out of a big white mug, he told her the details. He had never seen the Creep, and the method of getting the money changed all the time. "He's pretty smart," Leathers alleged. "Never the same twice—picking up the case or getting it to him. Sometimes I'll make three or four pickups and hang on to all the money. Then I'll get a call, and he'll tell me how to get the money to him."

"How do you do that?"

"Different almost every time." Leathers shrugged. "Sometimes I leave it someplace, like on a park bench in a lunch box. But I ain't never mailed it or seen him. Always a different place and time."

"Any idea about who it is, Tom?" Dani inquired wearily. The encounter and the tension had drained her, and she wanted to get back to her room.

"Not an idea in the world, Dani—except it has to be some-body with the rodeo. I've picked up money in San Antonio, Cheyenne, and several other places. That narrows it down some, I guess." He suddenly peered at her, his faded blue eyes sharpening. "How come you're interested in all this, Dani?"

"I hate to get taken, Tom," she commented, but saw that he didn't buy that.

"And you just happen to carry a pistol?" he asked shrewdly. "Never mind. I appreciate your believin' me, Dani. But be careful."

"Tom, don't say anything about all this," Dani requested. "Just give him the money."

"Yeah, it'd be better for both of us. It made me think twice, the way he broke Tarzan's legs—not to mention what he done to Tilman Yates. A hairpin like that, he ain't gonna draw the line at anything."

Dani went back to her motel room. As she guessed, Sixkiller came by, and she filled him in on what she had learned from Leathers. "We can cross out Megan and Bake. They were at the table with me when the call came," she mentioned.

Luke listened carefully, then worried, "It's not too good—that Tom knows about you, Dani."

"He won't say anything."

"You're too trusting. If you'd been through a little more, you'd know not to trust anybody."

"That's no way to live," Dani protested. "Tom's just as much a victim as the others. And we can use him, Luke. He can tell us about the next drop. I have a list of those he's gotten money from. Now we can set a trap. It's the best thing that could have happened."

Sixkiller looked at her, taking in the clear eyes and the fresh-ness of her face. "You'll learn better, I guess. But I hate to see it. Keep that gun handy. "A thought struck him, and he asked,

"When you pulled the gun on Leathers, were you ready to use it?"

"Why—" Dani faltered, then seeing his expression, retorted, "I didn't have to use it!"

"Next time you might," Luke warned. "Listen, if you're not prepared to use it, don't take it. I'll do the shooting, if it comes to that."

"I can handle it!"

"No, you can't," he denied her words at once. "You're too proud to admit it, but you can't do the job. Ben said lots of times you're mad because you can't be a man, no matter how hard you try."

Dani was furious. She got up, flounced across the room, and threw the door open. "Good night!" she snapped.

He moved across the room, leaving at once, and she slammed the door behind him. "Ben Savage!" she muttered angrily. "He knows a lot about women!"

She showered and went to bed, but sleep did not come quickly. For an hour she lay there, trying to convince herself she was going to sleep, but then she would either begin to think about what Leathers had said—or wonder if Luke and Ben were right about her.

The phone rang so unexpectedly that she jerked convulsively. Glancing at the clock, she saw that it was nearly two-thirty. She stared at the phone, fighting back a dark fear that lurked in her.

"Hello?" She said, finally picking it up.

"Dani, I told you not to be clever." It was the same voice, but this time there was an angry thread in it.

"I don't know what you're talking about!" Dani insisted.

"Sure, you do—but you won't do it again." Something that sounded like a giggle came to his voice, and he whispered, "Better see to your horse, Dani."

The phone went dead, and Dani leaped out of bed, trembling so violently she could hardly find the light switch.

Biscuit!

An image of the faithful horse flashed in her mind, and she began scrambling into her clothes. When she was dressed, she grabbed her purse, drew out the .38, then after checking the loads, left the room.

She wanted to break every speeding law in Houston, but knew that it wouldn't help to get stopped. Her mind raced, and she had to fight down the fear that tried to rise in her like a dark cloud.

He must have been watching Tom and me, she thought. *It's the only way he could have known about me.*

She braked the truck and was out of it almost before it stopped rolling. The parking lot was empty, and she ran at once to the area where Clyde kept his stock. Clyde had offered her the use of it, explaining, "The stalls will be empty tonight. I'm having new stuff put in tomorrow. Plenty of room for your horse." There was nobody in sight as she darted down the long runway that led to the stockpen. The silence of the place frightened her, and when she got to the line of stalls, her eyes sought the rust color of Biscuit.

He's gone! was her first thought, and she gave a little cry as she ran to the stall where she'd put him.

But Biscuit wasn't gone.

He was lying on his side, his mouth open as he gasped for breath, his eyes wide and rolling.

"Biscuit!" Dani cried, and fell to her knees at his side. She was weeping, her hot tears rolling down her cheeks and onto the nose of the dying animal.

"Biscuit—don't die! You can't die!"

But he was dying. As Dani held on to his head, he gave one surge of his head, seeming to respond to her voice. For one moment she thought he was going to lick her hand, as he had a thousand times, but he was too weak. Even as she watched, his eyes glazed over, and his head drooped with a grim finality. His body shuddered once—and then was utterly still.

Dani could not hold back the flood of tears. She cuddled his head in her arms, weeping over the horse as if he were a human child.

The grief that welled up inside her was like nothing she had ever known. None of her close family had ever died, and the death of a distant aunt had meant little more than formal sorrow.

But this was hell. It was a helpless rage at the one who had done it, and the tearing wound in her spirit was worse than any cut made by a knife.

Never again to hear his whicker when she came laughing to give him sugar cubes.

Never again to have him nip at her arm playfully as she passed by.

Never again to feel his muscular body as he careened around a barrel, or to slap his heaving flanks, laughing with delight when he brought her back with a winning time.

Never again.

The quietness of the stables was broken now by her deep sobs. A huge brindle bull lifted his head from a stall down the way, peering curiously at the figure in the obscure darkness. He failed to identify the sound and dropped his head, ignoring the weeping that continued for a long time.

13
Feeding the Ducks

Clint and Ruth drifted into the snack bar a little after nine on Wednesday morning. Stopping abruptly, Clint stared at the crowd, then remarked to Ruth, "Never saw so many people here at this time of the day. Wonder what's up?"

Ruth shook her head, but before she could answer, Clyde Lockyear came over, wringing his hands. His mouth was formed into a large O as he said, "Oh, my! What a terrible thing!"

"What's wrong Clyde?" Ruth asked in alarm.

"You didn't hear? It's Dani's horse—someone came in and killed him last night. Looks like poison! What a terrible thing!"

Ruth and Clint stared at him in shock, then Clint asked, "Who did it?"

"Nobody knows, Clint," Clyde replied. "Dani came in and found him by herself."

"Oh, no!" Ruth exclaimed, biting her lip. "She loved that horse so much!"

Several others gravitated toward Clint, all nervously trying to talk, as people do after a bad accident. After listening for a few minutes, Clint raised his hand, protesting, "Wait a minute! One at a time!" He turned to Hank Lowe. "Let's have it, Hank."

Lowe gave him a summary of what had happened and ended, "Dani's in pretty bad shape. She loved that animal."

"Where is she?" Ruth wanted to know. "Maybe I can help."

Fran Lockyear responded with a shrug. "I don't think anyone can help—not unless she can bring that horse back to life. Anyway, Dani's with the law now. Same cop who came when your horse was ruined, Clint."

"He couldn't find his nose with both hands!" Clint snapped. Then he forced himself to speak more calmly, "You better stick close to her, Ruth. She's not hard-nosed enough to take a thing like this." He turned and walked off abruptly, but Ruth remained.

Megan had stood on the outskirts of the group, feeling like an outsider. She noticed that Boone Hardin had done the same and she moved to stand beside him.

He looked up, his eyes hard. "Anybody that'd do a thing like that ought to be shot! I'd be glad to do the job myself." He gave an angry look at Clint Thomas as he disappeared. "*He* don't care nothing about nobody, does he? Nobody but himself."

Megan pointed out, "He may feel more than he shows, Boone. Men are like that sometimes—afraid to cry."

"Cry! Him?" Boone moved his hand in a vicious chopping movement and uttered a harsh laugh. "He wouldn't cry if he saw his own mother drop dead in the street!"

Megan made herself look over the crowd. As if only half-interested she wondered, "Why do you dislike Clint so much, Boone? Is it just because he's made it to the top?"

Boone hesitated, glancing at her sharply. But when he saw that her attention was on the crowd, he answered, "Yeah, that's it. All of us feel like that about him."

He got up and left the room, and Megan studied him as he vanished through the door. She was a close student of human behavior and recognized raw hatred when she saw it—and she had seen it in young Hardin more than once—always directed at Clint Thomas. She tried to solve the puzzle of what lay behind his resentment, as she listened to the talk that ran around the small group. Could one of them be behind the killing?

Clay Dixon was farthest away, but she heard him say to Rocky James, "Now maybe she won't be so stuck-up. She always thought she was too good for us."

Wash Foster twisted his head to stare at the big cowboy. "She tied a can to your tail, didn't she, Clay? Maybe you killed the horse just to get even."

"Shut your mouth or I'll shut it for you, Foster!" Dixon doubled up his huge fists and glared at the smaller man. He was a formidable figure, and Foster drew back at once, turning to talk to Fighting Bill Baker.

Ruby said, "I guess this will end Dani's barrel racing. She doesn't have another horse, does she?"

"She can use mine," Fran Lockyear offered abruptly. Noting the look of surprise on several faces, she snapped angrily, "Well, what are you all staring at?"

"Never knew you to be so generous, Fran," Bake responded evenly.

"It won't cost me anything." Fran shrugged and then looked at Clyde with a sullen expression. "It ought to make *you* happy—keeping that little religion nut around."

She whirled, and when she had stalked out of the room, Bake gave Lockyear an odd glance. "What did she mean by that, Clyde? You been putting the moves on Dani?"

Lockyear flushed, his small eyes blinking. "You got a mind like a sewer, Bake! I like the girl, that's all. But skirt chasers like you and Clint wouldn't understand that. You always got to have another scalp to hang on your belts!"

Dempsey blinked at the unexpected attack. "Whoa up, Clyde!" he cried. "No reason to fly off the handle."

But Lockyear gave him an unforgiving look and left the snack shop without a word.

"Plumb touchy," Rocky James said. He was a powerful man, though short, and a look of speculation entered his hazel eyes as he added, "Funny thing, when you throw a rock at a pack of dogs, the only one who'll holler is the one you hit."

Ruth Cantrell gave James a look of disgust. "Is this all you've got to do, Rocky? Stand around and bad-mouth people?" She was pale, and spoke nervously. "Well, I guess this settles it."

"Settles what, Ruth?" Ruby asked.

"Why, nobody else will refuse to pay up to this criminal! I can't risk my horse, and neither can you, Ruby."

Ruby nodded slowly. "I guess that's right. We can't stay with our animals all the time." A thought came to her, and she proposed, "Say, why couldn't we keep our stock together and hire a guard?"

"That's about what Clint tried, and look what it got him." Bake Dempsey shook his head doubtfully. "We're all scattered out, Ruby. Maybe we could do it at night. But we'd have to pay high for a good man."

An argument ensued, so Megan got up and left the room. Ruth joined her outside. "Megan, have you talked to Dani?" she asked.

"Just for a few minutes." Megan nodded. "Luke Sixkiller called me and told me about it. He thought some woman should be with Dani. And Hank's right. She's really hurting." Grief touched Megan's eyes, and she quietly suggested, "She's going to need us, Ruth."

"It's all my fault!" Ruth uttered in despair.

"Your fault? How is it your fault?"

Ruth wanted to tell the story of Dani's identity, but felt bound by her promise. "Oh, I don't know what I'm saying, Megan! Where is she?"

"In Lockyear's office. Let's go wait for Stark to finish. I don't want her to be alone."

While the impromptu conference in the snack bar was going on, Luke Sixkiller stuck close to the body of Biscuit. He had been awakened before dawn by Dani's call. She had woodenly told him the bare facts, and he had dressed and gotten to the Dome in twenty minutes. Lieutenant Stark had looked up with irritation, through his rimless glasses, as Luke had barreled through the door to Lockyear's office. "Wait outside," he'd ordered sharply.

"You all right, Dani?" Luke had asked.

"I'm all right, Luke," Dani had spoken mechanically, and the set of her face told him at once that she was in shock. She had tried to smile, but failed. "Wait for me outside until the lieutenant is finished," she had requested.

Sixkiller had felt inclined to stay, to let Stark know what was going on, but it was not his decision. He had left the office and gone at once to where two men crouched over the body of the dead animal. One of them was Clyde Lockyear, and the other was a tall, rawboned man with salt-and-pepper hair. The second man was drawing a sample from a large vein.

"What happened, Clyde?" Sixkiller asked.

Lockyear briefly explained, "Looks like it might be another case of horse killing. Luke, this is Mr. Venable from the police lab."

Sixkiller sat on his heels, watching the tall man as he carefully stored the sample in a metal container, then began inspecting the body. "Maybe it was his heart," the Indian suggested. "I had a horse go like that once."

"Maybe." Venable's brief word was typical of a police reaction, and Sixkiller knew it would be pointless to question him further. He waited until the examination was over, then stood up as the other two rose to their feet.

"That's all I'll need," Venable commented. He packed his kit, and when Lockyear asked him what he thought, he said, "You can get the report from the officer in charge tomorrow."

"Talky bird, ain't he?" Lockyear muttered angrily. Then he looked down at the horse, shaking his head. "Too bad! Too bad!"

"Anybody see anything this time, Clyde?" Sixkiller asked. Lockyear explained how the pens had been almost empty. As the stock dealer nervously went over the thing, Sixkiller's eyes were moving over the area. "I guess they looked around for clues."

"Sure, but there wasn't nothing. But I don't think it was a heart problem," Lockyear declared positively. "Dani would have noticed something. It was too sudden." He ran one hand over his thinning crop of hair. "It had to be some kind of poison to work so fast. A shot, probably."

Sixkiller got what he could out of Lockyear, which wasn't much. Then he asserted, "We have to get this horse buried. I don't want Dani to see him again."

Lockyear gave the burly Sixkiller a sudden sharp glance, but only offered, "I'll take care of it, Luke." He glanced down at Biscuit's body, adding quietly, "Lost a few myself. Ain't never easy to say good-bye to a good horse or dog." After pondering that, he exclaimed, "Hey, I've got a little place about ten miles out of town. Just twenty acres and a shack. But there's a little creek with some cottonwood trees lining the banks. How about if I have the horse buried there? Got to move him, and it wouldn't cost much to get a backhoe in there." His round face looked worried, and he nodded. "Might make her feel better."

Sixkiller put a hand on the small man's shoulder. "That's a kind thought you got there, Clyde. You do it."

Clyde had brightened up and scurried off to take care of the details, and Sixkiller had gone over the area carefully. He didn't expect to find anything, and he didn't. Finally he walked back to the office, finding Ruth and Megan there. The three of them talked quietly. Ten minutes later the door opened, and Dani came out, followed by Lieutenant Stark. Dani looked exhausted, her face wan and pale. "Come along, Dani. Ruth and I will take you to your room," Megan ordered.

"All right."

The curious deadness in Dani's voice caught at Sixkiller, and he told her, "I'll be along after a while." He watched the women disappear down the hall, then inquired, "What's it look like?"

Stark took off his glasses, wiped them with a white handkerchief, then replaced them. He stared at Sixkiller, trying to decide whether or not to answer. Finally he shrugged. "I don't know what it looks like. Let's see—you're Sixkiller?"

"Yeah."

"Then you can do your own guessing. You had enough practice in New Orleans." Stark allowed himself to smile briefly. "I caught you on TV when you nailed the Marconi brothers. Thought I recognized you when I was here about Thomas's horse, but I wasn't sure."

"So you checked with the department?" Sixkiller prompted. "Well, I was a bad boy, Lieutenant. Got a three-month suspension."

"Funny way to spend your time—getting stomped by those crazy bulls," Stark remarked dryly. "But as to what I've got, the answer is nothing. My guess is somebody came in and gave the horse a shot of some kind of deadly poison. Wouldn't be too hard, I guess. Place was almost deserted. All he had to do was walk up and give the shot."

"Wouldn't whoever did it have to know something about horses? I mean, wouldn't he have to hit a big vein or something?"

"Maybe. I'll talk to some people and find out." Stark jammed his hands into his pockets and stared at the floor. "I don't like this thing. I've got a feeling it's going to get bad."

"Yeah, me, too. If Dani had walked into the guy killing her horse, he could have nailed her." Luke hesitated, aware of an urge to let the policeman in on what they were doing, but decided to talk Dani into telling him.

"The guy ever ask you for money?" Stark inquired.

"No. I've only been here a little while and haven't made any money. I wish he would. It'd give me a way to get to him."

"Nobody is giving me anything," Stark noted moodily. "I can't find out who's paying off, and the ones I do know won't trust me. If he gets to you, Sixkiller, no heroics and no private stuff. You come running to me, all right?"

"Don't worry, Stark. I'd like to drop the whole thing in your lap." Sixkiller and the officer parted, and on his way to the parking lot, Luke felt about as helpless as he'd been in a long time. *Got to be some way to nail this guy!* he thought, anger making him drive recklessly.

He went directly to his own room, called Savage, and gave him a quick report. "She's hurting, Ben. Don't know what will happen."

"Stay close to her, Luke," Savage responded at once. "She's going to have to face up to this thing. Wish I was there," he grumbled.

"She may call it off."

"I hope not." Savage pointed out, "She's already in a spin over shooting that guy. Can't handle it. Now if she folds over this, she'll never be able to face things."

Sixkiller paused, thinking it over. "Right. I'll keep you posted, Ben," he promised.

He put down the receiver and made his way to Dani's room. Ruth answered the door at once, and he entered to find Dani sitting on one chair, Megan on the other. Megan caught his eye and made a hopeless gesture with her shoulders.

Dani looked up at Sixkiller, her eyes dry. "I think I'd like to rest a while," she told them.

Ruth said, "Sure, Dani. Call when you wake up."

The two women left, and Sixkiller sat down in the chair across the room from Dani. He relaxed and began to speak in an ordinary voice, as if nothing had happened. "I talked to Stark a little. He's a pretty good guy. I guess we better let him know what's going on." When Dani didn't respond, he sat there, his legs stretched out in front of him, his Stetson pushed back on his head. "You want to tell me about it?"

"No, Luke."

Dani sat there silently for so long he thought she'd never speak. Finally, she whispered, "Clyde told me I could keep Biscuit in one of his stalls. . . ."

Sixkiller sat there as she recited the events, sounding like a schoolgirl reeling off a rather boring lesson she'd committed to heart. Her only bobble was when she had to say the horse's name—which she could not do. Instead of saying "Biscuit" she would say "my horse," and then it was with a slight hesitation. But as she finished, Sixkiller was aware that she was hurt worse than she showed. He'd seen it before in men who learned to carry on, talking and going about their business when they were nursing a terrible emotional wound. And it worried him to think that most of them had cracked sooner or later.

When she finished, he wondered aloud, "What now?" When she lifted her eyes with a puzzled look on her face, he sat up, asking, "Do we hang in here?"

Dani suddenly got to her feet and began pacing the floor, her hands clasped tightly. She finally stopped and cried, "Yes!"

Sixkiller rose and went to stand in front of her. He sought to comfort her, "Dani, I'm sorry about Biscuit."

The name made her blink her eyes, and she stood there, struggling against the tears. Suddenly the memories came back, tumbling over one another, and she swayed slightly.

"I've had him—since I was a girl," she faltered. Then she could not go on. The tears refused to obey her will, filling her eyes so that she could not see. She held her shoulders stiffly in place, but they, too, betrayed her as they began to shake. She cried out, "Biscuit!" and the tone was one of heartbreak, of something forever lost. He saw that her feelings were deadlocked, leaving her wholly powerless.

Once Sixkiller had known something distinctly similar, when struck in the stomach, he could not breathe, speak, or move. "Maybe," he said quietly, "I can help." Reaching out, he took her shoulders and pulled her against his chest.

He felt the quick loosening of her body, and he was listening to the sudden onset of her weeping. He said nothing, but stood there holding her. Her hair was a rich lustrous auburn, with a sweet, flower-tinged smell. She was tall for a woman, with square, strong shoulders. There was a substance to her body; it was warm and firm in his arms. She pulled her head back and looked at him strangely, and he noticed her skin, lightly browned by the sun, and her lips, broad and on the edge of being full—the lips of a giving woman.

Without meaning to, he moved his head forward and kissed her. The salt of her tears lay on her lips, and there was a fragile, vulnerable quality about her. It was like no kiss he had ever known, and he did not realize that it was because he was not seeking something from her. For the first time in his life he was reaching out to a woman, trying to give.

She trembled, but there was in her very vulnerability a hunger for reassurance, and the strength of his arms and the gentleness of his kiss brought a sense of order to her.

Then she moved back, and the weight suddenly went from his arms. She straightened and gave him a full, quick look in which he witnessed a self-willed pride now deliberately shutting out the softer things he had seen.

She said only in a quiet voice under absolute control, "Thanks."

"For what?"

"For not taking advantage." She came up with the bare minimum of a smile, and her eyes were brighter, no longer paralyzed by grief. "Most men would have."

Sixkiller felt embarrassed. It always embarrassed him to have someone mention any good quality they saw in him. He nodded shortly and trying to sound tough, warned, "Yeah—well, don't count on any more chivalry. That's all I had in stock."

"All right, Luke," she said, but the smile grew broader, and she touched his arm in a trusting gesture. Then she took a deep breath, and spoke in a voice that was not yet quite steady, "Biscuit. A casualty."

Sixkiller nodded, then told her about what Clyde had offered to do about burying Biscuit. Dani listened, and when he was through, she quavered, "That's good, isn't it, Luke?"

"It's what I'd like for myself. Open plains, a creek murmuring, and the trees whispering over me."

She said quietly, "That's poetry, isn't it?"

He looked at her with defiance. "I never read the stuff! Let's go for a walk," he suggested.

They left the room and stopped at a convenience store for bread. Then Sixkiller led her to a small park with a pond. As they reached its banks, a flock of ducks fluttered toward them, greedily seeking the bread.

"Had to bring you here," Luke commented. "I found a duck that looks just like Handsome. Think he could have made it from Dallas?"

Handsome II, as Dani called him, was built like a battleship and fought an eternal war against the horde of mallards. Dani smiled at him, saying, "He reminds me of a third-rate dictator for some reason."

The intense green heads of the male mallards almost hurt the eye when the sun brought out their color. The trees overhead put their green image on the blue water, and overhead fluffy clouds hung motionless. The smell of the water and the splashing and babbling of the ducks pleased Dani, and she said nothing more until all the bread was gone.

They sat on the small bench under the trees, and after a time of restful silence, Dani began to tell Luke about Biscuit, from the time he was a long-legged awkward colt. She had slept with him in the barn, sneaking out of the house. She'd taught him to carry a saddle, then gone through all the steps of training him. Stories of her high-school rodeo days followed.

Sixkiller sat watching her face until she finally ran down and said, "He was a fine horse, Luke. I'll always remember him. Nobody can take those memories from me."

Sixkiller was very still, so still that he could hear the tiny gnat near his ear, buzzing like a miniature chain saw. Dani looked at him, wondering at his silence. Finally he shared, "I've got me a little room. The good things that happen to me, I keep them there. It's kind of a secret art gallery." He looked into her eyes and smiled. "When the bad times come, I go to that room and look at the pictures." He hesitated, then turned to face her, putting one big hand on her shoulder. "And if I live to be an old, old man, stuck in a nursing home without a soul to care if I live or die—even then I can go to my gallery. And I'll pull out a picture of a beautiful girl with auburn hair, throwing bread to green-headed ducks on a blue pond."

Dani stared at him for a long moment, then whispered, "That's—very beautiful, Luke—like poetry!"

He got to his feet, glared at her, and snapped angrily, "I never read the stuff!"

14
Waiting for Megan

W here'd you get that outfit—at a garage sale?" Sixkiller and Dani were drinking coffee in her motel room, early on Saturday morning. She was sitting on the bed, with her legs crossed, balancing a notebook and chewing on the end of a pencil. Sixkiller slumped in a chair, looking at her morosely.

Dani glanced down at the faded top, which had once been red but was now a rather sickly shade of pink. It had always been too large, but it was comfortable, so she had used it as a lounging outfit, along with a pair of patched shorts worn thin by many washings. She responded, "You don't like my outfit, go to Neiman-Marcus." Then she looked up, took in his relaxed figure, and snorted, "As for that, you look like a bum. Don't you have another outfit, Luke? Or are you just trying to get sympathy so you can go on welfare?"

He ignored her jibe, only excusing himself with, "I'm not given to foppish attire." Then he came out of his chair and went over to the coffeepot and poured a cup of very black coffee into the small paper cup furnished by the motel. It was held in a brown plastic holder, and he glared at it, complaining, "What a thing to put coffee in!" Going back to his chair he grunted, "All right, let's go over it again."

Dani looked down at the white sheet before her, then shook her head. "All we've got in the way of physical evidence is the two blackjacks. Identical. Made by a firm in Cleveland. They sold over ten thousand of them last year, mostly through catalog sales."

"That's a lot of busted heads," Sixkiller pointed out. "But they don't have any serial numbers, and anyone can buy one without a permit." He sipped the coffee, then suggested, "Maybe I ought to ask Ruby about it."

Dani shook her head. "Not yet. She may have done the job herself."

"She'd be capable of giving Clint a rap on the head. But I don't see her breaking the horse's legs."

"Because she's a woman?"

He gave her an amused look. "After arresting as many women as I have for murder one, I'm never surprised at what a woman would do."

She stuck her tongue out at him, then bit the eraser again, looking down at the sheet of paper. "All right, we've got the phone calls. But the voice wasn't one I could recognize. It sounded disguised, and Ruth and the rest of them agree. Nobody came close to recognizing it."

"I think we better have your phone rigged," Luke replied. "Someday we might be in court, and they can get a pretty good reading on voices these days. Not as definite as fingerprints, but they can scan them somehow and tell if the voice is the same."

"Okay. It's a long shot but long shots are all we've got. Now, Tom Leathers has come closer to this man than anyone else."

Sixkiller leaned over and pulled a doughnut from a box. "This is the last one," he remarked. Holding it up, he thought about it, then gave her a critical look. "You're getting fat," he teased. "I'd better eat it."

"I am *not* getting fat!" Dani rapped out. "*You're* just greedy. You ate four of those six doughnuts."

"Only to keep you trim," he excused himself. "I read the other day that women your age start going downhill pretty fast. You need me to look after you."

He grinned at her, and Dani thought suddenly that he *had* looked after her. Since Biscuit had been killed, he had been by her side almost constantly. Not that he was obvious about it. He was too clever for that she thought. But he had simply *been there*. Always with his easy talk, always taking the light tone. Thinking of it now, she saw how well he had handled her.

Handled me, she thought with a wry stab of insight. *He's not as rough as he wants people to think. Most men would have rushed around patting my shoulder and telling me not to cry. But since that moment when I broke down—when he kissed me—he's been looking out for me.* She thought about that kiss—had thought about it often—but could not decide what she really felt.

Looking at him, she saw what a masculine figure he was. It was not just the powerful frame, the arching chest, and the smoothly corded arms. Body builders had never attracted her. They seemed like freaks, with their small waists and absurdly pumped up arms and shoulders, and their absurd posturings made her feel slightly ill. They were, in Dani's opinion, no better than strippers in their ridiculous attempts to strut and pose.

No, there was none of that about Luke Sixkiller. He did pump iron, she knew, because he saw his body as a tool to use in his profession, much like the .44 he carried. Both of them were necessary in dealing with his clientele—the criminals of New Orleans—so he kept them both in good condition.

He's the most physical person I've ever seen, Dani thought, studying him overtly as he ate the doughnut. *He makes other men seem small. And it's not just his size, either. It's something inside him—that determination that won't let him quit.*

He saw her looking at him and cocked his heavy, black brow. "Well, what else we got?"

She ducked her head to look at the sheet of paper. "Your list," she said. "You want to go over it again?"

"I don't know." It was a list of names that he had given her after she had left the party to go out and plant the money in the pickup. "We don't know that the Creep is one of the rodeo people."

"I think he has to be, Luke," she argued. "He knows too much about his victims—like he knows about the picture hanging over Hank Lowe's couch, things like that. Ruth told me he even knew her maiden name, and she swears she never told anyone."

"He knew her name was *Savage?*" Luke questioned sharply. "Then we don't have to wonder how Ben got suckered."

"Ruth says she never told a soul."

"She's a woman, sweetheart. She could have told it and not even noticed." He ignored her angry look at his statement, adding, "Probably told Clint, at least."

"She swears she didn't."

"Maybe she doesn't remember." He gave her a sly grin, then said, "I know something about you. You've got a fishhook-shaped scar."

Dani's face turned a fiery red, and her mouth dropped open. "You've never seen that scar!"

"No, worse luck!" Sixkiller grinned. "You told me about getting thrown into that barbed-wire fence, when you were talking about Biscuit the other day by the lake. You said you had to have six stitches, and it left a crooked scar."

"I don't remember saying that!"

"How else would I know?" He shrugged. "We all do that, Dani. We let our hair down with those we trust. Ruth must have let it slip. But I guess you're right. We'll have to say that it's somebody in the inner ring. Still, it couldn't have been anybody who was in the room that night."

"I wish you'd been looking around while he was talking to me on the phone. That's the *only* sure thing."

"What does that mean?"

"It means that whoever it was must have slipped out of the room while I was taking the money outside to the truck. He saw Tom and me, Luke. I think he must have seen me holding a gun on Tom. That's why he killed Biscuit."

"You're guessing."

"Not altogether," she told him slowly. "I talked with Tom. He felt so bad about Biscuit! And he said that when the Creep called him to get the money, he was different."

"How different?"

"He was angry—very angry, Tom said. And it had to be because I'd messed up his plan. I had a gun and was dangerous. That's why he killed Biscuit. But he had to have seen Tom and me. So he *couldn't* have been in the room after I left. So here's a list of people you saw after I left the room:

1. Clay Dixon
2. Boone Hardin
3. J. D. Pillow
4. Wash Foster
5. Ruby Costner
6. Clyde Lockyear
7. Hank Lowe"

Sixkiller commented doubtfully, "I saw all those, sure, but it was packed in that room. There could have been others in the back, where I couldn't see them." He closed his eyes, trying to remember. "I didn't see Clint or Bill Baker or Rocky James. Didn't see Ruth, for that matter."

"I asked her about it." Dani nodded. "She and Clint were dancing a lot. She thinks they were out in the larger room when I got the call."

"She with him all the time?"

Dani hesitated, then explained, "Not exactly. She went to the bathroom, and when she came out, he was gone. But he found her later." Dani looked a little embarrassed. "He'd gone to the other bathroom. Except for that, they were together all the time."

"Well, it's not much help, is it? Even someone in the room could have had somebody else working with him. Say he's hired Rocky James to keep an eye on Tom Leathers. Rocky sees you two, then comes back and gives the report to his boss."

"It could be," Dani agreed slowly. "But if this man is as smart as I think he is, he'll want as few people as possible in on the scheme." Then she shook her head. "The only *sure* thing is, anyone who was in the room when I was talking to the Creep can't be our man."

"I can't help you with that," Sixkiller admitted. "Guess I slipped up. I wasn't counting noses—not until you left the room."

Dani smiled ruefully. "I was pretty wound up myself, Luke. All I can be sure of is the people at my table—Megan and Bake. Clyde was still performing, and Fran had left. That's how it was when Tom came to tell me there was a call. And I could see them at the table while I was talking to the Creep."

"Still leaves lots of suspects," Sixkiller pointed out. He looked at his watch, got to his feet, and stretched. "We better get to the Dome. I've got a date with a bull named *Tombstone.*"

"And I've got my first ride on Big Boy," Dani agreed. She came off the bed, stretched her legs, then said, "I've got to get dressed."

Thirty minutes later they were pulling into the parking lot at the Astrodome. "Rodeo's over tomorrow," Sixkiller remarked, getting out of the Silverado. "We going to Fort Smith?"

"That's where most of the contestants are headed." Dani nodded.

"Well, if I don't make more money there than I have here, you'll have to take me to raise." Luke grinned. He moved away, and Dani went at once to saddle up.

She had been practicing on Big Boy for two days and was not yet sure of herself. He was a much taller horse than Biscuit—a rangy, iron-gray gelding. He was not, in her judgment as good as Biscuit, but Fran had won top money on him before she gave up barrel racing, so Dani knew that the fault lay in her.

After saddling up, she rode slowly around the open space reserved for the contestants, putting everything out of her mind except the race. Finally, Ruth came up on her horse to say, "Come on, Dani. Team roping's almost over. Time for us to do our stuff."

The two rode slowly toward the entrance, and Ruth reluctantly shared, "I got a phone call this morning—from you-know-who."

Dani shot a glance at Ruth. "When do you pass the money to him?"

Ruth hesitated, then admitted, "He didn't say, Dani. Just told me to get it ready. Only a hundred dollars." Ruth's squarish face had a puzzled look and something more than that. "Dani, he's never before cut his price."

"Was that all he said?"

"N-no," Ruth stammered. She gave Dani a quick glance. "He said that Clint was cheating on me."

"Ruth! You don't believe that?"

"I don't want to," Ruth confessed. "But Clint's always been a man to chase women. Up until now he's been faithful, but lately he's been acting strangely." They passed into the building, but Ruth didn't ride to where the other girls were getting in place. Pulling her horse up, she explained in a sad tone, "He's worried, Dani. I think he's lost a lot of money gambling. He never talks to me about it, but Clyde says he's in pretty deep."

"How does Clyde know? I thought he had no use for Clint."

"He doesn't—but Clyde's a big plunger himself. Didn't you know that?" Ruth shook her head, her dark eyes bitter. "The difference is that Clyde's got the money to lose, and Clint hasn't. It's scary, Dani! Clint makes a lot of money, but he doesn't have a dime saved. If he got hurt, I don't know what would happen!"

"What about the rest of it?" Dani asked. Big Boy was moving nervously, but she pulled him up shortly. "About the woman."

"He asked me if I knew where Clint was last night. But I lied about that, Dani."

Dani gave her a quick look. "He was with Megan. We both knew that, Ruth. He's helping her with her book."

Ruth sat there silently, her head bowed, and finally she admitted quietly, "He says it's more than that, Dani. He says they're having an affair."

"That's not true, Ruth!"

"Oh, I know you think she's got religion, Dani," Ruth said bitterly. "But I don't know, Clint knows women. If he wants her, he'll go after her."

"Don't believe it, Ruth. It's not fair to Clint or to Megan. Talk to him about it."

"I—I'm afraid to," Ruth replied. She lifted her dark eyes, which were filled with misery, to meet Dani's. "I can't lose him, Dani! I can't!"

The announcer called for the first barrel racer, and Dani pointed out, "You're next. We'll talk later, Ruth."

Dani's mind was on what Ruth had just said, and she did poorly when her turn came. Ruth took second place, but when Dani tried to talk to her, she seemed tired and withdrawn. "Talk to Clint," Dani advised her. "It's just some slimy trick the Creep has come up with." Then a thought came to her. "Come on to church with Megan and me tomorrow, Ruth. Luke's going, too."

"I guess it can't hurt," Ruth agreed, but there was a doubtful look in her eyes, and her square shoulders sagged as she rode away.

Sixkiller sat with his back braced against the pew, his black eyes zeroed in on the minister. From time to time he would glance to his right, where Dani sat with Ruth beside her, then to his left, where Megan sat, her back stiff. They had met for breakfast, and he had half expected Ruth to change her mind, but she had not.

As the sermon went on, Luke tried to examine his own feelings. He was more than a little surprised at himself, for since there had been some unpleasant experiences at a small church on the reservation, he had kept clear of religion in any form. He had made a separate peace on the matter, deciding that some people were religious and some were not—then having classified himself as one of the *nots,* he had declined to show any interest in church. He had seen so much violence on the force that he could not hang onto the streak of gentleness that was buried deeply inside.

But something was working on him. Outwardly he maintained the same hard-nosed attitude, but he was an intelligent man, and he had never been able to shake off the notion that evolution was a humbug. His Indian ancestry and heritage gave him a "spiritual" cast, in the more general sense of believing in things that could not be measured in a test tube. He was aware of the physical world in a way that most people are not, and it seemed inconceivable to him that the great dance of the stars overhead was some sort of "accident."

He knew this agitation had something to do with Dani Ross. When he had first met her, he had remarked, "Just another Jesus freak. She'll get over it." As he had watched her, though, she had not "gotten over" it, but had kept the same even frame of mind.

Luke associated most religion with some sort of mental or emotional instability, much in the same way that rationalistic intellectuals of the eighteenth century insultingly branded the early Methodists *enthusiasts.*

Luke moved his eyes, taking in Dani's smooth face, the intelligence of the gray-green eyes, and the sensitive lines of the wide mouth. He had seen her quick intelligence in action many times, so her faith was a puzzle to him, as it had been to others. *She's smart as a whip, looks like a million dollars, and she's got enough drive and stubbornness for ten men.*

Sixkiller knew that Dani Ross had rocked his little theological boat, for she had shown him a razor-sharp mind and a well-balanced emotional makeup—and a steadfast set of moral convictions that nothing could shake.

The sermon was brief, but once again, Luke felt something working inside him, and when he shook hands with the minister as they left the church, he found it difficult to meet the man's steady gaze. "I see you're back again," the minister noted. Then he added suddenly, "I'll be praying that God catches up with you soon."

Startled, Sixkiller blinked but could not find an answer. Later, when they were sitting in the restaurant where they had gone for lunch, Dani commented on this. Her eyes twinkled as she said innocently, "The preacher has your number, doesn't he, Luke?"

"He's been reading that poem too much, the one where Jesus is a bloodhound chasing a sinner."

"That's 'The Hound of Heaven.'" Megan nodded. "I didn't know you read poetry, Luke."

"Never read the stuff."

"Then how'd you know about it?" Ruth asked.

Beleaguered, Sixkiller shook his head stubbornly. "Probably somebody read it to me at the mission school. All I can remember is that it was pretty strange. Making Jesus into a bloodhound!"

"Oh, Jesus has lots of symbolic forms," Dani reminded him. "He's called the Lion of Judah, for example, or the Good Shepherd."

"Yes, but *bloodhound?*" Luke protested. "And God doesn't run around chasing people. People are supposed to seek God. Even *I* know that much, Dani!"

Dani took a bite from her chicken-salad sandwich as she thought about it. Then she said, "I can think of at least two places in the Bible that say God does pursue man. Jesus himself said one time, 'For the Son of man is come to seek and to save that which was lost.' And he said in John, 'No man can come to me, except the Father which hath sent me draw him. . . .'"

"And that part you read to me last night, Dani," Megan inserted, "with the lost sheep and the shepherd who goes out and looks for him."

Sixkiller took a vicious bite from his cheeseburger, feeling himself hemmed in. "Well, I don't see it that way. God's supposed to be able to do anything, isn't he? So if he's seeking me, why hasn't he found me?"

Dani said gently, "You've left out one thing, Luke. We're like God."

He stared at her with surprise on his coppery cheeks. "What does that mean?"

"It means that when God made man, he made him with a free will. Man's the only part of God's creation who has one. God has a will, and he gave man a will."

"I don't see what you're getting at," Ruth lamented. "Animals can decide things."

"But they can't *pray*, Ruth," Dani interposed swiftly. "They can be taught to do things, and they have marvelous instincts. But they're not like us. There'll never be a time when we won't be alive. A billion years will pass, and you and I will still be somewhere."

"That's a little scary," Ruth said. "I don't like to think about it."

"You find it scary because you're bound by time. But don't you like to be with those you love? Well, that's what we're headed for, to be with God. He *is* love, and there's no fear in that."

"There is if you're not sure you're going to make it," Luke countered, his eyes intent on Dani. "If the Bible is true, not everyone is going to heaven."

"All who want to will, Luke." Dani paused, searching for the best words. The other three sat there, watching her carefully. "It's like this," she said finally. "God could have made a race who *had* to serve him. But what would he have? A bunch of robots. Would you like a lover who *had* to love you? Of course not, and neither did God. I don't know why he made man, but I suspect it was because he wanted fellowship."

"That's an odd idea!" Megan exclaimed. Then she smiled. "But I like it!"

They finished their lunch, and as they went to the matinee, Dani saw that Luke was silent. He seemed to be pondering something.

"I think that bloodhound is on Luke's trail," Megan stated. She had followed Dani to the horse lot and was watching her saddle Big Boy. "He'd really be something, if he were converted."

"He's something now." Dani smiled. "But I know what you mean."

"Dani—?" Megan waited until Dani turned to face her, then said, "Thanks for everything. I never knew what peace was until you led me to Jesus."

"I'm glad!"

Then Megan confided, "Maybe we won't have to do this rodeo bit for long."

Dani asked instantly, "You have something, Megan?"

"Just a hunch. I'll tell you about it later." She reached forward and gave Dani a hug. "Be sure you win! I'll be up in the stands hollering 'Praise the Lord!'"

Dani smiled after her race, for she took first place. Everyone stopped her but she wanted to find Megan and go to her room. After Luke rode his steer, making a good time and taking a second, she found him.

"Luke, I'm going to my room. But I can't find Megan."

He snapped his fingers, then reached into his pocket. "She said to give you this note."

Dani opened the small slip of paper and read: *Dani, I've got a lead. Will be back at the room after the rodeo. Don't go to sleep! We've got to talk. Praise the Lord!* There was another phrase, but Megan's scrawling handwriting was so bad she couldn't make it out.

Dani asked, "When did she give you this?"

"Just as I was getting on the bull. Came running in and said she had to leave."

Dani shook her head. "I wish she'd found me."

"You think it's something about the Creep?"

"I don't know. She hinted at something like that." Dani turned, repeating, "I'm going to my room."

"Check with you later," he called as she left.

Dani went to the room and showered. It was only nine o'clock, but already she felt nervous. For two hours she glanced at the door, but only once was she interrupted. Sixkiller came by to check on Megan. He listened as Dani spoke, then shook his head." She's talking with someone and forgot the time. You know how she does that," he reminded Dani.

"I suppose so. Well, good night, Luke."

She read for an hour, then finally turned the lights out, but sleep eluded her. Finally, just as she was dozing off, a knock on her door brought her bolt upright. She called out, "Just a minute—!" and slipped into her robe. When she opened the door and found Lieutenant Stark and Luke Sixkiller standing there, her heart seemed to freeze.

"Come in," she invited. When they stepped inside and stood there with grim faces, she asked, "What is it?"

Stark's thin lips grew even tighter. He blinked his eyes, then quietly stated, "It's bad news, Miss Ross."

Dani felt her head beginning to grow lighter, and her hands trembled. "Tell me."

"Well, Clint Thomas has been shot," Stark said.

"Is he dead?"

"Yes. But that's not all. . . ."

Stark shot a glance at Sixkiller, and Luke broke the news. "It's murder and suicide, Dani." He saw her face stiffen, but had no choice. "Megan shot him—and then herself. They're both dead."

15

Captain Little Gets Some Volunteers

Murders had become so common in Houston that they were usually relegated to the fifth page of the newspaper or to a footnote on the six o'clock news. But the death of a celebrity such as Clint Thomas was something else. The media swarmed like vultures, delighting in their ability to lay bare every sordid detail of the tragedy.

In exasperation, Fighting Bill Baker responded to a reporter who was pumping him, "Say, the guy's dead. Why don't you give him a break?"

The reporter stared at Baker as if he had said something stupid. "The public's got a right to know," the man had answered. Before breaking the sharp nose of the reporter, Bill exclaimed, "And I got a right to clean your clock!" Hauled into court for his misdeeds, once he had paid his fine, Bill had asked, "Can I get this same rate on some of them other lousy hyenas, Judge?"

Dani came in for her share of roving reporters. Since Megan had been her friend, she was targeted by all the television commentators. She refused to speak to any of them and finally got another room at the motel, under another name, to avoid them.

But Al Packard, the pride of the "Now!" program, outsmarted her. This burly, overbearing man billed himself as the first to get the "facts" on any story. His size, his overwhelming manner, and his connections enabled him to corner anyone he felt would add to his program; Packard bullied most people mercilessly, all in the name of journalism, though he had no training in that field. He had been an all-American linebacker for Texas A & M and capped that with a short career with the Houston Oilers. A knee injury had taken him out of professional football, but he used his controversial manners to become a sportscaster, then graduated into his own program. "Now!" dealt exclusively with sex and violence, never bothering with hard facts but filled with hints and innuendoes, delivered by Packard.

Dani never knew how he had gotten her room number, but no doubt it had been easy enough. She and Sixkiller had fled to the pond to get away from the reporters, but at noon they had returned to the motel. Lieutenant Stark had told them his superior had called a meeting with all the intimates of Clint Thomas at one o'clock at the police station, and Dani wanted to change out of her jeans.

Luke walked with her to her room, his own being only four doors away. Neither spoke to the large man standing in the side corridor containing the ice machines and the vending machines. But as Dani put her key in the lock and opened the door, a voice startled her by calling, "Miss Ross?"

Both turned to find the man standing just behind them. He was at least six four and must have weighed over 250 pounds.

His face was blunt, set above a neck so thick that it looked as though he had none. "I'm Al Packard," he introduced himself, then waited, obviously expecting the name to mean something. When neither of them spoke, he commented, "Need a few minutes of your time, Miss Ross."

Dani stared at him. "Are you a reporter?"

"I'm host of the 'Now!' program," he said. "You must not be from Texas, or you'd know it."

"Sorry, Mr. Packard." Dani briefly informed him, "I don't have anything to say."

It was the same line she'd used all morning, and turning her back, she stepped inside her room. Al Packard stepped in behind her, and when she turned, he was so close she bumped into him.

"Won't take but a few minutes." He nodded. "Now if you'll—" He broke off suddenly, for he found himself being shoved to one side. Wheeling quickly, he met the black eyes of Sixkiller. A quick flare of anger came into Packard's eyes, and he barked, "Don't crowd me, Mac."

"My name's not *Mac*," Sixkiller remarked. His face was emotionless as he stood looking up into the face of the hulking reporter. "It's *Luke Sixkiller*. You can use it on your program. As a matter of fact, why don't you and I go to my room and talk."

"I'm talking to her, Mac," Packard responded forcefully. "Maybe, if you're a good Indian, I'll mention your name."

At the deliberate insult, Dani saw a smile form on Sixkiller's lips. For all his thick shoulders, he looked frail beside the bulk of Al Packard. But something in the way Luke smiled made her nervous. Packard was on guard as well, for he had spent a majority of his life dealing with strong men who were out to maim him.

"Gee, thanks," Sixkiller said eagerly. He put out his hand. "I'd be glad to tell you what you want to know."

"Sure, sure—but later, all right, Chief?"

After this tolerant word, Packard nodded and took the hand Sixkiller held out. He gave it a hard squeeze, then half turned back to face Dani—when he found he could not. Sixkiller's hand had closed on his like a vise, and he grunted involuntarily.

"Why, you punk!" Packard laughed, his face red with anger. "Try to outgrip me? I'll break every bone in your hand!"

It was an old game to Packard, he had always been a strong man, especially in his hands. He had been a champion arm wrestler in his younger days, and though his legs were weak, and he had picked up excess poundage, he still retained most of the strength that had given him the nickname *Hooks* on the football field. It was his boast that once he got a hand on a runner, it was all over—and that was no exaggeration. He had used the strength of his hands to humble man after man, crunching each one's hands with a terrible grip.

Now he threw his full strength into doing the same to Sixkiller's hand. There was no doubt in his mind as to the outcome, for the hand of the smaller man was lost in his own huge paw. Harder and harder he squeezed—but nothing seemed to happen. Sixkiller's hand did not give, but remained solid and firm. It was like squeezing a padded piece of steel.

Packard threw every ounce of strength into his hand, and his face contorted with the effort. The two men seemed to Dani to be frozen into place. As she glanced at their hands, she saw Packard's whiten with the strain, his fingertips turning pale under the pressure. She glanced fearfully at Luke's face but it seemed almost relaxed.

Packard's mouth sprung open then, for something was happening that had never happened to him before. The hand of the Indian was contracting! Always before his opponent had collapsed under the force of his grip—but now Sixkiller's hand was like a white-hot band of steel closing on his flesh.

Desperately Packard fought to keep his hand from giving in, but there was something inexorable in Sixkiller's grip. Pain shot into the big man's hand, and he uttered a short cry of pain—which shocked him, for he had never been one to cry over pain. Yet the pain had not brought the cry from Packard, for he had known much worse in his playing days; it was something in the ebony eyes locked into his. As his hand collapsed and the bones began grinding with a fiery agony, something in Sixkiller's eyes leaped out at Packard, and the big man suddenly felt that not until his hand was a mass of broken bones would he be released. Frantically he lunged back, hauling at his right arm. For all his efforts, his arm might have been frozen in cement, for the pressure continued to grow, and the pain grew unbearable.

Dani was shocked when Packard suddenly cried out, "Let me go!" and fell to one knee, his left hand fluttering in a helpless gesture.

Dani took one look at Sixkiller, then stepped forward. "Luke, that's enough," she interceded quickly.

Luke glanced at her, and the fire in his dark eyes seemed to die down. He didn't let go of Packard's hand, but pulled him outside. Keeping the pressure on, he moved down the walkway, dragging the big man along. When he got to the steel stairs, he released the hand.

Packard, his face white and his eyes blinking, snatched it back, trying to move his fingers. There was blood on the tip of one of them, and he took the handkerchief from his breast pocket and wrapped it around the hand.

"You'll be sorry for this!" he mumbled. He would have said more, but he flinched as Sixkiller moved a step closer.

"You print anything I don't like about Miss Ross," Luke commented idly, as though he were speaking of a change in the weather, "and I'll put you in the hospital." He paused, then said pleasantly, "All right?"

Packard tried to meet his gaze, and he wanted more than anything in the world to smash Sixkiller's impassive face. He stood there, trying to make himself strike a blow, while Sixkiller waited, a look of expectation on his face. When he saw that Packard was finished, Luke asked mildly, "You need any help to get down those steps, Mac?"

Packard wheeled and stumbled down the stairs. Sixkiller smiled then and turned back to Dani's room. She was standing at the door, where she had watched the scene, her face pale.

"Let's make some of that rotten coffee," Luke suggested, taking her arm and stepping inside. "It's not much good, but it's the same stuff they use in the restaurant." He moved to the machine, and as he busied himself with the coffee, he chatted freely.

Dani moved to one of the chairs and sat down suddenly, her legs weak. As Luke whistled off-key at the coffeemaker, she studied him, not quite able to believe that he had not been affected by the encounter. When he brought her coffee, she took it, sipped carefully, and asked, "Luke, didn't that bother you?"

He blinked as though confused, then glanced at the door. "Oh, that bit with the big, bad wolf? Not much." He sipped his own coffee, then added, "He's not a bad one, Dani. He wouldn't last half a day in one of the bad sections of New Orleans. They'd have him for lunch." He changed the subject, and she knew that there was no way she would ever be able to take violence the way Luke and Ben did. They had gone through a hard school, and they had either had to grow hard or die.

"I'm going to miss Megan," Luke said after a while. "She was a good one. You two were really close."

Dani nodded, taking a quick swallow of the hot coffee to get rid of the lump that rose in her throat. When she finally got control, she shared, "She loved old movies, Luke, just like I do. We'd stay up half the night watching the Marx Brothers or even the Three Stooges. And she was always taping things with her video. She hid it in her room once and taped a bunch of silly stuff we did." Then she abruptly volunteered, "She didn't do it, Luke."

He rolled the cup around in his powerful hands, not answering for a long moment. Then he gave her an odd look. "Because she was a convert?"

"That's one reason I can't buy it."

"The law won't look at it that way."

"No, it won't. But it's not just that, Luke." She hesitated, then asked, "Do you think she did it?"

"Nope."

The simple expression from Sixkiller brought a light into Dani's eyes. "Why not?"

"She's not the type."

"The law won't buy that either, Luke."

"I'm not the law now," Luke slowly pointed out. "If it was my case, I'd pretty well ignore anyone who told me she didn't do it because she wasn't the type. Even before she got converted she wasn't the type. She wasn't a killer—and she wasn't the type for suicide. But that's the way it'll probably come out when the cops here add it all up."

Dani shook her head in a fierce gesture. "No! Megan deserves better than that! We've got to get whoever really killed her."

"And Clint," Sixkiller reminded her.

"Yes, Clint, too." They talked about the case until it was time to go to the station. When they got there, they were directed to Room 216. The room was big enough for the ten or so people they found inside—all of them from the rodeo.

Clyde and Fran moved to Dani at once, both of them obviously nervous. Fran's lipstick, usually geometrically perfect, was smeared, and her mascara ran down onto her cheeks. Her speech was slurred as she cried, "What a terrible thing! I can't believe it!"

Dani caught the smell of liquor on her breath but had no time to answer. Fran was on a talking jag, and after mourning over Clint, began cursing Megan. "The little tramp! I knew she was no good from the time I saw her!"

Clyde took her arm, his own face weary and drawn with strain. "Shut down, will you, Fran?" he said tightly. "She's dead. There's no point in bad-mouthing her."

Fran yanked her arm away with a curse, but at that moment the outer door opened, and Lieutenant Stark walked in, accompanied by a large man wearing cowboy boots and belt. They moved to the front of the room, and Stark spoke, "Sit down, please." There was a scurry as they all found seats. "Thank you all for coming. This is Captain Little of the Homicide Squad."

The captain had an east Texas twang and a pair of small, blue eyes. He was lean, with a blanched face. "All right, I'll make this short as I can. You've heard some details on the TV, most of them wrong. Here's what we've got. The victims were both shot with a .38 colt revolver registered to Megan Carr. Thomas died of a gunshot to the head and Megan Carr of a gunshot in the heart. Both of them died instantly. The coroner puts the time of death between seven and nine o'clock last night," he pronounced flatly.

"Why, that was when the show was on!" Tom Leathers remarked grimly.

"Just keep quiet until I finish," Little ordered, giving the cowboy an impatient look. "The crime took place in an Airstream motor home parked in the area set aside for trailers. There was no sign of a struggle, and nobody reported gunshots." He looked around the room and took out a miniature cigar and peeled it as he went on. "But the stereo was turned up full volume—which was customary with Clint Thomas, it appears." He put the cigar between his teeth, pulled a kitchen match from his shirt pocket, lit it with one rake of his thumbnail, then touched it to the cigar. He took his time, and Dani felt suddenly that it was all an act—the tough cop playing cowboy.

"The body was discovered by a man named Boone Hardin. He says he went by to see Thomas, and when nobody answered his knock, he tried the door. It was unlocked, so he opened it and looked inside, finding the two victims. He was coming out of the trailer, on his way to report the shooting, he says, when he met another man, Hank Lowe. He told Lowe what had happened, and the two of them went to a phone and called the station. The time of his call was ten minutes after ten." He sent a puff of blue smoke toward the ceiling, then asked, "Any questions?"

"Where are Boone and Hank?" Bake demanded.

"They're being held for questioning. As soon as we're through in here, I'll have them released. Now, I asked Lieutenant Stark to get you here because you people have been close to Clint Thomas for some time. I'll be calling some of you in for individual questioning later, but right now I want some basic information. When I call your name, stand up and tell me two things. Number one, what's your relationship with the two victims, and number two, where were you between seven and nine o'clock last night. First, Clyde Lockyear."

Clyde stood up awkwardly, swallowed, then announced, "Well, Captain, I'm Clyde Lockyear. I furnish bucking stock for rodeos. I haven't known Megan Carr for long—only about six weeks. She was writing a story about rodeo, and we had coffee together while she interviewed me. 'Course I've known Clint for ten years or more."

"You ever have any trouble with either one of the victims, Mr. Lockyear?"

Clyde opened his mouth to say something, changed his mind then swallowed hard. "Well—yes, sir, I guess so." He turned to Fran, saying, "My wife was married to Clint Thomas."

The captain's eyes drilled into Fran, and when Clyde offered no more, he insisted, "Tell me about the trouble."

Clyde countered quickly, his round cheeks flushing, "Oh never an actual *fight*, Captain Little. He'd have killed me, if it had come to that, I guess. It was always verbal. He'd make remarks about Fran—that's my wife—and I'd take it up. That kind of thing."

Little studied him, then asked, "Where were you when the murder was committed?"

"Why, taking care of the stock, Captain!" Lockyear looked surprised at the question. "I'm busy as a one-armed paper-hanger during a show. Got to get bulls, barebacks, and saddle broncs in place, then get them into the chute—it's a split-second kind of thing. You can ask anybody, I guess. I was right there all that time."

"All right. Mrs. Lockyear?"

Fran stood up, her face flushed. "Like Clyde says, Clint and I were married once."

"Why'd you split?"

Fran hesitated, then admitted reluctantly, "He left me for another woman." Anger laced her voice. "He always had another woman!" Then she blinked and licked her lips. "But I had nothing to do with the killing!"

"And where were you from seven to nine?" Little demanded, puffing like a furnace on the stogie.

"Why, at the show, of course! But I move around a lot. Sometimes I'm back with Clyde, helping with the books. Getting the right horse to the right chute at the right time—that takes some book work. Lots of people saw me."

"I see," Little acknowledged her words, then nodded. "All right. Bake Dempsey?"

Dempsey got to his feet, his face sober. "Don't really know Megan Carr, Captain. Just talked to her a few times."

"But you know Clint Thomas, don't you? Didn't I read that you've missed being number one the last three years, when Thomas beat you out for it?"

Bake stared at him, then stiffly answered, "Sure. Clint beat us all out. He was the best."

"Not what you said to a few witnesses."

"Why—sure, I brag a little," Bake answered quickly. "But it was just talk. And I didn't go near that place of Thomas's last night. I rode a bronc at eight-thirty."

"What about after that?"

Bake swallowed, and Dani saw that he was uneasy. "I got hurt a little. Went home and rubbed some liniment on and went to sleep."

"Any witnesses?" Little asked.

"I bunk alone."

Little gave him a careful look, then proposed, "We'll talk more about your movements."

"Ruby Costner?"

"That's me." Ruby stood up, her face set defiantly. "Let me put it all on the front porch. I don't know the Carr woman, but I used to live with Clint Thomas. He threw me out for Ruth Cantrell. I hated his guts, and I'm glad somebody took him out. I'd have done it myself, but I didn't want to wash clothes in a women's prison for ten years."

Her attitude seemed to interest Captain Little. He lowered the cigar, smiled faintly, then nodded. "Very clear statement. Can you account for your movements last night during the times mentioned?"

"No!"

Little flicked the ash off his cigar, then nodded again. "Maybe you'll remember more later, Miss Costner."

"Clay Dixon?"

Dixon rose, a sullen look on his face. "I'm Dixon. Don't know much about the Carr woman—except she was stuck-up."

"How do you mean that?"

Dixon shifted his eyes around the room and realized that plenty of witnesses were available to the policeman. "Aw, she wouldn't have nothing to do with me," he mumbled.

"And Clint Thomas? Any trouble with him?"

"Well, he broke a chair over my head a while back," Dixon conceded. "But I busted him when he took out after Ruby."

"Oh? You were Miss Costner's boyfriend?"

"Yeah, I was." He shrugged his big shoulders, admitting, "You'll hear it anyway. Me and Clint had a fight over her. I busted him up good that time." Then he gave the captain a nod. "And I was with Rocky James the whole time last night. You can ask him."

When James stood up at Little's request, he verified Dixon's testimony. "Sure, we went out after the rodeo and got drunk."

"But you're a bull rider aren't you? You couldn't have been with anybody when you were working the bull riding."

"Well—all except that time I was with him."

Little sorted through the rest of the crowd, and Dani saw that despite his garish dress, he was a careful man who missed very little. Finally he got to the end of his list, saying, "Miss Ross?"

"Yes."

"The Carr woman spent a lot of time with you?"

"Yes, Captain."

Little chewed the stub of his cigar, then crushed it in an ash-tray on the table. "No sense keeping the rest of you. Stay available for questioning."

"We can't stay in Houston, Captain Little!" Clyde protested. "The rodeo ended, and we've all got to make shows in other places!"

Little nodded reluctantly. "I guess that's right. But I want a phone number where I can reach every one of you. There's going to be an inquest, and you may have to come back for it. If I can't find you easy, you'll come back the hard way."

He waved a hand in dismissal, and they all filed out. As soon as they were gone, Little commanded, "Come with me," and left the room. Stark stepped aside for Dani, and the two of them left the large room, following Little down the hall to a door with a small sign, CAPTAIN AMOS LITTLE. When Dani stepped inside, she found Luke Sixkiller sitting in a leather chair, reading a tattered copy of *Field and Stream*.

He got to his feet and came to stand beside Dani. Both watched as Little walked behind the desk and plumped himself down. Stark moved to stand against the wall to their right, and Dani saw that he was unhappy.

"Well, Danielle Ross, I understand you're a private detective working to find an extortioner who is shaking down rodeo people," the captain challenged.

Dani shot a look at Luke, but the captain caught it. "Oh, I didn't find out from the lieutenant here." He pulled out another cigar and went through his little ritual, giving them time to worry. Finally he lifted his eyes to meet Dani's. "Nice the way you let us in on all of it."

Dani replied rather breathlessly, "Well, Lieutenant Stark did know that Luke had been a policeman in New Orleans."

"And Captain Sixkiller, he hunted our man up and told him all about it?"

"Well, no, not exactly—"

"Not exactly, my foot!" Captain Little suddenly smashed his fist against the desk, sending a glass resting on the edge flying. He ignored it, raking them with a pair of the angriest eyes Dani had ever seen, and his voice would have cut glass.

"You come waltzing in without a word to us poor suckers who try to do a job here, meddle around like a pair of comic-strip characters, playing cowboy, and now we've got two deaths on our hands!" He pointed his cigar at Luke. "Sixkiller, I don't expect any private detective to have sense, but you should have a little! What would you do to a pair who came on your turf making this kind of mess?"

Sixkiller conceded soberly, "I'd do just about what you're doing, Captain. Maybe worse."

His ready confession seemed to irritate the tall officer. "Don't give me any false humility, Sixkiller!" he snorted. "I talked to your superior officer in New Orleans, and he told me to stomp you hard."

"He doesn't like me," Luke maintained. "Hard to believe, isn't it?"

Dani saw the anger rising even higher in Little's eyes and interjected hurriedly, "Captain, it was my fault. Luke wanted to tell you what we were doing, but I wouldn't let him."

Little stared at her, then retorted abruptly, "I talked to a guy about you, too. Dom Costello in Boston." Costello was a police captain in that city, and Dani knew he had given her a good word. They had worked together on several cases when she had been with the attorney general's office, and he was one of the few men who'd treated her with absolute fairness.

"I hope he gave me a good reference," she declared quietly.

Little stared at her, his eyes scrunched together, then relaxed. He puffed on the cigar and shrugged. "He said you were okay—for a woman."

Dani knew Costello hadn't said that, but she smiled. "I am sorry, Captain, really I am. But I knew the rodeo would be over in a few days, and we didn't have a thing to give you." Then she asked curiously, "What's all this business with the timing—trying to find out where people were when it happened?"

Little gave Stark a glance, seeming to debate something. Then he rubbed his forehead in a weary gesture. "Megan Carr didn't kill Clint Thomas. And she didn't shoot herself either." He glanced up, seeing the quick reaction in both Sixkiller and Dani. "It's a frame."

"How'd you get it?" Sixkiller wondered aloud.

"The Carr woman was holding the gun in her right hand—" Little began, but Dani exclaimed, "And Megan was left-handed!"

"Whoever did it slipped up," Little confirmed. Then he allowed himself a smile. "I hope you two don't have any plans for a while."

Dani asked in surprise, "Why not, Captain?"

"Because you're going to work for me." He grinned openly. "I'm not going to pay you, but you're going to stick with the investigation until you nail this guy. Then you'll bring him back here, and I'll take all the credit. How's that strike you?"

Dani glanced at Luke, then smiled. "It's the best offer I've had all day!"

16
A Woman in Black

Dani went by to feed Big Boy early Tuesday morning and found the Astrodome being torn apart. All the rodeo gear was being removed, and she barely had time to speak to Clyde and Fran, who were almost ready to pull out with a trailer load of stock.

"We're on our way to Fort Smith, Dani," Clyde explained hurriedly. "You going to be there?"

"Yes, but I'm staying for the funeral."

She meant Clint's funeral, for she had learned the day before that Megan's body would be shipped back to her home in Pennsylvania for burial. Clyde's lips drew tight. "We're not staying, Dani. I may be a lot of things, but I'm not that much of a hypocrite." He nodded good-bye, saying, "We'll see you in Fort Smith."

He went to the big diesel, climbed behind the wheel, and pulled out, with Fran following in a brand new Buick Roadmaster. Dani waved at her, then went to take care of the big horse. He lifted his head and made a slobbering noise when she appeared, and she smiled. Reaching into her pocket, she got some cubes of sugar and fed him. The memory of Biscuit came with the action, but she had learned to accept that. Big Boy needed exercise, so she rode him for an hour, finding out that she was learning his movements better.

"We'll take a first at Fort Smith, Big Boy," she promised, patting him on the shoulder. He moved his head around, and she rubbed his nose, then slid out of the saddle and groomed and fed him. Afterward she went by the Greenleaf Funeral Home, where Megan's body had been sent after the autopsy.

Dani had never liked funeral homes or the whole business of funerals. There was something pagan in the whole thing to her—something vaguely anti-Christian. She could never pin it down, and did her duty, but the sorrow and grief that permeated the services, as a rule, did not reflect the hope she saw in the New Testament. She had heard the funeral directors' rationale: "It's a memory picture," one had said to her when she had refused to go in and view the body of one of her college classmates. "We make them look as natural as possible. It will be the last time you'll ever see your friend, so that memory will remain with you."

But it didn't work that way for Dani. When the memory of her friend came afterward, it gave her no comfort, for the waxen-faced girl in the coffin lined with white silk was not the happy, glad-hearted girl she had known.

Now, she had no desire to look at Megan's body. A handsome silver-haired man in an immaculate suit met her as she entered the funeral home, and if he was offended by her jeans and dusty boots, he gave no sign at all. "Miss Carr? Yes, right down that hall. Please sign the book, if you will."

Dani walked down the thickly carpeted hall, paused outside a room with a stand and the name CARR on a small card over it. She picked up the pen, then looked down at the names. There were only a few, but the body had only been at the funeral home several hours. Bake Dempsey had been there and Hank Lowe. A few others she didn't know. She signed her own name, then entered the room. To her surprise she found a short, strongly built man standing at the window. He turned at once as she entered, his eyes boring into her.

"I didn't know anyone was here," she excused herself. "I'm Dani Ross."

"You the girl Megan was friends with?" He had a strong face, with a high forehead where his hair had receded, and his lips were strong and determined. Dani could see a little of Megan in his blue eyes and the shape of his nose, but there was a hardness in him somehow.

"Yes. I only knew her for a little while," she explained. Then she asked, "Are you her father?"

"Rich Carr." He nodded. He studied her with careful eyes, then smoothed his hair down with a thick hand. The light caught on a large diamond ring as he lowered it. "Yes, she was my daughter."

Dani asserted, "I loved her very much, Mr. Carr."

Suspicion flashed out of him instantly. "How could that be? You didn't know her."

"I don't think that's always the true measurement of love," Dani responded slowly. She sensed in Carr a strangeness, as if he were holding himself in tightly for fear of showing anger. "Can we sit down? I'd like to tell you what Megan meant to me."

Carr sat down beside her, his back stiff and his face fixed. "What I mean about time is that I've known some people for years and never managed to get close to them. I suppose you've done the same."

"Yeah, I have," he agreed briefly.

"But sometimes we just feel drawn to people. We know more about them and trust them more after having known them only a brief time than we do others we've known for years. It was like that for me with Megan."

"How'd you two get together?"

Dani hesitated, intimidated by his hard manner. But she took the plunge. "I took her to church with me, Mr. Carr."

"Church? Megan wasn't religious. None of us are." He gave Dani a direct stare, challenging her, "We're all atheists."

Dani sat there silently, then gently conceded, "That may be true of your family—but Megan had an experience with God. It changed her completely."

"I don't wanna hear it!" Carr snapped. Getting to his feet, he moved to the window and stood staring out at the oaks on the lawn. Dani said no more, but sat there with her head bowed. She began to pray silently and lost track of time. She was thinking of the hours she had spent with Megan, giggling over old movies, sharing experiences, and especially of Megan leafing through her Bible.

"Well, let's hear it!"

Dani looked up with a startled expression. Mr. Carr had come to stand over her and was staring down at her angrily. He saw her hesitate, then contended, "I don't believe a word of that Bible, but I wanna know what went on with you and her. I think you messed her mind up! Come on, what happened?"

Dani began to speak, though the words came with difficulty. She went back to her own experience, speaking of how she'd found Christ and how God had been with her ever since. Carr stood there, his feet planted, eyes skeptical, but he said nothing. Dani told him about her time in the silo, when it looked as though she and the others were going to die at the hands of a maniac. She told him how she'd put a woman she

243

loved in jeopardy of life imprisonment by discovering that she had killed someone. She even told him about killing the gunman in New Orleans and how it had almost destroyed her. Then she began to speak of how she had met Megan. Finally she told Carr how Megan had called on God in the little church. "I can't tell you how happy she was, Mr. Carr! Not only just then, but every day!"

Carr listened as Dani ended, "She kept saying how peaceful she was—and it was true!"

Carr suddenly turned and walked back to the window. He said nothing for a long time, then spoke in a muffled voice, "She called me." He didn't go on for what seemed like a long time, but when he turned, his face was contorted. "She told me all you just said—but I wouldn't listen. I—I told her she'd lost her mind and not to come home until she got religion out of her system."

Dani rose and went to Carr. "I know. She told me."

"She hated me, I guess, the way I talked to her?"

"No, Mr. Carr. Megan loved you very much. She thought you were the finest man who ever lived."

"She said that?"

"Yes, many times."

"Even after I bawled her out for getting converted?"

"Especially then," Dani told him. "Won't you sit down? There's so much I'd like to tell you about Megan."

They sat there for an hour, and Dani talked most of that time. The Spirit of God was in her, and as she spoke of the cross and of Jesus' death she saw what the gospel can do. Carr listened, incredulous at first, but he could not doubt the honesty of the girl who spoke. He knew people well, and he understood that this young woman was telling him the absolute truth.

Finally Dani confided, "She was filled with joy, Mr. Carr. I'll miss her so much. But I'll never grieve over her, for I'll see her again." Tears were in her eyes, and he saw them glistening there as she whispered, "Christians never say good-bye, you know!"

Seeing tears in Carr's eyes—which reminded her so much of Megan's—Dani explained, "I never shove anyone toward God, Mr. Carr. But Jesus said—'And I, if I be lifted up, will draw all men unto me.' I feel that's what's happening to you."

"Me? Become a Christian?" Carr asked huskily, ineffectually trying to laugh. "I'd be laughed at all over Philadelphia!"

"Do you care about that? Isn't what you're feeling right now the most honest thing you've ever known?"

He hesitated, then a look of wonder came into his eyes. "You know it is!" he whispered. "What *is* it that's happening to me? Is this what Megan felt?"

"Yes. Maybe a little different." Dani nodded. "A wise man once said something like, 'Every human being has a God-shaped vacuum in his soul—and he'll never know a moment's peace until God fills that space.' That's what becoming a Christian means, Mr. Carr. May I tell you how to let Jesus Christ come in and give you that peace?"

As Carr struggled and tried to say no Dani remained silent. Finally he blurted out, "I don't know how! Tell me!"

Thirty minutes later she was standing outside the funeral home, feeling drained, completely exhausted. Carr had followed her to the truck, and he asked anxiously, "You'll come?"

Dani nodded. "I'll be there. I'm no preacher, though."

Carr had called on God and finally had been able to smile and report, "I'm all right!" After Dani had given him her New Testament and asked him to read it through, he had demanded, "Will you come and help with her funeral?"

Dani had agreed at once to fly to Philadelphia, but now she was wondering if she'd been wise. Carr gave her a close study. His face was pale, and his eyes were red with weeping. "It won't be pleasant," he quietly informed her. "None of our friends are Christians. Most of them won't like what you'll have to say about Megan."

She smiled and then moved forward and kissed his cheek. "You'll be with me, won't you? That's all I need." Then she climbed into the truck, started it, and waved as she pulled away. "Read that Bible, Mr. Carr!" she shouted.

Carr waved back, then looked down at the worn New Testament. He opened it, read a few words, turned, and walked slowly back inside, his eyes on the book. He bumped into a young woman, who gave him an indignant look. "Sorry," he muttered, scarcely taking his eyes off the page. He disappeared through the door and went back to the room. He halted, then walked over to the casket and looked down.

For a long time he stood there, the New Testament in one hand. Finally he reached out and laid his hand on the lustrous black hair.

"Hello, Megan—," he whispered, and to his intense surprise, instead of grief, a well of joy arose in him, so strong that he could scarcely stand. Finally he looked down, and the words he'd heard from Dani came to his lips: "Christians never say good-bye!"

Clint Thomas's funeral the following Wednesday contained every element that Danielle Ross despised.

She went with Ruth, who clung to her. They had been escorted to the small private room, where Dani had looked down at Thomas's face. She had not intended to take part in this, but Ruth was so unsteady that Dani was afraid to release her hold on the woman.

The face in the casket only superficially resembled the Thomas she had known. The natural lines had disappeared, and with the eyes shut, all the lively spirits were gone. *Clint looks younger—but like a statue,* Dani thought. He was wearing a new, ornate cowboy shirt, one he would never have chosen in life, and she had heard one of the cowboys whisper in awe that a pair of eelskin boots costing $500 had been put on his feet!

Dani closed her eyes and felt glad when Ruth finally turned away. They went at once to a private room off the main auditorium, reserved for family of the deceased, and the funeral began as soon as four men in dress clothing wheeled the heavy bronze casket into place at the front of the auditorium.

The place was packed, and Dani recognized at least half a dozen celebrities sitting close to the front. Most of them were from show business or were sports stars, and she realized instinctively that they had been placed in the front for publicity purposes. Cameras clicked often, and their flashes reflected in the huge crystal lights overhead.

The front of the auditorium was a mass of flowers, and the heavy, cloying odor of them smelled unpleasant to Dani. Soon an organ began playing, very softly, and she recognized the strains of an old country-gospel song.

A famous, sultry country-Western singer came out, beautiful in a Western skirt and vest, and sang a poor rendition of "There Will Be Peace in the Valley." When she finished, she waited for the applause, realized there wouldn't be any, and left in confusion.

Two other thick and sentimental songs were sung by famous country-Western singers. Then the minister rose and came to the microphone. He was one of the most famous preachers in America, his image filling millions of TV screens each week.

He was a dramatic speaker, his eyes sparkling, his hands constantly drawing images in the air, and he told a story well, though Dani found his message shallow. He did not touch on the nature of death, the finality of it, or the possibility of judgment to follow. Instead he spoke with warmth and enthusiasm of the goodness and richness of life.

Then he managed to tie all life's joys to Clint Thomas, who was, he said, a man who understood life! Finally he dropped his voice to a whisper, saying, "This man is not dead! He will never be dead! As long as one cowboy rides a wild bronc to the last bell, and the pickup man comes by and takes him off—Clint Thomas will live!" A smattering of applause greeted his words, but the minister held his hand up for silence.

"Clint Thomas rode until he heard the buzzer sound! He made a good ride! And now—the Great Pickup Man in the Sky has taken him! Let us rejoice that he's now riding better horses in the green pastures where he'll never get thrown!"

Sixkiller was sitting beside Dani. He leaned toward her, whispering in her ear, "If you let this jelly bean preach my funeral, I'll come back and haunt you!"

Out of all the "mourners" who packed the auditorium, fewer than fifty gathered around the open grave at Restview Cemetery. Dani and Luke stayed with Ruth, taking their seats under the green canopy that swayed over the open grave. They were the only ones sitting; the others stood around the tent, looking inside.

Dani saw the long, black hearse disgorge its contents, and the eight pallbearers took the weight of the bronze casket. All were riders, including Bake Dempsey and Bill Baker, who manned the forward end of the coffin. They moved across the dry, brown grass, guided by the silver-haired funeral director, their faces brown and their hair slicked down. Moving under the tent, the director maneuvered the casket onto the thick, web-like strands mounted on a heavy brass framework. Carefully he let it slip forward until it was poised over the open grave; then he nodded, and the undertakers moved outside the tent. Another nod and a man stepped to the head of the casket.

It was not the famed television preacher this time, but a small man who pulled a black book from his pocket and began to read a formal ceremony.

Dani paid no heed to the familiar words. She was looking at the people instead, knowing some of them. One she had never seen before wore a black dress and had a black hat that seemed out of place. Dani studied her carefully. For some reason, the woman looked familiar, though Dani felt certain that she had never seen her before.

The stranger was not large and was slender of build and had very black hair and the dark skin of the south—perhaps Spanish or Mexican. She was staring at Thomas's casket with a pair of large black eyes and seemed hypnotized by the words the minister was reading in a rather mechanical fashion.

The woman was somewhere in her early forties, Dani judged, and attractive still, despite the lines in her face and the hands that were rough from hard work.

Tears were in her dark eyes, and she mopped them away with a tiny handkerchief. Suddenly she looked across over the top of the casket, and her eyes met Dani's. At once she flushed, then dropped her eyes.

Something in the gesture triggered a faint memory in Dani, and as the minister closed his book and began a prayer, Dani whispered to Luke, "Take Ruth back to town, then come back for me."

After the final amen, the three of them rose, and Sixkiller moved off with Ruth. The crowd drifted slowly toward the cars, which were parked on a gravel road a hundred yards away. The mourners were subdued as long as they were close to the swaying tent, but as they moved away, they began speaking more naturally. Dani drifted along, keeping to the rear, always with an eye on the woman in black. A clump of cottonwood trees rose to the left of the gravel road, and as the car doors began slamming and engines came to life, the woman went to stand in the shade of the trees. The cars sped away, raising a curtain of dust that came back as powder. Some of it came to rest on Dani's hair, but she paid no heed.

All the cars left, with the exception of a gray Toyota bearing the icon of a rental agency on the door. Dani waited for the woman to move away from the trees, but she did not. Finally, Dani walked across the dry grass, coming to stand a few feet behind the woman, who was standing with her arm against one of the trees, her face pressed against her forearm. Her back was heaving, and Dani heard her sobs.

"May I speak with you?"

At Dani's words the woman whirled and gave her a startled look. She wiped her eyes on the limp handkerchief, then shook her head. "I don't want to talk to any reporters."

"I'm no reporter. I was a friend of Clint's."

The woman had started for the Toyota but paused and looked more carefully at Dani. "What do you want to talk to me about?"

Dani took a wild guess, based solely on the impression that she had gotten during the funeral.

"I want to talk to you about your son, Mrs. Hardin."

Instantly, the woman cried out, and lifted her hand to her throat in a protective gesture. She stared at Dani. "How do you know me?"

Dani said gently, "I know your son. You *are* Boone's mother, aren't you?"

"Yes, I am."

"Could we talk for a little while, Mrs. Hardin?"

"I—I suppose so." Mrs. Hardin questioned, "How do you know Boone?"

"I'm a barrel racer. Boone and I got acquainted not too long ago. But I'm afraid he's in trouble, Mrs. Hardin."

"You can call me Faye." The woman shrugged, then gave Dani a frightened look. "Boone didn't have anything to do with Clint's death! He couldn't have!"

"The police are holding him. He was seen coming out of the trailer where Clint was shot."

"No! He couldn't do it! Not Boone!"

Dani didn't want to alarm the woman, but she knew that the police were going to be pressured. Any time a murder made the front page, the police became a target for many people who wanted to see instant results. Dani knew that Captain Little was aware that a murderer was loose and was likely to hold on to Boone Hardin. She explained that carefully to Faye Hardin, then offered, "I'd like to help Boone, Faye. If you'll tell me why he hated Clint Thomas so much, maybe we can do something."

"He didn't hate him!"

"Several times I heard him say things about Clint. Others have noticed it. It's going to come out when they're questioned."

Dani waited, and finally Faye Hardin's face seemed to grow softer. "He doesn't hate him. How could a boy hate his own father?"

Dani had half expected this, but when the other woman spoke it, it came as something of a shock. As for Faye's question, she knew that many young people hated their parents for various reasons. "Did Clint leave you when Boone was young?"

"He left before Boone was born." The voice was soft as she confessed, "I'm weak—so weak! Maybe I ought to hate him, too, like Boone says he does. But I never did! Never. I loved him always!"

Dani knew it all then, though not the details. A brief romance that had meant little to Clint Thomas. A child was born, a boy. He found out his father was Clint Thomas, a famous rodeo performer. And he spent his life learning to ride so he could outperform the father who left him.

Faye Hardin needed little urging, and she laid out the history of her tragic life—and that of Boone—pretty much the way Dani had guessed.

"Boone wanted to be like his daddy, miss," the sad-eyed woman explained. "That was all. He didn't hate him!"

But Dani knew that young Boone Hardin was in for a hard time. She thought of the watchful eyes of Captain Amos Little, and as she tried to assure the tearful woman that things would be all right, she found she didn't have confidence in her own words.

When Luke came back, she told him the development, and he promptly asked, "You going to tell Little?"

Dani nodded slowly, "No choice, Luke. Let's go do it now."

They left the cemetery, and as the pickup disappeared in a cloud of fine dust, a backhoe started up with a hoarse cough. It moved slowly toward the grave, where two men had taken down the tent and were loading it into a truck. The driver of the backhoe waited until they moved the astroturf covering, then stepped on the gas pedal. The yellow machine raised its shovel, looking something like a steel dinosaur as it bit into the raw red dirt and dropped the bite into the open grave.

17

Late Movie

As the two-engine plane touched down, Dani gave a sigh of relief. She knew it was foolish, but she could never let all her weight down in a small plane. It had been a white-knuckled flight for her from Oklahoma City, where the big jet from Philadelphia had set her down.

Ducking her head as she emerged, she spotted Luke at once and gave a wave. He came to take her hand, and as she stepped down to earth asked, "You make it all right?"

"Fine." The earth was good and solid after the bumpy ride, and she savored the concrete that held her firmly. Luke got her suitcase and led her to the Ford. Leaning back in the seat, she sighed and relaxed.

As he drove from the airport to the motel, he spoke idly of Fort Smith. "This is a good town. I used to come over here and rodeo when I was a kid. This used to be the gateway into the Indian territory of the Cimarron Strip. All kinds of bandits and road agents."

"This is where Judge Parker had his court, isn't it?"

"Yep. He hanged forty-one men in his day. Used to stand in his office at the window and watch the gallows. But he had to be rough, I guess. He sent his marshals into the territory, and lots of them didn't come back."

He turned off into the Holiday Inn and took her to room 211. "Had to be the second floor." He shrugged. "Nothing left on the first. Let's get a burger."

Dani changed into her riding clothes, then they went to McDonald's. After they had eaten and were on their second cups of coffee, he asked, "How was the funeral?"

Dani nodded, but there was a sober expression on her face. "I'm glad I went. It would have been hard for Mr. Carr, if I hadn't." She sipped the black coffee, thinking about the funeral. "It wasn't in a church. I guess none of the people there had been to church for a long time. And Mrs. Carr had asked a friend of hers to do the funeral. It was pretty grim."

"Not as bad as the one Clint got?"

"Yes, it was. Not so rah-rah and filled with platitudes. I think he was some kind of New Age disciple. He never came right out and said so, but he hinted around that Megan would be back in some other form."

"Reincarnation, huh?"

"Yes." Dani smiled slightly. "When I got up to give my 'trib-ute' to Megan—which is the way Mr. Carr managed to get me in—I was scared stiff! There I was, the only Christian in the place! But I decided before I arrived that there was no way I could please anyone there, so I just put my head down and flew right at it!"

"What was the title of your message? 'Turn or burn?'" Luke grinned.

"Oh, it wasn't that bad!" Dani protested. "I just told them what Jesus had done for me, then I told them how Megan had gotten saved a few days before she died."

"How'd that go down?"

"I don't think they recovered in time to tar and feather me." The memory of the looks of shock on the faces of the people came to her, and she smiled more broadly. "Well, I came right out and admitted that I believed in God, in the fact that Jesus Christ was the only way to get to heaven, and in the resurrection."

Sixkiller studied her, liking the fresh glow on her cheeks. She was wearing a green shirt he'd never seen before, and it picked up the green in her eyes. Her hair was windblown, and there was a fullness and richness in her that he always admired. He wanted to tell her so, but realized it was not the time, so he said instead, "I'd better tell you something before I lose my nerve. I've been thinking about Megan. Can't get her out of my mind." He drew a line around his coffee cup with a thick finger, his face sober and more thoughtful than Dani had ever seen it. "She got a raw deal—but I keep thinking about how happy she was after she prayed in church that day." He shifted his shoulders, gave her a sudden direct look, then added slowly, "I always thought religion was something for old ladies—but I can't think that anymore."

Dani knew a flash of joy, for she had longed for this man to find God for a long time. Wisely she didn't say much, but she put her hand on his thick wrist, feeling the corded strength of the man, and finally she acknowledged, "I'm glad you saw that in Megan, Luke."

He expected her to preach to him, but she sat there, her hand on his wrist—and he admired her as never before. "Well, I guess that bloodhound is after me, Dani," he admitted sheepishly. "Can't see how a hard number like me can cut it, but something's going on. Say, wouldn't ol' Ben Savage laugh his head off, if I got religion?"

Dani responded instantly, "No, he wouldn't. Some might, but not Ben. He's going through some of this himself."

"Savage?" Luke stared at her. "He sure keeps it to himself."

"It's a pretty private matter, Luke. Between you and God, mostly."

He stood up, telling her, "I got Big Boy put up. You want to go out to the fairgrounds?" She nodded, knowing that it was time to let the seed lie fallow for a time.

The Fort Smith rodeo was more of the old school, she soon discovered, than Houston. For one thing, it was not held under a roof, and this reminded her of her younger days of high-school and college rodeo. The air felt cooler in the mountains, with a tang that reddened the cheeks and made everyone feel better. The arena was set up on a high mound, and it was a stiff climb from the cars to the entrance gate.

"Guess we better get in the grand entry." Luke nodded. The familiar smells of horses and leather came to Dani as she followed him into the chute area. They passed the trailers bunched together, and Dani caught a glimpse of Hank Lowe's big Holiday. Cindy and Maury were playing beside it, and she waved to them. They waved back wildly, yelling something that she couldn't make out.

When Luke took her to the horse pens, Dani saddled Big Boy and mounted quickly. Everywhere riders were moving, and you could tell which ones would be in the grand entry, because their horses were fancily turned out with the parade saddle and other trappings. Big Boy moved restlessly under her, and she guided him to a place in the line that was forming. Ruth greeted her, and Dani pulled Big Boy in beside her. "Hello, Ruth," she returned the greeting. "How are you?"

"All right, I guess," Ruth answered in a fashion that meant she was not. Her naturally bright eyes were dull, and she had a washed-out expression. "You just get in?"

Dani had no time to answer, for the parade master was yelling at them, and the line moved forward. The stands were full, and the riders all smiled and waved their hats at the spectators, who applauded enthusiastically. Dani noticed that only with an effort Ruth summoned a smile. As soon as the parade was over, Dani suggested, "Ruth, let's go out to a really fancy place for supper tonight after the show."

The other woman hesitated, then explained, "I told Maury and Cindy I'd take them to the park for a picnic tonight before the show."

"That'll probably be more fun," Dani agreed at once. "Are you giving them a hand with their schoolwork?"

"Oh, a little." Ruth seemed embarrassed by the question, and after the parade she disappeared.

Dani did fairly well in the barrel race, coming in second, behind Ruby Costner. After she put Big Boy up, she went to watch the steer wrestling and was pleased when Luke took a first.

"I think it was all an accident," Luke commented, coming to stand beside her and slapping the dust out of his shirt. "I fell off the horse, and the steer happened to take a turn right into where I was headed. I had to get him down, or he would have trampled me." But he was grinning, and when she complimented him, he allowed, "You know, Dani, this stuff gets in your blood. I'd forgotten how it can get to you."

"Maybe you can give up catching crooks and give Bake a run for the number-one slot."

"Too old," he claimed regretfully. "I'm already over the hill. Thirty-five is old as the hills in this game. Which reminds me,

Boone's bunking with me again. I can't get over it—Clint being his father."

They walked away from the grandstands, finally deciding to go for a Coke. The refreshment stand was not crowded, and when Luke bought two giant-sized Cokes, they moved to the parking lot under the shade of a large walnut tree.

"I thought Little might hold Boone on suspicion," Luke reported. "He's the best bet so far."

"He didn't do it."

"Your womanly intuition tell you that?"

"No. You don't think so either."

Sixkiller took a long pull on the straw, then shook his head. "I've listened to the kid a lot since the killing. He had a love-hate thing for Clint. When he was in the hate mode, he might have done it in a blind rage. But he could never have killed Megan and faked a suicide."

"I guess Little knows that. He's really on the spot, isn't he?"

"Yeah. When the victim is a celebrity, it's always that way."

They both felt depressed, perhaps because there seemed to be so little chance of ever finding the killer. When the rodeo ended the next day, Dani said, "It's pretty hopeless, Luke. We might as well go back to the office."

"Well, most of the guys are going to Baton Rouge. That'll be a close place to quit from."

But after the final matinee, Tom Leathers came around as Dani was giving Big Boy a grooming. He stood watching her, talking about the rodeo. Then he spoke in a hard tone, "Well, he called again."

Dani's head jerked suddenly at his words. "You mean the Creep?"

"Yeah. Called thirty minutes ago. I was helping load the bucking stock for Clyde, and Wash came to say there was a call for me at the office."

"What did he say, Tom?"

"Said to go pick up cash from some of the performers."

"Which ones?"

"Bake, Ruby, Clyde, and J. D. Pillow. Said he'd called them, and they'd have the cash when we get to Baton Rouge."

"Did he tell you what to do with the money?"

"Naw. Said to hang on to it till he called again." He straightened up, gave her a sudden look, and started to speak. Then he apparently changed his mind and walked away.

Dani put Big Boy in the stall, grained him, then went on a search for Bake Dempsey. She found him grooming his roping horse. "Bake, did you get a call from the Creep?"

He paused in his motions with the currycomb, giving her a startled look. "I guess you got one, too?"

"Not this time. Tom told me. Was there anything different about the call?"

He studied the question, then shook his head. "About the same, I guess." Suddenly he threw the currycomb against the side of the stall, making his horse rear up. Ignoring him, Bake savagely cried, "I was hoping we'd heard the last of him!"

"Why would you think that?"

Bake picked up the currycomb, then gave her a sheepish look. "Oh, I had a nutty idea about him."

"You thought maybe it was Clint himself?"

A startled look came to Bake's face. "Yeah, I did." He squinted at her suspiciously. "You have the same idea?"

"It occurred to me," Dani admitted. "It could be any of us, Bake."

"Aw, not a woman," he objected quickly. "It's not a woman who calls."

"I could have an accomplice. I could have been in it, with Clint doing the calling."

Bake grinned at her sourly. "You out to destroy my faith in women?"

"It could have been Megan," Dani mused. "But now we know it's neither of them. Still it's got to be somebody in tight with us."

"Maybe it's me," Bake suggested, giving her a sly look. "I could be the Creep as well as anybody."

Dani didn't smile. "It could be you, Bake. It could be you who killed Clint and Megan."

Bake's face grew angry. "Come on, now! Why would I do that?"

"You think Captain Little hasn't gone over it?" Dani shot back. "He'd be saying, *Let's see now, who would benefit from the death of Clint Thomas? Why, that cowboy, Bake Dempsey! He'd be number one!* How much will you make now that Clint's not around to be champion?"

Dempsey stared at her unbelievingly. "You think I'd kill a man so I could win a contest?"

"Men have been killed for a lot less, Bake," Dani pointed out. "But Little has probably thought up a motive for the rest of us. And some of them aren't too hard to find."

"Like Ruby—because he dropped her?"

"Yes, or Fran. She really hated him for divorcing her."

"And Clyde hated him because Fran was still really in love with Clint."

Dani gave him a look of surprise. "You're pretty sharp, Bake. I didn't think a man would have noticed she was in love with him. But that's right. And it goes on down the line. Clint took Ruth from Hank Lowe. And now we know he deserted Boone and his mother, so that gives Boone a motive. Clay Dixon hated him for lots of reasons—Clint stole Ruby from him, was a better rider, and smashed Clay's head with a chair.

"I'll give you one you may not know," Bake confided. "A few years ago Wash Foster was a great rider. Matter of fact, he was neck and neck with Clint for the championship. At the finals, Wash got a killer bronc. He'd never ridden him, but Clint had. When he mounted the horse, Wash asked Clint how much rein to take, and Clint said to take the shortest rein he could, that the horse would keep his head high." Bake's eyes narrowed, and he shook his head. "The horse came out, and first thing he did was put his head right between his front feet. 'Course Wash wasn't ready for that, and he got snapped off. Fell right in front of the horse, and like I said, the horse was a killer. He smashed Wash so bad he was out for over a year— and he was never no good after that."

Dani nodded slowly. "And he blames Clint for it?"

"So would I!" Bake bit off the words. "No matter how close we are in the rankings, we always help each other that way. You should see the looks Rocky James gave Clint!" He caught her bewildered look, and shook his head. "You didn't know about Wash and Rocky? They're cousins."

"That's not much kin to hate a man for."

"It is in the hills of Tennessee, I guess. That's where they come from, and Rocky's a pretty surly cuss. He's stomped a few men that I know of. Used his boots on one. Would have killed him, if Wash hadn't pulled him off."

They stood there, suddenly silent, and then Dani questioned, "You going to pay up, Bake?"

"Nothing else to do, is there?" Unaccustomed gloom scored Bake's face. "All I've got is my ability to ride a horse or a bull. I put that on the line every time I climb aboard. No matter how good a man is, Dani, he's at a bad disadvantage with an animal that strong. And his hooves are about the same as concrete. If he kicks you in the head, it'll probably kill you. If he kicks you in the arm or leg, he'll probably break bones."

A grim smile touched the cowboy's broad lips. "There's an old myth around that says a horse won't step on you. I wish it was so, but it just ain't! A bucking horse is wild and half out of his head with fright. All of us have had hoofprints on us at one time or another." He broke off, gave her a self-conscious look, then allowed, "Well, it's a hard life, Dani. And all it would take to put me out of it would be one broken knee. Yes, I'm going to pay up. If that makes me a wimp, then it'll just have to be that way."

Dani shook her head, "I wasn't judging you, Bake." She hesitated before putting her hand on his arm. "Megan's death hit me pretty hard, I guess. Something in me wants to strike out at something, to get even. But there's no good in that. You only hurt yourself when you let bitterness take over."

Bake was caught by her words. He considered them, then shrugged. "I wish I could do that, Dani, but I can't. No matter how hard I try I can't just toss things off." Then he added, "I guess you Christians have to do that, huh?"

"That's what the gospel is, Bake. If I did what I wanted to do, I'd probably take revenge. But the Bible teaches that when we become Christians, Jesus Christ comes inside of us. And he loves sinners, so if we let him have his way, we can love them because he's inside."

"What if you don't let him?" Bake asked, a puzzled frown on his face. It was not like anything he'd heard in his brief visits to church.

"Then we have to pay for it!" Dani admitted wryly. "And it hurts, Bake! Once you've known the love of Jesus and the Spirit of God inside, when you offend him, it's mighty lonesome!"

"Oh, he runs off and leaves you?"

"No, no more than a loving father or mother would abandon a child who'd done wrong." Dani struggled for a way to explain; but all the theology she'd learned at seminary seemed to be too complex. Finally she explained, "Bake, I have a wonderful father. His name is Daniel. All my life he's been there when I needed him. We've always been very close. But sometimes, when I was a little girl, I'd disobey him. When I did, it wasn't so bad when he paddled me." Her eyes grew warm as she spoke of her father, and she smiled ruefully. "I could take that. But it was the look in his eyes, when I'd see that I'd really hurt and disappointed him! Boy, that was what ate my lunch! So it wasn't that I'd get a paddling, and it wasn't that I was afraid he'd chase me off. It was just that when we weren't close, because I'd let him down some way—it always broke my heart, and I'd find myself going to him, crying, and asking him to forgive me."

"That's pretty nice, Dani," Bake said. "You're telling me God is like that with you?"

"He's like that—with *everybody*, Bake. That's the way he *is*. Nobody is really *right* until they know God. That's what we're made for."

Fighting Bill Baker came scurrying across the dusty pens, calling out in his terrific bass voice, "Hey, Bake! Ya think we better get them horses loaded now, or whatta ya think?"

"Guess so, Bill," Bake answered. He was a tall, fine-looking man as he stood there, with the sun catching the lights in his curly red hair. His dark blue eyes regarded Dani carefully, and finally he said, "You're nice to have around, Dani. If I didn't know you were spoken for, I'd maybe throw my hat in the ring."

"Spoken for?" Dani asked in surprise.

"Why, I figured you and Luke were together," he countered. When she shook her head, he smiled. "Well, you could have fooled me. I didn't want to get that guy riled up. He'd pound me into the ground! Well, see you in Baton Rouge on Monday, Dani."

Dani said her good-bye, then went back to the motel. She showered, then watched *Flying Aces,* a Laurel and Hardy comedy. Right in the middle of it, she was swept with a sudden sense of loneliness. She had watched one of Laurel and Hardy's old films just a week earlier—and at their antics Megan had collapsed with helpless laughter. Dani could almost *feel* Megan's arms, for the girl had shrieked and clung to her, laughing helplessly until tears ran down her cheeks. They had watched *three* old comedies, staying awake until almost dawn, then had gone for pancakes and bacon as the sun came up.

Dani struggled with the grief that swept over her, the frustrating sense of loss that was like nothing else. But as the fat man and the skinny man cavorted on the screen, both of them long dead and buried, Dani could not control the tears. She got out of bed and turned the movie off, then washed her face and sat down at the small table. When she came to the sixty-ninth Psalm, the words seemed to leap out at her:

> Save me, O God; for the waters are come in unto my soul. I sink in deep mire, where there is no standing: I am come into deep waters, where the floods overflow me. I am weary of my crying: my throat is dried: mine eyes fail while I wait for my God.

She let those words sink into her heart, thinking, *This man knew what it was—he felt just as I feel now.*

She began to pray, and the grief began to ebb, leaving in her spirit a warm and comforting peace. Finally she read near the end of the psalm: "I will praise the name of God with a song, and will magnify him with thanksgiving."

She closed the Bible and went to bed, and the last thought in her mind before she slept was *Thank you, Lord, for letting me have Megan even for a little time. Now she is with you, and I will see her again someday!*

18

Sixkiller's Hour

The Baton Rouge rodeo didn't start until Monday, so both Dani and Luke slept in the day before. They got up at nine, met for a leisurely breakfast, then loaded Big Boy in the trailer. Dani led the way out of town, with Luke following her in Ben's Ford. The leaves were changing early, their red, orange, and brilliant yellows turning the mountain slopes into a crazy quilt. On Interstate 40 from Fort Smith to Little Rock, the hills lifted on either side of the highway, holding it carefully in a valley. As they passed by Lake Dardanelle, Dani noticed the huge, squat form of a nuclear stack belching forth white spumes of vapor. *They could have put that thing in an ugly part of the world, instead of spoiling a nice place,* she decided.

At eleven she spotted a small white church on the highway just west of a little town with the poetic name of Mayflower. A whim took her, and she pulled off onto the graveled parking lot. Sixkiller pulled in beside her and got out to ask, "Car trouble?"

"Nope. It's time for church."

Sixkiller looked around at the small church, then back to her. "Ross, you are a piece of work!" he attested, but didn't argue with her. The two of them went inside and instantly became the target of all eyes. There were no more than thirty people in the unpadded pine pews, and every one of them turned to watch as Dani and Luke took a seat.

The minister, a young man in his twenties, came at once to greet them. "I'm Dale Houseman. Glad to have you in the service," he offered shyly. He was thin and wore a threadbare suit with broad lapels—a style that was years out of style. "You're just driving through?"

"Yes," Dani smiled at him, and he blushed.

"Well, just join right in." He hesitated, then bit his lip nervously. "I hope you're not going to be disappointed. This is only my second Sunday as pastor. I—I haven't had much experience."

Luke looked at the young man and suddenly put out his hand. "Turn your wolf loose, Preacher!" he said loudly. "You got a prime sinner here to practice on!"

Pastor Houseman was taken aback, for a small sound of giggling followed Sixkiller's announcement. He swallowed hard, then nodded. A smile touched his lips, and he assured Luke "Jesus came to save sinners."

He turned and walked quickly back to the pulpit, nodding at an elderly man wearing a new pair of Big Smith overalls, who jumped up and cried, "Let's all stand and begin our service by singing hymn number one twenty-six. Everybody sing, now!" The pianist, a smiling young woman with bright eyes and not much musical talent began playing with enthusiasm.

Dani stood with the others and tried as best she could to get into the worship service. But she had difficulty. Not only was the piano player completely without a sense of timing, but the song leader was apparently tone deaf. He sang every hymn off-key, but was happily unaware of it. Dani felt heartily glad when the song service was over, but soon found that the sermon had to wait on a program by the youth. They had been, it appeared, to a camp outside of Little Rock, and the pastor wanted them to share their "testimonies" with the church.

A more reluctant crew Dani could not imagine! The smallest ones simply stood there, staring blindly out at the congregation, and the older ones were kept on the griddle until they said something good about their experience. Dani suddenly remembered that she and Rob, her brother, had been put through the same torture once after a Christian camp, and she had resolved that if she had anything to say about it, she would never lay such a burden on mere children!

Finally the preacher came to stand in the pulpit, and his hands trembled so violently that he dropped his notes—several pages of them—before he could even read his text. Finally he retrieved them, and with his face pale as paper read a few verses in a voice that threatened to break at any moment.

"My text is found in the Book of Daniel, the seventh chapter." He began to read, and to Dani's dismay, continued through the entire chapter. He was a poor reader, and the chapter set forth a vision seen by the prophet. It was filled with great beasts—lions with eagle's wings, a bear with three ribs in his mouth, a leopard with four wings and four heads, and one especially fierce beast with ten horns.

When Reverend Houseman had waded through the entire chapter, he said, "We will begin our study of the meaning of Daniel's prophecy, starting with verse four, where we left off last Sunday morning. . . ."

For forty-five minutes Dani sat there, her backside growing numb from the hard slats of the rough pew and her mind dulled by the intricate points of the sermon. She felt completely embarrassed for bringing Luke to such a service. It had been in her mind to expose him to the simple gospel, but she saw that young Pastor Houseman had been afflicted by what she called the prophecy virus, the tendency to become so enamored with the prophetic element in the Scripture that one could talk of nothing else. There was something almost diseased to it, and she had seen some bright young Christians who were faithful and productive servants rendered practically useless as they read innumerable books, attended prophetic conferences all over the country, and became too busy to carry on with the work of their churches.

Dani saw a sweet spirit in the young pastor, and she suspected that he had fallen under the spell of some highly gifted and magnetic teacher who was caught up in prophecy, whose work he was rehashing.

Finally he began to run down, and Dani heaved a sigh of relief. She had not dared look at Luke, thinking that he was planning to bawl her out for dragging him in to hear such a crashing bore.

Then the young man admitted, "I don't really know what your needs are. But I know what your answer is." He spoke earnestly for no longer than four or five minutes, telling how Jesus Christ had changed his life. "I hope that none of you will leave this place unsaved. Remember the Scripture says in Acts seven, verse fifty-one: 'Ye stiffnecked and uncircumcised in heart and ears, ye do always resist the Holy Ghost. . . .'"

As the pastor spoke those words and paused, Dani felt Luke's elbow strike her arm. Turning, she saw that his face was twitching, and his lips were trembling. Glancing down, she saw that his strong hands were clasped together, but even that didn't conceal the tremor in them.

The preacher, unaware of the impact of his words, went on, "These were the words of the first Christian to die for Jesus, you will remember, and as he died he cried out, 'I see the heavens opened, and the Son of man standing on the right hand of God.' When they stoned him to death, he cried out with a loud voice, 'Lord Jesus, receive my spirit.'"

"If you need to be saved," Pastor Houseman invited, "come forward, and we'll pray for you."

Pastor Houseman got the shock of his young life—for the broad-shouldered Indian dressed in Wranglers and a black cowboy shirt got up and stepped out into the aisle, treading on Dani's foot in the process. When he got to the front of the room, with tears running down his cheeks, he conceded, "I guess the bloodhound has caught me, Preacher. Start praying!"

Dale Houseman didn't have the vaguest idea what the cowboy meant by that, nor did he know what to do with the seeker. But an elderly woman in the first row did. She threw up her hands, shouting, "Glory to God and the Lamb forever!" Then she flew to Sixkiller and shouted, "Sonny, get on your knees!"

Dani sat there trembling as people crowded around Luke and began praying at the top of their lungs. As many as could get close put their hands on his shoulders or head or any portion of his body they could reach.

Dani wanted to scream, *No! That's not the way! You'll scare him to death with all that emotionalism!* But it seemed out of control, so she just slipped to her knees and began to pray for Luke. She was accustomed to quiet, dignified services, and the cries and moans of the people near Luke distracted her. But she prayed anyway—harder than she knew—for suddenly she was aware of a hard hand on her shoulder.

Startled, she looked up to see the elderly song leader standing over her, tears running down his brown cheeks, but with joy in his bright blue eyes. "You can shout now, Daughter!"

he cried. "Your man's done come through! He's washed by the blood of Jesus! Praise God!"

Dani could not get up, so he put his hard hands under her arms and pulled her to her feet. "Ain't that a sight, Daughter!" he exclaimed, waving toward the front of the church.

Dani stared at Luke, who was surrounded by the entire congregation, it seemed. His face was wet with tears. Dani had never seen him show *any* emotion to speak of, but now the barrier he kept between himself and the world was down. He suddenly lifted his hands and looked upward, and she heard him cry, "Thank you, God!" The worshipers joined in, and to her total surprise, Dani heard herself crying out to God with an unusual fervency.

Then the song leader said, "Go on, Daughter! Give your man some help!"

He gave Dani a little shove, and she moved down the aisle, her eyes fixed on Luke. He saw her coming, and his eyes leaped toward her. Then she ran to him, crying, "Oh, Luke! Luke!"

She could say no more, for she was weeping with great, choking sobs, holding on to him with a fierce strength, and his powerful arms drew her close. They stood there, suddenly unaware of the laughter and shouting of the other people. Dani had longed for Luke to know God, but had had little faith. He had been so hard and unyielding!

Now, as she finally stepped back and looked up into his eyes, she saw something new. Those eyes were still black as night—but there was a softness in them, and she reached up and touched his tear-stained cheek, whispering so quietly that only he could hear it, "Welcome home, Luke!"

To her surprise, afterward Dani discovered that her memory of the rest of that day was vague and fragmentary. She remembered well that Luke had insisted on being baptized—

right then! They had all gone to Lake Conway, where Pastor Houseman immersed Luke in plain view of several bass fisherman. Dani had the presence of mind to use Megan's video camera—a gift presented to her by Megan's father—and that scene was there for them to watch. She got one still picture with her Minolta, and it was enlarged and placed next to the portrait of her Civil War ancestor.

But after the baptizing, she could not remember details. She led the way through Little Rock, then took 167 past El Dorado and on into Louisiana, but it was all a blur. She could remember that many times Luke passed her in the Ford, pointed to a small cafe, and they got out. As they drank coffee, he talked, his face lit with excitement, and he asked her questions—Bible questions, some that she had trouble answering.

They got to Baton Rouge late that night and both checked into the Courtyard, but got little sleep. He took her out to Shoney's, and they ate breakfast—and still he talked.

Finally Luke grew quiet and she sat there, staring at him. "Luke, I'm so tired I can hardly sit up!"

He looked at her, then agreed, "Me, too. But I'm too excited to sleep." He closed his eyes, but almost at once opened them. "What happened, Dani? How come I got saved at that little church?"

Dani had thought about it a great deal. She disclosed, "I think it was partly for my sake, Luke. I had some pretty firm opinions about how people came to God. They had to go through certain steps, and if they made them all, they were saved." Then she laughed and put her hand on his arm. "But you broke every rule, Luke Sixkiller! All of them!" Shaking her head she said, "It was a terrible song service. I thought you had to have beautiful worship. It was an awful sermon! Poor Pastor Dale! And then when God *did* start dealing with you, oh, my! What a mess!"

"It just about scared me to death," Luke admitted. "I went to a Pentecostal-type church once, when I was just a kid. I thought they were all nuts!"

Dani bit her lip, then conceded, "I would have said it more gracefully, Luke, but I thought about the same. But no more! I learned something today, Luke. God can use any method he wants to—And he can throw any of *our* methods out the window."

Luke spoke thoughtfully, "That really was a dull sermon. I didn't understand one word of it. But when he read that Scripture about 'You do always resist the Holy Ghost,' it was like getting shot in the heart! That did me in, Dani, and when he talked about the guy seeing Jesus—I don't know, it just was like. . . ."

"Was like what, Luke?" Dani asked quietly.

"Well, don't think I'm nuts," he declared, his face intensely sober. "But just for a second, well, it was like *I* could see Jesus, too! Oh, not plain, maybe, but I thought he was there, looking at me, and I started to cry." He looked at her. "Dani, I haven't cried since I was ten years old!"

"That's—that's *beautiful*, Luke!" Dani exclaimed. "I'm so happy for you!"

He nodded. "Dani, I see what you've been going through. About shooting that guy." He thought hard, then looked down at his hands. Looking up he acknowledged, "It's going to be pretty tough, being a detective of homicide and a Christian."

"Don't worry, Luke." Dani smiled. A thought made her lips grow soft, and she said, "You're under new management, Luke. No telling what God will do with you!"

19
Deep River

The LSU Rodeo and Livestock Show was held in John F. Parker Coliseum, a large, stucco, domed arena on the campus of Louisiana State University. After riding in the vast universe of the Astrodome and under the open skies in Fort Smith, Dani felt cramped and uncomfortable here. There was no chance to practice, so on Monday night, she shot out into the arena at full speed, then spotted the barrels, much closer than she had anticipated. Ruth had tried to warn her about this, but she overreacted, yanking Big Boy's head around much too soon. It confused the big horse, and he swung to the right instantly. The timing was off, and when he careened around the barrel, he struck it solidly, sending it rolling. This upset Dani, and it didn't help matters when the next two barrels went the same way.

Face burning with embarrassment, she ducked her head and drove Big Boy at full speed out of the arena. She came to a halt, slipped off to the ground, and patted Big Boy's neck.

As usual when she lost, she wanted to scream or kick something, but she kept it bottled up inside.

Then a voice cried, "Hey, that was great! You got all three of them!"

Whirling, she found Ben Savage nodding with approval. He was wearing a pair of slacks, a blue knit shirt, and a pair of disreputable Nikes that had once been white.

Dani opened her mouth, prepared to scream at him, then realized that he was needling her. "It takes lots of practice," she conceded with a casual shrug. "Some of the girls go for days without getting a single barrel, but I can usually nail at least one."

He came over and stood in front of her, his hazel eyes alert. His coarse black hair was unruly, and he seemed to move easily, betraying no sign of the beating he had taken. "You okay?" he asked casually, his broad gash of a mouth relaxed.

"Yes, Ben." She studied him carefully, not wanting to show how glad she was to see him. "How about you?"

"Guess I'll live through a couple more clean shirts," he answered. "Still a little stiff." He eyed Big Boy cautiously, then confirmed, "I have an exaggerated respect for large animals. In fact, I'm scared spitless of them."

She laughed. "Let me put him up, then we can go talk." She unsaddled Big Boy, put him in a stall, then suggested, "Let's walk for a while." She led him out, and as they strolled under the huge live oaks decked with moss, she spoke animatedly. They found a bench in front of one of the classroom buildings and sat there, Ben listening as she told him about Megan. He only made a few comments.

Dani gave him a strange look and began, "Something happened on our way here from Fort Smith." She paused, suddenly aware that she wanted very much for Savage to understand. He saw her trying to arrange her thoughts and wondered what was coming. Finally she disclosed, "Well, Ben, we stopped at a little church outside of Little Rock—and Luke was converted."

Ben had expected almost anything else, and he blinked with surprise. He tried to adjust his concept of Sixkiller to the sudden image of the man that her words had stirred—but he could not reconcile the two. Dani, he saw, was waiting for him to speak, and he stated quietly, "I know you're happy about that, Boss."

Dani wanted to say, *I wish you'd come to that place, Ben!* but did not. She spoke of it, giving Savage the details, then ended, "It's going to be tough on him, Ben."

She was, he realized, asking him for support. "Sure. But he can make it. Luke's a pretty stubborn fellow. Gets his head down and runs at it—whatever he does. Might not fit in the regular pattern, though."

"You're right about that, Ben." Dani realized that Savage had expressed his promise to do what he could for Luke in his new way. She warmed to him, wanting to put her arms around him, to hug him hard, and say, *That's my Ben!*

But she did none of these things, afraid that if she let herself go, she would pass over some sort of invisible and tenuous line that lay between them. Instead, she shook her hair in a restless gesture, got to her feet, then blurted out, "Let's go watch the bull riding. Luke's giving Bake Dempsey some competition."

They walked back into the arena, coming to stand close to the chute where Clyde was dealing with a huge brindle-striped Brahma with heavy, blunt horns and a massive head. The animal's hump was almost level with the top of the chute.

Suddenly Sixkiller stood beside them. "Ain't he a little darlin'?" he said, grinning at Savage. "How you coming, Ben?"

Savage stared at Luke, then back at the bull. He nodded and answered, "I'm doing all right." He stared at the bull, who raked his horns across the wooden frame of the chute with a loud bang, then shook his head. "Good luck."

"Thanks. Let's go out to eat as soon as I win first place." He left and mounted the chute, then settled himself carefully onto the bull. He set his grip, then nodded, and the gate swung open. The animal went into a tight, cyclonic spin, but Luke stayed aboard until the buzzer sounded. He came off, hitting the ground hard, and when one boot caught in the dirt, sprawled headlong.

Dani's hand caught at Ben, and he felt her nails bite into his arm.

The bull saw Luke and made a dive at him, but somehow Hank Lowe slipped between the bull and Sixkiller. At that instant Rocky James made a dive at Luke, seized him by one arm, and with all his strength snatched him up and hurled him to the left. The bull caught a glimpse of Luke, but Lowe jumped at him, slapping him in the face with his hat. The bull stopped in confusion but suddenly lowered his head and charged so quickly that Hank had no time to dodge. As the bull got to him, he grabbed the near horn with both hands and vaulted over the bull's head. The crowd broke out in star-tled yells and wild applause. The hazers moved in, roped the bull, and dragged him from the arena.

Dani moved without planning it, going to Luke and ask-ing in a not quite steady voice, "Are—you all right?"

"Sure." Luke turned and threw his arm around Lowe's shoulder, giving him a hard hug. "Hey, I owe you a steak for that."

Then Ruth was there, coming from the rear, and her lips were trembling. She seemed to be unsteady on her feet, and

Hank had to reach out to grab her. She held to his arm, gazed at him, and finally quavered, "I thought you—"

She couldn't finish, but a light came into Hank Lowe's eyes. "No problem, Ruth," he comforted her, then took a deep breath and smiled broadly. Without letting go of her shoulder, he ordered, "Well, you folks better move out of here. That next bull is on his way."

Ruth loosened her hold, but as she moved out of the arena, Ben affirmed, "I guess that was pretty good, Ruth. He saved Luke's bacon, didn't he?"

"Yes—but who's going to save him?" She shook her head. "When did you get here, Ben?"

The two of them talked, but later when Savage, Sixkiller, and Dani went to Chris's Steak House for a late supper, Ben remarked, "Ruth looks pretty down. Pretty hard jolt, losing what she wanted most."

Dani didn't comment, and Luke only maintained, "She'll be all right, Ben." Then he shook his head, grinned slightly and asked, "You hear about me? I'm ready to start passing out tracts on the street."

"I'm glad for you, Luke," Ben said instantly, and a warm light filled his eyes as he smiled at Sixkiller. "You'll be a winner with God, just like you've been one with the department."

Luke was taken aback, for he had expected that Savage would be cool, if not antagonistic to his new life-style. "Thanks, Ben. I know you mean that."

The two men said no more, but Dani felt happy. She sat there between them, and soon they began talking about the case. She went over all they had, and when she was finished, Luke explained, "It's not going too well. I don't see how we can flush this guy out."

"Only two ways to motivate folks," Ben advised slowly. "Either a carrot or a stick. But his carrot is the money he's raking off—and we don't have a stick to use on him."

As he spoke, Dani had one of those moments of revelation. Suddenly something had popped into her mind and she reported, "Hey, I think I know how we can motivate our man."

"With a carrot?" Savage asked, one eyebrow high.

"No, with a stick."

"Dani, how are you going to use a stick on him, when you don't even know who he is?"

"That's my idea," Dani continued. "Now listen to this. . . ."

The two men listened intently as she outlined her plan. As soon as she finished, both began to shake their heads. At the same moment, they exclaimed, "No way!" and Ben said, "It's too risky."

But Danielle Ross would not be denied. For over an hour the three disputed the idea. Finally Ben shook his head wearily. "I don't know why I argue with you! I never win."

"We'll have to build in lots of backup," Luke warned. "And the thing that bothers me most is that backups are never very close. You might have to handle this guy yourself, and—"

Dani observed slowly when he paused, "You don't think I can use a gun."

"That's it." He nodded. "And *you* don't know either."

"Well, I'll probably know before this is over," Dani pointed out practically. Then in a businesslike fashion that covered the agitation that had already begun to stir in her, she insisted, "Now, let's get this thing firmed up!"

Dani caught Bake Dempsey the next afternoon just as he was going to get his horse for the calf-roping event. "Bake, can you do me a favor?"

"Well, I got to get ready for—"

Dani cut him off, "Oh, not *now*, Bake! But after you finish, will you give this note to Ben for me?"

Bake's mind was on the event, and he nodded absently, saying, "Yeah, sure, Dani."

She turned and ran out of the chute area. Bake stared at her, his attention caught by her excitement. "Wonder, what's her hurry?" After the calf roping was over, he saw Ben talking to Ruth. "Hey, Ben," he cried, taking the note out of his pocket and handing it over. "Dani asked me to give you this."

"Thanks." As Bake walked away, Ruth asked, "Do you think this will work, Ben?"

"Maybe. But I don't like it." Then he shook off the frown that creased his brow, and glanced at her. "We'll catch this guy, Ruth."

Ruth gave him a wan smile. "Doesn't seem to matter too much now, Ben. Clint's gone." She looked very tired, and when she left him, he suddenly kicked the dust in an outburst of violence he could not contain.

"Women!" he complained bitterly, then wandered back toward the chutes, stopping when Tom Leathers called, "Hey, Savage, come here, will you?"

The call came at nine o'clock. Dani had not left her room, afraid she would miss it. About eight she had gotten hungry but had ordered a sandwich from room service. She had paced the floor nervously and was still pacing when the phone went off, the shrill ring making her jump.

She put her hand on the phone, took a deep breath, then picked it up. "Hello?"

"Hello, Dani."

"Oh, it's you!" Dani made her voice weary. "I thought I'd hear from you. How much do you want this time, you bloodsucker?"

"Oh, I didn't call to talk about money, Dani." A chuckle sounded and he said, "That surprises you, doesn't it? Can't you even guess why I'm calling?"

"No. What is it?"

"Why, I've got a friend of yours with me." There was a pause, and the sound of some sort of struggle, after which she heard the Creep say, "Speak up or I'll cut your throat!"

Dani stood there, fear beginning to have its way. This was not the plan! Then she heard another struggle, and then—

"Dani! Don't come here! He's not—"

It was Luke's voice! Dani gripped the phone so tightly that her hand ached, and finally heard the hateful voice complaining, "Your friend isn't very cooperative, Dani. But you'll be more reasonable, won't you?"

"What—what do you want?"

"Why, you know that, Dani! A smart lady like you?" Dani stood there, paralyzed, and the voice, muffled as it was, grew cold. "Bring that evidence to me right now, or your friend will be dead!"

"Wait—!"

"No! I won't wait. You've got exactly one hour to get the evidence and put it in my hands! Listen, now, and I'll tell you exactly where to bring it." He spoke rapidly. When he was finished, he warned, "You bring the police, and Sixkiller is dead. You might get me, but I'll finish him off first. Now, you've got one hour—one hour, that's all!"

The phone went dead, and Dani stood there, her mind frozen, it seemed. But she shook her head, said a quick prayer, then went to the dresser and took out the .38. After she had belted it around her waist, she took out another gun, a nickel-plated .25 Beretta automatic. She pulled the clip out, checked the loads, then shoved it back in and levered a shell into the chamber. Then she went to the closet, pulled out a worn pair of calf-high boots, and pulled them on. Finally she slipped the Beretta into the piece of canvas she'd had a shoemaker tack inside one boot that afternoon. When she got up and walked, it felt uncomfortable, but not unbearable. She sat down on the chair, bent over, and pulled the automatic free, then replaced it. Feeling a little ridiculous, she picked up the Rapala filet knife she'd bought at a sporting-goods store and slipped it into the other boot, sheath and all.

Still sitting there, she prayed quietly for no more than five minutes, then rose, picked up an old black leather briefcase she'd prepared, and left the room. The Silverado sounded very loud as she started the engine, and as she pulled out of the parking lot of the Courtyard and turned off onto Interstate 10, she put everything out of her mind but the task ahead of her. She was not afraid for herself, which was a shock to her, but she felt terrified that Luke might suffer. She could not put the thought of Megan out of her mind and prayed again, *O God, don't let it happen to Luke!*

She took a right at the Essen exit and followed it until it crossed Perkins and became Staring Lane. The stars were out, she noticed as she drove carefully toward the river, and she wished they were not so bright, for darkness might well be her only ally.

Crossing Highway 30, she saw the low-lying form of the levee, then came to the dirt road that led to the top of it. When she left the street lights, there were only the headlights to make twin cones in the hot darkness. The smell of the river came to her, rank and strong, and she could see flashes as the moon and stars threw their reflections on the broad bosom of the river—the Mississippi River, the largest river in North America. People from the South called it the Old Man.

She kept one eye on the odometer, measuring off exactly 2.6 miles, and at once she saw the turnoff, on the river side of the levee, just as he had said.

Carefully she turned the truck onto the steep, slanting side of the levee and followed it until the land grew level. Then the road turned right and disappeared into a forest of willows that lay ahead. For a while the road itself was no wider than the Silverado, but it broadened out suddenly, and there in the twin beams of her lights, she saw a small, unpainted, one-room cabin with a white pickup parked in front of it. She stopped the car, turned the switch, then took a deep breath. Her hands were steady as she opened the door.

Just as her boots sank into the moist alluvial mud, a voice caught her: "Now, just hold it right there, Dani." She stood stock-still, and a bright light caught her in the face, blinding her. "Just put your hands on the cab!"

Dani turned and placed both hands on top of the cab. She could see the river in front of her, flickering with a million ripples, and then she felt a hand going down her side and flinched in spite of herself.

"Easy now! Ah! Here we are!" The weight of the .38 left her side, and the voice directed, "Now you can turn around, Dani."

When she turned, he kept the light on her, but chest high, not in her eyes. "You bring my little present?"

"In the cab."

"You just move real careful, now, and let me have a look." Dani moved to one side and was able to make out a dark form, but no more as he opened the door. He leaned over, took out the briefcase, then opened it. Inside were five audio cassettes and three videotapes, all in plastic cases.

"Now, you've got to convince me that these aren't just copies."

Dani said dully, "I was going to do that tomorrow. One time I ruined a video, and I asked Ben to take care of it."

There was a silence and then a low laugh. "Well, I think I'll buy it. Now, wouldn't you like to know my real identity?'

Dani nodded, and again he chuckled. Then he put the light up so that it shone on his face. "Now, Dani, you know who I am."

"Clyde!" Dani whispered.

Lockyear laughed and spoke in his own voice, "Dani! Dani! I really am disappointed in you! You'll never know how many hours I put in worrying that you'd tumble onto ol' Clyde!"

"Why, Clyde?" Dani asked. "You've got more money than you need."

"Dani, I'm a little pressed for time," Lockyear evaded her question. "But if you'll just move down toward the shack, you can join your old buddy Luke. We've got a little trip to make, and I'll entertain you on the way. Move down toward the house."

Dani stumbled down the rough pathway, the light from his flashlight piercing the darkness. When she was almost to the house, he ordered, "Now, take a right—out to the boat dock."

Dani moved to where an aluminum boat was tied to a rude dock, and when she got near the prow, Lockyear reported, "Here we are, Luke. Just like I said! I knew Dani wouldn't let her good friend down! Now, Dani, turn around and hold out your hands. And be careful!" The click of a hammer being drawn back was loud in the stillness and as she held out her hands he said, "It takes two hands to do this, but if you move, why, you won't need to be tied, will you now?"

She didn't answer but stood silently as he tied her hands tightly with a length of heavy cord. "Now, then, you get in the front of the boat with Luke, and we'll make our little trip."

The boat rocked as Dani stepped in, and she almost fell, but Clyde caught her. "Watch it now!" he warned, then steadied her. "Just move down with Luke."

Dani walked carefully to the bow of the boat, then sat down on the thwart beside Luke. In the brightness of the moonlight she could see that he was tied hand and foot and that blood was trickling down from his left eyebrow.

"Sorry, Dani," he apologized quietly. "My fault. I let him get behind me with a gun."

"It's all right, Luke," Dani comforted him and, moving awkwardly, managed to put her bound hands on his. "You mustn't take this on yourself."

There was the sound of a cord being pulled, and the outboard roared into life, churning the water and sending the smell of burning oil across to where they sat. Clyde kept it revved up, then throttled back. He put the light on Dani and Luke, announcing, "Here we go." He eased the boat out into the black water, and at once the power of the river took it.

"Strong current here," Lockyear remarked. "Used to fish here a lot. Long time ago, but it's still the same."

Dani smelled the rank odor of the river and felt Luke's body pressing against her. She knew that he was struggling wildly to free his hands. No hope of that, for her own wrists were fastened as if they were in a vise, and Clyde would have been much more careful with Luke.

The waves slapped the prow of the boat, the combined weight of Dani and Luke keeping it low. As they rocked up and down like a seesaw, Dani felt the Beretta pressing against her leg, but the light in Clyde's hand was steady, centering on her and Luke.

"Why did I do it?" Lockyear queried suddenly, his voice rising over the sound of the outboard. "I really don't know."

He sounded rather puzzled. "I suppose I must have enjoyed seeing the big heroes squirm!"

The bank they had left was now a vague, shapeless mass, and Dani could see the glow of the lights of Baton Rouge over the levee. Suddenly Clyde opened up the throttle, and the boat lunged ahead.

Luke said, "Dani, he's going to drop us in the middle of the channel."

"I know."

Luke pressed against her. "I'm sorry. Wish I'd played it different." Then he acknowledged, "Good thing we stopped at that little church. It makes a big difference."

Dani started to answer, but suddenly the outboard was throttled back. *This is it* leaped into her mind. She was certain Clyde would stand up to shoot them, and there would be one moment when she could act—that moment when he was getting to his feet.

The engine shut down completely, and Dani flexed her hands. She would have only one chance to draw the Beretta and no time at all to think. She sat there waiting.

Clyde piped up, "Well, I hate—"

Dani could not see him, for the light was in her eyes. But she felt the boat shift as he came to his feet, and the light moved down to the bottom of the boat.

With one motion, she reached down and thrust her right hand into the boot, and the handle of the weapon seemed to leap into her hand. She came up with it at the same moment that Clyde got his balance and swung the light upward.

He must have seen the gun, for he cried out, "What—?"

Whatever he might have said was drowned by the sharp, flat reports of the automatic.

Ben had warned when he'd given her the Beretta. "It'll take more than one shot, Dani. I knew a vice cop who had to use the twenty-five he carried strapped to his leg as a hideout. He emptied it into a pusher, and the guy took every slug—then pulled his own gun and shot the cop in the chest."

The air seemed filled with the sharp, angry *splatting* sounds the small gun made. Dani pulled the trigger as rapidly as she could, but most of the bullets went out over the water, for one of the first slugs had caught Lockyear, knocking him backward. He made a tremendous splash as he hit the water.

He was not dead, for as Dani dropped the Beretta and drew the filet knife, she heard the gurgling cries of the wounded man. She turned and cut the rope that bound Luke's hands, crying, "Cut me loose! He'll drown!"

Luke cut her loose, and Dani made a dive at the flashlight, which had fallen into the boat. Sweeping it up, she shone it over the dark waters, spotting Lockyear at once. The boat was drifting away from him, and she could see his arms thrashing the water. She was not good with engines, but she was an excellent swimmer.

Time to find out if all those Red Cross lifesaving courses were any good! she thought. She threw the light on Luke, who was cutting his feet free, then called out, "Luke—here!" She tossed him the light, then kicked off her boots.

"Hey—" Luke cried out in alarm. He juggled the flashlight, almost losing it, then surged to his feet. "Dani! Don't do it! This river is treacherous!"

Dani dared not think about it. She jumped over the side, and the warm waters covered her head. At once she felt the power of the current but stopped to listen. She heard Lockyear's thrashing and threw herself into a strong crawl. Almost at once, she heard the sound of the outboard start up, and at the same moment, her hand struck Lockyear. He grabbed at her, pulling her down, but she doubled up and kicked free by driving her feet into his chest. Somehow she made him out as he came up and grabbed him from behind. "Be still!" she shouted. "We're all right!"

Those courses did work, after all! Dani thought as she kept the two of them afloat. It would have been hard to swim, but all she had to do was keep their heads above the surface. Lockyear lay still now. Whether he was dead or just letting her keep him alive, she didn't know.

Then the boat came drifting close, and the light flashed in her eyes. Thankfully she felt Sixkiller's strong hands. "Take Clyde first," she told him, and Lockyear's body was hoisted as if he weighed nothing.

She heard the body fall into the boat; then she held up her hands and at once was pulled out of the grip of the river. Dani would have fallen, but Luke held her, putting both arms around her.

"We'd better see about Clyde—" Dani suggested, but he didn't release her.

The boat was rocking slightly, and he finally observed, "Well, I read somewhere if you save somebody's life, you're responsible for her as long as you live."

Then he laughed and so did she. "It would be a full-time job, I'm afraid!"

Luke had released her and was starting to bend over to examine Lockyear. But he paused, gave her a serious look, then retorted, "That would be just about right!"

20
"What Could Be in His Heart?"

A ll right, let's have it quiet!" Captain Amos Little's voice shut down the babble of voices that filled the room, and the group sitting around the large walnut conference table turned to where Little stood, at one end.

Dani, sitting at the other end, beside Luke, glanced to her left where Boone Hardin, Ruby Costner, Hank Lowe, Ruth Cantrell, and Fran Lockyear were ranged. They all looked bewildered, as did the four who sat across the table from them—Clay Dixon, Tom Leathers, Bake Dempsey, and Bill Baker. Ben sat in a chair along one wall, next to a man named Edgar Dalton, one of Little's men.

"What's this all about, Captain?" Clay Dixon demanded. "You can't pull a man out of bed and drag him to the station without a warrant!"

Little gave him a sudden hard look. His eyes were red-rimmed, and fatigue put more lines in his face than nature had. Dani saw that his temper had not improved since she had left him two hours earlier. She had called him as soon as she and Luke had gotten Lockyear to a hospital, and he had flown from Houston in his own plane at once. Getting in at two, he had grilled Luke, Ben, and Dani for hours, then sent Ben and Luke to get anyone they could find who'd been paying Lockyear.

"I can arrange a warrant," Little grated, his eyes fixed on Dixon. "You can spend a few days in the tank as a material witness."

"Hey, wait!" Dixon broke in. "You don't have to do that."

Little considered Dixon, obviously weighing some dire plan for the cowboy, then ordered, "Keep shut." He looked around the table. "I've got no jurisdiction in this state. The chief of police has allowed me to come, and I wanted you here. Some of you have been paying extortion money to Clyde Lockyear. Before he's charged and extradited to Houston, I wanted a hearing. A few things need to be cleared up. Edgar, go bring him in."

The man sitting beside Ben rose and left the room. Fran Lockyear stared at Little, her face pale under her makeup. "There must be a mistake, Captain," she complained. "My husband has been paying money himself. I know! I handle the cash, and he's been paying big money for months now. I was even there when he gave it to Tom Leathers to be delivered."

"Mrs. Lockyear, if you'll just wait, you'll have a chance to ask questions." As Little said this, Dalton came in with Clyde Lockyear. "Just have a seat, Lockyear," Little directed, indicating a chair beside him.

"You can't do this!" Lockyear sputtered. He was wearing the clothing he'd gone into the river with, and it was limp. He glared at Dani. "You can't force an injured man to go through this!"

Fearing the worst, Dani had sat in the emergency room of the hospital while they worked on Lockyear. Blood had covered his left side, and it was the greatest relief she'd ever known when the young doctor had come out saying, "He's not hurt much. Bullet hit a rib and plowed some meat off his side. Just a bad scratch." Luke had held her steady when her legs had gone weak, and even now she was still filled with wonder at how minor the wound was.

Ben had found them there, heard Luke describe the shooting, and then had grinned. "I told you, Boss, those popguns won't do. If you'd hit him dead center with three or four of the bullets, he'd still be alive and kicking."

Now, looking at Lockyear, Dani thanked God that he was alive. He looked smaller in his wrinkled clothing, and a thread of fear laced his voice as he argued loudly with the captain that he had a right to call a lawyer.

"You're not under arrest, Mr. Lockyear," Captain Little explained, a smile tugging at his lips. "As soon as this meeting is over, you will be arrested, and *then* you can have your call."

"I don't understand why we're here, Captain." Bake Dempsey had a puzzled look on his face. "I mean, you've got the goods on him, haven't you? I hear you found enough evidence in his trailer to prove that he's the man who's been clipping all of us."

Little shook his head. "There are a couple of angles I want to bring out. But for the moment I'm going to ask Miss Ross to say a few words. She's been working with my department on this matter, as one of my assistants."

Luke pressed his knee against Dani's, and she knew he was laughing inside. Little had been livid when he found out what had happened, promising to have her license revoked. It had taken a lot of explaining and a promise that Lockyear was going to be tied up like a Christmas turkey for him to take back to Houston before he'd grudgingly agreed. Dani returned the pressure, realizing that if she didn't come through, Little would bury her.

Getting to her feet, she smiled at those around the table. "Thank you, Captain Little. First, let me say Captain Little must be credited with apprehending Clyde Lockyear. I've been around to carry out his instructions, but he deserves all the credit." Ben and Luke exchanged sly winks; both of them wanted to smile at Little, who was lapping it up as a cat drinks cream.

"And I want to apologize to those of you I've had to deceive. Going undercover means fooling everyone. You'll never know how often I wanted to confide in some of you—" At this point Little snorted, and Dani quickly continued, "But you do deserve to know what's happened. That's really what this meeting is for."

"How long have you known it was Clyde, Dani?" Ruth interrupted. "I thought you said you got a call from the Creep while you were actually with Clyde. He couldn't have called you if he was *with* you, could he?"

"No, he couldn't." Dani gave Clyde a slow look, then shook her head. "That's what threw me off. I suspected most of *you* at one time or another, but since I was with Bake and Megan at the table, and Clyde was singing when the call came, I crossed them off my list."

"Did he have somebody working with him?" Bake asked, then shook his head. "But that couldn't be," he said in a puzzled tone. "Because you always said it was the same voice that called you before."

Dani looked at Ruth, then said, "It wasn't Clyde who called, and it wasn't someone he hired to help him. It was the *first* Creep." A murmur ran around the table, and Dani announced, "It was Clint Thomas who called."

"No! He was with me!" Ruth was staring at Dani, her face gone perfectly pale.

"Not all the time, Ruth," Dani contradicted her. "Remember what happened?"

"Well, I went to the rest room," Ruth recollected. "And when I came back he wasn't there. But he'd gone to the rest room himself."

"No, he was making the call to me," Dani told her. "It only took two or three minutes."

Hank Lowe spoke up then: "Wait a minute, Dani. It *couldn't* have been Clint. I've gotten calls since Clint died. The same guy, no doubt about the voice."

Others began nodding, but Dani demanded, "What's Clyde's one great talent?" Several said something about Lockyear's singing but Dani shook her head. "Not just singing. He's a great impersonator. He can sound like just about anyone he wants to." Then she asserted, "I've suspected Clint for some time. Ever since his horse Tarzan was killed, to be specific."

"Why did you suspect him?" Ruth demanded angrily.

"Because of something he said. It didn't register at the time, but later it came to me. You see, Luke found a blackjack close to where Clint was supposed to have been slugged. But he didn't give it to the police." She ignored an angry grunt from Little. "You heard Clint, Ruth. He said, 'I've been hit on the head with a blackjack.' Later he asked Lieutenant Stark, 'Why don't you start looking for the guy who sapped me?'" Dani gave Ruth a sympathetic look. "Don't you see, Ruth? Clint *couldn't* have known what he was hit with. He had to have tossed that blackjack down himself."

"I remember that blackjack," Ruby chimed in. She nodded, adding, "We got a pair of them, just for a joke. I've still got mine somewhere."

"But—who broke Tarzan's legs?" Ruth asked.

"It had to be Clint himself," Dani explained.

"But *why?*" Ruth wondered. "Why would he do that? He loved that horse!"

"He needed money, Ruth," Dani spelled it out. "He kept pretty good records, which Captain Little confiscated earlier this morning. Clint made a lot of money—but not as much as he lost gambling."

Little broke in suddenly, "We found one note from a big-time gambler for twenty thousand. And it said if Thomas didn't pay up, he'd take a ride to the cemetery. It's pretty clear that he was milking you people to try and avoid that."

"What about the rough stuff?" Bake asked. "Clint couldn't have done all that, could he? It took a real roughneck to ruin Tilman Yates. And what about Ben?"

"We got that from Thomas's records, too," Little nodded. "He hired the rough stuff done. Never paid for the job though. He had the goods on a guy who was dealing some dope as a sideline, so he made him do the dirty work in exchange for keeping quiet."

"Who was it?" Ruby asked.

"Rocky James. You all know him."

"Rocky—!" Hank Lowe exclaimed. "I knew he was on dope, but I didn't know he was dealing!"

"He's a pretty rough one." Little nodded. "But he won't be dealing now, not for a few years."

"I thought I'd know Clint's voice anywhere. But it was always sort of muffled and pitched a lot higher. He fooled us all, I guess. So after Clint was killed," Ruby confirmed slowly, "Clyde took over his racket. Sounds like something he'd do!"

"We've got enough on him to convict." Little nodded with satisfaction toward Clyde. "Found all Thomas's records in his trailer."

"You had no right to search my place!" Lockyear shouted.

"I had a search warrant," Little said. "But I want a little more than an extortion conviction."

Lockyear suddenly shut his mouth. He glared at Dani and Luke, then stated loudly, "You're looking for a fall guy to take the rap for killing Clint Thomas and that woman. But you won't pin that on me!"

Dani saw a half-doubtful look in Little's eyes, and quickly suggested, "Let me go over a few things. Who did kill Clint Thomas and Megan Carr? To be frank with you, almost everybody in this room had some sort of motive."

"Aw, come on, Dani—!" Hank Lowe protested. "Thomas was no bargain. He was a womanizer and would ruin his best friend to win. But that's not the same as saying we'd knock him off."

"That's right!" Boone Hardin's face was twitching, and he looked very young as he added, "I guess I hated him plenty. He abandoned my mother and never acted like I was alive. But even if I killed him, I couldn't have killed that lady!"

Dani saw several nodding agreement and pointed out, "Most of you had a motive of sorts, and you all had the opportunity. Thomas's motor home was close enough to the arena for any of you to go there, kill the two of them, then go back and be seen."

"Take a pretty hard nut to do that, Dani!" Hank Lowe protested.

"You're right, Hank. A hard nut is what we have to deal with." Dani's face clouded, and she seemed lost in thought.

Then she shook her head. "Somehow I've always felt that whoever did the extortion killed the two victims. But I couldn't pin the Creep down! That is, until yesterday."

"How'd you do that, Dani?" Bake asked. "You didn't follow Tom when he made a drop of the money."

"It was in the note I gave you."

"The note for Ben?"

"Yes." Dani pulled a slip of paper from her pocket, and read it: "Ben, Luke and I have got the physical evidence we need to wrap this up. And it won't be for extortion, but for murder one! I'll hang onto the evidence, but you get Little and some of his men here tomorrow. I'll hand the evidence over to him, and he can nail him. But warn them to be careful. He's killed two people and has nothing to lose."

"Well, I gave it to Ben," Bake told her slowly. "So how did that solve anything? How did Clyde know you were on to him?"

"Why, you gave *me* a note for Ben, too!" Tom Leathers volunteered in surprise, and several others piped up, "Me, too!"

Dani looked at Clyde, who was glaring at her. "I was pretty sure that it was one of you, but I didn't know *which* one. So I gave the same note to every single one of you. You got the note, Clyde, and then you knew what you had to do."

Lockyear began to stutter, and he shook with anger. "All right, I did take over when Clint was killed. And I did take you and Sixkiller out in a boat. But you can't prove I did any more than that." A grin came to his lips, and he nodded with satisfaction. "You can't even get me for attempted murder. You shot *me*, Miss Detective. I was just taking you across the river to a safe place until I was sure I had all the 'evidence' you claimed to have!"

Fran was staring at her husband, loathing on her face. Then she attested, "Captain Little, I know this man. He's been a flop all his life. Wanted to play cowboy, and he hated Clint because Clint was what he'd always wanted to be. He wasn't even jealous because I'd been married to Clint."

"Some say he was, Mrs. Lockyear," Little broke in.

"No. He never loved me. And he's not a killer. He's not even man enough for that! He might have had Clint beaten up, but he'd never kill anyone."

Dani alleged, "You're wrong there, Fran."

"Prove it!" Lockyear shouted. "You're just guessing!"

Dani looked at Lockyear, then slowly explained, "I was guessing for a long time. And all the time I had the answer right in my room."

Bake looked up, his handsome face startled. "In your room?"

Everyone was staring at Dani now, and she spoke with a trace of sadness. "I always felt that I was missing something from the note I got from Megan. The one she gave you to give me, Luke." She thought for a moment, then went on. "Her handwriting was terrible. That's why she always used a tape recorder and a video camera instead of writing things down. Let me show you the note. She turned to an overhead projector that had been set up; then switching it on, she placed a slip of paper on the glass.

"I doubt if you can read it. It says, *Dani, I've got a lead. Will be back in the room after the rodeo. Don't go to sleep. We've got to talk.* That much I could read," Dani said. "But the last sentence I could never make out. Not until two days ago. When I finally deciphered it, I soon knew who had killed Megan, and the one who killed Megan also killed Clint Thomas." Then she turned and pronounced, "Clyde, you murdered them both."

"You'll never prove it!" Lockyear objected defiantly. "I was in the arena the whole time the rodeo was on! I can prove it. I've got witnesses."

"But you weren't in the arena *before* the show started, Clyde," Dani pointed out. "You were in Clint's trailer. And you killed him."

"That's crazy! I didn't like him, but I don't kill everybody I don't like! And I wasn't in that motor home before the show!"

"What did the last line say, Dani?" Ruth asked suddenly.

"It said, 'If you get bored, watch the stateroom scene.'"

A puzzled look appeared on most faces, and Dani shared, "Megan and I were both crazy about old comedies. Laurel and Hardy, Buster Keaton, and most of all the Marx Brothers. The most famous scene in all the Marx Brothers movies is the stateroom scene. Megan and I had watched it three times. When I finally figured it out, I ran the movie and found this message from Megan."

"I've seen that!" Bill Baker piped up. "Where they keep piling more and more people into the little ship's cabin. That the one?"

"That's it. It's a scene from 'A Night at the Opera.' I want you to see a few minutes of it."

Dani stepped to the VCR, and soon the old black-and-white movie began flickering across the scene. The group watched, bewilderment on their faces. "Don't see what this is for!" Dixon grumbled. "Just a crummy old movie!"

But then the old film disappeared. Megan Carr's face appeared, and she grinned, saying, "Hi, Dani! If you don't find this tape, you're no detective!" Then she sobered. "Listen, I've been tying this thing together. And Dani, it's going to blow your mind! You'll never guess who the Creep is!" Her eyes sparkled, and she cried out, "It's Clint Thomas! I've got the goods on him!"

As she began explaining how she had discovered his identity, Dani grew sad. When she had first seen the message, she had not been able to hold back the tears, seeing the vibrant life and joy in Megan's expression. *If she'd only waited!* Dani had thought painfully.

"I took a hint from you, Dani," Megan was saying. "I got the idea of following someone who was paying the Creep off when he put the money down. So I went to one of the victims. I knew Clyde was getting clipped pretty good, so I decided to talk to him. He said Tom Leathers took the money, but that he'd make up some excuse for doing it himself. So he did. He called me two days later, and I followed him, then waited around. It wasn't hard. Here's what I got on film."

Megan's image disappeared, and the screen was filled with a scene taken in front of some sort of building with a large green yard and white benches. Clyde came into view, sat down, then after a while, got up and walked away, but he left a small briefcase. Megan's voice came as he disappeared, "There's the bait. Now let's see who the rat is."

The film stopped, then came on abruptly. "Here's our rat!" Megan announced. There was no mistaking the man who walked up to the bench, picked up the case, then walked away without looking back.

"That's Clint!" Ruth whispered. "I—I can't believe it!"

But nobody heeded her. All were staring at the screen, for Megan was back, this time in a motel room. "Well," she said, "now we know who the Creep is. But I want to nail him for keeps. I hate to do this to Clyde, but I want all the credit. Clyde's going to be on 'Candid Camera.'" She waved toward them, looking into the camera. "Clyde called me to find out what I'd discovered, and he's coming over. I need his help, because to tell the truth, I'm a little shaky about this. Clint's had some guys pulverized, and I don't want to be next. I need a man, and Clyde will do."

The film stopped and began again abruptly. This time it showed Clyde coming into the room. The light was poor, but as he stood in the middle of the room where Megan had focused the camera, there was no mistaking him. When Megan told him about Clint, he went wild. Megan looked nervously at the camera as Lockyear paced the floor. Finally, when he stopped she confided, "I want to get him, Clyde. But I need some help."

Lockyear agreed grimly, "Anything to get him!"

"I'm going to confront him with this, Clyde, but I'm afraid of him. Will you go with me?"

"Let's do it!"

Megan seemed to hesitate, then told him, "I've got a gun, but I don't know how to use it."

"Give it to me. I know how." Megan crossed the room, took a revolver from a drawer of the dresser, then handed it to him. "Let's go to his motor home, Clyde."

"That's good. You be there about five. He's always there before the show. I'll meet you there. He's got a VCR, so we can hit him with this film." There was an unholy light in Lockyear's eyes that the camera picked up. He put the gun in his pocket then left.

As soon as he was gone, Megan looked into the camera. "I guess I ought to wait for you, Dani, but I want it all tied up. I'm going to use my radio, so I'll have it all by the time I get back tonight."

Dani turned the machine off, then turned to Clyde. "But she never came back. Because *you* killed her, Clyde."

Lockyear stared at her, then insisted doggedly, "Okay, we went there. But Thomas wasn't home. I had to make the show, so I told her we'd do it later. But she said to give her the gun back, that she'd do it herself. So I did."

"You didn't think you should mention a little thing like that to the police?" Little asked. He was studying the rumpled suspect in a manner that seemed to disturb Lockyear.

"I—I knew somebody would think I was in it, because I hated Clint. But I didn't kill him—or her either. I didn't go in that motor home that night! You can't prove a thing!"

Dani shook her head. "I've got one more thing for you, Clyde. It's a cassette recording." She punched the button on a cassette recorder she'd placed on the table and stepped back as the voice of Clint Thomas, speaking over the sound of the stereo, came into the room. It started in the middle of a sentence, and the voice was mad with rage.

Clint: ". . . You two think you're up to?"

Megan: "We want you to see a few minutes of this video."

Clint: "What's Clyde doing here?"

Clyde: "I'm here to see you go to jail, Clint old buddy!"

Clint: "I'll break your neck. Just let—hey, now, what's with the gun, Clyde?"

Megan: "Just watch the video, Clint. Then we can talk."

As the tape ran, Little stared at Clyde Lockyear's face. He had spent years watching faces, and now as the scene unfolded, he drew his conclusion. Clyde looked startled as the recording began. As it progressed through the part where the video was shown and Clyde taunted Clint with getting caught, the stockman's expression changed. A sickly light came into his eyes, and he began to tremble. Suddenly he put his face in his hands and began to weep.

The tape ran on, and then Clint's voice cried, "You little punk! You don't have the nerve to get on a bucking horse! I'll take that gun and make you—"

The shot could be heard over the sound of the stereo.

Megan's voice cried, "You've killed him!"

A second shot.

Silence for a time followed by the sound of movements, of rustlings and footsteps. Then nothing.

Clyde got to his feet, his face contorted. "He was no good! And I didn't mean to shoot him! He would have killed me, if he'd gotten the gun away from me! It was self-defense!" He looked around the room, and for one moment he looked haggard, a pitiful little man who had stepped off a cliff into a nightmare. "I—I had to kill her! She'd seen me kill Clint. I didn't want to! Then I went through Clint's things, and I found his book with all the people he was swindling. So I decided I'd do it. I'd do what *he* couldn't do!" Then a crafty look came into his face. "You'll never convict me," he cried. "I'll get lawyers. They won't let you use these tapes!"

"But we can use what *you* took from Clint's motor home," Little reminded him.

"What? I didn't take anything!"

"Then how did Clint Thomas's championship buckles get in your trailer?" Little asked. "Plenty of witnesses to tell how much he thought of them. One witness will testify he saw them in Clint's motor home the afternoon before he was killed. But when we searched your place, Lockyear, we found them hidden with Thomas's book of records. The only way you could have gotten them was to take them from Clint Thomas's desk, where he kept them."

Suddenly Clyde Lockyear began cursing and raving, his eyes insane with rage. Little barked, "All right, you're under arrest for the murders of Clint Thomas and Megan Carr." He informed him of his rights, then said, "*Now* you can call a lawyer. Take him away, Edgar."

When the policeman closed the door, momentarily they could still hear Lockyear's screams, before they died away.

"How did you get that recording?" Little demanded. "She wasn't wired. We'd have found that on her body."

"Remember she said, 'I'm going to use my radio?'" Dani asked. "Megan had a special radio. It *was* a radio. A very small

one, that played AM and FM stations. But she used it sometimes in her work. It had a small tape recorder built into it and
a powerful mike. When she interviewed people, she'd have
the radio on, sometimes, then turn it off to do the interview.
But when she turned it off, that turned on the tape recorder.
I think she took it with her and at some point took it out of
her purse and put it down on the table. Clyde didn't see her
do it. That's where it was when Ben went by to check it out."

"My men missed it?"

"It was just a radio, Captain. There was nothing to show
that it was anything special."

"I'll have a little talk with my boys," Little replied grimly,
and obviously the "boys" were in for a rough session. Then
Little lamented, "It's all circumstantial."

"It's the best I could do," Dani reminded him simply.

For the first time, a smile creased Amos Little's lips. "You
did just fine, Miss Ross. You ever want to be a real detective,
you come to Houston. I'll fire a couple of the waffle-fingered
clowns I got and put you on."

Ten minutes later the room was empty except for Dani, Ben,
and Luke. The captain had informed them all that they would
probably be called as witnesses when the trial was held. There
had been a trying time for Dani as most of the cowboys came
to say good-bye. Hank and Ruth had left together, and Ben
had said, "Wouldn't be surprised but what something might
come of that. Good man."

Then Dani asked, "What about Clyde?"

"Oh, he's going where the dogs won't bite him." Luke
shrugged. "But capital punishment's out of favor. All the evidence is circumstantial. I'd say he'll get life, but be out in ten
to fifteen."

"What could have been in his heart?" Dani whispered.

"He wanted what he couldn't have," Savage recognized. "I feel sorry for him. Know what that feels like."

Dani gave him a swift glance, but his smooth face told her nothing. She said, "I guess we can go home now."

Luke announced, "I guess I'll stay with riding bulls for a while."

"But the case is solved," Ben objected.

Sixkiller looked embarrassed. "Well, I got to stick with Boone a little longer. He's in pretty bad shape."

Dani smiled and put her hand on his arm. "That's good of you, Luke!"

"There's a rodeo in Conway. I think I'll talk the kid into going with me. Then we can sort of drop in on that little church where I got saved."

Dani was pleased. "You'll be a flaming evangelist, Luke Sixkiller! Give me a call when Boone gets the glory! Or better still, bring him back with you to New Orleans. We've got to celebrate your new calling."

Savage watched them, saying nothing himself. Finally when the two others walked out, talking about the Lord, he stood there, thinking hard, before he shook his head with a strange gesture, then followed them.

21

Greet the Brethren

Dani watched as Ben fished for blue crabs, his hazel eyes turned to slits by the glare of the sun. He was wearing his favorite lounging outfit, a pair of faded denim cutoffs and a T-shirt with the picture of an old steam engine and the words *Durango and Silverton Railroad* written in ornate calligraphy underneath. He was standing knee-deep in the lake holding on to a short length of weathered cord that dangled into the water, his tanned face serious.

Something tickled Dani's right leg, and she glanced down to see a red ant marching across her thigh. Quickly she reached down and brushed it away. She lay there in the sun, soaking up the warmth and idly watching Savage.

As he stood poised, waiting for the line to stir, Dani studied him from behind her dark glasses, thinking of how much time they'd spent together during the past two weeks. She'd spent a great deal of her days relaxing, going almost daily to her parents' home off the shores of Lake Pontchartrain, riding a spirited mare named Lady a friend was keeping there during a long vacation. She'd spent time with her sister, Allison, going shopping with her and enjoying the things Allison made her do—such as going roller-skating. Somehow Ben had been there for a lot of it. The roller-skating, for example, had been fun, for he'd come home with her father for dinner, and Allison had insisted on his going along. Allison and Dani had laughed themselves sick as he'd fallen flat time after time, going around the rink rubber-legged, his arms flailing. When they were both holding on to his arms as his feet skidded wildly, he cried out, "Wait! I think I've got the hang of it!" Then he burst into a graceful routine, including leaps in the air that they'd seen only from Olympic champions. Dani shook her head, saying ruefully to Allison, "We should have known! Anybody with the timing and grace to be an aerialist *would* be great at something like roller-skating!"

The line in Ben's hand moved slightly, and instantly he lifted the cord, removed the palm-sized blue crab that clung to the piece of meat tied on the end, and dropped it into the bucket that floated at his feet. He peered into the bucket, then picked it up and waded back to the shore. "This ought to be enough for supper." He set the bucket down, moved to where she was lying on an old quilt, and plumped himself down beside her. He gave her outfit a critical look and shook his head sadly. "Don't you ever read those fashion magazines?" he asked. She was wearing a pair of lime green shorts and a red halter top. "Where'd you get that outfit? At a rummage sale?"

Actually he thought she looked great, though she wasn't a raving beauty, he decided as he gave her a critical inspection. "You better make it as a private detective, Boss."

"Why?"

"Because you'd never make it as a fashion model," he announced, then shook his head sadly. "Too much figure. To be a top-rate model a woman's got to look like she just got released from a concentration camp. No curves allowed. Anyway, your face, Boss, just won't do." He reached out and put his hand under her chin, raised it up, then plucked her sunglasses off for a better look. "Nope. Face too square—mouth too big—crazy colored eyes." He held her face for a moment, then commented, "Good complexion though."

She stared at him, laughter in her gray-green eyes that reflected the water and the sun. "Thanks a lot, Ben. I was going to hit the salons tomorrow. Now you've saved me all the heartache of rejection."

He held her chin a moment, then dropped his hand, saying briskly, "You look pretty good for an older chick." Then he lay back and covered his eyes by throwing the back of his left hand over them. "Any more of those bad dreams?" he asked casually.

Dani shot a quick glance at him, then shook her head. "Not a one. Guess Dr. Savage's Cut-Rate Psychology Course was worth all I paid for it." Then she grew serious, her eyes changing with her mood. "I think about Megan a lot." She came to a sitting position and watched as a brown pelican sailed by, as stately as a galleon. Then a flight of six egrets, flawlessly white and sparkling, moved across the cloudless blue sky.

She rolled over, reached out and grabbed his coarse black hair, turning his face toward her. "Maybe I've gotten hard, Ben," she confided. His hazel eyes were watchful, filled with some sort of emotion she could not understand. "I've heard that can happen to people." She released his hair, and rolled back to stare at the sky, saying, "I tried to kill Clyde Lockyear."

"No, you tried to save yourself and Luke," Ben contradicted her instantly. "If there'd been any way to stop Clyde besides shooting at him, you'd have taken it. *That's* when a guy needs to worry, when he begins to *look* for a way to hurt somebody. And you're not in much danger of that, Boss. Too bad we live in a world where there have to be soldiers and policemen—but David killed his ten thousands, didn't he?"

Dani sat up, surprised as always when Savage quoted the Bible. For some reason he seemed slightly ashamed of the knowledge. "Come on," she said, getting to her feet. "Let's go to the house. You're supposed to help Allison with her acrobatics."

They left the lake, and when they got out of the car, Daniel Ross came to report, "Got something in the paper you'll get a kick out of."

Dani took the *Times Picayune* he held out, and Ben came to stand beside her.

"'Homicide Cop Hits the Glory Trail,'" Dani read the headline aloud, then laughed with delight. "Oh, Ben, it's Luke!"

Savage stared at the picture of Sixkiller. Luke was behind a pulpit, holding up a Bible in one hand and pointing a stern forefinger. "Oh, boy!" Ben chuckled. "The boys down at the station are going to *love* this!" He found the picture extremely funny, and even Dani had to laugh.

"It says in the story," Dani's father continued, "that he's preaching his first sermon tonight. Think we all ought to go?"

"Wouldn't miss it for anything." Savage nodded. Running his eyes down the page, he read, "Says here he's going to attend New Orleans Baptist Theological Seminary. Going to be an evangelist."

"There was a Methodist preacher back in the late eighteen hundred's named Peter Cartwright," Dani's father replied thoughtfully. "He ran into some pretty raunchy folks. More than once he had to stop preaching and warn a man to behave, or he'd have to leave. Then if the troublemaker didn't stop,

Cartwright would march down, grab the man up, and toss him out bodily. "A smile crossed his lips. "Guess Luke's got the physical qualifications for that sort of thing. May need it, too, if he goes on the streets of New Orleans, preaching. Well, we'll all go give him our moral support. He's preaching at Victory Tabernacle over on the east side of town. Pretty rough section, so don't wear anything formal. As Mark Twain put it, the trouble starts at seven."

Victory Tabernacle was a large, white frame building set in the middle of a section of New Orleans that had once been predominantly white middle class, but now was changing to a mixed lower-class population. The houses were trying to stay middle class, but many of them had given up and were simply running down.

But if the houses and the streets themselves were going downhill, Victory Tabernacle was not. The paint was fresh, the green carpet of grass in front clipped, the shrubs in front of the building sculptured, and the parking lot free of papers and broken glass.

As he parked the van between a Ford pickup pulling a blue bass boat and a '57 Chevrolet, Daniel observed, "Looks like a good crowd." They moved across the lot, joining several latecomers, mostly locals wearing the standard uniform of jeans, T-shirts and Nike running shoes. When they stepped inside, a young black man wearing about the same uniform came to say, "Got some seats 'bout halfway down." They followed him and squeezed into two of the dark oak pews—Dani and Ben on one, Daniel, Ellen, Rob, and Allison in front of them. Rob, at seventeen, had had to be threatened with the loss of the use of his father's car before he'd agreed to come, but now that he was settled, he seemed interested in the phenomenon.

They were just in time, for as they settled themselves, Luke came out from a door to one side of the front of the auditorium, accompanied by a tall young man wearing a pair of slacks and a tan sports shirt. Luke looked about as uncomfortable as a man could possibly look, and Dani whispered, "Ben, Luke would rather be going up a dark alley against a homicidal maniac than be here!"

Savage nodded, but then the song service started. On one side of the stage was a group of musicians, playing guitars, piano, drums, and keyboard, and the young man with Luke stood up and said, "Let's just praise the Lord."

There were no songbooks, but a young woman threw the lyrics on the white wall behind the pulpit by means of an overhead projector. The first songs were peppy, almost what one might hear at a high-school pep rally. Some of them had a steady beat that caused one to unconsciously sway from side to side. Then the pace slowed, and all over the auditorium, people were lifting their hands and with closed eyes were singing quietly but fervently.

Savage studied the congregation with a practiced eye, but most of all he watched Dani, cutting his eyes toward her. He himself felt terribly out of place, with his hands held at his sides, not knowing any of the songs. But Dani, he saw, was relaxed. From time to time she would lift her hands in a simple gesture of praise, but more often she would simply fold her hands, lift her face upward, and with her eyes closed sing the simple choruses in a clear contralto voice.

Savage felt relieved when the singing died down and the pastor came to introduce the speaker. He spoke only briefly, stating that he had known Luke Sixkiller only a few days, "But I have come to respect him and to love him as a brother in the Lord."

After mentioning Luke's career as a policeman and his fine record in the army, the pastor summoned him, "Luke, come and tell us what the Lord has done for you. And let's give the Lord a hand for giving us a new volunteer in *His* army!"

Sixkiller came to the platform and stood waiting until the applause died down. As he began to speak, Dani found that her hands were clenched together so tightly that they ached, for she feared that Luke would freeze up. Leaning forward, she noted his dark blue suit and maroon tie, the same sort of outfit he wore when on duty with the homicide squad. He said with a small grin, "Well, I may as well make one correction in that introduction. I'm not officially a member of the New Orleans Police Department. I was suspended a few weeks ago—for police brutality."

A tall black man two rows in front of Dani suddenly stood up and yelled, "Yeah, Sixkiller! And I hope they bust you for good!"

Sixkiller stared at the heckler, then smiled and nodded. "Hello, Ace. Still shooting up?" A laugh followed his words, and another very muscular black man stood up and cried, "Sit down, Ace, before I give you some brutality!" He waited until the heckler sat down, muttering, then invited, "Now you git right on with yoah preaching, Mr. Sixkiller!"

"Thank you, Eddie," Luke responded. "But I don't guess you're going to get much preaching tonight. I heard my grandfather tell about an Indian preacher once who only got two dollars in the collection plate after he preached. When someone complained, 'Not much collection, Chief!' he only said, 'Not much *preach!*'"

A light wave of laughter went over the congregation, and when it passed, Luke told them, "I read in the paper that I'm going to be an evangelist. Some newspaperman has a good imagination, or else he's the son of a prophet, because I never said that. Right now I'm just waiting to go back to work with the NOPD, but something happened to me three weeks ago, and tonight I just want to tell you about it. . . ."

Luke began in a conversational tone, telling how he'd grown up on the reservation in Oklahoma. He told of his early school years, then of his stint in the army, and finally of the years in homicide. It was all done in an easy, relaxed manner, and he was careful to include several incidents from each period, some very humorous, using himself as the butt of the stories, and some sad, as when he lost his partner of six years in a shoot-out in the ghetto.

Then he spoke of recent days with the rodeo, but made no mention of Dani by name. He spoke of how he'd run from God, and suddenly he began quoting from Francis Thompson's poem "The Hound of Heaven." A silence fell over the room as he recited:

> I fled Him, down the nights and down the days;
> I fled Him, down the arches of the years;
> I fled Him, down the labyrinthine ways
>   Of my own mind; and in the midst of tears
> I hid from Him, and under running laughter.
>   Up vistaed hopes I sped;
>   And shot, precipitated,
> Adown Titanic glooms of chasmed fears,
> From those strong Feet that followed, followed after.
>   But with unhurrying chase,
>   And unperturbed pace,
>   Deliberate speed, majestic instancy,
>   They beat—and a Voice beat
>   More instant than the Feet—
> "All things betray thee, who betrayest Me."

"I don't know much about poetry," he said, looking directly at Dani, "but I know about running from God! And Jesus

Christ caught up with me just three weeks ago, in a little church in Arkansas. I friend of mine lured me into the place, and I found that morning what I'd been looking for all my life. . . ."

He spoke simply of his experience, and when he was through, he paused. The silence was palpably thick, and his voice was a little choked, as though he were keeping it under careful control. "I'm no preacher, but I *know* something came into my life that morning, and I know it was Jesus Christ, the Son of God. I know what it means to have peace."

He closed the service simply, by presenting Jesus Christ as the answer for anyone who felt that the Hound of Heaven was after him. As soon as the music started softly, from all over the auditorium, people got up out of their seats and filled the altar.

It was a moving moment for Dani, and she stood clinging to the back of the seat in front of her. She watched as Luke spoke with a young woman, obviously a woman of the streets. She was weeping, and finally the two of them bowed their heads and prayed. Slowly Luke moved from one to another, some of them obviously hardened by the life of the ghetto.

Dani's parents left before the altar service was over, but she told them, "I want to speak to Luke."

"I'll bring her home," Ben offered, and the two of them waited for over an hour as the pastor and the people of the church dealt with those who had come forward. Finally they saw Luke shake the pastor's hand, and then he came toward them.

"Saw you earlier," he noted, his face suddenly showing strain. "I'm about as tired as I ever was."

"Let's go get something to eat," Dani suggested quickly. The three of them left and crowded into Sixkiller's Porsche. They found a restaurant and ordered cheeseburgers. Dani discovered that she had to do most of the talking at first. Ben was quiet, and Luke seemed exhausted. But as he ate, he brightened up.

"I didn't expect to see you guys tonight," he said with a grin. "Probably wouldn't have showed up if I'd known it."

"You had some distinguished folks in your congregation, Luke," Ben remarked. "I saw Two-edge Frank, Poppa Van Dyne, Boudreau Topps, and quite a few of your old customers."

"I saw them." Luke nodded. "None of them came to the altar. I thought they might be waiting for me outside."

"It was marvelous, your testimony, Luke!" Dani blurted out. Her eyes were bright, and she spoke glowingly of how he could reach people whom no other preacher could touch. Sixkiller shook his head, smiling doubtfully, but soon the two of them were talking of the invitations to speak he'd already gotten. Dani had her own ideas, and they were so caught up in the plans for the future, neither of them noticed that Ben Savage was not saying a word.

After a while, Ben got up, announcing, "I've got some stuff to do. See Dani home, will you, Luke?"

"Hey, we're ready, Ben," Luke said. "We'll dump this chick, then you and I can talk."

"No. I've got an errand. See you both later."

Sixkiller watched him go with surprise. "What's with Ben? He acts like a cat with a sore tail."

Dani suddenly understood. *We left him out,* she thought. *We made ourselves into a little holy club and left Ben on the outside.* The thought saddened her, but she didn't explain it to Luke. Instead she pointed out, "I've got to go home."

"Sure."

Luke took the long way to Dani's parents' home. He drove across the Lake Pontchartrain Causeway, a long sliver of concrete that dissects the lake. He drove slowly, and when they exited, he laughed. "Remember how I had you and Ben staked out down there, waiting for that serial killer?" He gave her a sly look. "I'll bet Savage really got into that, pretending that the two of you were lovers parked beside the lake."

Dani sniffed. "It was all in the line of duty."

Luke scoffed, and then Dani giggled so hard that when he pulled up in front of the house and they started for the front door, Dani teased, "Don't make so much racket! They're all asleep!"

When they reached the door, she turned and held her hand out. As his own closed on it, she said simply, "Luke, I'm so very *proud* of you!"

The moonlight fell on her face, turning it to old silver, and her eyes were almost luminous. Sixkiller fell silent, then shared, "I found a verse this morning that I didn't know was in the Bible."

She stared at him, for the comment seemed irrelevant. "What was it?"

He didn't answer, but stood there, his tough face made gentle by the softness of the moonlight. His lips, long and mobile, suddenly smiled. He said, "It's in First Thessalonians five, verse twenty-six."

Dani frowned, her lips pursing delightfully. "I don't know that offhand."

"It says, 'Greet all the brethren with a holy kiss.'"

Dani tried not to smile as she replied, "Oh? Well, when you find one of the 'brethren' you can give him a holy kiss."

Sixkiller moved his head forward, so close that he could smell her perfume. "I found another verse. It's in First Peter, chapter five, the fourteenth verse. Do you know that one?"

"No," Dani said, looking into Sixkiller's dark eyes.

"It says, 'Greet ye *one another* with a kiss of charity. . . .'"

Dani was suddenly very much aware of the fact that her heart seemed to be beating faster. To cover her sudden nervousness, she noted, "You're becoming quite a Bible scholar."

Sixkiller moved yet closer, and now she could smell his shaving lotion and was aware of the warmth of his hand over hers. "Then there's Second Corinthians, the twelfth verse of the thirteenth chapter."

"What—does it say?" Dani whispered.

"Greet one another—" Gently Luke put his arms around her and pulled her close. Her hands fluttered at his arms, and she tried to speak, but his firm lips fell on hers. She felt very small and helpless, for his arms were powerful, but at the same time she knew she was safe and secure. She found herself lifting her hands and placing them on his neck, and for one long moment she lay against him. It was not a demanding kiss, and she sensed the gentleness that lay deep inside Luke. It was there, as she had always guessed, covered by a hard manner, but there all the same.

Then he drew his lips back and finished the quotation, ". . . with a holy kiss."

Dani started to speak, then found she had to clear her throat. The kiss had somehow disturbed her, and with a lighthearted comment she tried to cover up the emotion that was still with her.

"I think you'd better save your 'holy' kisses for the 'brethren,'" she said.

Sixkiller shook his head. "That would be too complicated." His arms did not relax as they held her firmly. "I've been listening to all this stuff about the feminist movement. Gets harder and harder to tell the men from the women, you know?"

"You know I'm a woman, Luke Sixkiller!" Dani laughed softly. "You don't go around holding any of your buddies like this!"

Sixkiller answered in a shocked voice, "Heaven forbid!" But then he shook his head. "I'm not really a Bible scholar, Dani. So for right now, I'm just going to take the verses I like. I'll work on the one that says 'brethren' after I get to seminary."

He pulled her closer, saying in a dangerously casual tone, "Right now, I'm staying with the simple verse. Remember it? Second Corinthians thirteen, twelve?"

Dani nodded, "I remember—and I'm afraid I'm going to hear it a lot in the future."

"Say it for me, Dani," Luke commanded.

She looked at him with her eyes enormous in the moonlight—then she said softly, in the most gentle of all tones, "Greet one another with—a holy kiss!"

The moonlight fell in long silver bars on the white house, softening its outlines and making it look like a house found in an old, old story. After a while, the single shadow became two; then the car started up with a hoarse cough and roared away.

Dani stepped inside the door just as her father came out of the study. He blinked at her over his glasses, asking, "What have you been up to, Daughter?"

Dani went to him, put her arms around him, and kissed his cheek. Then she turned and walked to the stairs. She was halfway up when she seemed to realize she hadn't answered his question. She turned, and a smile came to her mouth, making her eyes bright as she answered, "Doing? Why, I've been studying theology, Dad," she replied. Then she turned and disappeared as she moved to the upper landing.